The House of Memory

The Helen Rose Scheuer Jewish Women's Series

The House of Memory

❖ ❖ ❖

Stories by Jewish Women Writers of Latin America

Edited by Marjorie Agosín

Translation Editor: Elizabeth Rosa Horan

Stories translated by

*Susan Bassnett, Dina Castillo-Mendoza,
Joan E. Friedman, Dick Gerdes, Roberta Gordenstein,
Elizabeth Rosa Horan, Celeste Kostopulos-Cooperman,
Andrea G. Labinger, Alexis Levitan, Martha Manier,
Giovanni Pontiero, and Margaret Stanton*

The Feminist Press at The City University of New York
New York

Published by The Feminist Press at The City University of New York
City College, Wingate Hall, Convent Avenue at 138th Street,
New York, NY 10031.

www.feministpress.org

First edition, 1999.

Library of Congress Cataloging-in-Publication Data

The house of memory : stories by Jewish women writers of Latin
 America / edited by Marjorie Agosín ; translation editor, Elizabeth
 Rosa Horan ; stories translated by Roberta Gordenstein . . . [et al.].
 p. cm. — (The Helen Rose Scheuer Jewish women's series)
 Stories translated grom Spanish and Portuguese.
 ISBN 1-55861-208-4 (hc. : alk. paper). — ISBN 1-55861-209-2
 (pbk. : alk. paper)
 1. Latin American literature—Jewish authors. 2. Latin American literature
 —Women authors. 3. Jewish literature—Latin America. 4. Latin American
 literature—Translations into English. I. Agosin, Marjorie. II. Gordenstein,
 Roberta. III. Series.
 PQ7087.E5H68 1999
 860.8'09287'098—dc21 99-10658
 CIP

Steven H. Scheuer, in memory of his mother and in celebration of her life and the 100th
anniversary of her birth (1995), has been pleased to endow the Helen Rose Scheuer
Jewish Women's Series. *The House of Memory* is the sixth named book in the series.

Publication of this book was made possible, in part, by public funding from the National
Endowment for the Arts.

Text design and typesetting by CompuDesign, Jackson Heights, New York.
Printed on acid-free paper by McNaughton & Gunn, Inc., Saline, Michigan.
Manufactured in the United States of America.

05 04 03 02 01 00 99 5 4 3 2 1

To Josephine, Raquel, Sonia, Helena, and Frida,
the women in my life
who taught me to write and to sing.

Contents

Part Two
The Sign of the Star: Immigrants and Strangers

Part Three
On the Border: Forging Identities

Acknowledgments

I am grateful to each of the writers whose work appears in *The House of Memory* for her beautiful writing and her generous spirit.

This anthology unites for the first time in any language the voices of Jewish women writers of Latin America, and I celebrate the courage and vision of The Feminist Press and of its publisher, Florence Howe, who made this anthology a reality. Special gratitude goes to my editors, Jean Casella, who has a privileged sensibility and a power to transform confusion into clarity, and Marna Miller, whose patience, dedication, and fine editorial work made an invaluable contribution to this anthology.

I extend my special thanks to the many translators of this volume, and especially to Roberta Gordenstein and Elizabeth Rosa Horan, for their commitment to this literature and for their gifted and respectful translations.

As always, my love and gratitude to Alida Brill and Steven Scheuer, whose generosity has made this book possible and who have allowed me to explore the rich traditions of Jewish writing in the Americas, this time through the voices of my sisters.

My husband as well as my two children serve as a constant reminder of the tenacity of love. I thank them for their presence and for their unconditional support of my work.

Marjorie Agosín
Wellesley, Massachusetts
December 1998

Introduction

This anthology originated from my own experience as a writer who was impelled to acknowledge and explore her special identity as a Latin American Jewish woman. Many of the nuances of this identity first began to reveal themselves to me, as they did to several of the other writers in this collection, during the era of the military dictatorships in my native Chile. In the countries of the Southern Cone—Chile, Argentina, and Uruguay—the 1970s and 1980s were a time of widespread terror, tortures, and "disappearances." As a Jew, I was joined with my ancestors in a history of persecution, resistance, and exile, which we suddenly found repeating itself yet again before our eyes.[1] As a woman, I was joined with my sisters in groups like the Mothers of the Disappeared, charged with the task of preserving the memory of loved ones who had been lost.[2] As a Latin American, a Chilean, I was irrevocably joined to the plight of my country, although my family had safely fled to exile in the United States. And as a writer, my only weapon was my words—my ability to bear witness to the scenes of horror as well as the deeds of courage and dignity, while never losing a sense of astonishment. As I struggled to find a way of living, of surviving amid the daily news of horrors, a saying from the cabala became very meaningful to me: *Tikum olam*, which means "mending the world" through good deeds. Words are the means I have with which to help mend the sufferings of the world—words that implicitly emerge from the distinctive perspective and voice of a Chilean Jewish woman living in exile.

In the 1990s, I was inspired to reflect upon my condition as a Latin American Jewish woman writer in a more profound and personal way as I undertook a singular project—to write my mother's memoir, to revive and recreate the memory of a living mother who tells her story to her daughter. I listened to my mother's stories of growing up during the World War II era in a small town in southern Chile inhabited by fifty Nazis and three Jewish families, and later to my father's stories of his parents' flights from Odessa to Istanbul to Marseilles to Chile and his own final exile to the United States.[3] From these stories was born a desire to penetrate more

deeply into the terrain that had shaped my own identity—the space of Latin American Jewish experience.

I found in that experience an enigmatic and complex heritage of Ashkenazim and Sephardim; of orthodox and reformed, *conversos* and Marranos,[4] of utopian immigrants, impoverished refugees, and desperate exiles,[5] all immersed in a collective history, but for the most part alien to that history. The history of the Jews in Latin America remains largely unwritten, filled with secrets, with forgotten memories, with stories yet to be told.[6] While the Jewish presence in the Americas is as old as the European conquest of the New World,[7] it had and continues to have the dimensions of an alien presence, watched over and separate, often all but invisible except for the times when it is brought to light as the special target of prejudice and persecution.[8] The uncovering of this history is a vast and complex task, because in spite of certain commonalities each community possesses its own idiosyncracies of experience.[9]

The history of women has also in many ways been a hidden history, not only in Latin America but all over the world. Silenced by the historical patriarchy, the distinct experiences and contributions of women have seldom found their way into the history texts, nor, until quite recently, have the voices of women been published and read on a large scale. Yet this distinctively female history is also an integral part of my own identity.

It is through literature, to a great extent, that history is recorded and understood. And it is through the study of related works in concert and in context that the idea of a literary tradition is formed. With a few notable exceptions, critical works have yet to view the literature of Latin American Jewish writers as forming a distinct and noteworthy tradition.[10] And until now, no collection has brought together the work of these women writers and made them available to English-speaking readers.

This anthology has been created to remedy a lack of knowledge about, and availability of, an important body of literature at a time when there is a growing curiosity in the English-speaking world regarding this work. And on a more personal level, it has been brought to life to acknowledge a tradition of which I can now recognize I am a part; to pay homage to the writers who have inspired and nourished me, and who have taken my hand and accompanied me on my journeys of identity.

Breaking Our Silence

The House of Memory: Stories by Jewish Women Writers of Latin America does not attempt any prior classification of what this hybrid and complex identity

means—of what it signifies to be a woman and a Latin American and a Jew. Nor does it seek to create a type of double or even triple "ghetto" for the writer who is Jewish and Latin American and female. As Margo Glantz writes in her work *The Family Tree*, even the most unique and distinct cultural experience opens out into the universal:

> Whether we came from nobility or not we all have our geneologies. I descend from Genesis not out of pride but out of need. My parents were born in the Jewish Ukraine.[11]

Yet this collection *is* being created at a moment when, partly in response to the fascist dictatorships of recent decades, Latin American Jewish identity has begun to assert itself, to reinvent itself—to recognize itself as a hybrid, pluralistic, and multicultural, and shaped by complex cultural and historical forces. The work of Latin American Jewish writers reveals consciousness of a new form of *mestizaje*, or cross-culturalism, where Central and Eastern European and Middle Eastern heritages blend with the traditional Latin American—which itself combines Iberian, Native American, African, and other influences.[12] Robert DiAntonio and Nora Glickman have noted the effect of the Latin American Jewish writer's complex heritage:

> The Jewish writer in Latin America is always and has always been torn between conflicting loyalties. From this tension is born their dynamic and insightful literature that enriches the mainstream of modern Latin American fiction, as it underscores the unique and multifaceted nature of Judaic literary history.[13]

This collection is also being created at a time when Latin American *women* have begun to discover their voices in a way that curiously parallels the experience of Latin American Jews. The resurgence, in the 1970s and 1980s, of testimonial works written by women, including indigenous women, such as Rigoberta Menchú's *Me llamo Rigoberta Menchú y así me nació la conciencia* (tr. *I, Rigoberta Menchú*) and Domitila Barrios de Chungara's *Que me dejen hablar* (tr. *Let Me Speak!*), appears as the expression of highly marginalized voices.[14] On a large scale, during this same period, women—who were still viewed as creators of children and cakes, not of art—emerged into literary life. In the countries under fascist dictatorship, life was always marginal and secret, but many women found a refuge of freedom in literary workshops, where it was possible to express oneself, tell one's stories. The voices of an entire group that had been maintained

in silence in a collective isolation were finally speaking to one another, and being heard.

Emerging out of silence, at the same time, have been the voices of writers who reflected the growing self-awareness of both these segments of Latin American society: for the first time, many significant works have begun to be produced by Jewish women of Latin America. Many of these texts have been autobiographical novels or poetic memoirs drawing on both personal and family experiences, such as *Las genealogías* (tr. *The Family Tree*) by Margo Glantz, *Cláper* (published in English under the same title) by Alicia Freilich de Segal, and *Músicos y relojeros* (tr. *Musicians and Watchmakers*) by Alicia Steimberg. These innovative literary forms draw in elements of fiction, poetry, autobiography, and biography—as if such a hybrid social and cultural experience demanded the creation of new, hybrid genres.

As Latin American Jews, these writers faced the task of reclaiming and rewriting the story of their heritage and reevaluating their particular condition of *mestizaje*, which is different from the conditions of the indigenous or the Spanish or the other non-Jewish European peoples in Latin America. As women, they faced challenges of recovering a censored and almost invisible history, and of reasserting the particular experience of their gender, which is different from the experience of Latin American Jewish men.

The Latin American Jewish woman writer exists in a twofold condition: that of a marginal woman writer within (not one, but two) patriarchal cultures—cultures that grant prominence to a masculine voice; and also that of a marginal Jewish writer within a predominantly Catholic culture. This position of double marginality—the marginality produced by gender as well as by heritage—has given birth to a literature that constantly questions itself, and that questions not only its own identity but the nature of the very forces that shape identity.

The dilemma signified by being a Latin American Jewish woman writer is the singular question of this anthology. To respond to this question, one needs to ask many other questions: What does it imply to write as a woman, as a Latin American, and as a Jew? Are there certain concerns that are central to the writing of Latin American women—or Jewish women? And the main question: Is there really a tradition of Latin American Jewish women writers? These questions, too, only lead to other questions. Yet, through the stories included in this anthology, it may be possible to outline the terrain in which these narrators learn their reality, assume it—or, perhaps, invent it.

The writers gathered in this anthology are all distinguished authors, successful within their own cultures. They constitute some of the most interesting and innovative voices of contemporary Latin American literature. Many of them are well-known figures, such as Clarice Lispector of Brazil or Margo Glantz of Mexico. Others, like Sonia Guralnik of Chile, are just beginning to be known. In spite of being from different countries and different generations, and in spite of writing in a diverse variety of literary forms, all share certain qualities as Latin American Jewish women writers. They are threads in the same fabric.

The majority of writers in this collection begin, in one way or another, with their beginnings, with their families: the father, the mother, or the grandmother who came to Latin America as part of the great Jewish diaspora. They have paid more attention to their lineages, in general, than have Latin American Jewish male writers, and they have revisited, in particular, the generations of women in this diaspora, rescuing female experience from obscurity. But these writers are doing more than simply recording family history. For them, the family is both the microcosm that helps them write the history of their culture, and the mirror that helps them name themselves and discover their own identities.

Curiously, the theme of anti-Semitism and the experience of persecution surface explicitly in only a handful of these stories. Rather, these stories implicitly question the position of Latin American Jewish women in a space that is both familiar and alien, that is ours but at the same time not ours—the distinct identity that needs to be recovered, understood, and transmitted.

These stories are acts of faith that seek to recover memory and belief and connect them with an identity; to return to the historical past and reshape its stories in the present; to anticipate the future, when the fables of the past will be reinvented anew. The literature of the world is, in effect, a great book of memory, and these writers respond, with rare courage and candor, to the universal question of how to filter and transmit memories, how to insert into this powerful book of memory the texture of a singular and complex human experience.

Memory and identity, exiles and returns—they echo in voices of these wandering women, makers of dreams and the work of the word. These voices are the ones that will tell the stories of their people, that will continue to sing in a language that has the smell of journeys, the color of the shadows of other times. They are voices that once spoke in Yiddish, in Polish, in Russian, in Hebrew, in Ladino, but that arrived by chance in

The House of Memory

Latin America, Spanish- and Portuguese-speaking America, and learned to speak in languages new to them. They are the voices that did not succumb to oblivion, that survived the flames of Auschwitz and the death squads of Peron and Pinochet, that refused to submit to the historical silencing of women. They are voices that say, "I also exist, and I am not from here, and in this ambiguity I live and invent myself; I believe; I write; I am."

Recording Our Genealogies

The recording of memory, the invention of memoir, and the dualities that are entailed in the process—what is remembered, how it is remembered, and who articulates the memory—are central to many, perhaps even most, of the works produced by Latin American Jewish women writers. The writers appearing in the first section of this anthology, in particular, participate in this activity of recovering, reshaping, and recording memory. They imbue the everyday and the particular with historical significance, telling the story of a people through the stories of individuals. They cross pasts and presents, writing about fictional or fictionalized family members in order to rediscover the springs of their own identity.

Argentine author Alicia Steimberg, who began to write in the 1950s, was one of the first women writers to include in her writing elements that identified her as a Jewish writer, elements that explored the Jewish experience in Latin America. Yet she recalls that she had been writing for more than a decade before "the stories which were told in my household began buzzing around in my head." When she began to write about her family, it was "like turning on a faucet."[15] The novel that resulted, *Musicians and Watchmakers*, published in Spanish in 1971 (and excerpted in this anthology), is a key work in the literature of Latin American Jewish women writers.

Musicians and Watchmakers draws upon both family and national history. Nora Glickman is correct in pointing out that the novel is a work of transgression, questioning the sentimental myths of the nuclear family as well as the heroic myths of the literature of the Jewish peasant who arrived to colonize Argentina motivated by ideological conviction.[16] In contrast to these myths, Steimberg gives us unforgettable characters—real people, flesh and blood beings. In *Musicians and Watchmakers*, she recreates the Barrio Once of Buenos Aires in the 1940s and the conversations of her aunts, cousins, and grandmothers, full of fears, hopes, and prejudices. The novel highlights, among other things, the generational conflicts that are

produced between those Jews who arrived in the diaspora and those who were born in the New World. And it records stereotypical gender roles but at the same time subverts them: the grandfather is the central authority figure in the family, but it is the grandmother who manipulates, behind the darkness and the shadow, the destiny of the household.

Musicians and Watchmakers is a text that makes memory its redemptive thread but also raises powerful questions: What does the poor emigrant remember of the diaspora? What happens in Jewish families desperate to improve themselves and become part of a petite bourgeoisie that is generally anti-Semitic? What roles did women really play within families and within the larger culture? Such questions would continue to dominate Steimberg's work, and her exploration of such themes would influence other Jewish women writers, not only in Argentina but in other Latin American countries as well.

The Family Tree (the slightly variant title given to the book published in Spanish as *Las genealogías*) by Margo Glantz, first published in Spanish in 1981, is already considered an essential and canonical text of Mexican Jewish literature. It inspired a series of works by Mexican women on similar themes, which together have come to comprise an important presence in Mexican letters.[17] What unites these writers is the obsessive concern for recovering personal memory and, along with it, the collective memory of the spirit of their origins. In *The Family Tree*, the daughter boards the symbolic imagination of the father and mother and accompanies them on their journey from Russia to Mexico. Glantz exhibits a great passion for voyages, for remote cartographies, for the coasts of the Black Sea and the swells of the wide Atlantic, as well as for the pleasure of remembering and absorbing all those places that can be encountered only through memory. But her work is far more than a simple work of documentation or nostalgia. She invokes the presence of Jacob and Elizabeth Glantz in Russia, but on invoking it, approaches her own presence in Mexico City. *The Family Tree* inhabits a border zone, carrying on a dialogue that transgresses the limits of past and present, joining the memories of yesterday in a faraway land with the recovery of those memories in the Mexico of today. For Glantz, memory is a way to return to the past not only for its own sake, but in order to understand the present.

The Family Tree does not follow a linear structure, but rather follows the course of signs and symbols that carve a path through memory, where the events of the past spill over into the present. Some of the events are

recalled with a kind of excessive certainty, as if to rescue them from the denial of oblivion, while other events remain in an interesting state of amnesia and cloudiness. It is in this zone of ambiguity, where the author chooses to remember or omit details, that Glantz invents a new way of distinguishing memory from pure recollection—and of touching the often invisible texture of memory.

The works of Latin American Jewish women writers employ diverse methods of embracing genealogies. Published in Spanish in 1987, *Cláper* by Venezuelan Alicia Freilich de Segal seeks to reconstruct a usurped identity and explore its present-day legacies by interweaving the visions of father and daughter. The narrative of this novel, excerpted here, fluctuates between two landscapes: The first is the landscape of the father's memory, the abandoned Europe, the Polish shtetl of an earlier era, with characters reminiscent of Sholem Aleichem and Isaac Bashevis Singer and the paintings of Marc Chagall. The second is the landscape of the New World in the radical 1960s, with its sense of foreignness and "otherness," but with its geographical and human exuberances. And *Cláper* also explores a third landscape, a landscape of chiaroscuro, a borderline and ambiguous terrain between the two worlds. The novel achieves its maximum power when the threshold is crossed, when the experiences of the father and daughter echo one another—as they do in the opening pages, when each, in his or her own youth, longs for independence. In that border zone, the voice of the father and daughter fuse, metaphorizing the experience of the new land, the joining of the cross and the star.

It is interesting to note that Alicia Frielich de Segal, Margo Glantz, and Alicia Steimberg, who all write about the experience of the emigrant, include in their texts words from the languages of their ancestors— Yiddish, Hebrew, Polish—and also recreate by means of the Spanish language the cadences that are the legacy of those other linguistic heritages. Other Latin American Jewish writers also use such formal devices. The Spanish of Latin America, already altered by the indigenous languages of the hemisphere and by the languages of other emigrés, is thus further reshaped and enriched by the languages of the Jews, the language itself reflecting the fluid *metizaje* of the culture.

Argentine writer Ana María Shua continues the line first traced by Glantz, Segal, and Steimberg. Shua's memoir *The Book of Memories*, from which this excerpt is taken, is family history; it recounts the story of the Rimetka fam-

ily, a typical family of emigrant Jews, in which the majority are tailors, peasants, mystics, and gypsies. But Shua's memoir acquires a unique dimension and complexity through the positioning of the author in her text. In this memoir, Shua relates the experiences of earlier generations of the diaspora, including the grandfather who emigrated to Latin America— but at the same time she places herself at the central axis of the story. She is both the author and the protagonist. Moving backward and forward through time, she interweaves the voices of herself as an adolescent girl and as an adult woman, recreating herself at every moment, and constantly questioning what is written, what is remembered, what is said and what is not said, what is certain and true.

In this transgressive spirit, the memory of the Rimetkas is reinvented upon being written by the granddaughter, Shua herself. Shua is audacious in revising memory; instead of being the daughter who listens and faithfully records what is said, she is the daughter who invents what is heard. In an act of feminist defiance, Shua implicitly disobeys the word of the age-old patriarchal tradition, which says that a woman cannot even study the Talmud. Shua takes it upon herself to question and *re*write the Book of Memories that is kept by her family.

Like Ana María Shua in Argentina, Sonia Guralnik in Chile found her voice against the backdrop of a silence of a country where free expression had been effectively gagged. In this time of fascist repression, Guralnik recorded in a personal notebook, "Writing has become a witness of my own conscience." She describes her search for a language in which to write about what was happening in her country:

> In Russia I spoke Russian, the language in which I learned to read and to write. At home we spoke Yiddish. Here in Chile, Chile of America, I had to learn Spanish, the language in which I think and write and invoke the wars—the First and the Second, the Holocaust, Israel recently created with its own wars. But I want to speak also of another war, without declarations or missiles. I am really an expert in wars, but how can I explain this fratricidal war by night in which we lived buried alive? It is since those wars and their losses that I begin my battle with words. It is in those afternoons of silence that I write about my disappeared nephew, my daughter absent in exile.[18]

For Guralnik, as for many other Jewish writers, the era of fascist dictatorships in the Southern Cone echoed the era of the Holocaust in Europe. The dictatorships' methods of terror and torture and their policies against all "foreigners" and "others" resembled the policies of the Nazis; the thousands of persons in Argentina and Chile who were "disappeared," rounded up in the night to be jailed or killed, were like the vanished Jews of Europe, who were herded and transported and vanished into the "night and fog," never to be seen again. Writing about this chapter in their families' pasts became a subversive way to write about the present. In her provocative and memorable story "Sailing Down the Rhine," Guralnik brings past and present together by writing of a present-day encounter with the violent and insane past of Nazi Europe. The story maintains a powerful narrative unity and at the same time creates a somewhat surreal atmosphere, as the experience of this trip along the Rhine uncovers different layers in the memory of the protagonists. The river flows but this fluidity is unreal; its smooth surface belies the currents of pain and fear that lie beneath, in the depths of memory.

In this story, the silent terror of the camps—Auschwitz, Dachau, Bergen-Belsen—is broken by the victims. Guralnik humanizes the victims, gives them histories, memories, and voices. They recognize that they are not anonymous inhabitants of the camps just as they also recognize the ones who victimized them. Although this is the only story in this anthology set entirely outside of Latin America, it relates to situations that occur today in the countries of the Southern Cone, under now-democratic governments that have given amnesty to the torturers of the fascist years: victims walking in the streets or traveling on trains or ships also find themselves recognizing their torturers.[19] For Guralnik, the story seems to have been a way to bear witness to the silenced victims of the present as well as pay tribute to the silenced victims of the past, the inhabitants of the camps. She finds yet another way to build a bridge to the experience of her ancestors.

The novelist and anthropologist Teresa Porzecanski, a generation younger than Guralnik, explores similar themes. From Uruguay, a country that also suffered atrocities during military dictatorship, she too reaches back to recall the Holocaust and earlier pogroms. In "Rojl Eisips," the past invades the present through the mind of an old woman who is shut away in an old-age home. The narrator arrives at the home looking for her in order to deliver a letter. But Rojl Eisips never reads the letter, because she lives

suspended in a kind of unreal time, without a present and without a future. She lives entirely in her memory, which journeys through a past filled with pain and loss—the fires of pogroms, lost relatives, abandoned houses, women fleeing after the devastation of wars. Her memory is fixed on these horrors; she cannot escape them to live in the present.

As the narrator listens to Rojl Eisips, these memories become part of her own memory as well—a part of her. Porzecanski thus configures a collective memory, a genealogical tree of pogroms and holocausts, of disappearances and fascist dictatorships. She shows that the historical past of one's people is always part of their present as well.

The literature of the Mexican Angelina Muñiz-Huberman is preoccupied with the themes of Jewishness, cabala, and mysticism, as well as the position of the Jew within the confluences of time and history, especially the position of the Jew in the New World. Muñiz-Huberman's work does not search for identity in genealogies and familial alliances; rather, it tackles Judaism from a historical perspective, focusing particularly on the Sephardic Jews in their series of emigrations. Characters from Spanish and Latin American history appear frequently in Muñiz-Huberman's work, including the Spanish Inquisitors, Saint Teresa of Avila, Bartolomé de las Casas (the sixteenth-century Spanish missionary priest who sought to end the enslavement of the indigenous Latin Americans), and later, the young Jewish women Anne Frank and Etty Hillesum, who both perished in the Holocaust.

Angelina Muñiz-Huberman draws upon the work of Jorge Luis Borges, who was fundamental in introducing the contemporary presence of cabalistic and Sephardic texts into Latin American literature,[20] although like other Latin American Jewish women writers, she seeks her own relationship with mysticism through the feminine voice. It also draws upon the cabalistic tradition in which the writer orders her own universe, comprehends it, in order to later teach it through telling and retelling stories.

"The Portuguese Synagogue" is a disturbing and beautiful story—a story that dislocates and reshapes language and displays a lucid knowledge of history, especially the Holocaust. The narrator is a traveler who sits in the Portuguese synagogue of Amsterdam, and there, within the realm of God and of prayer, appear all the scenes of violence that have passed through the space. The symbolic imagination becomes a means of invoking the presence and articulating the experience of women whose deaths were imposed, women who tried in vain to understand the chaos of the

universe and time breaking up. Both Etty Hillesum and Anne Frank wrote diaries and tried to bring order to the disorder of history, to pacify the uncertainty of all the imposed deaths, and to celebrate life; here in the empty synagogue, the narrator yearns to do the same. "The Portuguese Synagogue" puts a human face on the horrors of history, and explores responses to all the holocausts and to the particular and universal genocides of the world. It is a text that, like all the work of Angelina Muñiz-Huberman, reads like a poem; it is an ode to pain and suffering, but also to spirit and life.

Costa Rican poet and short story writer Rosita Kalina draws upon cabalalistic tradition in her story, which refers to the legendary figure of the golem, a kind of robotlike creature brought to life to do humans' bidding. The golem in Kalina's story is a conciliatory spirit that comes to help the children in school so that they will more easily learn the Hebrew alphabet and the teachings of the Talmud and of cabala. When the golem achieves his purpose, he disappears—or, perhaps, is reincarnated in the spirit of the rabbi. "Golem" resides in an ambiguous, miraculous space that testifies to the possibility of creating magic through the religious spirit.

Within the tradition that draws upon the memories of ancestors are many works that reveal a strong element of humor. Humor—especially a subtle, ironic, and sometimes tragicomic humor—has been an almost essential characteristic of Latin American literature written by women. This phenomenon seems emphasized even more in the literature of Latin American Jewish women writers, whose work often combines elements of two traditions: the wise humor of Sholem Aleichem, the trenchant folk humor of Isaac Bashevis Singer, and the magical ironies of Gabriel García Márquez or Isabel Allende.

Angélica Gorodischer is a distinguished Argentine writer known particularly for her work in the field of science fiction—work that is at the same time austere and abundant, baroque and subtle, quotidian and wildly imaginative. Gorodischer's story "Camera Obscura" begins with a family photograph, the portrait of Grandmother Gertrudis that occupies the most important and visible site in the main room of the house. But here the photograph is not so much an object of sacred memory as a symbol of transgression. The famous Grandmother Gertrudis is one of the ugliest women in the family. Through the voice of both a male and a female narrator, we discover that Gertrudis, in spite of her reported ugliness and her

difficult and circumscribed life, proved that she was both beautiful and free when she ran off with the very same photographer who took her portrait. This explicitly feminist story subverts the assumptions of the patriarchy and shows how a remarkable woman can overthrow the male dominance of memory, as a male narrator is forced to admit: "Now it turns out that my grandmother Gertrudis is an important person and it is forbidden to speak badly of her in this household" (96).

Clarice Lispector is among Brazil's preeminent writers and one of the great voices of Latin American literature, acclaimed for her original and lyrical language, for her comprehension of things that go beyond the immediate and the tangible. Curiously, although her work certainly touched upon her Jewishness in a variety of ways, Lispector has rarely been viewed in her own country as a Jewish writer—her very critical acclaim and popularity perhaps preventing such recognition of "otherness." But Grace Paley, one of North America's most distinguished Jewish writers, has remarked upon the impact of Lispector's heritage:

> Lispector spent the first two months of her life in the town of Chechelnik, in the Ukraine. This is a small short fact. The interesting question unanswered is, at what age did she enter the Portuguese language? And how much Russian did she bring with her, and Yiddish? Sometimes I think that this is what her work is all about, one language trying to make itself at home in another.[21]

Lispector's brief *cronica* or "chronicle," as she called it, "No More Worries," exemplifies a return to the Jewish past in which she grew up and to the superstitions that must have been a part of her household. (There are many Jewish sayings in this brief piece that I myself heard as a child in Chile.) This intensely humorous piece also reveals the hybrid nature of Clarice Lispector's upbringing and her writing: Jewish from the Ukraine and yet Brazilian to the core. (In several interviews, Lispector has said how much she loves the Portuguese language.) In "No More Worries" the stolen statue of St. Anthony that will bring bad luck to a spinster exists vis à vis Jewish lore together with the Brazilian lore of the northeast, the region of Lispector's childhood. Labeled both a sorcerer and a mystic, Clarice Lispector illuminates cultures and ethnicities while she enriches our opportunities to laugh and to dream.

The House of Memory

Reflecting Our "Otherness"

Without leaving behind the concern with memory or the quest for roots, many Latin American Jewish women writers have focused more directly on the experience of being Jewish within a society where the Jew remains, always and irrevocably, the "other." As their work reflects this strange and unique experience, it at the same time hints at the universal experience of the foreigner and the refugee—of being different, of not having the correct credentials, of being despised and misunderstood. By showing the damage wrought by prejudice, the stories of these writers make a powerful case for tolerance and humanity.

The best-known work of Chilean writer Ana Vásquez is preoccupied with political violence, state-sanctioned terrorism, and its effect on families. In the story "The Sign of the Star," written especially for this anthology, Vásquez deals with another kind of violence and the damage it wreaks. She captures the feeling of what it can mean to be Jewish in Latin America through the innocent and vulnerable presence of a little boy. The story, while possessing a profound tenderness, is also fiercely devastating: gradually, it unleashes a description of the horrors of the Holocaust, and of the anti-Semitism represented by the schoolchildren who are unable to understand and accept otherness, unable to comprehend that the little boy does not go to church on Sundays and that he can be Jewish without necessarily having a strong dogmatic religious presence. In this story, Ana Vásquez succeeds with absolute sincerity in recreating the pain suffered by so many Jewish children in Chilean schools, amid the indifference of parents and educational authorities.

Through the voice of a confused and frightened little boy who searches for meaning in his disorderly, dejected, and fragmented identity, Ana Vásquez creates a story opposed to the concerns of some other writers, who search for a type of unifying place between a Spanish Catholic/indigenous *mestizaje*. Vásquez captures with clarity the meaning of "otherness"—what it signifies to inhabit a different space and to be marked from an early age by a heritage that brands the individual as a stranger in his own land, and eliminates him from the collective conscience of the country.

Mexican writer and filmmaker Rosa Nissan, like Ana Vásquez, explores the impact of "otherness" through the eyes of a child in the early chapters

of her beautifully rendered autobiographical novel *May You Make a Good Bride*. The narrator is a young girl named Oshinica, a member of the Sephardic community of Mexico City, who lives in a predominantly Catholic neighborhood and attends a Catholic school. There is some humor on the surface of Oisha's story, as she recounts her childlike perceptions of the rituals of an alien religion. But beneath the humor lies the heartbreaking tragedy of a child who, unable to tolerate the persecution and loneliness that results from her difference, is driven to deny her own heritage: Oisha dreams of guardian angels and saint's day parties, practices crossing herself and studies for her first communion, and hopes that God will forgive her whole family for the fact that "the Jews killed Christ." To her classmates' taunts she responds: "That's a lie. I'm not a Jew. I say my prayers and make confession just like the rest of you" (130).

Nissan, capturing with consummate skill the voice of a young girl, reveals the difficulty—and at times, the hearbreaking sadness and self-denial—that come with being a Jew in a society steeped in the rites of the Christian world. This deceptively simple story profiles the constant schism of Latin American culture, which despite its multiculturalism retains a Christian hegemony in which Jews will always be outsiders—even if they do not wish to be.

Like Vásquez and Nissan, Chilean writer Barbara Mujica writes of a protagonist who searches desperately for the chance to become an accepted part of a society that has excluded him. In "Gotlib, Bombero," a Jewish man seeks to become a volunteer firefighter—an honorary position that has historically, in Chile, conferred great prestige upon its occupants. Living in the city of Antofagasta, a provincial and prejudiced territory, Gotlib waits like a child and hopes almost despairingly to be admitted to the local brigade, which from the time of its founding has declined to accept Jews.

Mujica succeeds in capturing the desire to belong to a restricted organization, to occupy forbidden space—to become, if just for a moment, an insider rather than an outsider. Much more is at stake in this story than membership in the local brigade, and Mujica captures, as well, the deeper meaning that underlies Gotlib's longing, his tenuous faith in possibility, and the lingering doubts he feels at the outcome of the story's events.

If the stories by Vásquez, Nissan, and Mujica show the short-term and long-term impact of prejudice, the story by Argentine Alicia Kozameh

goes a step deeper, to reveal the upheaval and disintegration within the soul of a woman struggling with her position of "otherness." The text of "Alcira in Yellows" is unique in its view of the internal turmoil and self-censorship, the profound terror of feeling oneself foreign to the rules of the society. Alcira's condition has been shaped by a society where anti-Semitism is only one of many forms of brutality. It has been aggravated by a family that reared her with conflicting messages regarding her Jewish heritage: her grandmother pushing it upon her, her father denying it altogether in an effort to force his family to assimilate. "Alcira in Yellows" reveals, in innovative form, the costs of denying human beings their freedom and their identity.

Reina Roffé, a successful Argentine novelist who left her country due to the censorship imposed by the military authorities upon publication of her book *Monte de Venus* (1976), is one of the few writers to return to the most ancestral and ritualistic roots of the Sephardic community. Roffé's tender and powerful story, "Exotic Birds," unmasks the lives of women in closed communities—in this case, Aunt Reche, a fragile but enduring soul who constantly returns to the port of Buenos Aires in search of "the family members," the Sephardim who came from Morocco. This story suggests the arduous struggle of those Jewish women who wished to flee from the confining communities imposed upon them in their native lands, then find themselves desperately trying to penetrate into the rhythm and time of the new communities. Most deeply, it reveals the constant battle of the woman fighting to belong on her own terms.

Of all the Jewish rites that have made their way from the Old World to the New World, the ritual of kaddish—the prayer of mourning—is the most austere and memorable. It is a ritual situated in the zones of heart-rending pain, a ritual full of vulnerability and tenderness. Around this ritual, the Chilean writer Graciela Safranchik constructs a wonderfully complex and moving story of a bourgeois Jewish family gathered together to acknowledge not only the deceased father but also the surviving mother and the memories that unite them all.

"Kaddish" is narrated by different voices, offering the reader the possibility of hearing, in the midst of the awesome silence of death, the voices of the living, the personal and collective remembrances of a family reunited through the rituals of death. It is a family made up of loving children and others, more aloof, who, facing the greatest finality of life, return

home to say kaddish and continue the ancestral ties to their relatives and their race.

This shattering text is more than a statement about what death means for the Jew; it becomes a beautiful and lyrical meditation about life, memory and recollection, recalling ways of being and of living, of accepting an existence in which all human beings must face pain and death. Through her story, Safranchik explores transcendental questions as well as practical ones: What can we do to live in a better way? How can we reach old age with dignity and make peace with the certainty of death? How can we retain our memory of times and people who have left us?

Such memorable meditations join this work to the best literature of Latin America, which poses the eternal question of death. However, "Kaddish" carries that theme to a new level, where the consciousness of the living is linked with that of the dead—and finally, joined more literally, as the mother follows the father to the grave:

> Once again these chants are rending our souls, perhaps that's why she made me sing when we were alone, to imagine how they'd sound when we brought her here. The two stone markers will be facing each other. Papa reserved the plots. He wanted her with him, soon, as soon as possible. But I don't believe she is quite ready to follow him. Is he what she's following? Is that why she chose to die so abruptly? Is it something you can decide? (194)

In carrying on a dialogue with the essential and the eternal, Safrancik, like so many of these Latin American Jewish women writers, has shaped new forms that stretch the boundaries of language's ability to express the mystical, the spiritual, the intangible, and the profound.

Revisioning Our Identities

The legacies of a turbulent and wandering past marked by the scars of prejudice become a literary force in the work of Jewish women writers of Latin America. With courage and vibrancy, these writers have managed to reshape and readdress their own origins and identities within the context of the Spanish language and the Latin American world. It may be the very historical invisibility of Latin American Jewish women writers that, paradoxically, has afforded them the freedom to reconceptualize and explore identity: written off as an insignificant minority, seldom defined except in

stereotypes, they had no choice but to define and create themselves, to discover for themselves the complex meanings attached to being a Jewish woman of Latin America.

Margo Glantz invents a highly original and playful premise through which to explore questions of identity. "Shoes," a new story, alludes to a genealogy very different from those published a decade ago. This story is an exquisite mixture of sensual description, humor, and history, a wonderfully original autobiography shaped around the author's great obsession with finding and wearing the best Ferragamo shoe. She explores the etymology of the word *shoe*, and the confluences between the history of this material object and her own history. She reveals that from the time of Moses and Deuteronomy, it was said to the Hebrews: "I have made you walk through the desert for forty years and your sandals have not worn out under your feet." Exploring her own genealogies, she confesses that she was the daughter of poor Russian immigrants but now wishes to travel in the world of the well-heeled—thus her obsession with the Ferragamos. In Glantz's innovative and audacious vision, even such an object as a shoe becomes a powerful icon of personal and cultural identity.

Luisa Futoransky, an Argentine writer, poet, and translator who now lives in Paris, joins with her contemporaries who travel back in time to trace numerous journeys and returns. "The Melancholy of Black Panthers" does not, however, dwell in a personal genealogy of certain memories, but rather presents a genealogy common to all exiles who share the silence of the stranger. In addition, she focuses her story on the experiences of women: Through the story of generations of powerless women, who arrived in different parts of Latin America abandoned and desolate, Futoransky tells how human beings dislocated in time and place might lose their reason and faith. She offers a tribute to the meaning of the lives of those women who arrived desperate, in search of a new memory and a new identity; who arrived mute, without language, with an unspeakable past. Finally, "The Melancholy of Black Panthers" postulates what it means to always be a writer in translation; translation from other languages, from other times and places: "Arriving in one language, living in another, and writing in a third" (213). In doing so, she recognizes that the story of these lost women is part of the story of her own identity.

Introduction

In addition to being gifted writer, Ruth Behar is a distinguished figure in contemporary cultural anthropology. In her book *Translated Woman*, she explores the different spaces formed by borders—between North and South America, between the Old World and the New World—and their effect upon language, upon the principle of the word. In the piece written for this anthology, "In the Absence of Love," Behar reverses the journey of immigration, seeking to recover the essential roots of her being. Returning from the United States to Cuba, she recreates the rituals of her heritage: at the cemetery of her ancestors, faithful to custom, she covers their graves with stones. She returns to her parents' home with the question, "What will happen to the one thousand Jews who remain in Cuba?" Cuba, for many of them, was never intended to be more than a temporary home. (Many Jews went to Cuba in the 1940s only to await their visas for the United States, and in the 1960s, the Jews who emigrated had "Repatriated" marked on their passports.) Behar searches for the homeland of her grandparents, for that Cuba which perhaps does not belong to her but which she wishes to make hers—and in that search she seeks herself.

The work of Miriam Bornstein evokes, with both power and tenderness, the condition of life in the borderlines—in a state of constant crossings and uncertain beginnings. Bornstein, like many Chicana authors, uses both Spanish and English to tell and retell her story. She recounts, with vivid imagery, the lives of her ancestors, from Poland to Mexico to the United States. Her story recreates vanished worlds—worlds of rivers that need to be crossed, like the Vistula in the Old World or the Rio Grande in the New World. They are rivers of memory, as well, that flow with the tenacious desire to remember. Bornstein is a writer who is determined to live and flourish in her own borderlands—the borderlands of language and memory. Involved in a constant search for home—whether it is Poland or Sonora, the shtetl or the desert—she remains a stranger in most lands, and yet is always welcome in the landscape of her own remembrances.

In my own work *Always from Somewhere Else: A Memoir of My Chilean Jewish Father*, I recount the many journeys of my father and his family—from the Ukraine, to Istanbul, to Marseilles, to the small Chilean town of Quillota, to Santiago, and finally to the United States. But in doing so I explore not only my father's experience as a constant exile and stranger, but also my own. I include this piece in *The House of Memory* because I believe that it helps to bring the anthology full circle, and reveals many of its spiraling

and intertwining themes: we begin with the stories of our ancestors in the Old World and the New World; we travel through our experiences as women and as Jews in Latin America, and we end our journey with an effort to shape and define and describe our own identities—only to discover that our destinations, in so many ways, return us to our points of departure. For what are we, after all, but the living legacy of our ancestors?

Ester Rebeca Shapiro Rok continues to develop this theme of the discovery of self through an almost obsessive pursuit of origins, of family stories. She sums up this experience in the opening lines of the piece included here, "From Belarus to Bolondron: A Daughter's Dangerous Passage":

> In telling the story of my Cuban Eastern European Jewish American self, I listen closely to a competing cacophony of ancestral voices carrying 150 years of oral history and living memory, because among them I discern the currents of my own life.

Like many other Latin American Jewish women writers, Rok thus participates in a twofold relationship with the stories of the past—as both gatherer and transmitter, listener and teller. As she retraces her family's journey through multiple exiles and decodes various family secrets, Rok is particularly aware of how she brings her own perspective to these stories, reshaping them as she retells them in her own way: "I insist on scrambling the official story and casting my central protagonists in contradiction to the cherished myths our family still lives by."

The character of Tia Consuelo is part of this family mythology. She is a powerful and complex character, an exceptional woman struggling to find her place. Like Aunt Reche in "Exotic Birds," she is bound by constraining social codes and was often misunderstood by her family. But she is more defiant than Aunt Reche; although Tia Consuelo still hangs on to some traditions, she also represents transgression and courage, passion and freedom. And for Rok she has a special significance: she is the closest thing Rok has to a role model for the new woman in the New World.

To the initial question of whether or not there exists a tradition of Jewish women writers in Latin America, I would clearly respond in the affirmative—and the stories in this anthology show just how rich, how varied,

and how powerful that tradition truly is. It is a tradition of women whose passion and obsession is to approach the rhythms, the secret murmurs of memory.

These writers are voyagers, wanderers through time and space. They are the keepers of the past, the inheritors of places and languages, the keepers of time. They have a way of being in the world that places them in a position where the history of ancient times is joined to the postmodernism of today. They were born, for the most part, in the Western Hemisphere, but they carry with them the cultural baggage of all the lands of the diaspora. They write in Spanish and Portuguese and English that includes echoes of Yiddish, Hebrew, Russian, and Polish.

These writers articulate an experience that is essentially personal, but also record the social and cultural history of a people. These are women who tell tales, and in the telling make reference to the burning of heretics in the Inquisition, the murder of Jews in the Holocaust, the torture of millions in Argentina and Chile—and thus, by means of the word, they bear witness. They are women witnesses; they fasten themselves to memory and through writing give a legitimacy to the history of women and of Jews in Latin America.

The work of these writers testifies to the fact that it is women, as the Mexican writer Elena Poniatowska has noted, who maintain the strongest relationship with the memory of the marginalized.[23] These writers speak for the legions of mute men and women, of the outsiders and the oppressed. They speak in a voice that begins as a murmur and becomes what Támara Kameszain calls a whispered conversation.[24] They move beyond the oral tradition that has been sustained through generations and enter the language of the text; they record the silenced voices, for the first time, in the great book of memory—a book that tells the stories of others, but also of themselves.

Writing, in the best Talmudic tradition, is practiced as a way of ordering one's identity as well as belonging to a tradition. By making their voices heard, these women, silenced and marginalized, have created for themselves an identity and a tradition in which they belong. Through their work, these writers, exiles and outsiders, have built for themselves a home, in the house of memory.

Translated from the Spanish by Roberta Gordenstein

1. Latin American Jews enjoyed relative tranquility in modern times until the period of sinister military dictatorships that dominated the countries of the Southern Cone and Paraguay and of Central America in the 1970s and 1980s. In Argentina, military fascism restored the strong anti-Semitic rhetoric that was part of the legacy of Peron and of its Nazi immigrants, and Jews were tortured beneath portraits of Hitler. In Chile, Jewish intellectuals and doctors, especially psychiatrists, disappeared with greater frequency than non-Jews during the period of mass terror that followed the ascent of military dictators in those countries in 1973. These periods of terror brought back to Latin American Jews memories of the fear and destruction of Europe under the Nazis. On the treatment of Jewish "dissidents" during Argentina's "dirty war" see Marguerite Feitlowitz, *A Lexicon of Terror: Argentina and the Legacies of Torture* (New York: Oxford University Press, 1998), 63–88, and Argentina, Comisión Nacional sobre la Desparación de Personas, *Nunca Más: The Report of the Argentine National Commission of the Disappeared* (New York: Farrar, Straus, Giroux, 1986). Direct documentation on the experience of the victims can be found in the archives of the Asociacion Mundial Israelita for the years 1976 through 1979, and in Jacobo Timerman, *Prisoner Without a Name, Cell Without a Number* (New York: Random House, 1990). On the disappearances of Jews in Chile see the report of the Truth and Reconciliation Commission published by the Vicarate of Solidarity, Santiago, 1986, 23.

2. The "Mothers of the Plaza del Mayo" began to create a movement in Buenos Aires in 1976 to demand to know the whereabouts of their missing children, who had been "disappeared"—abducted by the Argentine military and never seen again. They stood as a living witness to the government's crimes. See Jo Fisher, *The Mothers of the Disappeared* (Boston: South End Press, 1989) and John Simpson and Jana Bennett, *The Disappeared and the Mothers of the Plaza: The Story of the 11,000 Argentines Who Vanished* (New York: St. Martin's Press, 1985).

3. I eventually shaped these stories into two books: a memoir of my mother's life called *A Cross and a Star: Memoirs of a Jewish Girl in Chile* (Albuquerque: University of New Mexico Press, 1995; paperback New York: The Feminist Press, 1997) and *Always from Somewhere Else: A Memoir of My Chilean Jewish Father* (New York: The Feminist Press, 1998), which is excerpted in this book.

4. *Conversos* were Jews who converted to Christianity and Marranos were Jews who practiced their religion in secret after publicly converting. Both acts took place, for the most part, under threat of death or banishment by the Inquisition in Europe or the New World.

5. The fact that Jews fleeing the pogroms and the Holocaust of twentieth-century Europe settled in Latin America as well as North America is reasonably well known. Less familiar are other large-scale immigrations: in 1889, for example, the Jewish philanthropist Baron Maurice de Hirsch established in Argentina colonies that were endowed with a socialist and agrarian ideology, aimed at creating a type of kibbutz on the vast pampas and creating the interesting phenomenon of the Jewish gaucho. See Judith Laikin Elkin, *The Jews of Latin America* (New York: Holmes & Meier, 1998), 107.

Introduction

For more on the history of the Jews in Argentina, see Haim Avni, *Argentina and the Jews: A History of Jewish Immigration* (Tuscaloosa: University of Alabama Press, 1991). More recently, in 1956, when many Jews were expelled from Egypt after having been part of one of the most important and distinguished communities of the Arabian diaspora, they also directed themselves to Latin America. These Sephardic Jews from the Middle East, returning to their Hispanic roots, have tended to be very quickly admitted to places such as Brazil, Venezuela, and Argentina, where they also coexist in harmony with their neighbors from Arab countries such as Syria and Lebanon, united by the Semitic tradition. See María Antonia Bel Bravo, *Sefarad: Los Judíos de España* (Madrid: Silex Editores, 1997), 322–89. Also see Paloma Díaz Más, *Los Sefaradíes: Historia, lengua, y cultura* (Barcelona: Riopiedras Ediciones, 1994).

6. Latin American historians have in the past devoted insufficient attention to the presence of Jews in their region, perhaps because as a statistic, this presence appears to be of little importance. The 1 percent of the population of Latin America that is Jewish (according to *The United Nations Demographic Yearbook*, 1996) has remained catalogued under the general rubric of "otherness." However, since the 1970s, interest in the theme of Jewishness, and texts on this subject, have proliferated among Latin American scholars. (Interestingly, this attention to Jewish history has coincided with a resurgence of anti-Semitism in many parts of Latin America.) Notable among these texts is the book by Judith Laikin Elkin, and also Selly Dayán de Mizrachi, *La saga de los Sefarditas: Del Medio Orienta a Panama* (Sociedad Israelita de Benefencia Shevet Ahim, 1986); Moshé Nes-El, *Historia de la comunidad israelita sefaradi de Chile* (Santiago: Editorial Nascimento, 1984) and *La inmigracion judía a Chile: 1920–1970*, coloquio 47 (autumn 1982); 73–82; Jeffrey Lesser, *Welcoming the Undesirables: Brazil and the Jewish Question* (Berkeley: University of California Press, 1995); and Robert M. Levine, *Tropical Diaspora: The Jewish Experience in Cuba* (Gainesville: University Press of Florida, 1993).

7. Of the ninety men who journeyed with Columbus on his first voyage, six were Jews. This first voyage of Columbus, in 1492, coincided with the mass expulsion of the Jews from Spain, and the new route he discovered offered opportunities for emigration to the Jews who refused to convert to Catholicism and who, by chance and by their willingness to move, saved themselves from the flames of the Inquisition (which would also soon burn all too brightly on the newly discovered continent). See Elkin, prologue and chapter 1, and Bravo, 91–120. For more background on the expulsion of the Jews from Spain see B. Netanyahu, *The Origins of the Inquisition in Fifteenth-Century Spain* (New York: Random House, 1995).

8. For the most part, Jews who emigrated to Latin America in the twentieth century had arrived with a firsthand knowledge of the evil fruits of prejudice and totalitarianism that fueled their dedication to societies built on tolerance and freedom. These values created a polarization between the Jews and the fascist regimes of the 1970s, where Jews often numbered high among the "subversives." See Feitlowitz, 63–88.

9. The presence of Jewish communities in places as unexpected as the Dominican Republic, where during World War II the dictator Rafael Trujillo encouraged the immigration of Jews in order to "lighten" the race, and the cruel irony of the situation in places like Argentina, Chile, and Bolivia, where refugee Jews have lived side-by-side with refugee Nazis, constitutes part of a complex and varied history.

10. Books of interest that refer to Latin American Jewish women's literature include Lois Baer Barr, *Isaac Unbound: Patriarchal Traditions in the Latin American Jewish Novel* (Tempe: ASU Center for Latin American Studies, Arizona State University, 1995); Judith R. Baskin, ed., *Women of the Word: Jewish Women and Jewish Writing* (Detroit: Wayne State University Press, 1994); and Hélène Cixous, *Reading with Clarice Lispector* (Minneapolis: University of Minnesota Press, 1990). Important works on Latin American Jewish writing in general include Robert DiAntonio and Nora Glickman, *Tradition and Innovation: Reflections on Latin American Jewish Writing* (Albany: State University of New York Press, 1993); Nelson H. Vieira, *Jewish Voices in Brazilian Literature: A Prophetic Discourse of Alterity* (Gainesville: University Press of Florida, 1996); and Leonardo Senkman, *La identitad judía en la literatura Argentina* (Buenos Aires: Ediciones Pardes, 1983).

11. Margo Glantz, *Las genealogías* (tr. *The Family Tree*) (Mexico City: M. Casillas, 1981), 13.

12. *Mestizo* or *mestiza* means, literally, "half-breed" or "half-caste," and is used to describe a person or culture formed through a blending of distinct racial or cultural backgrounds. Much of the population of Latin America is *mestizo*, having both indigenous and European blood.

13. DiAntonio and Glickman, *Tradition and Innovation*, 4.

14. See Rigoberta Menchú, *I, Rigoberta Menchú: An Indian Woman in Guatemala*, ed. Elisabeth Burgos-Debray (London: Verso, 1984) and Domitila Barrios de Chungara with Moema Viezzer, *Let Me Speak!: Testimony of Domitila, a Woman of the Bolivian Mines* (New York: Monthly Review Press, 1978).

15. Preface to *Musicians and Watchmakers* (Pittsburgh: Latin American Literary Review Press, 1998), 9–10.

16. See DiAntonio and Glickman, *Tradition and Innovation*. For more on the utopian Jewish communities of Argentina, see note 5.

17. Years after the publication of Glantz's *Las genealogías*, Elena Poniatowska's text *La "flor de lis"* (Mexico City: Ediciones Era, 1988), narrated the history of her family and especially the arrival of her mother to an exotic and distant Mexico. *Novia que te vea* (May you make a good bride), by the film producer Rosa Nissan, excerpted in this anthology, would also continue revising and recreating an essentially feminine memory.

18. Sonia Guralnik, personal letter to Marjorie Agosín, 1995.

19. Such a coincidence forms the premise for Ariel Dorfman's well-known work *Death and the Maiden* (New York: Viking Penguin, 1992).

20. The majority of Borges' early stories explore mysticism through cabalistic interpretation. See Edna Aizenberg, *The Aleph Weaver: Biblical, Kabbalistic, and Judaic Elements in Borges* (Potomac, Maryland: Scripta Humanistica, 1986).

21. Introduction to *Soulstorm: Stories* (New York: New Directions, 1989). Lispector's Jewish identity is discussed in Nelson H. Vieira, "Clarice Lispector: A Jewish Impulse and a Prophecy of Difference," in *Jewish Voices in Brazilian Literature*.

22. Cabala is a mystical Jewish system of interpretation of the Scriptures, encompassing the belief that every word, letter, and number of the Scriptures contains mysteries. The movement probably arose in France in the eleventh century and spread, especially to Spain, where it gained influence in the time of the Inquisition and the expulsion of the Jews from Spain.

23. Talk delivered at Wellesley College, Wellesley, Massachusetts, September 14, 1997.

24. *El texto silencio: Tradición y vanguardia en la poesia sudamericana* (Mexico City: University Nacional Autónomo de Mexico, 1987).

Part One

The Family Tree:
Ancestors and Traditions

From Musicians and Watchmakers

Alicia Steimberg

My grandmother knew the secret of eternal life. It consisted of a group of such simple rules that it was incredible that no one other than she herself knew about and practiced them. Sometimes we would participate in the ritual, thus guaranteeing ourselves, if not complete immortality, at least a good dose of it.

One of the ceremonies of this cult consisted of boiling Swiss chard and eating it immediately, sprinkled with the liquid from the concoction mixed with the juice of two large lemons. In the most perfect enactment of this rite, you would boil the chard beneath a lemon tree. When it was ready, you would make a cut into two lemons that were hanging from the tree right above the pot, so that the juice that fell on the chard would retain its vitamins, without losing a single drop of its nutritional value.

My grandmother said that ninety percent of human ills came from constipation. At home we all suffered from it, and there was a continuous coming and going of prescriptions to ward it off. Despite her wisdom in this area, my grandmother suffered from constipation more than anyone else. Whenever she managed to move her bowels, she would walk around for a while with a big smile on her face, and she would tell everyone about it. She was even known to crack a joke, or recall springtime in Kiev.

Those spingtimes came after really hellish winters. Just when it seemed as if the cold and the snow would last forever, one morning she would draw the curtains and watch torrents of water flowing past her window. As soon as the water had passed, the sun would suddenly burst forth, everything would erupt into flowers, and the woods would fill up with wild cherries. Sweet cherries, not like the ones we get here. And that's how it

would be the next day, and the day after that. Not like here, with these springtimes that don't even know what they are.

That's how my grandmother would describe her native land, whenever the activity of her bowels put her in a good frame of mind

＊　＊　＊　＊　＊

I don't know if Otilia ever deluded herself into thinking she was pretty. Perhaps one summer afternoon, while she was crossing Nueve de Julio Avenue in a streetcar with her fiance, a good-looking guy who resembled Clark Gable and was younger than she. You probably want to know how she caught him. It happened at a dance, where she and her next-in-line sister each nabbed a boyfriend.

The boys were friends. They hadn't been in Buenos Aires very long, and they earned a living as best they could. They also enjoyed the usual pastimes of bachelorhood. For thirty cents they could have a wonderful time on a sunny day: ten cents for the streetcar to the public beach, ten to get back, and ten for a salami sandwich. Stretched out in the sunshine, sporting their wool bathing trunks, their little mustaches, and their innocence, they would talk about the future:

"Hey, man, you gonna get married?" asked Clark Gable.

"Um, . . . no," the other one answered. "I'm gonna travel."

Nevertheless, the weddings took place only a month apart, shortly after the conversation at the public beach. Otilia got married first. (How the pretty girl envies her ugly sister's good fortune!) I witnessed Grandma's preparations. She stationed herself out on the patio of the house in Donato Alvarez, next to a bag full of little rolls. She cut them all in half and smeared them with something. On the folding tables they set up that night on that same patio, platters bloomed with little rolls, bottled orangeade and beer. I don't know if there was anything else, because I hardly even managed to get close, and when I did, I had to put up with my aunts' sloppy kisses and tell them what my name was, how old I was, and if I loved my little brother.

Nor was I able to observe the glorious moment when the brides took leave of their family homes and acquired the privilege of being supported by their husbands. The guests piled up around the bridal canopy, which was illuminated by an electric bulb. Clark Gable and his friend were tall guys; they had to tip their heads slightly to the side under the canopy, while the little lantern rested on top of their Vaselined hair. Despite this

minor inconvenience, everything turned out fine. On tiptoe, stretching out my neck to no avail, I heard the rabbi intone the praises to God which began the ceremony.

I was just a little girl, but I already understood that you were supposed to get emotional, that the jasmine-scented breeze came from the garden next door (because at my grandparents' house there were only some red wildflowers that didn't smell at all), and that more than one guest disrespectfully turned around in the middle of the ceremony to cast watchful glances at the folding tables. At the first of these weddings I learned something: I didn't have to stay until the end of the ceremony to get from the wedding canopy to the food tables. That's what I did the first time, and I nearly got trampled.

Some years earlier another marriage had been celebrated in that house, a marriage from which I was born, and three years later, my little brother (yes, I loved my little brother). After Otilia and Amanda's weddings, Grandpa got sick and I stopped going to the house in Donato Alvarez. I had no further news of him until they took me to La Chacarita cemetery (because my grandfather, an atheist, a socialist, and a vegetarian, was cremated according to his explicit wishes and doesn't repose among our other relatives in the Jewish cemetery). They didn't tell me before taking me to the cemetery that Grandpa had died so as not to upset me. We stood for a while looking at a little box which couldn't possibly have contained Grandpa. Otilia and Amanda didn't go to the cemetery on account of their "condition." My cousins were born, also a month apart: first the son of Otilia and Clark Gable. They went off to live in General Pico, and we lost sight of them for a while.

Thus ended a long and difficult period for my family, but one that was lovely and full of fun for me. I would sniff the cookies that Grandma baked in the kitchen; I would watch Mele, Otilia, and Amanda rehearsing didactic plays for the Socialist Party Theater Group; and I would see a windmill emerge on the canvas Mele was painting. The canvas didn't interest me as much as the palette, covered with all kinds of colored stains and peaks.

＊　＊　＊　＊　＊

Otilia and Clark Gable set themselves up in a room, in which they crammed a double bed and a couple of little night tables, a dining room table with chairs, a wardrobe, a cupboard, and a side table. In a vase that

she called the "centerpiece," Otilia put a bouquet of artificial flowers that she had made herself. When the Chipmunk was born (we called him that because of his chubby cheeks), they also had to squeeze in a crib.

Motherhood didn't make Otilia more beautiful, but it did make her fatter. It was no longer possible to visualize her as she had been during her engagement: skinny in her blue linen sailor dress, white spool-heeled shoes, and a mane of hair with little spitcurls on her forehead. Clark Gable, on the other hand, was even thinner than before, but still good-looking, wildly happy, and a great prankster.

Once in a while Clark Gable's mother and sister would come from Entre Rios to visit the couple. As married women, they enjoyed a certain amount of leisure and could travel for pleasure. They had screechy voices, and they practiced a form of birth control that consisted of repeatedly jumping off a table onto the floor after "having relations" with their husbands. They were famous for the number of miscarriages they provoked: in that family no one had had fewer than thirty or forty.

Otilia and Amanda, by hook or by crook, had become married ladies. Otilia chose names for her children from the social pages of El Hogar. The same names as the children of Senora Peralta Ramos or Senora Martinez de Hoz. She avoided those that were too obviously Catholic, such as any combination with Maria. Amanda, who had fewer pretensions and who was more sentimental and a great interpreter of tangos, gave her children more popular names. They were called Evaristo, Azucena, and Greta. This last name, which might be considered an exception, was a concession to her enthusiasm for foreign actresses.

With the business of the names, a long family tradition was broken. All Otilia and Amanda's female cousins were named Dora; all the male cousins, Leon. To differentiate, they were classified as Dora, Dorita, Ugly Dora, Big Dora, Little Dora, Uncle Jose's Dora. Then there were Leon, Little Leon, Big Leon, Leon the Watchmaker, and Leon the Lawyer. When they all got together, there was never any confusion: each one knew very well who he or she was and who all the others were.

With three of her four daughters already married, Grandma was happy. At other relatives' weddings, which didn't take place beneath the grape arbor, but rather in rented halls, she had her picture taken with her daughters, sons-in-law, and grandchildren, all dressed up and with new shoes. I learned to distrust the smiles that abounded at those social events. As soon as Grandma returned home from the party and put on her housecoat, her true colors emerged. Her face reflected an existence full of suffering,

yoked to the side of a silent husband and daughters who fought like wild beasts, feeding on their insatiable bitterness. The four of them were, according to what I overheard from their arguments, bitches, vipers, egotists, imbeciles, tightwads, and evil incarnate. I watched them, trying to discover those qualities in their faces, but without discerning much except that they were fat and ugly.

After each fight they would break off relations forever. But they got back together after each wedding and wake, displaying tender smiles, too much rouge, and their kids, and they eventually patched things up. For a while calm would reign. We'd organize a picnic. Everything would turn out badly, plagued by ants, mosquitoes, and packed buses. "When poor people try to have fun . . ." Mele would say. She was the one who got married late. Like her sisters, she was very fond of dramatic scenes. Grandma would try to lift our spirits by telling us funny stories that happened to other people: Some guy's business failed and he ended up on the street; someone else's trip got screwed up; another one had to leave school for financial reasons; yet another gave birth to a sixth daughter. She would laugh until she choked, never noticing if anyone else shared her mirth.

The same things weren't funny when they happened to her. Then she'd fall into a bitter depression, the grayish circles under her eyes would become more prominent, and she would take the event as further proof of her ill fortune.

In spite of her own unfortunate experience, she was a great advocate of marriage. She advised her girls to go to parties wearing beautiful, very low-cut dresses, with lots of jewels (real or costume, the main thing was that they should glitter), and to keep an eye out for the boys. Mustn't be a ninny. She'd say: "Young man, I'd like to introduce my daughter." The victim, taken by surprise, had no time to consider that not only did he not know the person to whom he was being introduced (which in itself is quite normal), he also didn't know the person making the introductions (not so normal).

This strategy never failed. The candidate would blush, offer his arm to the girl, and ask her to dance. Her mother would sit down next to the other mothers, who peered at her out of the corner of their eyes. It was pure envy, since their own daughters stood like wallflowers at the other end of the room, pretending to be thrilled chatting among themselves, while the others were already trying on their trousseaux or pushing baby carriages in the park.

The House of Memory

* * * * *

On certain afternoons we had visitors at the house in Donato Alvarez. My aunt and uncle from Constitución would come, give me wet kisses, et cetera, and ask that stuff about loving my little brother. Once they brought their grandson along to play with me, but he was coughing a lot, so I wasn't allowed to get too close. I watched him from a distance, sitting on the bottom step of the stairway that led to the terrace. When everyone was distracted, I climbed the entire staircase. When I reached the top, I lost my footing and tumbled down to the bottom, landing on top of Otilia, who was waiting for me with arms outspread. I hit her in the nose with the heel of my shoe. After that, she glared at me with hatred in her eyes, applying rags soaked in vinegar to her injury. She didn't say anything to me because I was just a child, but I'm sure that, from that moment on, I too became a bitch, a viper, an egotist, tightwad, imbecile, and evil incarnate, like all the other women.

My grandfather, the only man in the household, didn't generally participate in the conversations. Everyone remembers how he used to give orders to his daughters. Whenever he noticed them looking very happy, laughing a lot, or acting goofy, he'd give them a laxative. He was of the opinion that all strange behavior was the result of intestinal disorders. "Do you remember," Grandma would say whenever she was in a nostalgic mood, "how Papa drove you crazy with Josselin tea?" and she would shake with laughter.

When Grandma immigrated from Kiev to Buenos Aires she was eleven years old. They sent her to school, where she learned Spanish very well. She sang tangos like a sick bird:

Sca-a-ars (trill),
Indelible scars from a wou-ou-ound . . . (trill)

She never spoke of how she ended up marrying Grandpa. She gave birth to her daughters quite easily, one after another. They always arrived before the midwife, anxious to be born and start quarreling. There were some very bad times. Unemployment. Evictions.

At a charity ball, money was collected, as it was for other poor families, to help them get a new house. *El Hogar* published a short article about that ball. Taking advantage of the occasion, several of the girls made their debut into society. A few courtships began. In subsequent social notes appearing in the same magazine, there were pictures of their engagements,

marriages, and announcements of their first babies' births. The young mothers selected names for their little celebrities, the same names that Otilia's children bear, even today.

Before they were married, Otilia and Amanda were salesgirls at La Piedad department store, where they extolled the beauty of the bathrobes and housecoats to their customers. Mele, the one who was slow to marry, never worked outside her home. Sometimes she would sew or do housework, and when she was done, she'd go off and paint. She painted flowers, sailboats at sunset, Dutch landscapes with tulips, and haystacks beside country houses. She copied them from some postcards she had.

On Sundays we'd all have lunch at Donato Alvarez. Otilia and Amanda's fiances would be there. The men livened up the atmosphere: they were talkative, they'd bring bottles of wine, and they'd sit you on their laps so you could demonstrate how you were learning to read. The women didn't fight. I would recite verses, taste Papa's port, and announce that I loved my little brother. . . .

❋ ❋ ❋ ❋ ❋

Grandpa slept on a sofa in the corner. No matter how early one arrived, everything was always in perfect order: the bed made, the floor swept. Grandpa read *La Vanguardia*, books by José Ingenieros and Juan B. Justo, and essays on vegetarianism. He'd sit me on his knees and make me spell out: *l-a-v-a-n-g-u-a-r-d-i-a*. Afterward he'd send me out to the patio to play. He had a large mustache whose ends pointed up and whose shape he maintained by sleeping with something called a mustache guard.

Grandma slept in another room, which was very untidy. On top of the table, among dirty cups and bottles of medicine, you could see the twin arches of her false teeth in a glass of water, and her corset, much larger and more complicated than those of her daughters, with laces and whalebone everywhere.

Grandpa belonged to the Socialist Party. Firmly divorced from religion and family traditions, he devoted himself to instilling revolutionary ideas in his daughters. He taught them that everyone was equal, Jews and non-Jews alike. The little girls learned to sing the "International" before they knew "Rock-a-Bye Baby." He never managed to make them vegetarians. He had to content himself with eating his greens at the far corner of the table, casting an occasional disgusted glance at the stew that they devoured. He taught them to love work—not by example, however, since, thanks to a combination of bad luck, periods of crisis and unemployment,

his ill health, and his brothers' selfishness, he didn't live a very active life, although it was full of all the appropriate maxims and readings. In their peaceful moments, the four girls would sing:

*The sewing machine
sings its hurried song,
while the good woman
sews and sings along.*

Mama was the only one of the four with any schooling. "We starved to death so you could study, bitch," her sisters frequently reminded her. "Studying is the only thing that keeps me from blowing my brains out for having to live with you, vipers," Mama would answer.

She was the first to get married, and, loyal to her father's ideas, she did so at City Hall. I was told this, since in those days children didn't witness their parents' marriages. On the wedding night, one of my classmates explained to me, the man puts his front thing into the woman's front thing and he leaves a little juice that makes a baby in the woman's belly. If he gets carried away and leaves too much juice, it could turn out to be a very big baby, like her uncle who weighed fifteen pounds when he was born and his mama almost died. It could also happen that, after nine months, when they sliced the mother's belly open and took out the baby, there might be a little unused juice left inside the mother. In that case, after a while, another baby would start to grow, and that's how you could get a little brother and always have to tell people that you loved him.

Grandpa's other daughters weren't as loyal to him as Mama was. As soon as they realized that they weren't going to get anything (I mean husbands) out of the committee meetings and the Socialist Party Theater Group they went off to look for them, without any scruples whatsoever, at Jewish parties and weddings. I don't know how Grandpa, who was always saying that religion was the opiate of the masses, must have felt, standing before the lighted wedding canopy and listening to praises of the Jewish God at his daughters' weddings. As far as all his other ideas were concerned, Otilia very clearly and frequently said that he could stick them up his ass. Jewish husbands weren't "equal" to the others, they were better, since they didn't spend their lives playing pool at the cafe, and if they had a fight with you, at least they weren't going to call you a "dirty Jew."

"I'm so glad I married a Jew!" Otilia said. "You should see how Clark Gable worries about his wife and children! Big Dora's daughter married a

Christian. She said she was "in lo-ove" (sarcastic tone). And so? What did she get out of it? She's sure sorry now, poor thing! No, not poor thing, stupid thing! Because not a Sunday goes by that he doesn't lose every penny at the races. No wonder she has to suffer so much and sew for other people, poor thing, just so they can eat!"

As she spoke, Otilia finished polishing her nails dark red and waved her hands to dry them.

Evening was falling. Like flames, Otilia's nails passed before my eyes, and from the back of the patio came the smell of the sulfur that Grandma was burning to disinfect who-knows-what.

* * * * *

Doctors don t know anything, Grandma used to say. "They're businessmen. They don't care about taking good care of you; they want to hurry up and finish so they can go on to the next patient."

She and the four beasts spent their lives consulting doctors, because no doctor was any good. They preferred "naturists" and homeopaths, because, as they would say, "they cure with natural things," although they never followed any of the treatments for very long.

There was one doctor whom they respected more than the others. He had his prescriptions filled in the only pharmacy in Buenos Aires where they had the Elixir of Eternal Life, and where they displayed the following publications in the window: "War to the Death Against Toxins;" "Wheat Germ, the Germ of Life;" "The Sedative Properties of Black Molasses;" "Live to Be One Hundred with Daily Visits to the Bathroom;" and "Keep Death Away with Ten Lemons a Day."

The doctor placed the utmost importance on anything that was consumed by mouth, but he combined his dietary recommendations with general advice on hygiene, publishing both in a brochure. Each patient received one of these brochures along with the appropriate medication for his or her ailment. It was recommended that one sleep with the windows open, even in the middle of winter; that one wash one's hands before eating; that one avoid all contact with other people's saliva (here there was a little note about the number of microbes that two people exchange with a single kiss); and that the following practice be observed:

"Moisten sexual organs with cold water every day."

After having been respected and consulted by the family for quite a while, this doctor was replaced by another one (Otilia's discovery) who

cured all illnesses with different sorts of enemas, a method that she found truly harmless.

It was kind of a pity, because the first one was—how shall I put it?—more eclectic.

They would sit down next to our beds, look at us sadly and move their head a certain way, bending their necks first to one side and then to the other, so that their skulls bent alternately toward each shoulder. They would listen to the details of our illness and murmur: "Poor little boy. Ay, ay. Poor little girl. Oy, oy, oy." Papa's sisters weren't like my maternal aunts at all. They were long-suffering, respectful, and they didn't engage in arguing in front of other people. Sometimes they would run into the beasts when visiting our house. "It's been so long, girls! Can you believe it?" They weren't as close to us as Mama's sisters were: we always looked upon them as the visiting team. As soon as they left, the local gang would rip into them without compunction, recalling the time when Papa's family was starving to death in the Jewish section of Entre Rios. There were nine siblings. "Nine who lived," Grandma clarified, immediately bursting into one of her paroxysms of laughter. Grandma swore that Papa's mother fed her children a staple diet of angel hair pasta in milk until they were fifteen years old, and that's why they all turned out weak and sickly (my father's premature death confirmed that fact, according to her).

I don't know if the story about the milky soup was entirely true, but I can attest that my paternal grandmother believed that this was a nutritious childhood dish. All dried up, dressed in mourning, and with sparse white hair, she'd serve it to me in her kitchen, while in the dining room the adults entertained themselves with port and cookies. It was a sweet soup with milk skin floating on top and a few bits of angel hair pasta that got stuck in my throat. With considerable effort (because she could barely speak Spanish), my grandmother explained that the soup was good; if I didn't eat it, I was bad, and if I ate it all, I would grow up to be big and strong. . . .

<p style="text-align:center">✳ ✳ ✳ ✳ ✳</p>

You're going to kill me, Grandma said. You're going to finish off the few years of life I have left." She said this in a suffocated voice, weak and intense and tremulous at the same time, as she placed her fist on the table in a feigned blow since, according to her, she was so broken down, so worn out, that she didn't even have the strength left to make a proper fist.

During these scenes she looked very hunched over, her hair in disarray, with a vacant expression and purplish circles under her eyes. After pronouncing each phrase she seemed to collapse, with her lower lip hanging out and trembling like a leaf.

Her phrases began in a low tone, almost a whisper, and rose up to a high pitch at the beginning of the last syllable, whose vowels were stretched out long enough to achieve (without losing the rhythm) an even sharper pitch than at the beginning. That is to say, an ascending tone:

You're going to k-i-i-i-l-l . . .
(and in a descending tone):
me-e-e-e.
(and again, voice rising):
You're going to finish off the few years of life . . .
(descending pitch):
I have . . . le-e-e-e-f-t.

The fights Grandma had with her daughters were different from the ones they had among themselves. The beasts fought like equals, and none of them seemed lessened by the experience. They spoke plainly: "You want to screw up my life, you bitch, you viper, but I won't give you that pleasure." They were young, vigorous women who had nursed from none other than my grandmother herself and who had been nourished by a naturistic-vitaministic-anti-constipationistic regimen. Their mother, on the other hand, was old and quite worn down by the life she had led (always sacrificing herself to raise her daughters).

I never figured out how the fights began because I wasn't there (children should be spared violent scenes). I drew closer when the shouts penetrated the closed door and crossed the patio. Then I'd spy from behind the door, or I would go right into the room and no one took notice of me. At those moments the accusations usually referred to very ancient matters, and Grandma would be receiving the fatal blows.

The blows were almost always of the verbal variety. Only once did I see Grandma receive a punch in the arm. I waited to see if she'd be felled by lightning, but strangely enough, Grandma seemed to calm down with the impact. She rose from her chair (she almost always fought from a sitting position, due to her extreme weakness), and she left the room, rubbing her arm.

From the first fight I ever witnessed, during which Grandma announced, as usual, that she was dying, to her actual death, twenty-five

years ensued. Only in the last few years did she modify her technique a bit. She no longer threatened to die, but rather she would ask for a cup of tea, grab the cup with tremulous hands, and spill the entire contents down the front of her blouse. A daughter would have to help her change her clothes, to keep her from catching a chill. Or else she would say, "All right, Otilia, all right, don't be that way." A clear wish for reconciliation. Proof that Grandma was tired of violence and honestly desired peace. Unfortunately, the one with whom she was fighting at the time wasn't Otilia, but rather Amanda. The confusion of names infuriated her daughter even more. "You pretend to be stupid," she shouted at her. "You want me to think you don't know who I am, that you've got me confused with that other snake!"

And it went on like that until that poor mother ended her sad days. According to her, she deserved a happier ending.

Translated from the Spanish by Andrea G. Labinger

From The Family Tree

Margo Glantz

Bashevis Singer says somewhere: "The Jews don't record their own history, they lack a sense of chronology. It is as though they knew instinctively that time and space are just an illusion." This sense of elongated, gelatinous, compressed time that has a single theme with multiple variations and cadenzas resembles my parents' lives, where endlessly repeated conversations can suddenly shed a spark of light on some happening that ideal historical time has never satisfactorily explained. Time is a space marked out and filled with the ceaseless chanting of prayers by which a devout Jew measures his life.

And also his death. Then they have to say kaddish, blessing the holy name of God and remembering the departed, all seated on the ground without shoes so as to get nearer to the earth and accompany the one who has gone on ahead.

"I used to go to the synagogue next to the ritual bathhouse to pray for my father. I was the only one who was able to pray for him in the place where he died. My brothers did it in Philadelphia," [says my father.]

"What did you feel?" [I ask.]

"A great warmth because I was sitting next to the stove and the old men were praying all day long, chanting psalms, and I felt less of an orphan there. First we read a chapter from the *mishnah*, the oral tradition, and then we said kaddish, praising God and remembering my father's name."

"What do you say in kaddish?"

"At least ten Jews have to come together to make up what is called the *minyan*, which is a congregation. That's the right number to hold whatever ceremony you want. "May his name be blessed forever and throughout eternity." That's what all poets hope for. There was a great poet who came

from my village, about thirty or forty years older than me, Simeon Frog. Whatever happened to him, goodness knows. My brothers went to Philadelphia, I only remember the younger ones, Moishe Itzjok who didn't want to hand over three and a half years of his life to the czar and emigrated along with Abreml who had just come out of the army where he'd served the full duration. In 1939 when I saw my elder brothers Meier, Ellis, and Leie, it was like seeing them for the first time. Leie told me that when they left they accused him of having given me a false kiss."

"Why was it false?"

"Because I didn't feel it."

"Your grandmother," says my mother, "was marvelous. When she got to the United States she traveled from one end of the country to the other to see her sons and she didn't know one word of English. She had all sorts of things written down on paper and she taught them everything and crossed the four points of the compass to see them."

"She loved your mother a lot," says Nucia rather sadly.[1]

"Yes, and I loved her too, she was a splendid woman, she never caused any trouble, she always tried to help and never interfered in a nasty way, always out of a desire to do good. Quite unlike a mother-in-law."

My grandmother is very indistinct in my memory. She was in Mexico twice, first in 1928 before I was born and then from 1936 to 1939. She died there. She was very ill in the last months of her life, while in mine she barely fills a fleeting space, one marked by a photo in which I am in the foreground and she is in the countryside. She is also part of a legend that enhances my father's life: when she was already very ill, my grandmother Sheine (or Sofia, according to her passport) waited until her youngest son, who was visiting Philadelphia, came back to Mexico before departing this life. At that time we were living in the Street of the Argentine Republic, number 96, in a three-story building with a courtyard where we used to play as children.

<p style="text-align:center">✳ ✳ ✳ ✳ ✳</p>

The new Jewish cemetery was near the Hill of the Star. The old one was near the Burial Vault of Griefs. My father remembers another cemetery when he was thirteen years old, just after the death of my grandfather Osher. Nucia was working for a wealthy relative in a mill, helping to count the sacks of grain that the peasants brought in at night.

The Family Tree

My father had to keep watch, but sometimes he would nod off to sleep, sitting next to the mill. The gentiles came and to wake him up they would pee noisily, sometimes down the slipway that fed the grain into the stone millwheels, from which Jacob had saved himself with a single leap. He was in the Ukraine, in a village called Krivoy Rog, about a hundred and fifty leagues from Novy Vitebsk, his native village; it was winter, and it was 1914 too, the year the war started.

One day he was going home in a *svostchik* (a small carriage) when he came to Sofievka, a Christian village with twelve or fifteen Jewish families and a burial vault. A great storm came up, an early spring blizzard. The coach driver and his horse found shelter in a stable, and my father went to see a relation, Eizel Jilbuj, who looked after the cemetery.

"I went to look for somewhere to spend the night. I knocked and knocked. Eizel was enormously tall, and used to stoop, and had a white, white beard. He came out carrying a lantern and angry and said to me: 'Yankl? What a surprise! Come on in.'"

"I went in feeling pretty frightened, because I knew it was a graveyard. In I went, the first thing I saw was this funeral bench where they strip and wash the dead bodies, with a little broom next to it. I felt a bit panicky and wanted to get out, but I couldn't, I had the night and the snow outside and dead bodies inside."

Eizel woke up his old lady, who put on the samovar and offered my father the customary glass of tea with a lot of sugar and then showed him where he could sleep, next to a window.

"I couldn't sleep. I lay down, all hunched up. I didn't know what to do. Then I shut my eyes tight and the old lady told me not to worry. I slept a bit, then all of a sudden there was a tall figure by my side, with a piece of rope and an ax in his hand calling me and I woke up. He was shouting and telling me we had to lasso the dead first and then he would cut their heads off with his ax. I shouted too, I yelled, and the old lady got up again."

The old lady came in and restrained the crazy old man with his long white beard; then she told him off (I guess she was very small, they must have been one of those classic couples where the woman is really tiny and the man is huge, but the woman is the one who shouts loudest) and she woke him up and took him back to bed. She explained: "'Eizel has started walking in his sleep. Ever since they took Yerujem off to the war.'"

Next day Eizel didn't remember anything about the night before. My father was still shaky, but his old relative offered him a splendid breakfast of bread and butter, herrings, semolina, tea and more tea, more bread and butter and jam; after that he took him out for a walk round the cemetery garden, showing him the paths and pointing out the children's graves, covered in flowers and almost buried in the snow, then he proudly pointed out the family mausoleums, he showed him how well laid out it all was and he said it all as though he were showing Adam round Paradise, a long time before the first sin and, obviously, a long time before the arrival of Eve.

Then he asked him if he would like to stay on for another night. My father replied hastily that he preferred to stay buried in the snow on the road home rather than spend another night among the dead.

It is seven leagues from Sofievka to Novy Vitebsk. In Sofievka there were just a very few Jews and a graveyard.

<p style="text-align:center">✳ ✳ ✳ ✳ ✳</p>

When Grandfather Osher died, Yankl went to stay with his uncle Moishe Haim, an unqualified mining engineer.

"My uncle was a wealthy man, he used to work in the coal mines, which was where most of the money came from in Krivoy Rog. He was very modern, he'd shaved off his beard, not like my father who kept his long like the old style Jews did. Your mother's father was modern too, he had a little pointed beard that you could hardly see. Before he went to work in the mines, my uncle had mills and supplied the military with food. I was with my cousin Ilusha, who was much older than me, they were very nice to me, they treated me like a poor relation. My girl cousins, I remember them well, they were tall, handsome, strapping girls, who went to private school, because in my village the state school only had six grades and they only took Jews who spoke Russian."

"Not Yiddish?"

"Not Yiddish, nor Ukrainian either. In Krivoy Rog there was a Jewish university, a yeshiva, and a gymnasium, that's what we called a high school."

"Not one city in the Ukraine," says mother, "had up to a million inhabitants. Odessa was really important, but there were only about four or five hundred thousand people living there. There were some other big cities, Kiev, Herzon, Nikolaiev, ports on the Black Sea, and Krivoy Rog and Kremenchug where your grandmother Sheine was born."

The Family Tree

"She was a very intelligent woman, even though she was uneducated, she couldn't read or write Russian, only Yiddish, and not very well either, but she was very intelligent. They didn't educate women in those days, even though she was born in a city. You have to remember it was midway through the last century," says my father.

"And what about the revolution. Where were you when the revolution happened?"

"That was a very interesting time in my life, the revolution caught up with me in Krivoy Rog. In 1915 I was in the village, and in 1916 and '17 I was in the city with my uncle, though the revolution didn't reach the little places, only the deserters made it out there. They went from the villages to the city too, and then because everything was in turmoil a lot of people came to our village, begging, there was no food in the cities, but out in the villages there was never any shortage of food. All those people belonged to the intelligentsia. Then some Zionist Jews came through who set up a little *ajshara* in my village, they were training settlements for those who wanted to go to Israel. This *ajshara* went on to Constantinople later, and when my mother and brothers went to Turkey in 1922 they saw them there again. They wanted to take them with them to Israel, but my mother preferred to go and join my brothers in the United States. They were very helpful to me, I read with them, I learned Russian well, and when the revolution reached our region I became a revolutionary."

Mother has been washing the dishes in the kitchen, but now she comes in and tells us to go to the table because tea is ready. We sit down and my father carries on talking enthusiastically. Before this I have spent days trying to persuade him to tell me something about his youth and he has refused because it all seemed uninteresting. Suddenly something strikes him:

"Before 1917 there hadn't been any pogroms in our villages, but everything came with the revolutionary movements. But I've told you all that."

"I've just come across something really interesting," says mother, "I think you'll be absolutely fascinated."

"Wait just a minute, Mother, Father's remembering things he's never told me about before. Let's hear what he has to say."

"Do you want tea?"

"Yes."

"The revolution. Sit down here, Margo, are you all right? The revolutionaries wanted to free the Ukraine, there were all sorts of groups, good,

honest people who wanted to help and bands of bandits trying to kill us all. Oh, yes, I've certainly lived an interesting life! The world war, the revolution, what an experience! Since everything was upside down, people used to come and hide out in my village, some very well-educated, very intelligent people, who taught me a lot. I'll say they did! They made me into a revolutionary. They were young men and women too, they must have been about twenty-two or twenty-three years old."

In 1921 he was in Herzon, where he took a course to become a teacher of Marxism, which he continued in Odessa in 1922.

"Once they sent me to Moscow as a delegate for the youth of Odessa at an agricultural congress, and I met Lunacharsky and Radek, the Bolsheviks. Lunacharsky had an aristocratic background, he came to attend the lectures on cattle shows and he brought an actress with him. Lunacharsky was an interesting man, he was tall like Radek. Do you know who Radek was? He came from Galicia."

"From Poland? Was he Jewish?"

"Yes, he was a Polish Jew, but he was part of the Russian revolution. I think his name was Rosenfeld, he was one of Lenin's Bolsheviks, Karl Radek. I met Zinoviev and Kamenev too."

"And Kalinin," says mother.

"I saw Kalinin too, but what did I have to do with the likes of them? I was just a lad, I saw them from a distance, I was interested in what they had to say, but I was too insignificant to be with them. I met a lot of leaders at that time too. Kamenev and Zinoviev were both Jews."

"Zinoviev was Trotsky's brother-in-law," adds mother.

"I had a lot of diplomas and certificates dating from that time, but when I was going through the Polish Corridor at Danzig I went into the toilet on the train and tore up all my papers, I don't know why. I was frightened and I tore them all up and lost the lot."

"Not all," I say smugly. "I've got some of them, they're all in bits."

"Like our lives." . . .

*　　*　　*　　*　　*

"A tall cossack and a short one passed by our house, their hands covered in blood, and my mother, crying her eyes out, washed their hands in a bowl." My father's mother wore broad skirts under which she hid my two aunts, Jane and Mira, girls of sixteen and seventeen.

"I was almost out of my mind, I walked (I was only a boy), I ran from

one place to another and crossed the town over the little bridge that led to the baths and I tried to shelter in my uncle Kalmen's house, he was my father's brother. It was 1917, I went into my uncle's house and I almost went mad, my uncle had a long curly red beard, all crimson with blood, and he was sitting with the blood pouring down and his eyes open. The fear of death still hadn't left him, perhaps he was still breathing! Beside him, wrapped in a sheet, were all the household utensils, everything made of silver or copper, the Sabbath candlesticks, the samovar. I was scared stiff, I had no idea what to do, I just ran out of the village like a madman. The pogrom lasted several days, I went out into the country and I found an abandoned well, deep, but with no water in it, and I spent several days in it. When I heard that everything had calmed down, I came out. Before that, I could hear the terrible cries of the girls and children."

It all happened so fast that one pogrom followed another.

"In those troubled times different groups were chasing one another and as they went thraugh towns and villages they laid waste to everything in their path."

It all sounds so familiar, it's like those revolts that our nineteenth-century novelists wrote about and like what you read in novels about the Mexican revolution, the revolts and the levies, the confusion, the sacking of towns and villages, the deaths.

"The Bolsheviks came back and we had some of the short rifles left by the bandits and some of the horses too; only those who'd been in the world war knew how to defend themselves, the rest of us were saved by a miracle. Many of the bandits were peasants who knew us, and they killed the people they stole from to make sure they couldn't be denounced."

Yasha hid in the house of a *muzhik*,[2] a friend of his grandfather's, Sasha Ribak. He had "an enormous mustache, like the poet Sevshenko" (the great popular poet of the Ukraine). My father stayed hiding in a corncrib, breathing through a hole, even as bandits stuck their bayonets into it. Ribak took him food and water and let him out when things calmed down a little.

"General Budiony's Bolshevik cossacks arrived. When things were a bit calmer, I came out. When it was dangerous I went back into hiding again. I remember Sasha well, he was verygood. I wrote a poem about all that, in 1920, in Russian."

"And what about your mother and your sisters, how were they saved?"

"We survived by chance, by luck. My mother and my sisters hid in the

top of the house, where there was a loft used as a storeroom, in the space under the rafters. As the groups were all chasing each other they hardly had time to look. They sacked and killed everything they found in their way. My mother was saved that first time because she washed the cossacks' hands."

* * * * *

Sometimes they show documentary movies in the Regis cinema and girls with dark curly hair file over and over again into a concentration camp, then sometimes quite deliberately they walk into crematorium ovens. Usually they look like me, and seeing those images has left me with a daily sense of guilt that clings, guilt at having escaped a number branded on my right wrist or the indelible mark of the yellow star that was sewn onto overcoats in Parisian winters. Even Max Jacob had to wear one when he went outdoors, despite the fact that he had converted to Christianity.

Someone interrupts my recollections and the guilt dissolves. It doesn't matter much whether you're a Jew or not, what matters is whether you're willing to fight against the herd instinct.

My father remembers the pogroms, my mother does not. Nucia only remembers the story of Ilusha, the brother who was to die during the Second World War through eating a potato when he was starving. Ilusha joined a group of other young students fighting bands of outlaws who were robbing and killing Jews in the villages. The group was counterattacked by White Russians who beat them savagely and decimated them. Ilusha went home suffering from tuberculosis. He was already doomed.

"During the Civil War," says Nucia, "the partisans and the bandits were interchangeable, there were red ones, white ones, green ones who followed General Zeliony (that means green in Russian), or the kolchakovets who followed general Kolchak, he was a White Russian who commanded a cavalry regiment. Then there was Makhno, the trade union anarchist and his Jewish assistant, Voline, who were active in the Crimea and southern Ukraine. Makhno was a real anarchist, he used to gallop by with his horses pulling little carriages called tachanki and waving a black flag."

His beliefs were clear enough, but when they passed through the little Jewish rural communities, his men ransacked everything, raped and murdered.

The groups may have been interchangeable and persecuted one another, and without exception, they all devastated the villages, those ten

or twelve Jewish villages near the one where my father was (Zholta, Kuschinsk, Zlochistaia and the rest), organizing pogroms "officially."

In 1918/1919, some of the young men from my father's village decided to defend themselves and hoped to join the partisans in the village grave-yard, building armed barricades among the graves.

"The bandits sent two or three spies to see if we had any defenses, and they saw us and came back with some cavalrymen and killed all the defenders."

"What happened to you?"

He smiles and says: "I hid behind the graves with five or six others and we all got away. Besides, the bandits were being chased by another group led by General Grigoriev, he was an aristocrat and a counter-revolution-ary, and he gave his cossacks the freedom to plunder and destroy every house they came to."

Behind Grigoriev there was another group, Bolsheviks this time, who were following them to "clean up the bandits in the village." Some of the partisans were caught and shot by the river bank.

"Sometimes even the Bolsheviks killed us and ransacked the place, because it was chaos then. Later they imposed some sort of order, and when the Civil War ended, the pogroms stopped too."

When peace was restored to the region, only 30 percent of the inhab-itants of those agricultural communities founded by the czar for the Jews were left.

Translated from the Spanish by Susan Bassnett

1. The author's father, Jacob Glantz, is alternatively called Jacob, Yankl, or Nucia.

2. A *muzhik*, from the Russian, is a peasant in czarist Russia.

From Cláper

Alicia Freilich de Segal

[The Father][1] I'm happy. Through the clean mirror, as through pure crystal, I see that at last, yes, at last the sun is setting and the first evening star has come out. Shabbat ends but my night begins. All I want to do is walk and walk. . . .

I'm leaving you, my dear village, and you're seeing me off without knowing it. There is such excitement in your shabby narrow streets. This time Isaac and Pesha are the ones being led to the house of prayers. She will have to dance around him seven times before they shatter the glass in remembrance of the destruction of the temple in the Holy Land by the evilness of Titus the Roman. Cursed be his name! After hearing the noise and seeing the shards of glass, then and only then will they be man and wife according to the laws of our Arbiter, Creator of the Universe.

You know something? It's unusual for a month to go by without a wedding in my village. Nu? I guess even in Paradise it's not good to be alone. Why did I decide to leave at the end of this Shabbat and not another? I've waited long enough, and the moment of destiny we forge for ourselves has arrived for me. . . .

But I have to pretend and hurry without rushing. Thank God nobody notices as long as my mouth laughs and my legs dance by themselves, which is of course what happens to everyone in my village when there is a wedding. If I let myself be dragged into the merriment and forget my trip, I'll have to wait until next fall and that's too far away; after all, I'm no longer a boy.

Is it true what they say, that a person's nature changes every seven years? If it is, then I've already shed my skin three times and I have reached the perfect age to break out of the shell forever. Forever? Do any

50

of us ever really abandon forever the place where we're born and play as children?

A little while ago, on Yom Kippur, as I circled my head three times with the sacrificial rooster—and yelled out the exorcism louder than a crazy man would—I offered God this animal as a substitute for my sins. The bird will go to its death, that's what *capurot* is, after all, while I shall live a long and peaceful life in America. Amen!

Oy yoy yoy! Here comes Meilaj the mute.—Whew! He just passed. Thank you, my sweet little God, for your help. That good simpleton has very sharp eyes and with this full moon. . . . Luckily he didn't see me. He was so absorbed with his whistling, announcing the wedding and inviting all Christians to come and see the beautiful bride. Have you ever seen an ugly bride? Everyone praises such beautiful happiness! So, while performing his assignment with virtuosity, the whistler didn't notice me, leaving, with a knapsack over my shoulders.

As I pass the temple, I've got to walk more slowly. Awaiting the predestined couple, the wide open main door allows me to see the Ark, which holds its treasure, the Holy Scrolls, on the very same dais where—oy yoy yoy!—so often, I've accompanied my Pappinyu at sunrise and sunset prayers.

God sits above and arranges it so that here, below, male and female may be joined at a chosen time. I know that all weddings are parties, but today the room looks more glittering than ever before. A couple of weeks ago from nobody knew where came a strange painter who decorated these blessed walls. And he never even charged us a cent! And, what's even more unbelievable, the drawings are intact!

I would look at him in silence because he was a man of few words. But one afternoon I took him some cider and sweet dough with raisins and he spoke! He was fleeing France. He just wanted to breathe once again the air of Liozno, in Russia, where his family lives. But, when he realized how far away it was, he chose to remain in Lendov with us—"Almost the same"— he said, smiling, never once taking his eyes off the enormous rooster he was coloring blue.

Magical! That's what it was. Magical! Without any books, he knew exactly how to draw the feathers of all kinds of different creatures! From his brushes emanated a violin with wings, and green priests suspended in midair above roofs, and a seven-branched candelabra flying like a burning bramble, and a yellow lion and red cows, and gigantic moons, without a single word. Colored shapes with soul!

The entire town was shaken. So? Nu? Who was this stranger? Marcus Chagalovich or Sagalij he called himself, I no longer remember. Of course the village divided into two irreconcilable camps. One accused him of being a profligate and a sinner because of the irreverence with which he depicted the Sacred Commentaries. "Downright pagan!" The other said he had given a false name. They pointed him out as one of the anonymous Just Men who in every era come to redeem the world. Of course that would explain why he knew more about the Laws than our own venerable teacher Aaron.

Anyway, the artist was scared off by the whispers and all the gossips. After three days, probably to avoid being cursed by them—God forbid!—without even saying good-bye, or even leaving a single footprint, he disappeared into the night, just as I am doing now, along the very same long road. . . .

[The Daughter] Luminous was the morning of her inauguration into the world! Without crossing checkpoints or oceans, and while living under the same familial roof, she took the road that divided Neighborhood from Milky Way.

She was not moved by her parents' objections nor, for that matter, did she share their mourning over the distant, yet to them, ever present news about the Suez Canal situation. Goodness, the way they moaned and carried on! You'd think these were their very own personal problems or something. . . .

The tree-lined path that leads to the main building with its high oval clock is both border and path to her liberation. There is a lot to see and many to be seen by. In order to accomplish this, she'll have to sway her hips and get rid of that skinny slouching profile, that "good-girl walk," Mom would say. A brave heroine, she had dared to break out of the family padlock, the collegiate gates, and the community fences in order to go beyond this door and enter the foremost university. God, does that sound great! Now she must walk proudly and provocatively in keeping with the mood of her deed.

At last! Left behind are those gaudy reproductions of Marc Chagall that hang all over the living and dining room walls. Where does Father get this obsession for buying any trinket that imitates the painter? Must be his small-town taste; like all hicks, he mistakes junk for real art. Real art is these stained glass windows, which, on this particular morning, shed a

special light, bringing them into harmony with the modern architecture all around it. What beauty! A splendid open gallery offers her famous muralists, painters, and sculptors in quantities that go far beyond her artistic appreciation, yet is a most fitting place in which to experience this radical moment dividing her existence.

And the school building? Is it really this two-storied gray box? It looks more like a convent. What cold and penumbral classrooms! Ah, but behind the building, what a glorious field of furry green grass! Why are the walls so bare? No color, not even a line. In fact, nothing hints at the presence of young bright students everywhere.

"They put us up here in this dorm run by nuns, but it's only temporary," explains Cristina Doglio.

The animated voices of the freshmen break the still silence:

"Hey, what's up?"

"Schedule's out . . ."

"Who's teaching philosophy?"

"We get to choose from English, Italian, French, and German!"

"Wow! Look at the syllabus for Intro to Literature. That's a lot of work."

Yes, it's a new and exciting pleasure. Left behind is the daily, cloistered existence of her home in San Leopoldino. Here is an open universe without walls, so varied, it offers itself unconditionally to her every wish. No wonder the school motto is "This lighthouse is here to conquer darkness."

[The Father] Oy gottenyu! When will I finally be able to leave Lendov? From afar I see Pinchas Gros, the only one of us who lives among the Gentiles and in the very center of town. He's a common man who doesn't even know how to write his name and celebrates the Sabbath alone. I must admit he sure has a great talent for fixing watches and glasses. So why does he live alone? And with a big goat in his backyard? They even use him to threaten children and sinners; after all, who could bear being locked up with that enormous beast and all the noise he makes?

I still have to cross the worn-out wooden bridge where young lovers walk arm in arm, until around midnight, when Don Josu lets loose his dogs and the lovers rush back to the drugstore. From the street, the lovers look through the open window and enjoy the concert.—Oh, I forgot to tell you, the drugstore houses the only piano in town, a treasure that none of us ever really saw but guessed was there. We all managed, at some point, to hear its notes. Standing in front of the colored containers of the drug-

store, each heard a different melody. Know what I mean? Only the town priest could enter that house of enchantment. Dressed in priestly garb, he used to go very often to the house with the piano. What did the priest do there? Was he by any chance a privileged cherub? Tell you the truth, I always thought that what interested him was the pharmacist's wife. . . . And now where do I hide? Out of Guitzer Street comes Batcha and her crude husband, that chicken guzzler. Oy veis meir! That's all I need! Bitter as bile that woman is. Why, she'd cut off my hand with her kitchen knife if she so much as suspected that I had said they're not among the best of families. Save me, sweet God! And please don't let the lovers of the mill see me either. . . . Ay, ay! One night, I too dreamt of love while caressing Janala's blonde braid, inhaling her clean dress, her knotted kerchief, and her bare lips! From that intimacy at the mill, thank God, not one was ever left pregnant, God forgive! . . .

Farewell, Pappinyu and Mommala! May no evil ever befall you. Without saying good-bye, without hugs or kisses, your son goes away but does not leave you. . . .

[The Daughter] She got rid of them. She never felt they were real men anyway. Little Jacobs, Moisheles, young Reubens. Always together since primary school. No comparison to these university hunks! Those others were sexless siblings. Angels and seraphs. Soulmates. Was any of them ever like these guys here? Machos with their meaningful glances and provocative gestures? That one over there, for instance, he could be in a Hollywood movie. He's got a Gregory Peck air about him! Ah! and the one next to him! Wow! He's the spitting image of Victor Mature! And what about that hunk of a professor? Exactly like Jorge Negrete! Slim, dark, elegant mustache, reminds me of my Charro singing:

Allá en el Rancho Grande allá donde viv-if-a
Había una ranch-er-iita que alegre me deci-aa
Que alegre me deci-aaaaaaa

Back there in the big raa-anch, back there where I once liiii-i-ved
There was a rancherita who joyfully would saaaaaa-ay
Who joyfully would saaaaa-ay. . . .

All this guy needs is a pistol and a big sombrero! My Mexican Charro's got nothing on him. . . .

Ahhh, those matinee movies at the Rex and the afternoon ones at the Anuaco! Great but lasted barely ninety minutes whereas university life will be four years of handsome men parading deliciously before her. Farewell my old-fashioned parents! At last I'm a free little bird!

[The father] Some hours earlier, during the pause between afternoon and evening prayers, as I counted the minutes, anguished by my upcoming departure, our humble house of God was a boiling cauldron. The faithful were gathering in small circles, as if they were still at their market stalls. They were busy arguing: How many had actually died in the Great War? How many had we lost when General Pilsudski repelled the Russian army at the battle of Vistula?

"We should not have participated. That was a big imperialist war and some of our people sympathized with the Bolsheviks."

"That's nonsense! Didn't we give the Polish legions a Henry Barwinski?"

"Yes, we did, so what? They paid us well for that one, didn't they, idiot?"

"Did you already forget that we were accused shortly after, and still to this very day, of spying for the Russians? Have they quit calling us rightists and anti-Polish?"

"You're the one who's an idiot. You don't even know that the Polish parliament protested that falsehood."

"Nu, so it protested, so? Did anything change? Why? Why do we have to serve in an army where we are always watched and never trusted?"

"Friends, friends. Don't insult each other, please, it's Shabbos!"

"I believe that nothing about this country should be far from our concerns."

"C'mon, we've been here for centuries and we're now citizens of the Polish Republic."

"Any alternatives, stupid? There is maybe somewhere else for us to go to?"

"Maybe."

"Yeah, sure."

"Nu, you stay here then. You'd rather put up with the slaughter of your brothers, the burning of your miserable little houses, and the fact that your sons will never be able to study in a Polish school than suffer a little hunger in the Holy Land or even over there in America. Yes, gentlemen, and in exchange for all the advantages you enjoy here, you have to give your blood to their wars! We're citizens, right? That's what you're saying, right? Sure . . . You poor misguided souls."

"Can you suggest a better place? Can you? Then let's leave right away!"

"There must be some place on the face of this earth where there are no swords or Cossacks or savage thieves. . . ."

Their yarmulkes seem about to explode with all the shouting and shoving and even hitting at times, believe me! But the cantor's deep and tender voice calls them back to prayer marking the end of the Sabbath and once again, they turn meek before the splendor of the supplication. I, on the other hand, without arguing, am leaving: Momma, Poppa, I really don't want to be either hero or martyr on the Polish battlefield or anybody else's for that matter. I want to live and die my life for me. . . .

[The Daughter] One afternoon, two months later, the students crowded together in the corridors to surround a bald young man with deep green eyes. At the same time, another one, thin, but with a noble expression on his face, is taken upstairs.

The group drowns them in hugs and tears. Even Professor Miguel Rosbaum, always isolated in his cubicle and covered in book dust, runs to embrace them. And Father Hernando, one of the most reserved students, talks on and on as never before.

"Who are they, Father Cornejo?"

"Famous people."

"From TV? movies?"

"The resistance. They're survivors. . . ."

"And what are they doing here?"

"Jesus, girl, are you Venezuelan?"

"Yes, by birth, and you?"

"Well, I was born in Spain but I, for one, know that the UN protested the exile of these young people. Also, that General Tarugo—what am I saying?—Marcos Perez Jimenez, the president himself, was forced to grant them visas even though one is an active member of the Communist Party and the other of Democratic Action Party. But, I've already said too much, my child. Around here, by God, even the walls have ears."

For seventeen years she had been insulated from her surroundings. Who among her people took part in those passionate struggles for freedom, liberty, the sorrow of exile and jail, the excitement of a hastily called meeting against the dictator? Being a real citizen meant finding refuge for the democratic activists: distributing food and books to the opposition, whatever sublime task she might be entrusted with. Such a noble cause justified the total giving of oneself, and she would eagerly sacrifice herself for this Venezuela of hers.

Cláper

Dad and Mom didn't have to find out. Why should they? What good would it do? Voluntarily isolated, they would die of worry if they knew. It was too late for them to accept the demands of a new life. How could these ignorant Polish peasants ever understand, these peasants whose work week is a universe limited to a taxi route—from Plaza La Rueda to the corner of Carmelitas—from shop to home and vice versa? How could they possibly understand?

[The Father] Dear Poppa and Momma,
I ask you: If the Polish Gentiles win all the wars they start and will start, what do I ever gain? Quite the opposite. I'm neither Catholic, Ukrainian, Communist, or even Lithuanian. I'll always be the loser because I am who I am. That's why I'm saying good-bye. So long, really. I'm leaving but am not abandoning you. And, anyway, I remain a fervent Pole in one thing: I worry a lot about the Germans. . . .
Only yesterday Pappinyu brought home from shul a guest. This one was even poorer than us! But to share Shabbat even with only a piece of onion and herring, water instead of wine, bringing a beggar to the table, is the opportunity God grants us to praise him. No one should go hungry on his day of rest.
The paternal words proclaim the arrival of my very last Shabbat at home.
"My friend, have you ever studied?"
"Mr. David, he whose name I'm not worthy of mentioning, gave me life to go to school when I was very little, even though my clothes were patched and torn."
"How lucky, my friend! Everyone: wash your hands and let's begin the blessings!"
I envy Poppa's voice, which becomes even more beautiful during the prayer:

And there was afternoon and there was morning. Sixth day. And heaven and earth were created and all that they contain. And having concluded His creation on the seventh, He rested and sanctified it because on that day He concluded his work. Blessed art thou, oh Eternal God, King of the Universe, who doth create the fruit of the vine. Blessed art thou, Our Lord God, King of the world, who sanctified us and graced us with Your precepts and granted us the Sabbath to sanctify the memory of Your labor of creation. . . .

As the prayer concludes we raise our glasses:
"Let us drink to life and for peace! L'chaim! Dear guest, make yourself

at home. Tell me, if you know how to study you're already rich, don't you agree?"

"Thank you. Yes, but dear family, you also should know that poverty sticks to your skin and is hard to get rid of. It clouds wisdom. . . . I did study some, but one has to live. . . ."

"Excuse me, but poverty is no dishonor. . . ."

"Maybe not, Rebbe David, but it can make you do bad things. . . ."

"Yes, but I believe those bad deeds can be erased with the mortar of good deeds."

"You really think so? I think that wherever you go, wherever you stop, poverty is always in the middle of everything. That's what I think."

"Will you do me the honor of eating this gefilte fish? And tell me, my friend, did you ever try to overcome it by working with a paintbrush or with a needle and thread?"

"One has to learn many things, Sir, and, no cloak is big enough to hide poverty."

"Nu, so how do you manage?"

"I manage. . . ."

A candelabra with two candles barely sheds enough light upon us, but the vast darkness is illuminated by Poppa's every sentence and the amusing answers of Haim Lisrak, our guest who is poorer than us.

Meanwhile, Momma and my siblings doze off exhausted. Since sunrise they've been throwing sawdust on the floor trying to get it to shine, rubbing out ashes, fetching water at the well, grinding and seasoning fish, getting dressed, blessing the candles. . . . Yes, Shabbos relaxes the spirit but sure tires the body!

"Have another drink, dear guest. It's cherry brandy. A little wine lightens the heart. May you never be poor of soul. May your children grow to study Torah, to marry and to do good deeds! L'chaim! As long as there is health. . . ."

"You know, Rebbe David, poverty is worse than fifty plagues combined."

"But god only hates the ignorant. . . ."

"That may be so, but there is no crueler joke of divine affection than an empty pocket!"

"Listen, Haim, even the poorest beggar with pants full of holes, with seven different coats and seven masks to go begging alms from the same rich man, can enjoy the honor of Shabbat."

"Tsk, tsk, tsk! I certainly won't argue with that, Rebbe. That's why I keep praying: Help me, God, send me the cure, I already have the ailment!"

Cláper

Outside my whole village is a single chant to God. Aromas of hot cabbage soup seeping into every corner. I don't remember when I decide to put an end to the dialogue. Anyway, if people who have read Scripture and have eaten at the same table don't exchange words on Holy Laws, they might as well kneel before an idol. Besides, these two have already argued enough. Before the prayer of thanksgiving for the food we had just received, I interrupt with a not very sacred matter: I ask Poppa to use his formidable influence to have the district bureaucrats fix the public baths. "Oy yoy yoy, my poor nose, Pappinyu! Phew! I've got to cover it tightly before I can even go in to empty out the waste containers. And you know what all the gossips say? That right next to the women's ritual baths, young ladies become pregnant! Seems that the very learned, who sing sublime harmonies and sway as they extol the glories of our lord, every night of the week, are actually reading passionate love letters that pretty young girls hand them, while emptying the leftovers into that smelly hovel . . . deep below this mystical village. . . . Poppa . . ."

[The Daughter] Was there ever a Sunday without guests at home? First in the house in San Jose and then the one in San Leopoldino. Any writer, speaker, delegate, or visitor who passed through Caracas was compelled to be a dinner guest in the small and modest apartment in the Edificio de Nuestra Senora del Carmen. A pretty incongruous name for a building that housed people with unusual traditions like ours, and which many a guest had ironically pointed out to their hosts. We lived there since the time Father almost went bankrupt. It was a place full of books, magazines, and phony Chagalls. Its only luxury was an Erard piano reflected in the glass cabinet full of crystal objects. These had been gifts from the Landaus, the Sponkas, the Erders, and others, when they moved into the lovely house on the same street eight years later, the house that had to be sold in a hurry to avoid foreclosure.

Today's luncheon is one of many. This one is given for the writer Isaiah Rainfeld. As usual, Don Maximo had already taken and brought him back from the business area of town: "Because one must try to distribute the books of this known intellectual however one can. Whether those buyers read the hardbound volumes or just use them to decorate their libraries is irrelevant. It's a fundamental act of charity to help a wise man. Besides, we'll need real dollars to pay for the American edition of poems of resistance in the ghettoes.

The House of Memory

During the week, the business on Pasaje Benzo between Madrices and Marron streets was in the capable hands of the missus. After all, isn't she the expert in buying and selling bras, half-slips, and panties! Her husband? Oh, he's something else! Culture on agile legs and convincing lips. Yeah, a regular walking encyclopedia. No denying that.

"We sold thirty-six books, Mr. Rainfeld."

"That's great, my friend."

"In three more days, we'll sell all seventy. We'll go to the big tycoons secluded in their enormous mansions."

"It seems to be easier to write books than to sell them, don't you think?"

"Nonsense. Relax. Nobody ever turns me down. No matter where I knock, you saw that yourself. They know that I have never traded with someone else's gold. I am not a smuggler. I don't charge a cent of commission for the sacred labor of helping the learned. Just as I learned from my father, David, may he have found peace. . . ."

The exquisite banquet the lady of the house prepared, almost at daybreak, overflows on platters. Gefilte fish, chicken soup and matzoh balls, nuts, cakes, grapes. The best of the best. "One must always honor the intellect!"

And now, the moment of truth has arrived. Could there be a better setting to bring up the issue of her great leap?

"Father, tomorrow I'm beginning my studies at the university. . . ."

"This isn't the moment to discuss . . ."

"I'm not discussing, I'm notifying."

"Tonight when there are no guests, we'll talk. . . ."

"Why wait? I already registered and in fact, I'm also going to be teaching at the Colegio Canada."

"I'm embarrassed in front of Mr. Rainfeld, he understands Spanish . . . you're so obstinate. . . ."

"That's a fact."

"A daughter of mine? Practically engaged? Should get involved in that dangerous place where Reds hide and the National Security guards go looking for them with guns? That's sacrilege! Please, Mr. Rainfeld, honored guest, excuse us and help yourself to more fish."

Nothing better to dissolve her anger at Father than the Louie Armstrong open air concert at the Concha Acustica de Bello Monte brought from heaven itself just for her! Instead of screams, the sensual poetry of Gershwin's Summerti-i-me and the living is e-ea-sy. . . .

Cláper

[The Father] Over there in Lendov, how many strangers had Friday and Saturday meals at my parents' humble table? Impossible to count. Occasionally, the guest might even be a modern freethinker from the city.

"But, Mr. David, Charles Darwin already proved that man is just another animal. . . ."

"What are you saying, young man? If that's so, then how come not a single animal ever produced a Darwinich, or whatever his name is ?"

"Rebbe, he's an English naturalist who, after observing the animal species, determined their degree of evolution. . . . No, sorry, nothing to do with our God."

"If a horse had something to say, he would speak. . . ."

"That's not what we're discussing, Mr. David. Beasts have their own way of expressing themselves."

"Yes, yes, they have tongues, that's true, but they cannot say a single blessing!"

"They express themselves in sounds and gestures."

"Young man, the ignorant is not the one who does not know, but the one who scorns divine knowledge. And don't you forget that! A goat has a beard, but that doesn't make it a priest. Does it?"

"Ah! Finally we agree on something. Sir, you do admit then that we are the higher ranked in the animal kingdom?"

"You said that, I didn't. Anyway, before you become too big for your own breeches, young man, remember that butterflies precede you in the kingdom of divine creation! . . ."

And so they might continue until the moon descended and the sun dazzled us. . . .

[The Daughter] Ahhhh! Her intoxication continues with the music of Jelly Roll Morton. . . . The mixture of sweet wine and wrathful words at the end of Mr. Isaiah Rainfeld's reception fueled her tenacious will to face her opponent and pursue the confrontation:

"Father, I beg you! Please try to understand my wish to have a career."

"I understand and cannot tie you to the house, or prohibit you from having an honorable profession. Quite the opposite, I want you to amount to something, not be like me, who never got a diploma, who could not study and so had to earn a living knocking on doors, peddling, selling schmates. What do you want from me, Kindele? I'm afraid for you! In that political environment of atheists!"

The House of Memory

"But, Dad, you're not even religious!"

"Yes, I most certainly am, in my own way. It's true I no longer pray every day and I don't do a full fast on Yom Kippur and no doubt because of that my Poppa is turning in his grave. But, I practice my tradition every moment of my life. And, as you well know, I've made a sacred cult of my mother-tongue, Yiddish. Have you ever known me to sleep away from home, even one night? Do I have children on the streets? Do I get drunk? Gamble? Other women? That's what you're going to be exposed to out there. I'm afraid for you and for your sisters. . . ."

"Please, please, try to understand. We can't stay locked up forever. Each of us has to forge her own life! You did it, or have you already forgotten? You broke with your family and crossed oceans!"

"That was very different, young lady! Don't confuse the issues! I stayed back in Lendov, just my feet left! Can you understand that?"

"No, not at all. Anyway, why not just pretend that I'm not leaving San Leopoldino either, just my beautiful legs are running in search of other roads?"

A seemingly never-ending dialogue was being repeated, but she decided that as of this night it was ending. Max's moist eyes and Rifka's long sad face, marked with silent resentment, her leave taking at breakfast.

Would it have been wiser to go to another country? With what money? Maybe she just lacked the courage to cut, really cut that heavy cord. . . .

[The Father] As I was telling you, at the end of Shabbat, I'm leaving, without a word. I have a foreboding that I'm saying good-bye forever to Nune the carpenter, Toiba the cripple, and Leib the hunchback. Oy gottenyu, how deeply my heart aches for Momma, the blanket that covers all my weaknesses.

And when at last, Lendov is behind me, I jump, practically fly to Magelnitze without spending even a minute in that ugly little town where I used to come so often to buy yarmulkes. Its very smell upsets me. You see, when someone from my village closes their eyes forever, he is wrapped in his talith,[2] covered in straw, and then sent in a carriage to this overcrowded cemetery. Its stench freezes my bones!

"Magelnitze is sacred because it's where the eternal house is," my father used to say. "It's the good place," my mother usually added. You know what I think? I think it's the only place in the entire world where someone from our village has a right to his own little piece of land! That's what I think. And anyway, this business of putting the dead in face down, boy, that really

buries a person! Even if they swear to me that it's the real garden of Eden, and it's where all the dead will be resurrected, I still prefer gardens that are above and not below ground. Above, always above. You know what I mean? Even with all the hunger, plagues, pogroms. Nu, what can I tell you?

I don't stop at Vialorovsker either, because I know for sure that one-eyed Zina lurks right behind that window. Poor girl, she's been waiting for me to become engaged to her for four or five years now. . . . I point my face to heaven and cross the main road like a thunderbolt. I couldn't bear to feel her rancorous gaze.

"Get married? But Poppa, I'm just fifteen years old!"

"So what? I got married at the same age and I'm just fine, no?"

"But that's not good enough for me. From a cat a scratch; from a child bride nothing but damnation."

"What are you saying, my boychick? To get up early and marry early never hurt anyone. You'll have a good dowry and time to study Scripture."

"Pappinyu, you know why the bear dances? Because he has no wife. Give him one and he'll stop dancing. They sing that one at the market, Poppa."

"But it's a lie, because a husband is like a king and all couples are fine after a year or so."

"No, no, and no. It's never too late to marry or to die, Pappinyu."

"Oy veis meir! May the one whose name is blessed forgive your affront, my son! You're very stubborn and I worry night and day about how you'll end up."

And while he wails, pulling hairs out of his long black beard, I run away to help Momma with the town fair where she buys us used clothes. . . .

[The Daughter] That whole week was full of tension and whispers. Finally, on Friday night, when the rest of the family sleeps, he speaks. He looks worried.

"Where does one begin such unpleasant business? My dear sweet daughter, I want to consult you on a very delicate matter." In a low voice: "Please don't get upset. But ah . . . Manuel Rabinovich, the engineer, destined to be your husband, and from such a good family too, grandson of wise people! Well, anyway, he asked for a dowry, a house, car, office, and if possible, some cash. . . ."

The father, knowing full well his daughter's wickedly complicated personality, has to tell her the whole truth. . . . Should he get a bank loan? What does she think?

Well, I'm not surprised. It is customary, after all. The problem is I still like him even after six months. Elegant, handsome, first kiss and out together, in a group, of course, to places like that fabulous Montmartre in Baruta with its European music and the naughty Pasapoga with its mambos and guarachas.

"Thanks for the warning, Dad. If I were you, I wouldn't do anything." Of course in historical terms, a dowry was after all a justifiable institution even under a Marxist focus . . . but it had nothing to do with love. "Tell me, Dad, how much did you make when you married?"

"Your mother with three cotton dresses. . . ."

"Well, that's just about what I think you should fork over. . . ."

At times, Max could seem primitive and abrupt in his reactions, but he had never been a good peddler. He was unable to sell his daughter. His smile, overflowing with impishness, signed a pact of complicity. On that point at least, there was never any argument.

[The Father] It's a long way to Warsaw. And to be honest, it was none too sweet. But then again, I guess it could have been worse. On the way to Prztyk and Gora Kalwaria, I befriended a couple of coachmen. I've heard it said that God should protect us from forced exile and from coachmen, but, even though these were pretty rough guys, I could tell they weren't totally stupid. Look, these unfortunate men travel for so long facing their horses, after a while they themselves become like animals.

Anyway, I really liked Nisale, the frisky one. After listening to all my Oy yoy yoyings over my calf pains, one afternoon he asked me: "Tell me, young sir, you seem quite learned, what do we really need our legs for? After all, to Hebrew school we are taken, to our wedding we are driven, to our grave we are carried, to the temple we never go, and in front of all pretty Gentile girls we prostrate ourselves. . . . So, what do you think, do we need them for anything?"

"Yes, Nisale. We need them to take us to America the Golden!"

He remained pensive. Probably not half as old as he looked with those smooth toothless gums. I took great care to keep to myself my ideas about the feet being the very center of a penitent's soul. Like Joel, the bearded one dressed in rags, who showed up one day at my village. "May his body be feverish for nine years!" "A pox on him!" "He should only grow like an onion, with his head buried in the ground!" they all cursed him. Only a few of the women gave him some stale bread and water, moved by his misfortune.

Cláper

To make a long story short, Momma, teary eyed, tells me about the great Joel, born in the big city of Vilna, whose voice, at thirteen, was already legendary throughout the country. He sang the prayers with the virtuosity of the chosen. One day a famous Gentile composer hears him at an event and, overwhelmed, begs the parents to allow him to be the child's teacher. Years later, while in the capital singing profane tunes, Joel meets Katiuska, a Polish princess. They fall madly in love. So at the age of twenty-two, Joel abandons his singing career and, rejected by his people, he who had been so pious and devout decides to atone for his sins. He goes from village to village dragging himself to each and every little broken down house until he gets to ours. What grief his broken down body bears! And even you two, my very own parents, watch him suspiciously between the slits of the window shutters.

Dear parents, in this letter I can finally tell you that as I felt his child-like face and white hair wandering feverishly around the alleys of my childhood, I was more frightened than I had ever been in my life. A leper without sores.

I was reminded of the story of the king and the two men who guarded his orchard: one blind and one crippled:

"I see some delicious ripe fruit but I can't reach it with only one leg," says the cripple.

"So what do you need two legs for? If you stand on my shoulders, we'll both eat juicy apples. I don't need eyes to taste them. Why should you need two legs?" And that's exactly what they did. When the king found out, he questioned his guards.

"Your Highness, how could it have been me? I can't climb or walk."

"Do you believe, your Worship, that I could have picked them without seeing?"

The king ordered the cripple to get on the shoulders of the blind man and then sentenced both to die.

Body and soul must always go together, Poppa. I have finally realized that if succumbing to pleasure sickens one's head, then one ends up with pain like Joel's and in an asylum in Warsaw. I will never be a cantor like my brother, nor a mohel like you, Pappinyu, much less one of those chosen to study God's words fifteen hours a day. Now and with this letter, I can finally tell you one of the reasons I left home without kissing you goodbye. Please try to understand. Just like you can't dance at two weddings at the same time, I don't want to separate my heart from my head. Poppa,

The House of Memory

Momma, dear little brothers and sisters, please don't cry when you think of me. . . .

"That's what we need our feet for, Nisale, to save ourselves in America. . . ."

Translated from the Spanish by Joan E. Friedman

1. The novel *Cláper* is constructed of two parallel, alternating monologues—those of a father who left his village in Poland after World War I to emigrate to the Americas, and of his daughter who comes of age in Venezuela in the 1960s. The identities of the speakers have been added, in brackets, to this excerpt from the novel.

2. A talith is a traditional prayer shawl.

From The Book of Memories

Ana María Shua

Almost Like America

Grandfather was skinny when he crossed the ocean. He was real skinny and young, too, and he wasn't a grandfather before leaving Tomachevo to cross the ocean. Grandfather didn't want to come. No one wanted to come here. This wasn't exactly America. It was a poor runner-up. It was dangerous for women. They were put to work as whores. But Granny wasn't a whore, she worked as a seamstress. Back then, men here wore large white scarves that were embroidered.

"You mean handkerchiefs that you put in your pocket? Embroidered handkerchiefs for blowing your nose?"
"Large handkerchiefs like the ones you wear around your neck. White scarves, they said. Can't you hear?"

Grandfather was never persecuted. Grandfather wanted to build America, but not this America, the other one, you know, the real one, the one up north. He was a tailor's apprentice and he was always well dressed. He'd wear those Russian smocks buttoned at the neck and the baggy pants buttoned down at the ankle (like the Cossacks wear in the Russian ballets), made of thick, well-tailored cloth.

And that's the way you'd find Grandfather dressed in Poland, where it was always cold and where everyone ate potatoes. But he was also a deserter. Potatoes on Monday, potatoes on Tuesday, potatoes on Wednesday, potatoes on Thursday, potatoes on Friday, and on Saturdays . . . ah!, that was something different! Saturdays! On Saturdays, fried

eggs and potatoes. One would think that Grandfather would've hated potatoes and, with all that meat in America, he'd never have to eat potatoes again. But potatoes are what he liked best. On Saturdays, fried eggs and potatoes.

"Which army did Grandfather desert from?"

"Who knows? Poland was full of armies. There was the czar's army, the Red army, the Polish army, the Polish National Guard. And the Poles supported the Red army and the German army. They all came and went and fought among themselves."

Then one day Grandfather was drafted. It was wartime. Grandfather didn't want to go to war, he wanted to go to America. His fiancée didn't want him to go either, she wanted him to marry her. So he deserted and hid in her house. He hid there for a year, right in her bedroom. And in her bed, too? Grandfather did that? What was he waiting for? He was waiting for the right document. He waited for anyone who got sick, or who might have an accident and die. He was always wearing his nice suit, hiding in his fiancée's house, and waiting for someone to die young so he could buy his identity papers, a nifty legal document belonging to someone who hadn't deserted.

"And what was his fiancée's house like on the outside?"

"It was a house just like any other house."

"And what was his fiancee's house like on the inside?"

"There's a picture of it in the Book of Memories. There's a rug on the ground, and on the rug there's a table, and on the table there's a sewing machine, and around the table there are some chairs, and behind them there's a large piece of furniture made of dark wood, maybe an armoire. And to one side of the table there's a rocking chair and on the other side an armchair."

"Are there pictures on the walls?"

"There weren't any pictures because there were no walls. And around the rug, everything was white, pure white, because it was sitting on the snow. And that's the way his fiancée's house was on the inside. There wasn't enough light inside to take a picture, so they took everything outside and put it in the snow."

Gedalia Rimetka died fairly young and he had a mustache. Grandfather took his identity papers to the American consulate, the real one, the one

up north, but they turned him down. Gedalia hadn't died young enough; he just wasn't young enough to be my grandfather. It was always cold in Poland, and it was always snowing. When the snow melted, everything turned to mud. Even the mud was cold.

Grandfather crossed through the mud in Tomachevo, but he really wanted to cross the ocean. So he went to the consulate of this poor America where, he was told, they didn't pay much attention, they didn't understand anything, it was all the same to them. That's America too, but not quite. What's important is to leave Europe, to be able to cross the ocean. Then it'll be easy to get from one America to the other America.

They didn't pay much attention, or they didn't care, or they didn't understand anything, and so Grandfather got ready to cross the ocean. Grandfather Gedalia Rimetka—always elegantly dressed but a little too skinny—boarded the ship in Odessa and started the crossing. They ate the skins of the potatoes, too. Potatoes, however, are full of carbohydrates. Why, then, was Grandfather so skinny? Because he only ate potatoes, and only a few at that.

"Are you sure it was Odessa? Immigrants didn't leave from Odessa? Check the Book of Memories, what does it say?"

"The Book of Memories says that when Grandfather Gedalia boarded ship he was seventeen years old and wore a short-brimmed hat."

The ocean was wide, the ship was Italian. The men slept together in the hold. Was it called the bilge? Grandfather Gedalia didn't know the word *bilge*. Everyone but he vomited everywhere. Gedalia, who was tall and skinny, watched his ship brothers vomit. There were Polish and Russian travelers, and Italians who had gotten on in Genoa. They ate a lot of pasta on board the ship. Lots of macaroni and potato dumplings, but no ravioli. Round pasta, flat pasta, Bologna-style fettuccine with meat sauce, or pesto. That's why by the time Grandfather reached America he wasn't skinny anymore. He gained forty pounds in twenty days. Grandfather ate a lot of pasta but he never got sick. After they reached Brazil, he also ate a lot of bananas.

They arrived first to Pernambuco, where there were lots of blacks and Indians, and it was hot. Grandfather didn't like it there. "This is America?" his fellow travelers asked. They felt deceived. Give up that mud for this mud? Doesn't look promising. Hot mud in America instead of cold mud in

Poland? And so they loaded up with bananas. At first they were green, then they turned yellow. Large bunches of mysterious bananas. And that's how a young, skinny, adventurous kid left Odessa and how a dour and fat Grandfather Gedalia arrived in Buenos Aires. He always refused to eat strawberries. They're every where in the forests. Bananas are another matter.

"And those on the ship who ate according to the Jewish religion, what did they eat?"

"Those on the ship who ate according to the Jewish religion didn't eat."

And, finally, they arrived. Buenos Aires was a much more acceptable America. It was comparable to Warsaw. It was a real city. He stayed at a hotel for immigrants. Friends were waiting for him. It was cold, not as bad as Poland, but a lot colder than it is now. The cold that the immigrants felt was another type of cold. They would stuff newspapers inside their clothes to stay warm. Newspapers kept you warm, like this, underneath your shirt, yep, whole newspapers.

He lived for a short time in Entre Rios, where the Jewish communities had been established. It was cold there too, especially in the mornings. His fingers would get stiff, numb from the cold, as he milked the cows. Yes, Grandfather wasn't elegant anymore. Grandfather Gedalia was good at making suits, he knew how to cut cloth and sew, but he didn't know how to milk cows or harvest flax. On the other hand, he knew how to ride a horse. And he quickly learned how to eat barbecued meat.

Afterward he went to the city. Then he sent for Granny, who had been waiting for him in Tomachevo, and he didn't put her to work as a whore but as a seamstress. Then he earned a lot of money. Then he collapsed and died.

"What do you mean, collapsed? Didn't Grandfather Gedalia sur vive that collapse? Applying hot and cold presses?"

"Grandfather Gedalia survived one collapse but died from another. That's life for you."

Grandfather, said Aunt Judith, was a son of a bitch and he shit all over us. Uncle Pucho said Aunt Judith was a liar and had a dirty mouth. Uncle Pucho never did like women with dirty mouths.

The Name Rimetka

The original Gedalia, the one who died in Poland, the one whose identity papers Grandfather purchased, the one who had died fairly young so that Grandfather's face would coincide with the one in the picture, but not sufficiently young enough to convince the consulate authorities of the real America, the one up north, well, that Gedalia was never called Rimetka exactly.

The surname Rimetka was the result of a combination of auditory expertise and orthographic arbitrariness of some civil servant who attempted to decipher a document written in another language by providing his own interpretation of a surname that he thought a foreigner from Poland should have, which occurred at the time he was taking down Grandfather Gedalia's personal information for the purpose of making his Argentine identification card.

Like so many other immigrants, the Rimetka family had acquired an intensely national name, a truly indigenous product, much more authentically Argentine than a correctly spelled Spanish surname, because Rimetka never existed in Grandfather's homeland, or in the original language or, for that matter, in any other country or time in history.

About Grandfather Gedalia's Personality

Grandfather Gedalia never wavered in his habits. Every day at five o'clock in the afternoon he would have a cup of English tea at the Richmond Cafe on Florida Street, where he would sit with his friends and watch the women go by.

Not once did he ever set foot in the Richmond on Florida Street. He always went to the Lion Bar instead.

It's possible that Grandfather never set foot in the Richmond on Florida Street (to set foot inside, in the strictest sense of the word) because he always sat at a table on the sidewalk outside. Perhaps he might have set foot inside the premises because he had to go to the bathroom. You might think he would have sat inside when it rained, but that's not true either. He simply didn't go there when it rained because the women wouldn't be out walking.

Grandfather Gedalia would go to the Richmond Cafe and the Lion Bar because he was a moneylender and he had clients at both places. He

would meet his Jewish clients at the Lion Bar and the others at the Richmond Cafe.

Grandfather Gedalia never charged interest on loans to Jewish people because it simply didn't look right. But he also never loaned anything to anyone without charging interest.

They never let moneylenders frequent the Lion Bar.

That's not true.

After he got older, Grandfather Gedalia would meet with his clients in the Pumpernickel, a snack bar that sold hamburgers. Grandfather Gedalia didn't like hamburgers, but he liked the Pumpernickel, mainly because they didn't have waiters and he could spend as long as he liked there without having to buy anything.

Pumpernickel almost rhymes with *kuentenik*. *Kuentenik* means something like moneylender.

Kuentenik doesn't have anything to do with the word *moneylender*.

Kuentenik is a type of peddler.

In addition to being a moneylender, Grandfather Gedalia was also a *kuentenik*. But he earned more money as a moneylender. As a *kuentenik* he had to do his work on a bicycle until he could afford to buy his first car.

Let's say Grandfather Gedalia would meet with other men in a bar or a coffee shop. They were probably his clients because Grandfather Gedalia never had any friends. There is no doubt that he would watch the women go by. Is everything right so far? Do you agree with what we've said?

No. Grandfather Gedalia was quite charming. He had lots of friends. Most of his friends were immigrants, like him, but he also had some Argentine friends. He was especially proud of them. Not every immigrant had those types of friends.

Many years later, when Grandfather Gedalia would meet someone who was a son of an immigrant he would immediately ask his name and then go on to say that when he was coming over on the ship he had met someone by that same name. Whoever talked to him for the first time found him to be quite charming and would begin questioning him at length about this person he had met in order to see if he or she was part of their family.

Grandfather Gedalia was always terribly stingy.

Grandfather Gedalia was not always terribly stingy.

When Grandfather Gedalia was young, he was very ostentatious. Only after the Crash did he become an Uncle Scrooge.

Grandfather Gedalia became a miser after his children had grown up.

The Book of Memories

When Grandfather Gedalia bought the Old House he was a real miser about some things, but in others he liked to flaunt his wealth.

Grandfather Gedalia had a Hispano-Suiza automobile and he would take us out for rides in it. And he had a winter coat of beaver skin made for me and we would vacation in Uruguay. In Pocitos. And if you don't believe me, there are pictures to prove it.

It wasn't a Hispano-Suiza, it was a Packard coupe and we called it "the Packard." We always spent vacations in Mar del Plata. And if you don't believe me, there are pictures to prove it.

If you can't see the statues of those seals, you won't be able to tell if it's Mar del Plata.

You can't tell if it's Pocitos either.

Grandfather Gedalia was an admirer of the Kaiser and that's why he gave Uncle Pucho the name of Isaac Guillermo. He also admired the Germans in general until, that is, the Second World War.

After the Second World War he hated and feared the Germans but he still continued to admire them.

Grandfather Gedalia was for Yrigoyen and that's why he named Uncle Silvester Hipólito, after Hipólito Yrigoyen, who was president of Argentina from 1916 to 1922, reelected in 1928, and deposed in 1930. He originally named him Shloime but the civil servant didn't understand, or he acted like he didn't understand.

Grandfather Gedalia wasn't interested in politics.

In Poland, Grandfather Gedalia was a Communist. After he got to Argentina, he became a materialist.

How was he going to be a Communist and still follow the dictates of his religion? After you become a Communist, there's no going back to your religion.

After that he just stopped being religious. But he followed tradition. Mainly to keep up appearances.

If so, then why did he throw Aunt Judith out of the house?

Aunt Judith always annoyed everyone, she was unbearable, she was foul-mouthed, so Grandfather Gedalia gave her the boot using her disrespect for our religion as an excuse. In reality, he was the one who wasn't religious.

That's a lie.

What's a lie? If he didn't give a hoot about religion or politics, why did he give Uncle Pucho a name like Hipólito? Because he didn't care one bit about politics. But he was for Yrigoyen just the same.

When Granny would say something, Grandfather Gedalia would

always add: she has a big mouth and so she talks. Other times he would say: there is a saying in the Talmud that goes something like this: when people are born stupid, they'll be that way all their lives and the more they talk the more you can tell how stupid they are. Then he would repeat the saying in Hebrew.

Aunt Clara's grandchildren went to a school that taught Hebrew. After that, whenever he would quote the Talmud, he wouldn't repeat it in Hebrew anymore.

Grandfather Gedalia and Granny loved each other very much.

Grandfather Gedalia and Granny had their own special way of loving each other very much.

When Grandfather Gedalia was hiding in Granny's parents' house in order to escape from the Polish army, he never said "she has a big mouth and so she talks too much."

Whenever Grandfather Gedalia didn't like her food, he would throw it on the floor, say, for instance, when there wasn't enough salt or it wasn't hot enough.

When Grandfather Gedalia would be talking and Granny interrupted him, his eyes would well up with tears and he'd look at her as if to say "Now that I'm finally old and decrepit doesn't anyone show respect anymore?" When Granny would be talking, Grandfather Gedalia interrupted her all the time.

Grandfather Gedalia sold things on credit.

What kind of things?

Anything. It didn't matter what it was, he just had to sell it on credit.

Is that what it means to be a peddler?

Yes.

At first he peddled his wares on the street, then he went around on a bicycle. But when he got his first car he didn't use it for work, only to take rides.

Grandfather Gedalia used to say that after riding his bike around all morning, a working man had a right to ask his wife to put salt on his food. This meant that if the food didn't have enough salt, a working man had the right to throw it on the floor.

When Grandfather Gedalia got very old, he couldn't eat salt because it was bad for his blood pressure. But he continued to eat hot food.

Selling things on credit was a peddler's life. All the peddlers belonged to a peddlers' co-op. The wives of the peddlers would take things from the co-op and pay for them at cost. But they never bought anything on credit.

Whenever Grandfather Gedalia would tell a lie, he'd pat his left knee.

The Book of Memories

Grandfather Gedalia suffered from arthritis in his left knee, which had become swollen and deformed, so he'd pat it all day long.

Grandfather had a business selling cloth in La Boca district. Back then, the cloth stores sold more than just silk, even though there were stores that sold fine yard goods.

Whenever the rainy southeast winds would hit La Boca, everything would become flooded, so Grandfather Gedalia would have his Great Inundation Sales.

He would always put his bolts of cloth high up on the shelves so they wouldn't get wet.

In order to sell the cloth at his Great Inundation Sales, he'd wet them down with a bucket of water from the back of the store.

Was he in business in La Boca before or after?

It was after Grandfather Gedalia quit as a peddler but before he became a moneylender.

Grandfather Gedalia was always a moneylender, even in Poland.

Grandfather Gedalia couldn't have been a moneylender in Poland because when he came over he was still very young.

There are people who charge interest while they're still in their mothers' wombs. There are people who, as they're being born, make mortgage loans to the midwives.

Moneylender is just an elegant way of saying loan shark.

There is nothing elegant about being a moneylender.

Grandfather Gedalia was a loan shark and a moneylender. And ever since he quit making his own clothes, he was anything but elegant.

Grandfather Gedalia favored Uncle Silvester because he always got up early and they'd play dominoes together.

Uncle Silvester was the only one of Grandfather Gedalia's sons with whom he preferred to talk; for instance, he would go into Silvester's bedroom, look at all of his books, and then ask him how much they'd fetch at the flea market.

I've also heard that one Sunday afternoon he took Silvester on the trolley and then bought him a ham sandwich.

Grandfather Gedalia never ate pig's meat because it was against his religion.

Grandfather Gedalia never ate pig's meat in public.

Grandfather Gedalia was a pig.

<div style="text-align: right">Translated from the Spanish by Dick Gerdes</div>

Sailing Down the Rhine

Sonia Guralnik

The air is warm and still there is no breeze, the trees hold their breath; everything is motionless waiting for the last passengers.

At the end of the dock a bus appears, advancing slowly until it stops by the boat.

A very tall woman is the first to step down. She wears thick-lensed glasses.

"Good morning, Frau Braun."

"Good morning, Captain."

"Allow me. I am going to count the tickets."

She notes his blue jacket, his white cap, under which some gray hair peeks out. The captain has fine lips, which are sketched between two vertical folds. He is young still, in this youth of gold buttons—just how old might he be? He has just grown a fine mustache, which he dyes black, that's for sure.

The little old women appear at the bus's door and begin to step down with great difficulty. Some lean on canes, others walk two-by-two, in a slow march. All wear lace-up boots, all have twisted legs, but each one presents her deformed hips in a different manner: at times the knees come together, at others they are incredibly separated. Those who have long legs wear short boots like a child's and those who have legs like short parentheses wear tall boots like a hunter's.

"I'm not getting on board!" one of them says. "The Rhine's water isn't as clear as it used to be. It's dirty." And she crosses her arms.

Another whispers, "I don't want to go. I get so seasick on boats."

An old woman uses a parasol to keep the sun, glaring from the street, away from her face. She squints constantly.

Sailing Down the Rhine

"Hurry up! Hurry up!" orders Frau Braun, clapping her hands. "The boat is waiting for us."

There's a yellowish old woman who wears a wide-brimmed hat and gloves. Someone makes fun of her.

"I never go outside unless I'm correctly dressed," she says, straightening out her gloves, "or else I could be confused with the servants."

They have placed four wheelchairs on the deck.

Madame Grete is quite fine. She wears a tiara in her hair and an ocher-colored shawl on top of her overcoat.

"Everyone here?" the captain asks.

"Everyone!" shouts Frau Braun from below. And she pushes onto the gangplank the old woman who gets seasick.

The old women sit in two lines on the main deck. They have been promised hot chocolate if they behave themselves. They hold hands and begin to sing with shrill little voices as the boat departs.

Their voices, growing faint as the noise of the motor increases, are suddenly drowned out.

The boat has left behind the houses and the suburbs with their chimneys, parks, bridges, and sown fields.

A young woman on board sells postcards to the tourists. Approaching the old women, she suddenly seems to grow older.

"They are postcards from the war. This is how Cologne was after the bombing raids. Only the great cathedral was saved," she tells them, and she passes the cards close to their eyes so they can see but not touch.

At noon, Frau Braun holds her chin high and makes the old women move on up to the top deck to get some sun. They all hold hands: "Hänschen Klein, ging allein," they sing as they move along. Madame Katz goes through her purse: her glasses must be there in the bottom. Madame Ursula hasn't been able to locate her teeth. Someone has taken them. How is she ever going to sip chocolate and nibble pastries?

They have stolen Madame Grete's watch.

"There's a thief among you," Frau Braun says, shaking her index finger. Then she turns to the captain, explaining to him, "they get confused, they imagine days, things, dates, they forget . . ."

"I don't forget," thinks Madame Katz. She bows her head to rid herself of the formless memory that has hounded her ever since she entered the nursing home. She has seen this woman somewhere else. Where? How can she remember? "Wasn't it in the spring of . . ."

The House of Memory

Suddenly her memory is invaded by the warmth of her daughter's body, and everything clouds over in a rush of unstoppable tears. She sits up quite straight. Again she goes through her purse. Who could possibly have taken my glasses? She is sure she had opened the drawer to get them before she left on the outing.

"I can live without my glasses. I no longer read," she thinks. And thinks. Frau Braun converses with the captain.

She is sixty, tall and strong; her short hair grows quickly. No one knows she was a torturer in the concentration camps. Nor does anyone have any reason to know. The old women fear her. That helps her maintain discipline. She is capable of tiny tortures that leave no telltale marks: she hid Madame Ursula's dentures, and she just threw Madame Katz's glasses into the river. Up her sleeve she has Madame Grete's watch and soon she will drop it into the milk. She will add salt to the chocolate, but no one will find out because old women frequently imagine things and besides, they never say anything during the commission's annual inspection at the Paradise Home.

Madame Katz continues to contemplate the captain. There is something about him that seems false, like this boat and this sunny, happy day. She looks at him more intently and suddenly a light illuminates her old eyelids: the black mustache is a fake. Mustache. MUSTACHE. That's it! The jailer at Bergen-Belsen. They called her Mustache. My God. They say she shaved every day, but even so a shadow appeared at noon. It's noon now. Hardly daring to do so, she looks over at Frau Braun, who has the sun in her face. . . .

"She took Annie from me," Madame Katz thinks with great difficulty. She pushes back the thick tears that come up from the pit of her stomach, the sharp-edged sobs that pierce the feelings of everything she has lived.

"No, you just can't imagine how they are," Frau Braun is talking to the captain. "They forget their way, it's difficult to manage them. At times they become mischievous like mice. . . ."

The captain looks at her.

Madame Katz has made up her mind. She shouts: "Frau Braun is the torturer at Bergen-Belsen! Frau Braun is MUSTACHE!"

Like the rustle of dry straw, the old women's voices begin:

"Where were you during the war?"

"In many places. And you?"

"I was also in Bergen-Belsen."

"In Auschwitz."

"I was in Dachau."

The old women roll up their sleeves.

"In Ravensbruck."

"I was also in Auschwitz."

"My parents were never buried."

One of the women tries to stand up. She is the one with the bowed legs and short boots. She falls. Madame Ursula begins to cry and shout.

Madame Grete stammers, trying to get the situation in hand, so that they'll listen to her, that's why she's the queen. She will do the talking.

They all mill around Madame Katz, while the old women farther back keep asking questions, still not understanding what is happening. Madame Katz drills on with her voice low and her perfect punctuation, each syllable distinct: "*She* is the one who mixes up our boots, *she* is the one who takes away our fresh bread and leaves us the scraps before we enter the dining room, *she* steals and destroys our glasses, *she* is the one who puts salt in our chocolate, *she* is the one who turns off the heat when you are shivering in the darkness. Ursula, *she* is the one who shouts behind our backs, the practical jokes, she calls them. *She* is the one who cuts the historical items from the paper, *she* is the one who tore my Annie away from me through the bars, in pieces she tore her from me.

In the distance, Frau pounds her hands together, distractedly. Definitely, this captain is very nice.

"Go wash your hands," she orders halfheartedly. And she turns back to the captain, commenting, "Look how their hands are stained with freckles. There is no way to hide these women's age once you see their hands."

The captain has gone up to the bridge.

Madame Katz keeps talking in a hoarse quiver. The old women nod to each phrase. Finally she says, "It will be after lunch." The whisper travels throughout the boat, the wrinkled whisper that is not heard.

Once again the old women have taken each other by the hands. But this time a current of life runs through them. The old branches straighten in the storm. Where were you, Auschwitz, my brother, Bergen-Belsen, my brother, on the third day they broke our legs. "Rheumatism," the reports called it after the war, what a laugh, rheumatism, my legs, the ones I used to show off and get whatever I wanted, and now they are turned outward.

Madame Ursula, afraid, her new skirt dragging across the floor, repeating, "Quickly, quickly, she's coming." They pull her up and head off to the

dining room. They can't wait any longer. All follow the movements of Madame Katz.

"Would you all please do me a favor and hurry up!" Frau Braun howls, planting herself before them with her hands on her hips. Madame Katz approaches and with her sharpened wrinkles says: "No. First we will form a circle and sing a round. Ready!"

"HÄNSCHEN KLEIN / GING ALLEIN / IN DIE WEITE / WELT HINEIN! . . ."[1]

The captain and two crewmen have looked for Frau Braun for a long time now and with no luck. The captain has to take charge of the old women. The boat has arrived in Koblenz.

Translated from the Spanish by Martha Manier

1. "Little Hans/went alone/into the wide/world! . . ."

Rojl Eisips

Teresa Porzecanski

Well, that's why I'm still carrying that awful letter in my pocket. Now and then its existence fills me with a dark longing to hold it again, to grasp the worn-out envelope in my hand. Then I slide my hand in, bit by bit, terrified, as if it were a trap. Since I really don't want to find it, I wish that my pocket's shapeless emptiness would push my hand into a corner.

But when I get home in the middle of the dense, rush-hour traffic, and an incomprehensible buzzing zigzags through my ears, and I know that I'm about to give in, that I'll really give in, I head straight for that envelope. I search for it quickly in my jacket. Touching it gives me an almost sanguine feeling of peace and quiet.

I silently repeat the name of Rojl Eisips, as if doing so would wing her on back, and I could see her again, in the flesh. Over and over I read the Hebrew letters, almost indecipherable now, as if its writer were forgetting, little by little, the strokes of the remote alphabet, the mazy signs flying from the pen. The envelope—what's left of it—is covered with the traces of fingerprints, with ridges inextricably intermingled and blended.

It's all because I found Rojl Eisips. I found her through the ambiguous directions that a close-lipped Lithuanian cobbler gave me. He managed to recall that he used to have a distant relative with that name, who was paralyzed, or deaf, or a hopeless case, probably the mother of a distant cousin he barely knew, or the child of a disagreeable aunt who used to work in a bank—he couldn't recall the name—on the third floor, accounts department. And I found that old guy, in turn, through a lonely seamstress who specialized in stitching lapels for suits, while I got her address from an former haberdasher, who remembered that once upon a time she had a neighbor—it was when she was living in a pension on Blandengues Street—

and the neighbor's name was Rojl Eisips, a cook, and maybe she was still there, full of life and raring to go.

All that, ultimately to come across this moldy woman of indeterminate age. Opening a single eye, suspicious, she stabbed the rancid air of the hallway. "And why would someone be wanting to see me? Me!"

The visiting nurse didn't bother to answer. First she looked over to me, her glance both guilty and sarcastic, with a grimace that curled up and settled in the left-hand corner of her mouth. A minute later, she made a gesture of indifference and left. There I was, facing the wheelchair, while the nurse moved away, unaffected by the clammy corridor.

And then we were alone, Rojl Eisips and I, in that contentious orphanage, the "Asylum for the Old." At that moment the old woman pointed to a chair for me, and made herself comfortable in hers, and I understood that we were, the two of us, looking onto eternity.

"In Jerusalem," I whispered, "right in the oldest part of the stone city," I added, "an old man, selling carpets, handed me a letter with your name and address on it. And he told me: 'It's very urgent. It must reach the hands of Rojl Eisips as soon as possible.'"

"You say it was a stone city, but very, very old?" asked the old woman, in an accent transformed by a variety of origins. And then, suddenly, as if struck by a subversive idea, she said, "Come, tell me everything, the whole truth."

Perhaps her deafness, the sleepy way she had of looking at me, made me realize that she would never understand.

Firmly, I insisted, "I have a letter for you. A letter sent by a simple carpet seller in Jerusalem."

But there suddenly came from her, from some unexpected place within her, a new voice—dark, like a barrel—with which she repeated and repeated her own question, even as she was circling in on some vague plot woven far back in her memory. Then, as if conquered by sudden and credible truth, Rojl Eisips invented laughter—laughter that rose from the pit of her stomach, as if suddenly something in her might split open, giving birth to a whirlwind of light and harmony.

"But of course, of course I know you, Anele," she said, with her new voice. "How could I forget my oldest granddaughter, the slenderest of all the daughters of my daughter Frida, who died in Latvia? Why, that's her face you have, just like your mother's. And those eyes. The very same eyes your foolish father had, God keep them in His glory. Amen."

"No!" I shouted, much upset. "I'm not your granddaughter. I only came

to give you this letter." And I extended to her the envelope, an action that then struck me as ridiculous, even absurd, in the gloominess of that place.

"A letter?" she laughed, motioning it away. "What letter?" Now she was showing her gums, which were almost empty, and as moist as those of a newborn baby. "I don't need any letter to know you. I know very well who you are, Anele. How many times did I feed you and tell you stories, while your mother returned to Latvia to search for that foolish father of yours. He wasn't going to leave Riga until they dragged him out. And they did. In '39."

Suddenly, the indefinable age of the old woman had gone back in time. Her entire body had now expanded, and the beginnings of youth swept over her—over her eyes, small but limpid, and her smile, which became more and more pastoral, until her words were now rushing out all at once, one after the next, scarcely intelligible. Almost without stopping they flowed out, soft and foamy, from between her girlish gums. All her relatives, long since gone, were returning through her in a mad rush for life, suspended in the eyes of Rojl Eisips, which were at once irridescent and flaming with love's ghosts unleashed.

I still managed to gasp: "An old man I met in a store, selling rugs . . . when he learned that I was returning to Montevideo he scribbled out this letter, and he asked me, he begged me, 'Deliver it to Rojl Eisips. It's urgent,' he told me, 'Rojl Eisips.'"

But now a group of Cossacks had invaded her birthplace, plundering religious objects, setting fire to it, her parents trapped inside. And now her aunt, who sold pastries in a market in Vitesk, had raised the little girl on her own. And now Rojl Eisips reached the port of Montevideo in January of 1922, with a pair of shoes and a small bundle of belongings, enough for her needs, to be a cook on a ranch in Colonia, and later moved to the capital, apartment 8 on Blandengues Street, then giving birth to five wise children by a ghostly husband, now deceased.

It was getting dark outside and Rojl Eisips kept on talking. A vague litany lent rhythm and movement to her words. Over and over the Cossacks were killing her parents. Once again the aunt from Vitesk was making pastries to sell in the market. Then a ship appeared on the horizon of the port, and a fifteen-year-old girl wearing a head scarf descended, toiling in a multitude of dishes and kitchenware, then becoming pregnant, then bearing five wise children. What had it all been? Nothing but this summary, spun over and over, with the rhythm of a fable, as afternoon wore into evening.

The House of Memory

Sometimes it was Rojl Eisips who was selling the pastries, but at the market in Vilnius, not Vitesk, and her parents were being killed by the Polish police, not in a fire set by Cossacks. Then it was her aunt who arrived in America, with the bundle of clothing and the shoes, and it was the five children who gave birth to Rojl Eisips.

I don't know why I didn't escape. I had to stay. There I remained, hour after hour, hypnotized, until night took over and managed to silence Rojl Eisips. Two obese, machinelike nurses moved her chair. It slid along without a squeak. And as she was leaving, the very last time, head tilted to one side, eyes still glowing, those childlike gums were still spread wide, still telling stories.

And that's why the crumpled letter is still in my pocket. That's why I haven't been able to deliver it. I really don't know why I'm still keeping it, there where I put it the first time, and handling it over and over. Maybe I'm afraid to open it and prove that Rojl Eisips is still here and I'm nestled within her. And the two of us are irretrievably sinking into one sweet, drawn-out sentence.

Translated from the Spanish by Elizabeth Rosa Horan

The Portuguese Synagogue

Angelina Muñiz-Huberman

In Amsterdam the words "Violence has a certain unity of form" suddenly came to me.

●

In Amsterdam I left the others and walked to the Portuguese synagogue. As if fulfilling a promise. As if seeking solitude: the nostalgia of a place. A place that can only be the center of the universe.

●

There with the enormous iron candelabrum in the ceiling: that was the exact spot. Where all acts converge. Where such an appointment with destiny is undeniable.

●

You cannot put off what you know is to happen. What else am I doing in the synagogue but waiting for the encounter?

●

Sitting on the bench of dark, dense wood. Polished by centuries of cloths rubbing against it. (No one sits down anymore. The visitors stick their heads in quickly and disappear.) (I do sit. I've been sitting for quite some time. So much time that the caretaker grows suspicious. He doesn't know what he suspects, but he suspects something just the same.)

●

I run my fingers along the smooth wood. I rest. I hear the sounds of the full synagogue. Packed with recent arrivals from Spain and Portugal. After the edict of expulsion.

The House of Memory

•

What would have occurred during the Nazi occupation? Silence. Silence. Silence. After all the windows and the urns were broken, one by one. Shattered, smashed to bits, crushed to pieces.

•

Etty Hillesum walked near the Portuguese synagogue before joining the condemned.

The appointment was sacred.

•

What are the sounds I hear? Those of half a millennium ago, or those of forty, fifty years ago?

Both.

•

Etty Hillesum approached God in her own way. But her confusion was great. She didn't know what to do with the evil of the world.

She decided to accept chaos.

To wound herself in order to become part of the nightmare.

•

Where I am sitting another "I" could have been sitting. One of those women who emigrated and attended the inauguration of the *esnoga* in 1614.

Things can happen or they can not happen.

Here, in the silence of an unvisited temple, the emptiness of God remains. Those who fled the Inquisition found their place and prayed. No one could flee the Nazis.

Two diaries, among others, remained, that of a girl and that of a young woman: Anne Frank and Etty Hillesum. Both interrupted.

I would rather be the woman who sat here centuries ago. Because Anne and Etty are too near. They scratch and tear at me.

That's not true. I wouldn't have wanted to be here in 1614 either. I wouldn't have ever wanted to be in any temple or in any other house of God. And yet, here I am, sitting in the Portuguese synagogue, an empty museum.

I'm the one who's empty.

•

I no longer have a time in which to live. History has shattered me. I do not believe. I do not think. I do not feel.

The Portuguese Synagogue

And what's worse: I'm not even an automaton.
And the appalling part: I still possess a weak moral code.
If I have no time, it's because I have no place.

•

I probably shouldn't stay in the synagogue. The caretaker is so anxious and so eager for me to leave that when all is said and done he will have his way. Because what am I doing here?

I am just occupying a small section of a long bench made of solid wood. I have installed myself here and I'm not going to move.

I'm beginning to feel my muscles relax, to feel a laziness, a forgetfulness. As if my body were merging with the wood. As if I were no longer myself. As if I had ceased to exist.

I float and am transported.

I could pass through the glass and become part of the blueness of the sky. The iron bars framing the air prevent me from escaping.

Would the victims have escaped this way?

From the prisons of the Inquisition, from the boxcars, from the barbed wire?

No.

No one escaped.

The executioners escaped.

•

Although she was a girl, Anne was more mature than Etty. I don't know that for a fact.

Etty was still deceiving herself. She clung to prayers and poetry. To let herself finally be dragged down the path of denial.

•

Is it true that she tried to pray in the closed Portuguese synagogue?

•

She could still believe. I no longer can.

Despite the presence of the sacred enclosure: a monument to the divine absence.

•

I had drawn away from the others: from those who run down the streets, through the museums. And, of course, who pedal their shiny bicycles.

The House of Memory

In order to rest in the simple light of the synagogue.
And to take flight.

•

Images captivate me, and from them I get my ideas. From glass and mirrors (even those veiled by black cloth). From kaleidoscopes and from stained glass windows.

•

Even though I confuse my memory with the memory others. Did it happen to you or did it happen to me? Is it your memory or mine?

•

I don't know my limits very well either. I don't know where I begin and where I am the others. I surprise myself with an imitated gesture, with a word belonging to someone else.

I go from one mimesis to the next.

So I don't know who I am. I just am. One of these possibilities. Nothing that can be concrete. A sketch of a person. Ambiguous, half-traced.

Ah, but it bothers me that they might recognize in me something that is not mine. After all, it's robbery.

•

Etty aspired to mystical perfection. I can't believe in it. In the midst of the horror, she became as transparent as air.

When she was able to escape, when it was still possible, she avoided it. She said: if my people die, I will die with them. She didn't want to be a survivor or a witness.

•

She thought to leave a final testimony: squeezed together with the hundreds of Jews who were going to meet their death, through some crack in the moving train she threw out a card on which she had written: "We go singing to the concentration camp."

•

But I don't accept it. Today, in this temple of so many tears, I don't accept going off to death singing.

Because it was not a chosen death.

It was an imposed death.

The Portuguese Synagogue

Violence on a whim.
Agony in the name of fun.
Blood spat out.
The body carried to new depths.
The naked scorned.
The soul slashed.

•

And yet, in the abandoned synagogue there is peace. Prayers are still suspended. In the air.

•

It's silence.
 What else can it be?
 Silence.

•

In the Portuguese synagogue in Amsterdam there are no walls. The space is as vast as the heavenly dome.

•

Destruction is present.
 The end of the world is hanging.
 The armies of darkness polish their high, black boots.

•

The polished, black boot comes down hard on the bare foot.

•

The soldiers' excrement spreads over the roundness of the earth.

•

The perfection of the circle is lost.

•

The Portuguese synagogue of Amsterdam remains.

•

Those who desecrated humanity descrated themselves first.

•

The House of Memory

They were the ones who swallowed their own vomit.

•

From the shit they proclaimed purity.

•

Etty was easily deceived.
 Anne saw the truth.

•

With a faint breath, both of them shook the paper army.

•

In the synagogue I want to explain the unexplainable. To reason out the unreasonable.

An invented existence could be so peaceful. Simply to let life go where it ought to go. Follow the natural order of things. Instead of having lived this wretched present moment, to resign myself to imagination.

Not to compare. To choose total separation from reality. And thus, to erase history. No issues, no anecdotes. To sink into the flow of mental images. To turn out the light forever. To turn on the darkness.

Since language doesn't serve to explain. Since the word has been broken. Since systems and institutions are hollow scarecrows. Since the ten just men are nowhere to be found. To what heaven do I rise?

•

To the one creating the rupture?

•

From chaos, what can arise?

•

It's true that I drew away from the others. From those who were traveling with me. From those who are still babbling.

And I sat down here, in the Portuguese synagogue. For such a long time. Such a painful time. To think that one day I would think again, that one day I would understand.

That light would begin to shine in my darkness.

That, like the mystics, I would be granted a revelation.

•

So that just that idea might endure: I would write on black paper one dark
night.

•

What a desperate coming and going. Gropingly. With the walls receding.
Blindly. With the tips of my fingers not feeling a thing.

•

To think it is possible to embrace the whole world in this warm space of
precious woods that is the Portuguese synagogue of Amsterdam.

•

Amen.

Translated from the Spanish by Martha Manier

The "Golem"

Rosita Kalina

On the day of his death we all went to see him because we remembered his enormous platinum beard and his black hat, that angular figure of a good-hearted man, like Don Quixote, battling the windmills.

Rebbe Israel always received us without really seeing us. He had a halo over his head and a strap in his hands. He prepared us for our Bar Mitzvah, killed the hens, chickens, and roosters that we brought him twice a week, and when he drank alcohol that was ninety-five proof, perfumed with a few drops of mint extract, from a glass tumbler, just like that and all of a sudden, he'd even dance the *sherele* sometimes. Rebbe Israel lived a block away from the Battleship Spain grocery store in a tumble-down shack with a courtyard for the hens who thrashed around in the middle of their death throes, pools of blood spurting from their jugulars. The courtyard where the animals were dying was grooved and narrow. Toward the back stood a cement basin, always trickling water from a spout to wash away the blood.

Not everything was red at the rebbe's house. Neither could we say that everything was white. When we sat in the schooldesks of the *cheder*,[1] some days the boys and others the girls, papers would fly through the air, fountain pens would dance over our heads, and water would fall from the sky without our knowing how. Everything was miraculous in Rebbe Israel's house, even the big lumps on our heads that he gave us when we forgot to put on our yarmulkes, and the tugs at the long *peyes*[2] of the most religious boys when they did not move earnestly enough while they prayed, or when they made a mistake in pronouncing some word, especially the name of God in reverse, which provoked the fury of the rebbe, who relied on angels to punish us with a wooden rod about half a meter long.

The "Golem"

In the rebbe's house no common language was spoken. He spoke to us in Yiddish and we half understood him in Spanish. He translated the blessings from Hebrew into Yiddish for us, and we acquiesced and repeated, repeated and acquiesced, as if we understood everything completely. In Hebrew we repeated like parrots the passage from the Torah that we'd have to read, and in Yiddish, like parrots, we'd learn the speech that would follow our confirmation when we became thirteen years old.

Sometimes we took revenge on the rebbe's magic and applied our own to him. Rebbe Israel used two talithim,[3] one for everyday use, and another for special prayers. The everyday one was smaller. Talith katan, he called it. He passed it over his head, making it rest on his shoulders, and didn't take it off, even during the summer. When the rebbe sat down, we tied the four long fringes to the seat, and you should have seen the commotion. The hens cackled, the ones who were jumping around in their death throes became quiet in order to hear better, the air wet itself laughing, and the angels discharged their fury with the magic wand, which was sharper and sharper, or with suddenly strengthened hand-slaps, instead of the usual blows.

One day a more elaborate revenge occurred to us: a hen that our mamas squeezed into a sack for us to take to the rebbe, a hen that miraculously passed over a Gillette razor that we pretended not to see between our trembling fingers. We kept the peseta for ourselves in order to go to the Teatro Moderno on Sunday, and it never entered our heads that the poor hen, sacrificed that way, ceased to be kosher, because we had thrown its neck backwards without removing the small feathers, or because we had not recited the brocha before passing her over the blade.

The series of films at the Moderno were like fables: Rin Tin Tin, the Phantom, the Lone Eagle, and Dracula against the River Lizards. When Fu Man Chu—the magician—appeared in person, we had to save more money. Then we took fewer hens to the rebbe. Our mothers were happy; they praised our eagerness to carry the bundle for them. They didn't know that our magic was making the hens from the rebbe's house disappear, immediately transferring them to the Friday night table, well-seasoned, tender, and cool, after spending a single night in the refrigerator with a block of ice from our house.

As we were saying, things became very complicated at the rebbe's house. We were twelve boys, all given to magic, and between the rebbe's miracle-working and our own, our Bar Mitzvah preparations were delayed. Of course, we needed six months of study. We had already spent three, and nothing had entered our heads. The pencils continued making pirouettes in

the air, the notebooks lost their pages, and every time more water slipped in through the walls, because the rebbe made water spring from the wall at the touch of his magic wand. We always returned home soaked like nocturnal frogs, and our mothers asked, "What happened? You bunch of bums!"

"No, Mama! It's just that the rebbe's basin overflowed and we helped him hold back the waterfall."

We were already halfway through our apprenticeship and we understood less and less each time. Suddenly, a new person appears in the rebbe's house. We look at him with distrust. A rival who knows a lot and has already left us in the dust. He was a small boy, quiet, with a mark on his forehead. Even when we asked him a question, the boy pretended not to understand. He was either very quiet or very foolish, so we did not worry about him and tried to pay more attention to Rebbe Israel's gibberish.

What a curious thing! From the time that boy appeared, we began to place phylacteries[4] on our left arms and on our foreheads. We began to understand the Hebrew a little more, and even what we would have to say in Yiddish. We even asked Mama if she had placed the *mezuzah*[5] correctly on the right-hand side of the door because we discovered that she had put it on backward, so we took it down, opened it to see what it said inside, closed it again to return it to its proper site, and began to kiss it when we entered or left the home.

Meanwhile, the strange boy kept growing and growing each day by leaps and bounds. We realized this because he was stretching out rapidly and we were not. In six months we did not grow even a centimeter, and he, on the other hand, was getting taller with the power of a beanstalk. *Caramba!* We invented a story: we baptized the boy "Golem,"[6] because although he understood what we were saying, he never spoke, not even a word. Surely the rebbe had created him with the earth from the little courtyard and the water from the basin, in order to help us with our notebooks, inkwells, and pencils. Unobtrusive, the "golem" moved among us, placed our pens in our hands, kept the pages of our notebooks in order, and even helped the hens to die quickly.

While the "golem" was growing, Rebbe Israel was becoming shorter. Each day he shrank by two or three centimeters, until he managed to measure the same as we did.

But the "golem" grew disproportionately and already managed to touch the ceiling. The reddish stain on his forehead did not disappear, but it no longer caused us any curiosity. We had lost our distrust of him, and his figure did not frighten us. Everything was magic in Rebbe Israel's house.

The "Golem"

Finally the long-awaited day of our Bar Mitzvah arrived. Seated with our coreligionists in the first row of the synagogue facing the Canada Dry plant, we waited our turn to be called to read the Torah. Rebbe Israel, at our back, administered affectionate pinches and shoves. We read with devotion the passage where the prophet Elijah rises to heaven in a chariot of fire, and we addressed the congregation in good Yiddish, as good as that which Rebbe Israel spoke and taught.

When days later we went to visit him to bring him a little token of appreciation, the rebbe had recovered his stature, but we did not see the "golem." We wanted to ask him, "Rebbe, where is the 'golem'?" but we thought that perhaps he had died suddenly because there was a great mound of dirt near the basin.

We learned later that the same thing that had happened to us had happened to other groups of young boys. They also saw the "golem." It's a shame that we have already forgotten the Yiddish and the Hebrew, and that Rebbe Israel has died. They covered him with white sheets, and twelve burning candles kept watch over the body, which was laid out on the floor, alongside the desks of the *cheder*. They say that when he died, a red mark appeared on his forehead, like the letter aleph[7].

But we did not believe it.

Translated from the Spanish by Roberta Gordenstein

1. A *cheder* is a Jewish religious school for younger children.

2. *Peyes* are long, uncut locks of hair worn in front of the ears, traditionally worn by orthodox Jewish boys prior to their Bar Mitzvahs.

3. A talith is a traditional prayer shawl worn over the head or shoulders by men during morning prayers.

4. Phylacteries are a set of small leather cases holding slips inscribed with Scripture passages, traditionally fastened to the forehead and left arm by men during morning prayers.

5. A *mezuzah* is a small piece of parchment inscribed with Scripture, placed inside a case and attached to the doorpost of the home, in accordance with Biblical instruction.

6. A golem, in medieval Jewish legend (and associated with cabala, the mystical system of Scriptural interpretation), is a robotlike servant, usually made of clay and brought to life by means of a charm, particularly the name of God.

7. Aleph is the first letter of the Hebrew alphabet, and a powerful sign within the cabalistic system.

Camera Obscura

Angélica Gorodischer

To Chela Leyba

Now it turns out that my grandmother Gertrudis is an important person and it is forbidden to speak badly of her in this household. So in spite of the fact that I and my entire family have always spoken badly of her, what I have had to do is shut my mouth and not say anything, not even mention her name. I ask you, who understands women? But I really can't complain: my Chaya is the very best there is. Next to her, I'm worth nothing; you have only to see her—like everyone in the community, who began to look at her with desire as soon as she turned fifteen; she was so blond and with those eyes and those manners and the way she has of raising her head, that there was not a single *shachant*[1] who didn't think of marrying her off in a good match, but a very good one, at least to one of the sons of old Saposnik, the one with the automobile repair shop, and by the time she was sixteen my mother-in-law was out of her mind with offers of this, that, and the other, and one had to aim very high. And that same Chaya, who married me and not one of those rich guys—although, frankly, I don't do so badly myself—is prettier at thirty than she was at fifteen, and you'd never know that she has two grown children, Duvedl and Batia, the spitting image of her, except that they have my black eyes; that very Chaya, who is always so sweet and gentle, turned into a wild animal when I said there was no reason the picture of my grandmother Gertrudis had to be on top of the fireplace in a gilded frame with decorations that must have cost her a pretty penny, don't deny it. And that particular photo, too.

"Don't mention that subject again," Chaya told me when I told her to remove it. "Don't even think about it. I put the picture there and that's where it's going to stay."

"All right, fine," I said, "but at least not that photo."

"And what other, tell me that, huh?" she said, "since it's the only one she had taken in her entire life."

"Thank goodness," I said. *"Zi is gevein tzi miss!"*[2]

I don't even want to remember what she replied.

But it's true that my grandmother Gertrudis was ugly, profoundly ugly: short, skinny, dark, bowlegged, cross-eyed, with round glasses that had blackened metal frames and a broken earpiece held together with some pieces of cord twisted together and tied in a knot, always dressed in black from the scarf on her head down to her slippers. In contrast, my grandfather Leon, so handsome, so huge, with that mustache like a king's and dressed like a gentleman, he seems to fill the entire photo, and his eyes gleam like two lanterns. You can barely see my grandmother next to him, which is an advantage. To top it off, she is surrounded by all her children, who were also tall and good-looking, the six boys and two girls: my uncles Aarón, Jaime, Abraham, Salo, and Isidoro, and Samuel, my father, who was the smallest of the boys. And my aunts Sara and Raquel are seated on the ground near my grandfather. And behind them you can see trees and part of the house.

It's a very large photo, on bristol board, sepia-toned, the way they were in those days, so that the gilded and decorated frame must have been very expensive, and it's not that I pay attention to those things: Chaya knows that she can indulge herself and I have never denied her or my children anything, and as long as I am able, they will have everything and will not be worth less than others—the very idea!

That's why it hurts me to have the photo on the marble fireplace mantel, but of course I can't protest much because it's my fault and only mine for going around talking so much. And why shouldn't a man be able to tell his wife things about his family, you tell me; you could almost say that she has the right to know everything that he knows. And nevertheless, when I told Chaya what my grandmother Gertrudis had done, half in jest, half seriously—I mean in a funny way in order to lessen the importance of the tragedy, and somewhat indignantly, as if to show that I know that what's right is right and that I haven't inherited my grandmother's evil tendencies—when I told her the story one summer night as we were returning from an air-conditioned movie theater and we had bought ice cream cones and were eating them in the kitchen, just the two of us because the

children were sleeping, she stopped eating and when I finished she pounded on the table with the spoon and told me she couldn't believe it.

"But it's true," I said. "Of course it's true. It happened just as I told you."

"I know," said Chaya, and she got up and stood next to me with her arms crossed, looking at me angrily. "I know it happened like that, you wouldn't have invented it. What I can't believe is that you are so heartless as to make fun of her and say that she was an evil woman."

"But Chaya," I managed to say.

"No 'but Chaya's' or anything," she shouted at me. "It's a good thing that I didn't learn about this before we got married. A good thing for you, because as far as I'm concerned it's a disgrace to find out at this stage of my life that I'm married to a brute without feelings."

I didn't understand anything, and she left, slamming the door and leaving me alone in the kitchen, alone and wondering what I might have said to make her so furious. I went as far as the door but changed my mind and returned. We've been married ten years and I know her very well, although rarely had I seen her so angry. Better to let her calm down. I ate up what remained of my ice cream and the other one, almost all there, that Chaya had left, placed the ones we had brought for the children in the freezer, wiped the table with the dishcloth, and left the dishes in the sink. I made sure that the door and window opening onto the yard were tightly closed, put out the light, and went to lie down. Chaya was sleeping or pretending she was sleeping. I got into bed and looked at the ceiling, which appeared gray with the light entering through the open window. I touched her lightly: "Chaya, *mein taier meidale*,"[3] I said to her, as I did when we were newlyweds.

Nothing. She didn't move or answer me or breathe more deeply or anything. All right, I thought, if she doesn't want to, she doesn't want to, she'll get over it soon. I put my hand back and closed my eyes. I was half asleep when I opened my eyes and saw the gray ceiling again because it seemed to me that I had heard her crying. But I must have been mistaken, it wasn't so serious. I fell asleep for real and by the following morning, it was as if nothing had happened.

But that day, when I return almost at nighttime from my business, tired and hungry, what do I see? That. The portrait of my grandmother Gertrudis, in its gilded frame with decorations on top of the fireplace.

"Where did you find that?" I asked, pointing my finger at it.

"It was on the shelf above the closet," she told me with a big smile, "with all the photos of you as a child that your mother gave me."

Camera Obscura

"Oh, no," I said, and stretched out my hands as if to remove it.

"I'm warning you about something, Isaac Rosenberg," she told me very slowly, and I realized she was serious because she always calls me Chaqui like everyone else does, and when she says Isaac, it means she is not very happy, and she had never said it before with my last name, except for one time. "I warn you that if you take that picture away from there, I will leave this house and take the children with me."

She really meant it. I know her. I know she really meant it because that other time she had called me by my first and last name she had also threatened me with leaving, she did that a lot, and we didn't have the children yet, and to tell the truth, things were not the way she thought they were, but it's better not to discuss that subject. I lowered my hands and put them in my pockets and thought that it was just a whim, and all right, let her do whatever she wanted, and that I would try to convince her soon. But I didn't convince her; I never convinced her and the photo remains there. Chaya got over her anger and said, "All right, let's eat. I made a rice kugel."

She makes it with my mother-in-law's recipe, and she knows that I like it enough to eat three servings, and I know that she knows, and she knows that I know that she knows. That's why she had made it that day. I ate only three servings but I couldn't stop wondering why Chaya had behaved that way, why she wanted to have the photo on top of the fireplace, and what was the matter with my grandmother Gertrudis that she caused such an uproar in my house.

Nothing, she had absolutely nothing, not even a name, a good, honest, Jewish name, Sure or Surke, like other people's grandmothers, no, sir: Gertrudis. She never did anything right or on time, not even be born, since my great-grandparents came by ship with three children and my great-grandmother pregnant. They came from Russia, but they had left Germany for Buenos Aires on the *Madrid*, and when the ship docked, at that very moment, my great-grandmother's labor pains began and they thought that my grandmother was going to be born on deck among the trunks and baskets and packages and people coming and going, although they still did not know that the one who was about to be born was a girl. But my great-grandfather and his children had to disembark because almost everyone else had already done so, and my great-grandmother remained above writhing and watching her family already on Argentine soil, and then it occurred to her that it would be best for her also to disembark so that her son would be an Argentine. Very slowly, little by little, grabbing the railing and with a sailor helping her, she descended. And

The House of Memory

in the middle of the gangplank, what happens? Yes, just at that moment, in the middle of the gangplank, my grandmother was born. My great-grandmother let herself sink onto the beams and right there, with the help of the German sailor who shouted something that no one understood except the other German sailors, and a woman who ran up the gangplank, my grandmother Gertrudis, my great-grandmother's last child, arrived in the world.

From the very beginning there were problems with her. My grandmother, was she Argentine or was she German? I don't think my grandmother's nationality mattered a bit to either Argentina or Germany, but the immigration officials were overwhelmed with regulations, which said nothing about any similar case, and thus did not know what to do. Besides which it seems that my great-grandmother was becoming more and more of a problem and in spite of having just given birth, she began to shout that her daughter was Argentine—as if anyone could understand what she was shouting and as if with that she were making a gift to the country where she had just arrived, and what a gift.

In the end, she was Argentine—I don't know who resolved this, or how, probably some civil servant who was in a hurry to go for lunch, and they recorded it at the port as an Argentine arriving from Germany, although she had never left there for here, and there was another problem when they asked my great-grandfather her name. They had intended to call the baby Ichiel if it were a boy, but with the pressures of the voyage it had not occurred to them that it might be a girl and a girl also needs a name. My great-grandfather looked at his wife, which it seems he always did whenever he had to make a decision, but her energies had been exhausted with the pains, the pushing, the descent down the gangplank, and the shouts over the nationality of her daughter, who through all this was bellowing on a counter while wrapped in her father's jacket.

"Call her Gertrudis, sir, it's a pretty name," said the immigration official.

"What?" asked my great-grandfather—in Russian, of course.

"My fiance is named Gertrudis," said the man.

My great-grandfather found out shortly afterward, upon leaving the port with his family, the luggage, and the newborn, what the official had said, because Naum Waisman who had gone to meet them with his two children and car had translated it for him, but by then my grandmother was already named Gertrudis.

"Yes, yes," said my great-grandfather, somewhat disturbed.

"Gertrudis, do you understand? It's a pretty name," said the official.

"Gertrudis," said my great-grandfather, as best as he could, pronouncing the *rs* badly, and so it remained because that's how it was recorded in the port.

About the other troubles, the ones that came after with the civil registration and the birth certificate, it's better not to speak. However, for a time all was quiet and nothing else happened. That is to say, things happened, but my grandmother had nothing to do with it.

It turned out that they stayed with Naum for a month until they got adjusted, and afterward they left for the countryside. There my great-grandfather worked as a farmhand, but in a few years he bought the little farm and made it prosper, at first with the entire family working from sunup to sundown, but later things improved and with hired laborers all went well, so well that he bought a few hectares more until he wound up having a good-sized piece of property.

At that time, my grandmother Gertrudis was fifteen years old and was already horrible-looking. She was cross-eyed from the moment she was born on the gangplank of the German ship, but now she was emaciated and bowlegged and seemed to be mute, so little did she speak. My great-grandfather had a ton of friends in the neighboring countryside and in the town where they went every Friday morning to stay until Saturday night at the home of a first cousin of my great-grandmother. But neither he nor his wife had great hopes of marrying off that ugly and disagreeable daughter—until my grandfather Leon appeared like a blessing from heaven.

My grandfather Leon had not been born on the gangplank of a ship, German or otherwise. He was born as he should be, at home, or more precisely, in his parents' house, and from that moment on, he always did what he should, when he should, and therefore everyone loved him and respected him and no one laughed at him and no one thought he was a disgrace to his family.

He was a widower, childless, when he appeared at my great-grandparents' house, the widower of Ruth Bucman, who had died a year before. It seems that they must have informed my great-grandmother of what this was all about, because she washed and combed and perfumed her daughter and advised her not to speak, although there was no need for that, and to always look at the ground so that he might not notice her crossed eyes, which was useful but also unnecessary, and so that he might see at the same time that she was an innocent and timid girl.

And that's how my grandfather Leon married my grandmother Gertrudis, not in spite of the fact that she was so ugly but precisely because she was

so ugly. They say that Ruth Bucman was the prettiest girl in the community, in the entire province, in the whole country, and in all South America. They say she was redheaded and had almond-shaped green eyes and a sinful mouth and very white skin and long, fine hands; and they say that she and my grandfather Leon made such a pair that people would turn around in the street just to stare at them. They also say that she had a devilish temper and she made life impossible for her father, her mother, her sisters and brothers, her sisters-in-law, her nieces and nephews, her neighbors, and the whole town. And for my grandfather Leon as long as he was married to her.

The worst thing was that she bore no children, not even one was she able to give her husband; maybe it was just to spite him, because it seemed that the poison of that woman reached even that far. When she died, my grandfather breathed a sigh of relief, slept two solid days, and when he awakened, he dedicated himself to resting, to polishing his mustache with brilliantine, and to going to town every day on horseback to visit the friends that Ruth had alienated from his house by way of her shouting and bad manners.

But things could not go on that way for long; my grandfather Leon was a real man and he was not made to be alone all his life, besides the fact that the house was falling apart and needed a woman's touch and the fields looked practically abandoned and some people had already begun to take a look calculating that my grandfather was going to sell for almost nothing. That's why, a year after the funeral of his wife, my grandfather decided to get married, and remembering the hell he had experienced with Ruth, he decided to marry the ugliest woman he could find. And he married my grandmother Gertrudis.

The fiesta lasted three days and three nights at my great-grandfather's farm. The musicians took turns playing in the barn and the women were not able to keep up with the cooking, even with the kitchen in the main house, the servants' kitchens and two or three stoves and ovens that had been improvised outside. My great-grandparents outdid themselves gladly. You have to understand that it was a cause for celebration, since they had managed to get out from under such a burden and marry her off to the best candidate for a hundred miles around.

My grandmother did not spend the three days and three nights at the party. The very day after the ceremony, she set to work to put her husband's house in order, and nine months later, my uncle Aarón was born, and a year after that, my uncle Jaime was born, and eleven months later,

my uncle Abraham was born, and so on. But she never stopped working. You have to hear the stories my aunt Raquel told of how she got up before dawn and prepared the food for the entire day, cleaned the house, and went out to work in the field; and how she sewed at night while everyone was sleeping and she made their shirts and their trousers and even her sons' and husband's underwear and the daughters' dresses and the sheets and tablecloths and all the linens for the house; and how she prepared candies and preserves for winter, and the way she knew how to drive the animals, bale hay, pack the bales together, and help to load the carts. And all this without saying a word, always silent, always looking at the ground so no one would notice her cross-eyedness. You have to admit that she lightened my grandfather Leon's workload, as small and skinny as she was, because she had the endurance of two men put together. By afternoon my grandfather no longer had anything left to do: he decked himself out and left for town on his best horse, with the deluxe harnesses my grand-mother had already fastened on, and since she didn't like to be around people, she remained at the farm and continued her routine, day after day. And so time passed and eight children were born, and my aunts say that even with her labor my grandmother never stayed in bed or missed a single day of work.

That's why what happened was even more terrible. Of course my grandfather Leon was no saint and he liked women and they liked him, and of course some ill-intentioned neighbor woman went to my grand-mother with tales, and she didn't say anything or cause a scandal or cry or yell, of course. And the fact that my grandfather suddenly remembered Ruth Bucman and went around for a few days with his tail between his legs didn't mean that my grandmother should have blamed him for his past deeds. I don't say that he was right, but those are things that a woman knows she has to forgive in a man, and frankly she didn't have the right to do that to my grandfather, she who ought to have been more than grate-ful because my grandfather had married her. And everything was crueler still if you think about the irony of fate, because my grandfather tried to surprise them all and give all his sons and daughters a present. And I sup-pose my grandmother Gertrudis too, of course.

One day, while the eight children and my grandfather Leon were eat-ing and my grandmother was coming and going with the casseroles and the platters, my grandfather told them that a traveling photographer had arrived in town, and everyone asked what he was like and what he was doing and how well he took pictures and whose pictures he had taken.

And my aunts begged my grandfather to take them to town to take a picture of each one of them. Then my grandfather laughed and said no, he had already spoken with the photographer, and the next day he was going to come to the farm with his cameras and his equipment to take pictures of all of them. My aunts laughed and clapped and kissed my grandfather and began to chatter among themselves to see what dresses they were going to wear, and my uncles said this was all women's foolishness and fancy ideas from the city, but they smoothed their trousers and looked at themselves sideways in the window glass.

And the photographer went out to the countryside and took a picture of all of them, that brown photo on Bristol board that is now on top of the fireplace of my house in a gilded frame with decorations and that Chaya does not allow me to remove from there.

He was blond, the photographer, blond, skinny, not very young, with curly hair, and he limped a lot on his left leg. He sat them all down outside the house, with their best clothing, combed and polished so that it was a pleasure to see them. All of them except my grandmother Gertrudis, who was dressed as always in black and had not even bothered to put on a decent dress. She didn't want to be in the picture and said no so many times that my grandfather Leon was almost convinced and didn't insist anymore. But then the photographer approached my grandmother and said that if anyone had to be in the picture it was she; and she said something to him—I don't know if they told me what it was and I forgot, or if no one heard and they didn't tell me anything—and he answered that he knew very well what it was not to want to be in any photos, or some such thing. I've heard the story many times but I don't remember the exact words. The thing is that my grandmother placed herself next to my grandfather, surrounded by their children, and they remained posed there for a long while and they smiled and the blond, skinny, and lame photographer took their picture.

My grandfather Leon told the photographer to stay there that night so that he could develop the photo and the next day he could take some others. Thus my grandmother fed him that night also. And he told stories about his work and the towns he had visited, what the people were like and how they received him and the strange things he had seen or experienced. And my uncle Aarón always says that he looked at her as if he were speaking only to her, but who knows if that is true because he would not have been the only one who realized something was going on. What definitely is true is that my grandmother Gertrudis sat down at the table with

her family, and that was something she never did because she always had to have everything ready in the kitchen while the others were eating in order to serve it on time. After they finished eating the photographer went outside for a smoke because no one smoked in that house, and my grandmother brought him a shot of liquor, and it seems to me, although no one told me this, that the two of them must have spoken of something.

The next day the photographer spent the entire morning taking pictures: first my grandfather Leon alone, then with the boys, then with the girls, then with all the boys and girls together, then my aunts alone with their well-ironed dresses and curled hair. But my grandmother Gertrudis did not appear, occupied in the dairy and in the house as always. But I imagined that—I who did not know her, I who had not been born since my father was a little boy who hadn't met my mother yet—I imagine her that day, hidden, spying on him from behind some door left ajar, while the meal was burning on the fire. These are only my own imaginary wonderings because according to what my aunts say, she never burned a meal or ignored anything in the house or in the field.

The photographer developed the photos and ate lunch in the house and in the afternoon he mounted them on the cardboards with an engraved border and the date, and my grandfather Leon paid him. When they finished eating it was already night, and he said good-bye and left the house. He had already loaded everything into the shabby carriage in which he had appeared in town, and from the darkness outside he again shouted good-bye to everyone. My grandfather Leon was happy because the photographer had taken some very good pictures of them, but it did not warrant his accompanying him beyond the door because he had already paid him more for his work than anyone else in town or on the farms. They all went inside and you could hear the horse moving away and then nothing else.

When someone asked about my grandmother Gertrudis—which until today my aunts and uncles argue about because each one says that he was the one who asked—my grandfather Leon said that surely she must be around doing something outside, and a little while later they all went to bed.

But the next morning when they arose, they found the lamps still lit on the tables and the gates left ajar and the door unlocked and unbarred. There was no fire or dinner prepared or breakfast ready or cows milked or water for drinking or for washing or bread baking in the oven or anything at all. My grandmother Gertrudis had run away with the photographer.

So now I ask, am I right or not when I say there is no reason for that picture to be on top of the fireplace of my house? "And if the children ask about it?" I said one day to Chaya.

"We'll see," she said.

They asked, of course they asked, and in front of me. Fortunately Chaya had the sense not to explain anything. "It's papa's family," she said, "many years ago, when his grandparents were alive. You see? Zeide, Bobe, Uncle Aarón, Uncle Isidoro, Uncle Salo."

And so she continued naming them and pointing to them, one by one, without making any comments. The children got used to the picture and no longer asked anything else.

Even I became accustomed to it. It's not that I agree, no, not that, but I mean that I never notice it anymore, it doesn't attract my attention, unless I am looking for something over there and I have to move the gilded frame with the decorations. One of those times I asked Chaya, who was nearby messing up the shelves of the cupboard: "Are you going to explain to me someday what possessed you to put that picture there?"

She turned around and looked at me. "No," she told me.

I wasn't expecting that. I was expecting a little chuckle and that she would tell me yes, sometime she would tell me, or that she would tell me right now.

"What do you mean, no?"

"No," she told me again without laughing. "If you need me to explain it to you, that means you don't deserve for me to explain it to you."

And that's the way it remained. We found what we were looking for, or maybe not, I don't remember, and Chaya and I never again mentioned the photo of my grandmother Gertrudis on the fireplace with its gilded frame with decorations. But I keep on thinking that it is an insult for a family like mine to have in such a prominent place the photo of someone who seemed like such a good wife, so hard-working, so involved in her home, and who one day ran off with another man, abandoning her husband and children just for spite, for no reason.

Translated from the Spanish by Roberta Gordenstein

1. A *shachant* is a matchmaker.
2. "She was too ugly!"
3. "Chaya, my dear little girl."

No More Worries

Clarice Lispector

—Everyone knows that sprinkling salt on the fire or hiding a broom behind the door can get rid of unwelcome guests.

—Everyone knows that a red ribbon tied round the patient's waist can arrest the progress of erysipilas.

—Likewise, if you hang a red handkerchief up in the bedroom, it can cause a vicious attack of measles.

—There is nothing better for curing hiccup than to take nine sips of water without pausing for breath. Or to turn up your sleeves. In the case of an infant, a tiny piece of damp cotton-wool should be placed on its forehead.

—If you bury chayote in the soil early in the morning, it will remove warts.

—If you spill sugar on the table, sprinkle a few grains on your chest and you will almost certainly come into money.

—Spilling salt brings bad luck, unless you throw a little over your left shoulder.

—Touching wood to ward off all evils is something everybody knows.

—To make sure that duck turns out tasty when cooked, it should be plucked in total silence. And to make sure that chicken is really tender and succulent, put three chickpeas or a clove into the pot.

—A seahorse, on the other hand, relieves asthma.

—And anyone with sweaty hands need only catch a toad and hold it for a few seconds and the perspiration will vanish.

—It is common knowledge that crossed knives can provoke a quarrel and the same is true if one passes salt across the table.

—A broken mirror should be thrown into the sea.

—Hats should never be placed on top of a bed or shoes placed under a chair.

—It is always better to put the right shoe on before the left one.

—A lock of hair should be tucked into the hem of a bride's dress.

—On departing, one should always leave by the same door one entered by.

—Anyone who sweeps the house at night and throws out the rubbish is also in danger of throwing out good fortune.

—When the hem of a dress gets caught accidentally, it is advisable to bite it in order to get a new dress.

—Yellow is the color of leap year.

—In order to safeguard the health of young children, one should tie a tiny sachet round their neck filled with tiny lizards' tails.

—A stolen statue of St. Anthony will get any spinster to the altar.

—Itching in the right palm is a sign that money is on the way.

—One should pay in coin when given a handkerchief or a knife as a present.

—A glass of cold water with three pinches of salt will ward off the evil eye.

—Certain looks can cause sweet peppers to shrivel up.

—When you lose something, tie a ribbon or piece of string to the arm of a chair or the leg or a table, to the handle of a jug, round a lamp, or whatever, and keep the little demon tied up securely until the lost object is found.

—Crosses marked with chalk on the soles of your shoes can prevent them from squeaking.

—A piece of cork in the frying pan turns the food a golden brown.

—Never open an umbrella indoors.

—Any little black bird coming through the window brings misfortune.

—A St. George's cross on the right-hand side of one's front door keeps trouble at bay.

Now then, if you start putting all these precepts into practice, you will have no more worries.

Translated from the Portuguese by Giovanni Pontiero

Part Two

The Sign of the Star:
Immigrants and Strangers

The Sign of the Star

Ana Vasquez

*To little Paul, who, one wintry day in Paris,
had to battle the demons and assume the sign.*

*To Luna María, budding, may she grow
putting forth roots in memory.*

"Iliusha, Iliushenka, precious little angel . . . Wake up! . . . You have to go
to school." Through his eyelashes he glimpsed her smile, so familiar yet at
the same time bewildering. He felt the caress of her black hair on his
cheeks. He hugged and kissed her.

"Mommy! Mamushka."

"*Colecho, colechito, colechón,*" She hummed, imitating his way of speaking
when he was a little child and could not yet manage to say *colegio* or *tejido.*
But with time, imitation had transformed itself into a language loaded with
secrets, which She used to awaken him, wrapping him in her warm ten-
derness, and tickling him on the soles of his feet to wake up his tiny toes,
and placing a cozy sock on his little left leg.

How many times would he evoke that morning, the one when She said
to him for the last time, "Iliusha Iliushenka," when he had to take the first
step—in spite of himself—to abandon that translucent and marvelous
world and enter that other world of suspicion and aggression, the world
of the grown-ups. He was at the door, holding Rosalía's hand, when She
ran to hand him the avocado sandwich, wrapped so carefully in stiff white
paper that it always seemed like a present to him. She straightened his tie
and kissed him on the forehead.

The House of Memory

The class began with its habitual murmur of voices. They sang the tables, "twice one are two . . ." Miss Guire reviewed the assignments and afterward stood on tiptoe to place the piece of chalk on the uppermost edge of the blackboard, and with that large, round handwriting that Iliusha tried so hard to imitate, wrote, *Pairs of Words*, and traced a vertical line dividing the entire space. She spelled each word, wrote *hair* here and *hare* there.

"What kind of sandwich do you have?" Jimmy asked him.

"Avocado."

"Show it to me!"

He was saved by the bell. Miss Guire stood up. "Come on, children, straighten the benches before going out for recess."

Small, Iliusha was one of the first in line. Jimmy and Fernando Flores were among the biggest; they went out at the end. "Wait for me, shrimp," Jimmy shouted at him. But Iliusha was wise to him, and, hurrying to join a group of teachers who were chatting in the sunshine, he unwrapped the white paper and cleverly stayed near them as he ate his sandwich.

Ever since they had been in kindergarten, two years ago, Jimmy and Fernando had found their special places. Fernando was the best fighter and he liked to make fun of the smallest ones; Iliusha learned quickly not to pass near him because he was an expert at tripping and there was nothing Iliusha could do, on the ground and bruised, facing an oversized bully who was laughing at him besides. And he also learned to guard his colored pencils and to gobble up his sandwich quickly. Freckle-faced and fat, Jimmy was the favorite of Miss Guire and all the teachers. He was son of the English vice-consul, and for Queen's College, which aspired to be an authentic English *colegio*, having someone from *the* embassy as a student was something like having a coat of arms whose prestige reflected upon everyone. Jimmy could forget his homework; it didn't matter. Besides, he already spoke the "correct" English of his family. He could knot his tie with the colors of Queen's any way he wished, and no one would scold him. And when he behaved too badly, Miss Guire would let his father know and go out with a smirk of satisfaction to wait for him at the entrance of the school. An exclusive deference automatically gave Jimmy a special position: he was untouchable.

Almost all the children in the class gathered at the rear of the schoolyard, near the quince trees, where the teachers hardly ever went and where no one could surprise them. There they were, stamping their feet

on the ground to shake off the numbness. Iliusha approached slowly, savoring the last bite of his sandwich.

". . . I can't go because Sunday morning we always go to Mass," Fernando was explaining.

"Me, too," said Marisa. "We go to Mass at noon."

Rubbing his freckled nose, Jimmy asserted that they were Protestants, and that was different.

"It's the same, but another way," someone said.

"It's better to be Catholic!"

"It is not!"

"Because . . ."

"Where did you get that idea?"

"It's just that Protestants . . ."

Jimmy, who was shouting loudest, dominated the argument. "And my father prays before we start to eat. It's a sin to eat if you don't pray first."

"Of course, you'll get sick!"

"That's God's punishment!"

"What is praying?" asked Iliusha in his delicate little voice. Fernando pointed at him, scandalized. "Lying midget, how can you not know what praying is?"

A wave of heat swept over Iliusha's face until he began to feel dizzy.

"Liar! Liar!"

Those staring eyes, pursuing him, interrogating. Why did he have to ask, as if he were at home, with Her, who always said to him, "Ask me all the questions you want." When would he learn to bite his tongue, to hold back? Now he felt even smaller, almost insignificant, under Fernando's accusing finger. "No," he answered, with just a thread of voice, "Really I don't know . . ."

"But aren't you Catholics?"

"No," he replied, softly.

"Then you're Protestants!"

"No, not that either."

"But you can't be nothing! You must be something!"

And then, from the depths of memory, a word reached his lips: "I'm Jewish."

"That's impossible," declared Marisa flatly. "Only dogs are Jewish. Because, of course, in the song about who killed Jesus, you have to answer, 'the Jewish dog'."

Fernando began to jump up and down. "You're a dog, bow wow, a Jewish dog . . ."

"And you don't pray?"

Iliusha shook his head. He had already admitted he didn't know what that was.

"Don't you go to church?"

He continued to shake his head: "Rosalía goes sometimes," he said, "but we don't."

"Who is Rosalía?"

"The servant." She was the only person he had heard complain, "Hurry up and eat, I'm going to be late to church." She had shown it to him, with its tower and the clock that never told time. But Mass had nothing to do with it. Rosalía went to church to meet her boyfriend.

"And you don't believe in God?"

"Who?"

"God!"

He hesitated, not knowing what to tell them. "I don't know him," he stammered, trying to excuse himself.

"Stupid!" Fernando shouted at him. "You're a stupid dog. No one knows him, you idiot! But people believe."

Iliusha was bewildered. Why was he the only one who had not heard of this man? "I don't know him," he repeated. He didn't understand.

"Come on, children," shouted Miss Guire. "Hurry up."

Believing. Why would you have to believe? Once, in kindergarten, he had gotten involved in a terrible argument about Santa Claus. "He doesn't exist," Iliusha asserted, because She had said so and She never lied to him. "It's Daddy who brings the presents."

"Can Father come down the chimney?"

"Those are just stories; in my house there is no chimney, and they bring me presents without any problem."

Fernando (who was already bigger) shouted at him, "Liar! I saw him, and I have a photograph. A photo with him, understand? And he has a white beard like this . . ."

"That's just a man who dresses up like Santa Claus, but he's not real." She had shown him when She took him to choose his bicycle.

"Liar! He had a sack with gifts and everything."

Iliusha was positive; he stated over and over that Santa didn't exist, but he couldn't find arguments to contradict the evidence of the photo, and

the other children also insisted that they had seen him.

"You have to believe," said Marisa. "If not, he gets angry and won't bring you anything."

She never lied and for that reason he was certain, but the others didn't want to hear it, the presents were more important. But when they finished first grade, no one believed in Santa anymore. "That's for babies," they asserted contemptuously, because now they knew how to read and they felt grown up. But no one remembered that Iliusha was the first to say it. Maybe this story about God would be forgotten also, just as they'd become convinced about Santa Claus. Rosalía talked about God and included him in everything, like something that is repeated over and over until it means nothing, scattering "heaven's sakes" and "oh, my God" between sighs and grumbles. Because She didn't talk that way, and because he loved Her, Iliusha tried to speak like She did and not like Rosalía.

All through the class he couldn't concentrate, worried about that man who seemed so important. He would tell Her about it as soon as he arrived home. Then She would take him in her arms and everything would be simple again.

At noon, the children got together again, trampling the dry leaves of the plane trees, telling each other stories, exchanging pictures and stamps. Iliusha walked distractedly, between Marisa and Carlos Cariola, asking himself why they talked about a Jewish dog in the song. Maybe there were Catholic dogs?

The house was surrounded by a little garden where there grew three trees, which She cared for as if they were old friends. There was the medlar, which was covered with orange fruit as bright as a picture in his storybook, a walnut tree, and in the back the noblest tree, as She always said, removing the ripe Damson plums carefully, "Try it, Iliusha, how sweet!" On the ground floor was the workshop with its machines, the room where his father dampened the hides and stretched them, stapling them across an enormous table, the entrance with two armchairs where the ladies might wait, the fitting room, and the office. Next to the walnut tree, an exterior stairway led to the house. On each step She had placed flowerpot stands with flowers. He ran up, two steps at a time, shouting "Mamushka, Mommy."

"She went out," answered Rosalía, sulking as always. "She said to tell you to eat all your supper—and don't dawdle."

"Where did she go? Tell me!"

"She went to get your little brother."

Finally, finally, he was arriving! Iliusha had waited so long for him! He went running into the room. Everything was just the same, the cradle next to the window. On the pillow he left his old teddy bear; it would be a present for his brother. He ran down the stairs and entered the shop. "Daddy! . . ."

The machines were silent. The seamstresses were warming their dinner in the kitchenette and putting their plates on a corner of the great table where they cut the hides. They smiled at him, as always. "He took your mommy to the hospital." The odors from downstairs were disturbing, strange: the damp hides, the distinct seasonings. "Don't worry, he'll be back tonight."

He forgot about the Jewish dogs, and about the man, the one in whom he had to believe but whom he didn't know. He ate with Rosalía, in the kitchen. "If you eat everything, and quickly, I'll let you listen to the radio play with me."

She didn't like this, and since his parents did not allow him to listen, he was sure it would be entertaining. He ate everything as quickly as possible. He even swore by God, placing his crossed index finger and thumb on his lips, as Rosalía showed him. If he ever betrayed her, he would burn in Hell, and that was the worst fate.

"Jacqueline is a nurse in Switzerland, remember? She has to take care of a very rich young man who is locked up in a clinic. It seems that his stepfather wants to kill him little by little. A matter of inheritance," she added to explain to him, but he had no idea what that meant. While the two eagerly followed the adventures of poor Jacqueline, hiding from the wicked stepfather in the Swiss mountains, Iliusha thought that it wouldn't be so terrible if they were a few days late in bringing his little brother home. That way he could find out what happened to Jacqueline. "I think they'll get married in the end," said Rosalía.

The stepfather approached the bush where Jacqueline was crouching. Would he discover her? "We're late!" shouted Rosalía. "Oh my God, run! Run to school!" He arrived almost breathless as Miss Guire was closing the classroom door.

"Reading class. Open the book with the blue plastic cover." A passage from *David Copperfield*, illustrated with a sketch of London, into whose dark streets Iliusha immediately ventured. "Since you arrived last, Elías, you are going to read first."

He stood up. He didn't do badly, but it was hard to make himself heard over the ones in back. This time his voice broke, and he finished the para-

graph with difficulty, moved by the adventures of poor David, helpless and alone. He felt he was going to burst out crying because of the pain the character was suffering, wandering about the sinister London of the engraving.

"Louder, Miss," ordered the tiresome Fernando.

"Come on, Elías, read it again, very loud!"

Iliusha held back his tears because that was just what Fernando wanted, to persecute him later, shouting that he was a sissy. After reading he sat down, losing himself in a daydream, a mixture of the adventures of Jacqueline and the drama of David Copperfield. Jacqueline was like his Mamushka, with Her smooth black hair. Instead of seeking his little brother, She was running over the mountain, with Her white apron and nurse's shoes, with the same frightened eyes She had had when he was dazed after falling off the swing. Iliusha looked like the handsome rich young man from the clinic, but it was David. Only She could save him; She had to descend the Swiss mountain—which he imagined as steep and violet-colored as the Andes—to search for him in the mysterious alleys of London. . . . "And maybe they'll get married in the end," said Rosalía.

The bell signaled them to put away their books and go outside. Iliusha walked like an automaton, following his companions, still possessed by the dangers threatening poor David, trying to imagine how She would arrange things in order to arrive on time. Again they stood next to the plane trees, quiet, watching him approach. He smiled at them, distracted.

"Elías," said Rodolfo Sánchez, the best student. He spoke as if his good grades authorized him to represent the others. "We want to tell you something." Iliusha continued smiling, without responding, without being completely present. "We've decided not to speak to you anymore," continued Rodolfo. "From now on, no one will be able to talk to you."

"Why?" asked Iliusha, brusquely forgetting the dangers David was risking.

"This morning you told us you were Jewish, right?"

"Of course, why?"

"My father says you belong to the race that killed Christ."

While Rodolfo pushed him out of the world, Fernando began to howl, "Jewish dog, Jewish dog."

It seemed like a nightmare to Iliusha. He was sure it was not true. "But I haven't killed anyone," he whispered.

"Not you, your family, they were the ones."

"But . . ." He couldn't continue, he didn't know what to say. He was

invaded by an impression of unreality, as if it were not he who was there, next to the plane trees, hearing his condemnation. "But . . ." he repeated, and then he was silent, doubting. Perhaps it was true.

As if they had all agreed, they turned their backs on him. Sticking out his tongue, Jimmy made a face at him: "Ha, ha, ha, you're in trouble."

He didn't know how he returned to the classroom. All he wanted that afternoon, what he desired for a long time, was to be born again. Not in his own house, but to another family—to be the son of Marisa's mother, for example, or of Mrs. Flores, even if that meant being as dull as Fernando. He would even have accepted being red and freckle-faced like Jimmy, as long as he had a respectable father. To free himself from that infamous heritage, to cease being Her child because She was a murderer. But then he would have to renounce Her tenderness, lose that marvelous voice which sang to awaken him. No, not that! It was too much. He was ashamed to have even thought it. He preferred not being at all, changing himself truly into a dog. He would no longer go to school. He would remain in the garden, beside the medlar tree, wagging his tail whenever She approached. But Iliusha knew that no matter how much he wished, he could not be someone else. If only he could go back in time, no further than this morning, when they were talking about praying. He would bite his tongue until it bled, he would clench his teeth with all his might, so that the cursed words would not escape. And if they asked him what he was, he would answer, "Catholic and Protestant, both at once. We go to all the churches, we pray all day long." And God? Of course he knew him, certainly he believed. He concentrated in order to return to yesterday, and his head ached so much he became nauseous. But nothing changed. It was today, in the afternoon, or it could have been any day after "it" happened. He had already said "it"; the abyss had opened.

Almost as if it were a game, they all took pains to respect his exile, and if someone accidentally spoke to him, another would give him a shove, to say, "It's forbidden." At recess they turned their backs on him deliberately. They walked faster in the street so that he couldn't catch up with them. Their glances slid over his as if he didn't exist.

Now Aunt Debbie was sleeping at his house. She kept him company in the afternoons, and what was even worse, she ate lunch with him. Not only was his Mamushka missing, but now he couldn't listen to the drama with Rosalía either, and poor Jacqueline remained hidden from him forever beneath the bushes. Daddy wasn't in his shop; he almost never saw

him. He returned late at night. Half asleep, Iliusha asked him about Her. "Soon she will come back. She sent you a kiss . . ."

Why didn't he break out in tears when they ignored him? Why didn't he run to Miss Guire to tell on them? Why didn't he say anything to his father, or tell Aunt Debbie when the two of them ate together, accompanied only by the sighs of his aunt, who blew her nose all the time? A frightening sense of shame swept over him, invading him. He observed his aunt, his daddy, he remembered Her, and he was certain, positive, that none of them seemed like the murderers in the movies. They couldn't be evil or kill anyone. It couldn't be true. In the depths of his being, he hated himself for believing them, for having doubted his Mamushka. Although he had not confessed it to anyone, he had wanted another family, and that was betrayal. "You must be patient," sighed Aunt Debbie. But she was lying to him; he knew that if She was not there, it was because of him. In bed at night, he asked Her to return and forgive him.

Something was preventing him from complaining, from accusing them. And not for anything in the world would he have asked them to accept him again. He was Jewish, and he couldn't and wouldn't erase what he was. He never learned to fight or defend himself, and it never occurred to him that perhaps there were other Jewish children in the school. He thought he was the only one. He returned home alone, pretending that he could only step on the center of the sidewalk tiles, that if he walked on the edges a horrible disgrace would occur. Sometimes children from other classes who were going his way would approach him, but if they spoke to him, he wouldn't answer. He didn't want to give them the opportunity to turn their backs on him. Somehow he had to make it obvious that he was Jewish, as if he were marked with a mysterious sign.

Recess was when he suffered most. It no longer bothered him to be alone except that he didn't want the teachers to realize. As the mornings were still cool, he invented a sore throat. "My mommy doesn't want me to go outside." He remained in the empty classroom. If Miss Guire returned in the middle of recess to correct the notebooks and found him there, alone and bored, it didn't matter. Because she didn't have to know that the others refused to speak to him. He opened the white package, ate his whole sandwich, carefully collected the crumbs scattered on the cloth covering the bench, and stood up noiselessly to throw them in the wastebasket next to the blackboard. Afterward, since he was bored, he reread his lessons.

In the afternoon it grew hot, and Miss Guire did not let him stay in the room. How could he pretend? How could he hide what should not have been seen? Half the school was fascinated by the spinning tops; they competed to see who could make them dance best. Iliusha observed them from a distance, playing in the corner by the quince trees. He strolled about, hands in his pockets, moving slightly closer to groups of children from other classes so that the teachers—who were observing distractedly while they chatted in the center of the schoolyard—might think he was with them. He listened to them momentarily without saying anything, for fear of a new denunciation, and then drifted away slowly to continue his walk. It occurred to him as he was wandering about this way that the others pointed to him behind his back: "That's Elías, the one who's an outcast because . . ." He walked looking down at his shoes, wrapped up in himself, as if hiding his eyes would prevent them from identifying him and he would become truly transparent, invisible. Afternoon recess became interminable. He would have liked to invent another illness for himself, but he only knew about sore throats. And he didn't want to exaggerate because then Miss Guire might not trust him. Sometimes he questioned whether she also knew he was Jewish. If so, why did she speak to him?

They were starting geography. Miss Guire drew something like a brown empanada and painted a thick sky-blue border around it. Underneath she wrote *island* and below that, *An island is a piece of land surrounded by water.* "Copy this in your notebooks!" Iliusha took pains to make his empanada just like the one on the board, and he copied the sentence meticulously. During recess he reread it, humming, as he did to Her songs. The next day Miss Guire added new and complicated drawings with several colors: a peninsula, a strait, a mountain, and a valley. Iliusha invented a distinct melody for each one of the definitions, while the others made the tops spin in the yard.

Monday, surprisingly, they had visitors in class. The children stood up and greeted them with a bow. "What is an island?" asked Miss Guire. No one knew, not Jimmy (who was English) or Rodolfo. Then Iliusha raised his hand and repeated exactly the definition from the notebook. It would not have occurred to him that an island could be one like Robinson Crusoe's; for him, "island" was something similar to "*Colecho, colechito, colechón,*" a song made of nonsense words.

"And the mountain? . . . The valley?" Iliusha knew all the definitions.

"Very very good, Elías, excellent."

"He deserves the Honor Board," said the gentleman visitor, with a good-natured smile and a very hoarse voice. The Honor Board was the maximum aspiration and pride of all the children and all the classes at Queen's, reserved for the best. Each class competed to have the most Honor Board students. Not even Rodolfo Sánchez was on the Honor Board for this month; Iliusha was the only one in the class.

"The representative," said Miss Guire. "An example." He continued sitting on the bench with his hands folded, without looking at anyone, pretending he didn't hear the whispers behind him.

He returned home, running, his heart beating louder than a locomotive. "Rosalía, Rosalía! Mommy's back . . ." She must have returned, certainly now. She would be waiting for him, She who divined everything. She would have forgiven him. Now She would be proud because the name of her Iliusha, Hers, appeared on the Honor Board. She would kiss him on the forehead, laughing, take him in Her arms, and they would dance, humming their secret songs. He would cling to Her neck while She spun around in a whirlwind. He would kiss Her. "Never leave me again; don't stop loving me." He almost felt Her smooth hands caressing his cheeks already. "Rosalía!"

"Why are you shouting at me; don't you see that I'm busy?" She turned her back on him just as the others at school did. "I'm behind with the meal."

Then he couldn't stand it any longer; he threw himself to the floor sobbing, pounding the boards with his clenched fists. It was essential that She and only She come to calm him. "I don't want to wait anymore. Let Her come back now. Now!" He heard his own yells. And Rosalía's, calling Aunt Debbie.

He sobbed desperately. It was impossible for him to swallow a mouthful. Aunt Debbie insisted that he drink a glass of warm milk with honey. "Your mommy told me you like it a lot. Come on, drink it and make her happy. You mustn't cry like that. Eat an orange, and this little chocolate bar." It had a salty taste.

She brought him to school. She took him by the hand, walking rapidly, and he was terrified because he couldn't walk in the center of the sidewalk.

"Auntie . . . what if I went to another school?"

"Queen's is one of the best schools in Chile. It's expensive but . . ."

"But?"

"Your father works very very hard to pay for it."

"Then if I changed he wouldn't have to work so much."

Aunt Debbie moved her head, smiling. "He does it out of love for you, so that you can speak English well . . . and for friends."

"Friends?"

"At Queen's you can make good friends."

Suddenly he realized he had forgotten to tell her about the Honor Board. He opened his mouth but his lips felt stiff, his tongue rebellious and immobile. He didn't feel like it any longer. His prize was for Her, not for Aunt Debbie. He wasn't even proud, as if nothing were important any more. Aunt Debbie straightened the knot in his tie and smoothed his hair with her hand. He went running into the school so his aunt couldn't touch him, there in the street, in front of everyone.

He remained standing next to the door, observing the yellowing gama grass, not thinking of anything, sad. He didn't want to explain why he wasn't returning.

"Teacher's pet," Fernando Flores insulted him, with a shove, "You'll do anything to get good grades!"

Iliusha didn't look at him; he barely heard him, concentrating on his battle with those black ideas that pursued him. It seemed to him that the episode of the Honor Board hadn't happened that morning, but a long time ago, in that other life where he could still ignore what he didn't want to know. They did the Pairs of Words again, and even though he knew them by heart, he didn't raise his hand or say anything. But when someone made a mistake, Miss Guire asked him, "And now, Elías." He would spell the word in English and give the translation correctly and without enthusiasm, with his eyes fixed on the cover of the bench. Absent. "Bright boy," commented Miss Guire. "Very good."

Just before going out for recess, they passed him from behind a folded paper with his name in red letters. He opened it: "JEWS TO THE CRE-MATORIUM." He paused, spelling out the unknown word. Miss Guire was waiting for him to close the door of the room. "What is a cremato-rium?" he asked her in his timid little voice.

"They are the ovens where they burn stray dogs." But faced with his frightened eyes, she took his arm. "It's for wandering and sick dogs; don't worry, they don't make them suffer. First they give them a shot to put them to sleep. Go out to play, Elías, you don't look good."

They were sending him to the crematorium. With the dogs. Between the flames and the dogs, asphyxiating him with smoke, like the inferno

Rosalía always talked about. Blindly, he ran toward the rear of the school-yard, where the group was, where Fernando was laughing. With his fists clenched. He wanted to push him out of his life, kill him, never see him again. Being a murderer didn't matter, since he was one anyway. He ran in slow motion, in a kind of nightmare where his legs could not move as quickly as he wished. Stripping himself of fear, he ran as if he were cross-ing a border.

He hurled himself on Fernando in a whirlwind of blows and kicks. He lashed out any way he could, blind with rage. David against Goliath. They rolled in the gama grass, shouting and insulting each other. Iliusha barely heard the teachers scolding him as they separated them. The two were bruised, faces bleeding, and Fernando's shirt was torn. They took them to the nurse's office to wash up, and then they returned to class.

"Now you're going to shake hands like two real gentlemen," ordered Miss Guire. "Come on!" In front of the whole class. Neither one moved. Iliusha did not feel the tears or his face burning. "Come on, fair play." Ritualistic words. Fernando stretched out his hand, "like a gentleman." Iliusha crossed his hands behind his back and stared directly at him. With hate.

"This can't be. Elías, you are disappointing me. Don't you want to shake hands?"

"No." For the first time, they heard him in the back of the room.

"Come on, apologize, shake hands and it will be settled." Fernando stepped forward. Iliusha backed up.

"No," he repeated.

"What's the matter, are you angry?"

He was not able to explain that anger is the last resort of the defeated, of the weak, of those unable to express themselves. Fernando could per-mit himself those noble gestures because he was strong, and because the whole class was on his side. Iliusha had only his anger to help him survive. Later, when he was a doctor and successful in life (as they say without knowing what they are talking about), he would still feel that ache in his chest, that anguish. As though at any moment they could again turn their backs on him, exclude him because of what he was. Maybe by then the cells of his body would no longer be the same, but at the bottom of his secret pain, in the deepest part of the adult Elías would be huddled little Iliusha, with his wound always open.

"Come on, Elías," insisted Miss Guire, "be nice." He squeezed his eyes shut to concentrate and remember Her. He knew She would be proud.

Perhaps now She would decide to return. "If you don't apologize, Elías, I am going to have to punish you."

He stayed after dismissal, writing fifty times, *Good boys are always polite.*

"What did Fernando do to you?"

"Nothing, Miss."

"He must have done something, Elías." He raised his head and returned her look without lowering his eyes, concentrating on biting his lips and holding his tongue because he had learned it was always best to keep silent.

"You have never been a fighter, Elías, that isn't like you. Tell me so I can fix it. . . . Answer me, Son." Hearing her his heart began to melt. She was the only one to call him "Son"; Miss Guire didn't have the right. He shook his head, with his lips shut tight and his eyes moist. He showed her the notebook with the fifty lines, took his bookbag, and fled without saying good-bye.

If Aunt Debbie was still in the house it meant that She had not returned.

"I was going to jump and I slipped on the grass, he explained."

"But how?"

"It was a game of running and jumping. Since I was winning they pushed me."

"They're so jealous," grumbled Rosalía. He accepted the hot chocolate his aunt served him. He could barely do his homework. He fell asleep, exhausted, and continued fighting in his dreams. Against everyone—dogs, dragons, demons. All of them, the others.

It was Friday. In the morning the entire school went to the movies. An English film. Wisely, Iliusha stationed himself in front of Miss Guire and slept through it. As they left, Fernando Flores passed by his side, bumping into him. "Scaredy-cat."

Elías turned toward him with an opaque glance: "It's forbidden to talk to me."

His aunt had prepared gefilte fish. Everyone said she was a famous cook. Even though he was only a child, she awaited his praise with a triumphal smile. But Iliusha had gotten so used to not speaking that now it was difficult for him to produce any sound; he had to swallow some saliva first and then let it go, like someone who hurls himself into freezing water. He didn't comment but ate it all up. "Do you want more?" He nodded his head. He ate a second serving and she smiled at him.

"Aunt, do you believe in God?"

"No . . . we don't believe."

"Why?"

"We have other ideas. There are so many discoveries, progress, science . . . "

Iliusha understood her small disparaging motion more than the meaning of what she was saying.

"Maybe we don't have one?"

"Of course we do, Jehovah. But we don't believe in those things."

"Aunt, Catholics, they believe, they go to Mass, they pray and everything. That's why they're . . ."

"Oh, Elías, what questions, what questions. You're right, a Catholic who does not believe in God and who doesn't go to Mass stops being a Catholic."

"But those of us who don't believe in God, are we still Jews anyway?"

It was too complicated. The only thing he understood, although he already knew it intuitively, was the certainty that he was different. He didn't know why, but that's the way it was.

"And if you don't believe, why do you wear that?" With his index finger he gently touched the six-pointed star that she wore hanging from a little chain, and at that moment he remembered that She also wore one. "This is something else. It's the Star of David." Like David Copperfield— and he imagined that David, small and alone, like himself. He remained quiet, lost again in his daydream.

Aunt Debbie sighed, drank her little bit of coffee, lit a cigarette. "Do you want to know why I wear it?" Iliusha nodded his assent. "Because your grandparents died over there, far away . . ." With her eyes fixed on a distant space, beyond Iliusha, she was not speaking to explain to him, but to herself. "It's my history, what ties me to them." Then she noticed his disturbed expression and took his hand. "A long time ago, on the other side of the ocean, some very bad people, very bad, forced the Jews to sew a star just like this one on their clothing, and they put it here—you see?— right on their heart. Then, when these evil men were in a bad mood, or things were not going well for them, they blamed the Jews and searched for those wearing the star to beat them . . . or kill them."

"And aren't you afraid to wear it?"

His aunt smiled, "Sometimes, but I ignore it and wear it anyway."

The sky was covered with huge black clouds. The heat was oppressive. "An earthquake is coming," forecasted Rosalía as she accompanied him to school.

The House of Memory

A boring class. Miss Guire talked about honor and loyalty, assuming they would realize she was referring to the previous day's battle. Iliusha was gliding in a kind of dream populated with fleeting images that escaped from him every time he attempted to retain them for an instant. A white wing, the backyard of his house filled with garbage, shining stars sticking to his clothing, thousands of little stones tumbling down on him, landing on him like a stinging waterfall. Images that galloped by, returning over and over, until he was exhausted.

He wandered, half asleep, through the schoolyard, and it was perhaps that mixture of worry and tiredness that prevented him from realizing the danger. Amidst the clamor of familiar noises, the students approached, lining up to return to class. The teachers surrounded the director, still commenting on the morning's exit. Absorbed, Iliusha walked at the back, automatically maintaining the distance between himself and the others, as if excluding himself were his personal obligation and no longer theirs. He discovered that one could believe and not believe. And at any rate, he didn't understand why, he would always be a Jew. He didn't hear them come close. When Fernando and Jimmy grabbed him roughly by the arms he couldn't manage to shout. As soon as they subdued him, Rodolfo Sánchez covered his mouth. He struggled but two others grabbed his legs and between the five of them they dragged him toward the rear, to that space between the quince trees and the wall where the gardener piled up the dry leaves. "We're going to burn you, damned dwarf," whispered Jimmy. "You'll die in sin. Heretic."

He believed them. How could he not believe them, if the day before they had sent him the paper about the crematorium, and just recently Aunt Debbie had told him the story of the evil men who killed those who wore the star? He didn't want to die. With all his strength he tried to free himself, desperate. They were panting. Somehow, he managed to set one leg free.

"Outcast!"

"Jewish dog. Hold him tight!"

"Grab his leg!"

They punched him in the face.

"First we're going to brand you with a J so you'll know why."

"Poor animals," She always said when She saw cows branded With the initial of the ranch owner. Poor things, how it must hurt them. He saw the pencil point coming closer; it was upon him, between his eyes. He twisted backward, terrified. "No, not that!"

And suddenly nothing.

He didn't know what they did to him, or how they found him, or the punishment Fernando and the others received. He came to in the nurse's office. What was his father doing there next to the director? "Mamushka," he murmured, and fainted again.

He lost consciousness, plunging into a deep and empty sleep, rising up at times, carried by delirium, sinking again into a slumber without memories. He barely felt Aunt Debbie washing his hands."And these red marks, poor little thing . . . what could they have been playing?"

Afterward, or maybe before, he opened his eyes and saw the doctor, motionless, as if he had always been there. He struggled on precipitous slopes, pursued by a Fernando, who had turned into a dog and was spitting flames. He fled through moving mountains that were suddenly fenced playgrounds and dead-end streets. He smelled the smoke, escaping from the crematorium. She was beyond. And then, *An island is a piece of land surrounded by water.* Who was singing? Was it She, encouraging him? Or was it Miss Guire, shaking the rod to punish him? Go back Iliusha! Hide! Flee from the devils. And he continued his wanton race, almost breathless, no longer knowing whether he was running to tear himself away or because he wanted to find Her.

He was hot, vomiting. "Poor little thing," said Aunt Debbie's voice. How many days? How much fever? Suddenly it seemed to him that Miss Guire was also in his room, next to the doctor, making faces at him. Now the wall was moving. It wasn't a wall but Fernando and many others just like him, menacing. Beyond, She stretched out her arms toward him, smiling, "My Iliushenka." The wall grew and grew, preventing him from seeing Her. His heart was beating madly as he searched for Her always, between the packs of hounds or in the yard with the quince trees, getting closer to Her. He was next to Her, under the blankets; he could almost touch Her . . . But no, now She was waiting for him beside the samovar, next to the blurry photo of his grandparents.

When the fever began to leave him, a cold sweat overcame him, chilling him to the bone. If he opened his eyes he saw a six-pointed star shining in the center of the lamp. He squeezed his eyelids shut, exhausted, trying to fall asleep again, to continue searching for Her. He was certain that if he found Her he would be saved. They would return together; they would never be separated again. And the pack of hounds would cross the space with stars on their foreheads and howls of joy.

Half awake, or maybe still asleep, he wished with all his might, with his whole being; he tried to catch his star. But if his father gave it to him it was because She would no longer return. Then he burst into tears because he didn't want to, couldn't, accept that. Dying, what a frightening thing. He cried because She was not at his side, because suddenly he realized that Her absence, while he was sick, was the confirmation of that horrible thing.

His father opened the blinds, and the brilliant light invaded his room, illuminating the blue of his blanket. He felt the warmth of the sun like a caress. They set him between the large cushions. They fed him broth. He managed to swallow a mashed banana with honey. How could he explain that mixture of impressions and feelings, the joy of the light, the taste of honey still on his lips. He breathed deeply. "I want my Mamushka's star," he begged his father, sure that he had it. His father shivered, hesitated, sat down on the bed and took his hands—"Her star . . ."—and embraced him.

He would wear it when he returned to school. Maybe, just maybe, it was a way of keeping Her, of feeling less alone, of being with Her forever. "And that way they'll all know what I am," he said.

Translated from the Spanish by Roberta Gordenstein

From May You Make a Good Bride

Rosa Nissan

Second Grade

Every night I kneel down next to the window, gaze at a star (which is probably my guardian angel), and say the "Our Father" for God, and a "Hail Mary" for the Virgin Mother. Even though I'm the daughter of Jews, I hope that I have a guardian angel who follows me around all day long, just like my classmates have. Today I prayed that I won't have to change schools; they want to stick me in an elementary school with only Jewish kids. (Where do they get so many of them?)

> Dear Lord, make it so that I get to stay forever at Guadalupe Tepeyac Elementary. Don't let them take me out for anything in the world, especially now when I'm going to go into third grade—the most difficult year of primary school. Only here at this school, and with your help, will I be able to get through it. I promise you that I'll do whatever you ask of me: follow the Ten Commandments, go on Saturdays to catechism classes, and then, the day that I die I will be the guardian angel of whoever you say.

> In the name of the Father, the Son, and the Holy Spirit. Amen.

At eight o'clock in the morning, before beginning our studies, we always pray. We put the palms of our hands together near our mouths, we close our eyes, and then we all recite our prayer in unison. And Our Heavenly Father hears us. With our right hands we make the sign of the cross, and then we sit down to study. Our desks are really nice; the top

lifts open and inside we store all of our school stuff. I have the top of my desk lid decorated with stickers: in the middle is Saint Theresa (I adore her), and on all four sides are other saints with flowers all around them. I spend all day giving them little kisses so that they watch over me.

When we complete our assignments or behave ourselves, the misses reward us with another sticker. I'm one of the best behaved, and among those who have the most stickers. I just have to hide them when I'm at home because my mom doesn't like them very much. Sometimes she catches me making the sign of the cross in the morning. The other day she told me, "I would prefer it if you would leave the classroom when the others are saying their morning prayers." But I couldn't possibly do that. The rest of the kids would ask about me, and besides, I like saying prayers.

Yesterday during recess everybody was making sand castles. I was backing up to make mine a little bigger when I stepped on another girl's castle. She got so mad, and then threw sand in my eyes and screamed, "Jew girl, Jew girl!" Hearing that really surprised me, 'cause most of the girls don't even know that I'm Jewish.

A whole bunch more came around and then they started yelling "You people killed Christ!" and they made the sign of the cross in my face, and just stared at me like I was the Devil himself.

I yelled back, "That's a lie. I'm not a Jew. I say my prayers and make confession just like the rest of you."

It's almost one o'clock in the morning. I can't sleep. I keep thinking about how they threw sand at me.

This dream of Hell keeps haunting me. Last week I dreamed the same thing. The fire kept coming back to my bed to visit me, over and over. The yellow flames lit up the darkness, waves of orange and red fire. Then tombs opened up like manhole covers. People came out of them to walk toward God—he's going to reward or punish us. I can see the lids opening up, the resurrected people starting to walk. "The final judgment. We'll all be there someday," said Mother Mary. "Then we will know whether we'll make it to Heaven, or whether we'll end up with a tail and horns." The ones that go to Hell will make little kids do bad things.

Last night the neighbors came down from the second floor and we played Lottery. I got the playing card with "The Devil," and I lost because that old bad guy just never got called. That awful little red demon was dancing

around with his evil eyes in my sleep last night. He's got this big iron fork that he uses to sweep the cinders around; he just comes and goes, wherever he wants. He gives me this look out of the corner of his eye, shows me his horns, and sharpens his talons on the burning edge of his blade. It just scares me to death to imagine that this could happen to me. Oh, I hope it doesn't come to that!

And why is it that we've got to go around naked? And with all those resurrected dead people no less! Oh, I would just die if they saw me naked, and if I then had to go out like that and have everybody see me. What an awful punishment! I'd run into all these people that died like a thousand years ago: Benito Juárez, Napoleón, Miguel Hidalgo y Costilla, my other grandma, Cinderella, Cuauhtémoc . . . And how in the world is he going to be able to walk anyway, when they burned off his feet?[1] It must be that we come back all in one piece; they say nothing is impossible for God. It might actually be fun, if I get to meet all of these people, but . . . naked? Oh, not that! How embarrassing! And without even anything to cover yourself up!

Love God over everything else. (I love Him and I pray to Him.)

Don't take the Lord's name in vain. (I'm not going to swear anymore. But if I do swear something that's not true, I'll cross my fingers behind my back, and it won't count.)

Honor your father and mother.

Keep the Sabbath and the Holy Days.

Don't kill.

Don't fornicate. (This one I'm skipping. Who even knows what it means?)

Don't steal.

Don't bear false witness or lie. (I don't tell too many lies. Besides, it's the worst thing I could do to my mom.)

Don't desire someone else's wife. (I don't understand . . . whose wife?)

Don't covet someone else's belongings. (That's an easy one, 'cause I never want what isn't mine.)

The House of Memory

If I just follow these, I'm sure I'll go to Heaven. The thing that I really like about the Ten Commandments is that they're the same for Jews and Catholics. Finally, something that's the same! I can recite them at home just like I can at school. At least I have that. It's easy to follow them, too, 'cause that business about me going to Hell is just too horrifying.

I want to go to Heaven and be an angel like on my stickers. I'd sure like to be one of the invisible ones. How fabulous to be invisible! Go everywhere, flying from here to there, seeing everybody without them seeing me . . . now if I could just get up close to kid's ears and tell them, "Don't pay any attention to the Devil! Give your Sundays over to the nice Old Man. Let other kids borrow your crayons, even if they break them." They say that the Devil comes and tells kids in their left ear to misbehave, and their guardian angel tells them in their right ear to behave themselves.

Those blond angels with the baby-blue robes and transparent wings live up in the sky and they get to see God, the Virgin Mother, and all the Saints, and talk to them. "Holy Cross, Holy Cross, make the Devil go away and Jesus come." Ol' pot-bellied demons—don't come around me— get out of here! Go away forever! I know that those little devils are really pushy and they keep coming back to your ear and saying, "Steal that pen, hit your sister, pull her braids, make fun of her!" Sometimes they convince you, because the Devil only teaches you bad habits, and those demons are very tricky.

My robes would be white; I'd fly around from here to there. I'd tell all the kids to be good, no matter what country they're from . . . but I'm not sure I'd want to be the angel of a Jewish kid, I'd rather have a Roman Catholic. Someday I'd take the highway up to the sky; I'd sprout beautiful wings like a butterfly, and from the clouds I'd throw buckets of water so that those below would feel like it was raining.

All the girls at school get presents and parties twice a year; once on their birthday, and then on their Saint's day. But Jews don't get to celebrate the day of their Saint. The teacher asked me when was my Saint's day. The only thing that I could think of answering was that I would ask my mom. I'm sure there's no Saint Oshinica. I'll look in the calendar; if there's a Saint Eugenia, I'm saved.

Since we live on Guadalupe Boulevard we get to see all the processions that come by every day toward the Basilica.[2] They go by singing and

dancing and laughing; they drink arm in arm, carrying their children, their sick people, their food, their blankets. Each group has a guy in charge that watches out and makes sure that they don't go so slow that the procession behind catches up.

When we can just barely start to hear them, we run out to the balcony; we don't seem to ever get tired of watching them. Sometimes the groups are three or four blocks long, and when they pass us by, that's when it starts to get sad. But on the days close to the Holy Mother's day, they come by one after the other, bearing different standards, all with the image of the Virgin of Guadalupe—the Mother of all Mexicans—framed in threads of gold.

They must be having fun, coming from places like Toluca, Querétaro, Pachuca, and lots more. When they pass by our house they start singing "Mañanitas," so happy because they're about to get to the place where the Virgin of Guadalupe appeared for the first time. Many of them are so full of emotion just from being so close, their eyes fill with tears. Others are already on their knees, even though there are still fifteen blocks to go.

The whole area smells like *gorditas*. And all around the Basilica there are women sitting on their little steps off the street, warming up these corn tortillas on clay dishes. They're small, about the size of a quinto coin (well, maybe a little bigger), and come in packets of ten, wrapped in colored tissue paper.

I wonder why it is that they sell so many of those special candles all around down there. They're the really long and pretty rose-colored ones, and they're decorated with little golden flowers.

Sometimes we go inside the church to hear the mass. And sometimes we just walk around the vendor stands. Then we go up the little hill that you can just barely see from the window of our house. At the top there's a little white house with a cross on top. It's right there where the miracle happened to the Indian, Juan Diego. He sure was lucky! I hope that someday she can appear to me. If it's a miracle, then it could happen to me, too. Later on we come down from the hill, and to get back home we take the train that goes all the way up Guadalupe Boulevard. That way we're not gone too long and Mom doesn't notice that we went down there again.

I believed them. I believed my parents when they said that it wasn't the Jews that killed Christ. "If they bother you again, tell them that Jesus was Jewish, that he made his Bar Mitzvah."

"Oh yeah, right, Dad," I said. "Like they're going to believe that! They'll just get mad."

Since my mom was to going to Monterrey to see my grandpa, Micaela hurried up with her chores and she took us down by the Basilica again. We met up with some of her friends. After a while, I heard one of them say, "I'm telling you, Mica, you shouldn't be working for them. The money they pay you isn't enough—it runs out just like water."

I pretended not to hear this. The truth is, I don't know what to say when I hear that kind of talk. And then, what if they start in with the whole thing about killing Christ, too? Everybody must know about that. We went into the church on the hill and I just stared at the crucifix. Really, look how they left him! Some lady who was kneeling by us was crying 'cause he was dripping blood. That poor guy! How could you not hate whoever did that—what terrible people! It's been so many years since it happened, but you still have to feel awful about it. If this lady who's crying by me knew that I was a Jew, I really think she could kill me. The good thing is that Micaela likes me and she's not going to go around gossiping and telling on me. And besides, you can't tell if someone is Jewish just by looking at them. Frankly, I'm glad I'm Jewish rather than Black. But even I feel pretty sad and guilty about it. Look how they nailed him to that cross! What horrible people.

On the corner where we live there's a fine goods store, and the owners Berta and Bicha are friends of my mom. They live in the back of the store on the ground floor. They make the most beautifully decorated cakes. Sometimes I just sit for hours watching how they do one layer and then the next. They even make the little figurines, with paint and wires, then the flowers—different colors like blue, yellow, and pink. I think the prettiest ones are the wedding cakes. But I can change my mind when I see the ones to celebrate a *quinceañera*, with its little figurine coming down the steps of a circular staircase.[4] I spend a lot of time looking at them, and at the yellow, pink, and blue powdered sugar.

Actually, the figurines don't look that great until we make them a little dress with a piece of tulle and attach it with a bit of frosting around the waist. Then we cover the pleats with the frosting from the decorating bag, and it looks just like a little waistband. That's when they really look elegant. Then we apply a little paint to make them dark or fair-skinned,

and they end up looking just like we want them to. Poor things! But they're always pretty.

Bicha and Berta are friends with a priest who gives catechism classes on Saturdays at the church closest to my home. A lot of kids go there; we learn how to pray, and ever since I learned how to cross myself I'm better at knowing which is my right hand, 'cause it's the one you have to use to make the cross. When we're all done they give us those licorice candies that I love so much. I've never missed a class because they cover for me and tell my mom that I'm with them helping decorate the cakes. I really want to make my first communion, and they're the only ones who can help me save myself from the final judgment; and even better, maybe God will forgive my whole family.

In our neighborhood, Colonia Industrial, there are a lot of other Jewish families; they've been my parents' closest friends since even before they were married. My mom introduced Max and his wife Fortuna. They've got kids, too, but I'm the oldest—we all get along great. Today my mom and some of the other ladies decided to go to a Jewish school that's over in another neighborhood, Colonia del Valle, to see if maybe all of us get together, the school will send a bus to pick us up. When we got home from school, we found out they had registered us.

* * * * *

Third Grade

All of these kids killed Christ too? They seem all right to me. They don't seem like they could have done it. Maybe they don't remember doing it. They play marbles and tag and freeze tag—everything I played in the other school. Could they really be like my old friends? You can't tell at all that they're Jewish.

Translated from the Spanish by Dina Castillo-Mendoza

The House of Memory

1. Benito Juárez (1806–1872) was president of Mexico (1857–1865, 1867–1872), particularly revered as a champion of Mexican independence and democratic reform and as the first national leader of indigenous heritage. Miguel Hidalgo y Costilla (1753–1811) was a priest who led a rebellion against Spanish rule; he was eventually defeated and executed. Cuauhtémoc was the son of Moctezuma, who was emperor of the Aztecs when the conquistador Hernán Cortés arrived in Mexico in 1519. It is believed that Cortés's men tortured Cuauhtemóc by burning off his feet in an attempt to make him reveal the location of Aztec treasures.

2. The Basilica of the Virgin of Guadelupe, which sits atop a hill in Mexico City, is the nation's most famous cathedral, dedicated to its most beloved native saint. The faithful believe that it marks the spot where, in the sixteenth century, the Virgin Mary appeared to an indigenous peasant, Juan Diego, and requested his help in bringing his people to Christianity. It draws thousands of pilgrims each year.

3. In Mexico and other Latin American countries, girls' fifteenth birthdays, or *quinceañera*, are marked with especially lavish celebrations that wecome them into adulthood.

Gotlib, Bombero

Barbara Mujica

Ernesto Gotlib lit a cigarette and put it to his lips. He inhaled fitfully, then coughed. The cigarette tasted bitter. He rapped on the side of the table with his right hand—an edgy little rap—and mashed the cigarette in an ashtray.

"Rebeca!"

Rebeca knew what he was going to say.

"You think they've got to me yet?"

"You just asked me that two minutes ago."

"So? That was two minutes ago. What about now? You think they've got to my name yet?"

"How could I know?"

Gotlib got up and looked out the window, but he did not see the brown and gray rocks clutching at the sky like gnarled hands. The rugged coastline extended in either direction in front of him. Waves smashed against craggy knuckles, then shattered. Slivers of seawater caught the fading light as they sprayed upward. Gotlib sat down in a different chair and lit a new cigarette.

"Just tell me what you think."

Miriam came in with dishes and started to set the table.

"Move your arm, please, Papá. It's in the way.

Gotlib moved his arm off the table so that Miriam could put down a dish.

"I don't feel like having tea today," he said.

"Teolinda baked *alfajores*."

"I know, sweetheart. I'm just not in the mood. My mind's not on food."

"But you should eat something, Papá."

Gotlib shook his head.

Miriam set a teacup by his dish anyway. He would change his mind, she thought. Papa loved the sticky, nut-filled cookies that the Argentine cook prepared.

"Come on, Papá," she coaxed. "It's five o'clock."

Miriam finished setting the table and went back into the kitchen.

"You should eat something, Ernesto," said Rebeca. "Whether you have a cup of tea or not won't influence their decision either way."

Ernesto sighed. "You think they've got to me yet?"

Rebeca shook her head. "God knows. How many of you were there?"

"Seven, I think . . . Me, López . . . let's see . . . Martinelli . . . that's three . . . Valenzuela . . . that's four . . ."

"What about Tomich? Wasn't he coming up this time?"

Miriam had come back with a plate of *alfajores.*

"Marcela Tomich told me they were going back to Santiago, Mamá. She said her father wasn't a candidate."

"So that's only four," said Rebeca. She tried to make her voice soothing as she reached over and squeezed her husband's wrist. "One less to worry about."

"No," said Gotlib. "I never counted Tomich. I knew they were leaving Antofagasta. His brother is in Santiago. They have a business there."

"Well, so . . . four. López, Martinelli, Valenzuela, and you."

"There's Petersen."

"He'll have a good chance. They're always impressed with an English name."

"Swedish."

"Whatever."

"Just as long as it's not Jewish. Just as long as it's not Rosental or Vainberg or Gotlib or something."

"Ernesto, stop it. This is Antofagasta, Chile. This is not Nazi Germany."

"They've never elected a Jew. Never!"

It was true. There had never been a Jew in the Volunteer Fire Department of Antofagasta.

"Papá, don't get yourself worked up."

But Gotlib was worked up. Tonight the entire department had met to vote. Only the most respected men in the city were invited to join the fire brigade, and since boyhood Gotlib had dreamed of being a fireman, a *bombero.*

As a child he had watched the incandescent fire engines racing down the streets. On either side, the proud flame tamers stood tense and bold.

Gotlib, Bombero

When they reached the burning building, they yanked out their hoses and shoved their ladders up against the blistering walls, then hurled themselves into the asphyxiating black haze to pull out endangered men, women, children, even pets. It was like a movie.

Don Mauro Mujica had been head of the brigade for as long as Gotlib could remember. A successful businessman who had rebuilt the family fortune that his mother had squandered on horses, Don Mauro had a reputation for tough-mindedness and hard dealing. At work and at the club he was reserved. He wore English-cut suits and smoked imported cigarettes. But the sound of a siren transformed him. The mask fell and the cool caution that characterized his business style gave way to temerity. He rushed into the flames, balancing on teetering beams, yanking out victims, securing walls, hauling up hose, yelling orders. At a fire, old Don Mauro—he had seemed old to Gotlib back then, although he must have been in his forties—turned bold and resolute. He had grit. He led his men into the most vicious fires. They respected him, and they elected him chief term after term.

After a victory, the fire trucks would return to the station, moving slowly now, but with sirens screeching, as the townspeople grouped on corners to wave white handkerchiefs and hail the firefighters as heroes.

On September 18, Independence Day, and on other festive occasions as well, the firemen paraded through town in their gleaming engines, led by the fire chief in his bright red car. Don Mauro was at the height of glory as he led the noisy procession with his young son seated beside him. Sometimes Maurito would ride with his father to a fire on an engine. Gotlib was about eight or ten when he began to envy Maurito, who was the same age as he. Gotlib had longed to sit on one of those huge, gleaming trucks just once—not beside his father, of course, for his own father could never be a fireman. But by that time, he had already realized that he was not of the same breed as the tall, fair, slim boy with the wide smile whose admittance into the elite brigade was a foregone conclusion.

Sometimes Gotlib hung around the fire station on a Sunday. Mauro Senior would have the Victrola on, and the firemen, many of them of Italian extraction, would listen to a tenor sing "Santa Lucia." Don Mauro was at ease on those Sunday afternoons, surrounded by his men. He poured burgundy from his uncle's vineyards while Maurito, in those silly shorts that all schoolboys wore and unanimously hated, galloped around the station house. Then someone would coax, "¡Canta, Maurito!" and the others would chant, "¡Canta! ¡Canta!" They kept a huge Mexican hat with

silver trimmings on a peg in the office and Maurito would put it on and sing "Jalisco, no te rajes." All the men would laugh, not only because they thought Mexican songs were hilarious, but because Maurito was the fire chief's son and he was a great little clown. Ernestito would laugh with them, but he would keep a little to the side, a little out of the way. No one ever told him to go home, but no one ever invited him to come again next Sunday, either. Someday, he thought, Maurito would be a fire chief just like his father.

"I suppose there isn't much of a chance," Gotlib was saying. "It's an honor even to be a candidate, Ernesto. And to have been nominated by Mauro Mujica, the chief's son!"

"That's right, Papá," said Miriam. "I'd say you stand a very good chance."

"So what do you think? You think they've got to me yet?"

Rebeca would have preferred to have her tea and *alfajores* and not talk about it anymore, but she knew that her husband's self-esteem was riding on this vote and that his nerves would not let his mind off the subject.

"Let's see . . . Tomich is going to Santiago . . . Santamaría . . . he'll get in. He's Don Mauro's son-in-law, and his father has been a *bombero* for years. . . . That makes six. . . ."

"What about Carrera?" asked Miriam.

"That's it, Carrera! Good girl, Miriam. How could I forget Carrera?"

Rebeca smiled at her husband. He adored the girls. His daughters were the most important thing in his life, far more important than this ridiculous vote. That's why, Rebeca thought, it was a shame he was making himself so sick over this business.

And yet, she understood. To be a fireman was to be one of them.

"Well, if they went in alphabetical order, they took Carrera first, then Gotlib, then López, Santamaría—no, Petersen, Martinelli, Santamaría, Valenzuela. They started at three-thirty. It's after five now. They've already considered your candidacy, Ernesto. They've probably all gone home for tea."

"Sometimes the debates go on into the night."

Rebeca sighed.

"What if they didn't go in alphabetical order?" Gotlib said.

Rebeca stood up and went to call her other two daughters. "Tea, girls! Teolinda made *alfajores* and there are buns and sweet rolls!"

She sat down again and turned to her husband.

"If they didn't go in alphabetical order, then I don't know."

"So," said Gotlib heavily, "maybe it's already been decided."

"Maybe. So go ahead and eat."

She poured tea into his cup. Two giggling teenage girls collided with each other and the railing on the stairs. They tumbled into the dining room. One kissed Gotlib on the forehead, the other kissed him on the cheek.

"*Hola*, Papá. How's the future fire chief?"

"Don't make jokes, Emi," said Miriam. "Papá's nervous."

"Nothing to be nervous about," said Emilia. "You're as good as elected."

"They probably laughed themselves silly, to think a Jew wanted to be a fireman," said Gotlib.

Miriam suppressed a guffaw.

"C'mon, Papá," said Sara. "Don't get melodramatic."

This time Miriam laughed out loud. "After all this family has been through, Papá! Do you really think the Gotlibs of Antofagasta will fall apart if you don't get elected to the fire brigade?"

Gotlib smiled and squeezed her hand. He knew she was right.

Logic told him she was right. But there was more to it than that.

The Gotlibs had been in Antofagasta for more than forty years. Ernesto's father, Joseph Gottlieb, had come to Chile right before the war. Hitler was showing his fangs, and Joseph's brother Herman, who had seen his neighbors slashed with knives and broken glass, insisted that to wait would be fatal. Joseph didn't think so. He had started out as a tailor, but had expanded into ready-to-wear. He had a shrewd head for money and had built up a thriving business, importing cheap goods from Italy and turning huge profits. He had six stores in Munich alone. To up and leave everything behind would be devastating. Herman said that if Joseph didn't go, he would go alone. He had friends in Switzerland and France, and he could get false documents.

Herman did not need to harp. Events convinced Joseph that his brother was right. Late one night in September, hoodlums hurled a bottle filled with blood through Herman's front window. The crash was deafening. Shards of glass flew crazily through the room. They mixed with crimson on the opposite wall and slid, carried by streams of blood, down the painted surface onto the floor, where red and glass formed splintery pools that glistened eerily. Trembling, Herman called for his brother. Joseph stood and looked for a long time. Then he held his brother Herman in his arms and both men cried.

Joseph returned home and helped his pregnant wife pack two light bags. They took a change of clothes, a few items of jewelry that had been in the family for generations, and pictures of their parents. Joseph went to the store on Winkler Street and took all the money out of the safe. Then he lovingly straightened the stacks of sweaters, the rows of jackets, the skirts, the scarves, the wool stockings. Before he left, he turned out the light. Joseph felt as though a cleaver were lodged in his chest.

There was hardly time to say good-bye to cousins and friends.

In the train, Joseph's wrists went limp and he felt nauseous, as though he were sinking into a sea of vomit. Eventually his wretchedness became so intense that he stopped feeling it. He looked out the window at the tiny farms and drab sky, and allowed himself to be lulled to sleep by the monotony of the movement and the landscape.

Herman, Joseph, and Joseph's wife, Constanza, arrived in Le Havre before dawn. They got on the first ship crossing the Atlantic in which there were accommodations available. They did not ask where it was going because it didn't matter. Later they found out they were headed for South America, and thought that this was as good a destination as any.

The crossing was smooth, but Constanza's pregnancy made it tedious. Constanza was in the stage at which even the smell of fresh cooked vegetables made her ill. The odor of fuel and seawater sickened her to the point of paralysis. The cramped cabin and the rocking of the vessel—slight though it was—made her feel as though she were caught in a rapidly spinning canister. She did not complain, but in those rare moments in which her head was clear, she saw herself running through a pasture hand in hand with the child that would soon be born. Under her feet she imagined the grass to be soft and dry.

The first port of call was Rio de Janeiro. There was a crowd of dark faces at the docks and Joseph thought that maybe they had detoured to Africa, although the steward assured him that he was in Brazil. The swarm of black and red and green and yellow seemed foreign and frightening to Joseph. Multitudes of black people in brightly colored shirts . . . ripe produce in crates and baskets . . . throbbing rhythms of portside musicians . . . smells both pungent and rancid. Joseph knew that Constanza needed fresh air and solid ground, but he and Herman decided to stay on board until the next stop: Buenos Aires.

Argentina appealed to them. There was already a German-speaking Jewish population there. There would be synagogues and schools for the

children. But a man on the boat named Eisenberg said that there was more money to be made in Chile, and besides, Chileans were tolerant of Jews. Argentina was full of Italians, and who knew what to expect of them? There were Italians in Chile, too, but they were a small minority, and besides, most of them were from earlier immigrations and so had fewer ties with the homeland. In Buenos Aires, according to Eisenberg, not only were there more Italian surnames than Spanish, but there were sections where the only language spoken was Italian.

Joseph and Herman considered the situation. Mussolini had helped Hitler bolster Franco in the Spanish Civil War, and now there was talk of a formal Rome-Berlin axis. Where there were Italians with close and recent ties to Italy, there would be anti-Semitism, the brothers reasoned. Eisenberg said that he had a cousin in the north of Chile, where there were lucrative copper mines. It was an area of vast wealth that attracted thousands of Chileans from other cities every year, and this new, affluent population needed goods: clothes, food, furniture, medicines. There was plenty of cash, but nothing grew or was manufactured in the north. Everything had to be brought in from outside. It was, Eisenberg said, a land of opportunity for a shrewd businessman.

Joseph and Herman disembarked in Valparaiso. There, they contacted friends of relatives of friends, who recommended them to a German wholesaler in Antofagasta who supplied the mines at Chuquicamata. His name was Uwe Rissel.

Joseph went to work for Herr Rissel, but Herman, who had been trained as an engineer, found work at the mines. Joseph was an excellent salesman, with years of experience, and although he was not pleased with the idea of working for another man, news from relatives in Europe made it clear that he was lucky to be alive and working at all.

Rissel had access to a huge inventory; he sold everything from radios to toothpaste, from refrigerators to perfume, from auto parts to ladies' panties, from penny novels to screwdrivers. His orders tripled and quadrupled within a year of hiring Joseph. By then, Constanza had had a baby girl named Ana Noemí, and Joseph was glad of the increased commission that Rissel gave him.

Joseph learned Spanish quickly. At night he listened to soap operas on the radio and practiced pronouncing the names of the characters in front of the mirror: "Roberto . . . Rrrroberto . . . Rrrrroberto . . . Raúl . . . Rrrraúl . . . Rrrrraúl . . . He bought a dictionary and read lists of words out loud

to Ana Noemí. (When she started babbling, he discontinued the practice for fear she would imitate his imperfect pronunciation.) He went to the local school and offered to pay a young teacher by the hour to give him lessons. The fellow gave him a child's book of grammar exercises and every afternoon during siesta, Joseph would write them out, letter by letter: *Tú vas. Quiero que tú vayas. Tú vienes. Quiero que tú vengas.*

Joseph had a knack for convincing the miners that they desperately needed products that they had never even heard of. He sent the neighborhood children to the mine stores to ask for Milagro de Lourdes Elexir or Melena de Oro Shampoo, products unknown in Antofagasta. A few days later, he appeared at the store announcing that he was the sole representative for Milagro de Lourdes and Melena de Oro.

In the meantime, Herman had begun investing in the mines. With the demand for metals caused by the war, he was soon making money by the fistful. He was the first of the two brothers to buy a home—a small pink villa by the beach, with a spectacular view of the sea from the living room and a spectacular view of the mountains from the master bedroom. Within a few years, he married a Chilean-born girl named Ester Anita Shapiro, and they had two children, Jaime and Meyer.

Joseph's son Ernst was born a year and a half after Ana Noemí and a month after his brother's son Jaime. Joseph and Constanza named their son Ernst Heinrich: Ernst after Constanza's father, who had died of cancer years before, and Heinrich after a Nazi torturer.

The child's middle name was a compromise. Rissel admired Hitler, although that did not prevent him from hiring shrewd Jews to make money for him. When he heard that Gottlieb's wife was expecting, he demanded that his employee name the baby Adolph. Joseph refused, arguing that tradition dictated that he name their son after a deceased relative. Rissel's color rose. It was a little thing to ask in return for all he had done for Gottlieb, he said. He might just have to look for another sales manager, he said. Gottlieb thought that Rissel was bluffing. The German had never made as much money as now. But Joseph Gottlieb could not take a chance. As a conciliatory gesture, he gave the boy a middle name that was acceptable to his boss.

Heinrich Himmler was just beginning to make a name for himself in Europe as head of the Schutzstaffel, or Black Shirts, but with luck, not even the boy himself would ever associate the Nazi's name with his own. Joseph had had an Uncle Heinrich who had died years before. Officially Ernst Heinrich was named after him.

Gotlib, Bombero

By the time he was four, Ernst was accompanying his father to Rissel's. By the time he was seven, it was he who went pestering store managers for the products that his father was promoting. At nine, Ernst Gottlieb had mastered one of the fundamental principles of business: create a need.

Joseph got his big chance when Chile broke relations with the Axis in 1943. German nationals were being forced out of the country and Rissel had to sell cheap. Joseph got a loan from his brother and took over Rissel, S. A. He renamed the firm Antofagasta Wholesalers, the most neutral, un-Germanic tag he could think of. Constanza stayed home and took care of the children and kept the books while Joseph hustled. By the late 1950s, Gottlieb had built Antofagasta Wholesalers into one of the biggest companies in the country.

Herman prospered as well. He had invested his earnings in beachfront property and was now the owner of houses, apartment buildings, and a hotel. He urged Joseph to put his money into land, but Joseph preferred to stuff cash into the mattress. "Where I can get at it easily if I need it," he said. Herman thought his brother was thinking like a Chilean peasant instead of like a clever European businessman, but nothing he said made Joseph change his mind.

"This isn't Germany," Herman prodded. "It's not like you'll have to make a quick getaway."

Joseph accumulated sacks and sacks of escudos. Soon there were too many to fit into the mattress, so he hid money behind pictures, under floorboards, in wells, in holes dug beside trees, and in a secret compartment under the roosts in the chicken coop. When Chile went into an economic crisis and changed from escudos to pesos, Joseph was left with bags of money that wasn't worth the paper it was printed on.

Joseph's son Ernst was a teenager when he started writing his last name G-o-t-l-i-b to make it conform to its Spanish pronunciation. At the same time, he changed his given names to Ernesto Enrique. Joseph did not put up a fight. In fact, he was glad. At last, he was done with Himmler once and for all.

Ernesto was articulate about his identity. He was a Chilean, he said, not a German, and he didn't want anyone mistaking him for a foreigner. He was proud of Chile, which had taken in thousands of Jewish immigrants before, during, and after the war. It was thanks to Chile's open-arms policy toward refugees that, instead of being thrown into a gas chamber, he had been educated in good private schools and had studied business at

the Catholic University of Valparaíso. (Wealthy Jews, like wealthy Masons and other renegades, had a tacit working relationship with the Jesuit fathers. The Catholic schools were the best in the country. Jews and Masons supported them generously; in return, the priests educated the infidels' sons. Each side kept out of the other's hair and neither asked too many questions.)

By the early sixties Ernesto had completed his degree and gone into his father's business. He no longer loved Chile because it had taken in immigrants during perilous times; he loved Chile because he was Chilean. Unlike his father, he spoke Spanish without an accent and with dialectal variants; he said *uté* instead of *usted*, *etái* instead of *estás*, *paco* instead of *policía*, *porotos* instead of *frijoles*, and *living* instead of *sala*. He ate empanadas on Sunday afternoons and had tea every day at five. Yet Ernesto Gotlib sensed that he didn't quite fit in. No one had ever said anything to him about being Jewish, but at the Colegio San Luis he had felt pangs of embarrassment in the locker room when his circumcised penis was in full view. He felt awkward at Mass and in religion class. When they talked about the one true faith, it mortified him. The first time he had to line up with the other little boys for confession with Father Reblando, he lost his composure and had to be sent home. He was certain that Father Reblando was going to call him an anti-Christ and blame him for the death of Jesus. After that, Joseph arranged for his son to be excused from some of the rites. Joseph had made sizable contributions to the school, and the fathers agreed to the arrangement. They were a tolerant bunch.

As a university student, Ernesto had been invited to parties, and friends often had him to dinner—and sometimes even to baptisms, first communions, and weddings. But whenever a classmate introduced him to his parents, he suspected that they were thinking, "Ah, Ernesto Gotlib, the Jew."

Ernesto noticed, or thought he noticed, that his friends never presented him to their sisters.

After college, when young men began to join their fathers' clubs—the Club de la Nación, the Auto Club, the Club Italiano—he began to feel excluded. Joseph belonged to the Unión Hebraica, and that was all right, but Ernesto yearned to attend dances at the Alianza Italo-Española, where the fire chief's pretty daughter Graciela rocked and rolled with the sons of the men who formed the elite of Antofagasta: the firemen. To Ernesto's mind, those boys were real Chileans. Some of them had foreign grandparents—Martinelli, Petersen, López (whose grandmother was Yugoslavian)—

but Gotlib was sure that they never felt like outsiders. Gotlib felt like an outsider because Gotlib was a Jew.

Joseph and Herman Gottlieb did not share Ernesto's discomfort. They knew who they were: German Jews who had fled Nazi Germany in order to save their lives. They spoke German or Yiddish at home and walked down the street with yarmulkes on their heads on Friday nights. On the Sabbath, their wives lit candles. They were grateful to their new country for taking them in, but they knew that they were foreigners, not Chileans. They were perfectly content to have dinner at the Unión Hebraica on Sunday night, and they encouraged their sons to attend dances there, make friends with Jewish girls, and settle down.

After the switch from escudos to pesos Herman lent Joseph money to rebuild his financial base. This time, he invested in gold. Herman was rich and Joseph would eventually be rich again, but what was money for, Joseph asked Herman, if not to pass on to children and grandchildren? The Gottliebs looked at their progeny and smiled.

But in 1970 the world of Joseph and Herman Gottlieb shattered. Salvador Allende was a candidate for president, and violence was erupting in the streets. When Allende was elected, Herman's fears mushroomed. The new chief of state set out to revamp Chilean society, nationalizing industries and enterprises—including the mines.

Herman, like others who had invested heavily in copper, lost everything. Joseph would have been pleased to give his brother money, but money was not the real problem. Herman's life was in shambles. He had started from scratch in Germany and built a business, only to lose it. He had started from scratch again in Chile, and now the prospect of starting over yet again was overwhelming. Herman was no longer a young man. The sleeplessness was wearing him down. The strain showed on his brow and in his voice, which frequently cracked and trailed off. Herman was sinking into depression.

In the streets, rock-throwing mobs attacked anyone wearing a business suit. Herman and Joseph Gottlieb did not consider themselves perpetrators of economic crimes. They had not inherited their fortunes; they had earned them through sweat and ingenuity. But the firebrands saw no difference between Joseph and Herman Gottlieb and the idle rich.

Herman and Joseph had the impression that they were reliving a nightmare. Herman became afraid to go outside, not only because thugs and hoodlums of all persuasions used politics as an excuse to throw potatoes

with razor blades embedded in them at passers-by, but because squatters were taking over homes. It was dangerous to leave a house unattended, even for a few hours. And who knew if you could trust your servants?

In the following months, inflation soared and strikes spread. In the stores, there was no kosher meat or any other kind of meat. For a ration of rice, housewives queued up from five o'clock in the morning once a week, on Thursdays. Before long, women were beating their empty pots in the plaza to protest the scarcity of food. Toilet paper became a luxury item. Shoes were unbuyable. Rumors spread that Chile, an important manufacturer of leather goods, was sending its shoes to Cuba. Herman bowed his head and with a meat cleaver slashed the toes out of the shoes of his grandson, Jacobo. Meyer's boy was growing, Herman explained as though he had to justify his actions. Jacobo's little foot needed room.

It was a September night when a bottle filled with blood crashed through Herman's front window and shattered against the opposite wall, splashing crimson over the lamp, the sofa, the cream-colored carpet. Herman had been sitting at the piano, picking out a polka he remembered from childhood.

Herman did not move. He sat for a long, long time and watched the blood stream down the wall before he felt his muscles contract and his throat grow tight and dry. His head ached terribly. He had lived this scene before. He wanted to cry, but he didn't. He just sat watching the blood serpent creep slowly, slowly down the wall.

When Herman's wife, Ester, came back from visiting with Constanza that afternoon, she found the living room a wreck. In the bedroom, she found her husband sprawled over the bed, his head blown to bits, teeth and hair stuck to walls and furniture, and blood, great pools of viscous black-red blood, seeping through the white bedclothes onto the floor. His note said simply that he had been through it all once before. He couldn't bear to go through it again.

On September 11, 1973, Allende fell. Some in the country rejoiced, but Ernesto Gotlib was in mourning. His father, Joseph, had died only two days before. The doctors said it was a heart condition, but Ernesto knew it was grief. Joseph and Herman had always been inseparable.

By then, Ernesto was married and all three of his daughters had been born. He, like many others who had opposed Allende, assumed that the country would return to democracy. When it did not, he ranted at the dinner table and drew up protests that he read at meetings of the brother-

hood of the Unión Hebraica. But with time, his furor cooled. Pinochet was a dictator, but the country was prospering. Store shelves were filled with imported goods and there was a huge demand for everything from radios to toothpaste, from refrigerators to perfume. Pinochet wouldn't last, he told himself, and in the meantime, he, Ernesto, was cleaning up. He had inherited his father's business, and ran it with the expertise of a person who had known how to sell before he had known how to walk.

Gotlib was a rich man. He owned not only Antofagasta Wholesalers but retail stores as well. And he did not hide his money in the mattress. He invested it. Over the years, he accumulated houses, condominiums, office buildings, an interest in a shipping company, and a tourist boat. He had three beautiful daughters and a wonderful wife. But still, something was missing.

Gotlib had influence because he had money, but the pangs of the locker room had never subsided. Did those men who were recognized as the city leaders appreciate his merits, he wondered, or did they consider him a pushy, crafty, upstart Jew? In the middle of the night, as the waves rolled softly onto the beach with a steady swish, Ernesto felt the eyes of his classmates on his circumcised penis. He heard the voice of Father Reblando. He saw the soft, blond curls of Graciela, the fire chief's daughter, resting on the lapel of . . . Aníbal López.

Now that his father and uncle were dead, Gotlib had loosened his ties with the Jewish European community in Chile. After the war and during the following years, waves of Jews arrived from Germany, France, England. But they were not like Gotlib. They were foreigners. Gotlib was Chilean born. Not only for himself, he felt, but for his dead father and uncle, he needed to be accepted as a real Chilean. He needed to validate their choice. He needed a sign for all the world to see that he was not only a citizen, but the best of citizens. He needed to be a fireman.

Miriam put down the tray of breads and cakes and massaged her father's shoulders.

She's a beautiful girl, thought Gotlib. "It's for her—for all of them—that I want this so much," he said to himself. "So that they shouldn't feel like outsiders. So that they should be comfortable mingling with the best of them."

Of his three daughters, Miriam was the one to whom he felt closest. Emilia, the eldest, was exotic and talented. She had huge brown eyes and

curly chestnut hair that framed her darkish face, and she played the piano like Arturo Rubenstein. (Well, Gotlib conceded privately, maybe not exactly like Arturo Rubenstein.) Gotlib smiled at his firstborn child, and she smiled back at him.

Sara, the youngest, was pert and sassy. The beneficiary of the battles Gotlib had fought with Emilia and Miriam and lost, Sara was allowed to wear makeup at thirteen and go on overnights with the Girl Scouts of Antofagasta. Her sisters had wanted to do those things; he and Rebeca had said no but had wound up giving in. By the time Sara was a senior member of Antofagasta Troop 1034 and began wearing lipstick, her parents had stopped resisting. Even so, Sara had grown into a fairly well-behaved girl, although more spirited and stronger willed than her sisters. She had long, light brown hair that she refused to cut, although Rebeca said it looked messy, and a few barely-there freckles that she tried to cover with makeup, even though Gotlib said they were cute.

Miriam was taller and thinner than her sisters. She had soft, blond, shoulder-length hair and eyes whose irises were blue on the rim and amber within. Her facial structure was less than perfect, but Miriam had an incandescence that brightened a room. Gotlib felt her fingers knead and soothe the tight muscles of his neck, and knew that God had truly blessed him. It was, perhaps, too much to want to be a fireman, too.

Sara was speaking: "It's not the end of the world if you don't get in."

"She's right, of course, Papá," confirmed Miriam.

"Anyhow," said Emi, "if you don't make it this time, maybe somebody will nominate you again next year."

Gotlib basked in his children's love for a moment.

"You know," he said, shaking his head, "it gives me a funny feeling to think that at this very moment they may be talking about me. They may be deciding about me."

"Probably not," said Rebeca. "They probably decided hours ago."

But Rebeca was wrong. At the station house, Don Mauro had just presented Gotlib's name.

"Any discussion?"

"A good man," said Don Dionisio. "In spirit he's been one of us for a long time. Since he was a kid, really."

"Anything else?" prodded Don Mauro.

No one made a move to speak.

"Are you sure?"

Don Ricardo looked rather sour. He was getting hungry and he wanted to go home.

Don Héctor scratched his eyebrow out of boredom.

Don Ignacio shook his head, but said nothing.

Don Mauro waited in silence for someone to come forward. Don Agustín yawned. They had been at it for a long time.

"Then let's vote."

The men placed their ballots in the box. When they were done, Don Alejandro, the brigade secretary, read them aloud, one by one.

Gotlib had finished tea, but he and Miriam remained at the table talking. Rebeca sat with them a while, then got up to get her sewing; with three girls in the family, there was always something to mend. Teolinda was clearing the table. Sara and Emilia had gone upstairs, but bolted down when they heard a knock at the door.

Gotlib jumped up, then forced himself to sit back down. One of the servants would get it.

Virginia, Teolinda's niece, came into the room.

"Señor," she said, "there are two gentlemen here to see you."

"Who?" Gotlib's voice was controlled. He was making a great effort not to appear upset.

"Don Mauro and his son."

Gotib took a short, tight breath. He hadn't expected a visit. He had expected a telephone call.

"Have them come in," said Rebeca.

"I'll see them in my study," said Gotlib.

But Don Mauro was peeping through the dining room door.

It was an indecorous thing for the fire chief to do, and Gotlib was confused. But Don Mauro was grinning widely and the younger Mujica was bounding toward Gotlib as though he couldn't wait another instant. Mauro—the son—embraced Gotlib before a word was spoken.

"Congratulations, Ernesto," said Don Mauro.

"Congratulations, *compadre!* Welcome to the *bomberos!*" The younger Mauro's smile was even bigger and warmer than his father's.

Gotlib was fighting back tears, but Miriam was making no pretense to self-control. She was crying openly. Sara and Emilia were laughing.

"See, Papá?" giggled Sara. "What did I tell you?"

Emilia, then Sara, then Miriam kissed their father.

Rebeca was last of all.

Gotlib hugged his wife close as he turned to Don Mauro and his son.

He opened his mouth to speak, but his throat was tight. Finally he said, "Thank you . . . thank you . . ."

Rebeca was the first one to regain her composure.

"May I offer you some tea and *alfajores?*"

"Thank you, but we can't stay," said Don Mauro.

"Just a cup of tea?"

"All right, just a cup of tea."

Rebeca signaled Teolinda to bring clean cups and to refill the pot.

"Can you . . . can you tell me if there was a lot of discussion?" asked Gotlib.

"No," said Don Mauro. "There was no discussion."

"Everyone knows you, Ernesto. Christ, you've been hanging around the station since you were in short pants. You've always been a part of the *bomberos.* That's what they said—that you've always been one of us. It was unanimous."

"Unanimous! But didn't they mention . . . anything else?"

Father and son both looked puzzled.

"No," said the younger Mauro. "Nothing."

Rebeca felt a new surge of joy. She got up and went to help Teolinda with the tea. She did not want to cry in front of her guests.

Miriam got up, too, to keep from laughing. "Silly old Papá," she said to herself.

Gotlib smiled, but a new worry was gnawing at his brain.

"I wonder if they really wanted me," he said to Rebeca later, as he got ready for bed. "What I mean is, did they really want *me*, or did they just think a token Jewish name would look nice on the roster?"

Alcira in Yellows

Alicia Kozameh

To all those who,
with respect and fondness toward their origins,
emerge from themselves.

Cadmium yellow the sun at the end of the summer of 1958, a March stained with darkened blots, when in some part of her brain, in the process of understanding, Alcira has deposited the certainty, the conviction of her five years: *I can feel them, I feel all of them, they are five, five years they say I am completing, and I believe it.* Filtered by vapors ascending from chimneys, distanced from any possible abstraction, adding mustard-colored waves of heat to the industrial and mortal sky of Rosario, the air observes Alcira. It examines her closely, describes her for itself, and tries to understand her. It animates itself to question her and analyze her parts and return her intact to her origins. *Thanks*, Alcira, without alternatives, must feel, *thanks to this air I remain whole, thanks to the air that circulates, that comes and goes,* that wanders through the neighborhood of her five years, thanks to this air she can recognize herself, have a certain idea of herself, in spite of the ambivalences, in spite of the multiplicity of messages, of stories and signs.

Search, Alcira, between the dark and parallel lines that cross the sky from one corner to the other, *between those electrical cables that terrify me when the rain lets go but that move me inside and fill me with those desires to laugh, to shake myself with joy, because they are musical staffs, they are my score, the last one they bought for me; those electrical cables are a gigantic staff that surrounds me and spins around me, goes crazy and wraps me up, makes me dizzy; the cables carry within them the movement, the speed with which my ten fingers move on the piano; they put that madness into my hands*

and shake them, make them vomit up the music. The scores that Alcira loves because they are music, and the scores that are intolerable for her because they are the instrument that her piano teacher brandishes, waves, in order not to permit her to interpret her own melodies. The ones she invents in the middle of those nights in which not a single sound is heard.

Search, Alcira. She searches for moments, situations, in the sky of her neighborhood, in which there may appear some similarity with the words she hears each day: from her father's mouth, from her mother's eyes. With the food she eats and the food she enjoys. With the faces, almost always round, of her cousins. With her mother's insistence on bathing her portion of meat with several scoops of milk curd under the satisfied gaze of her father, and the tense and lowered eyelids of her grandmother, descending as if to neutralize offenses, place results at a distance, change the direction of thought, during the long supper on the long dining room table of her house.

Alcira searches between her two feet squeezed against the grooves of the wide sidewalk, the sidewalk extended between the shadows of the tall trees open to above, searches for *why, why did grandmother sink her finger covered with rings into my belly, near my belly button, and say to me a little in Spanish, a little in her Arabic of Aleppo, and another little bit in Yiddish: "You listen to me well, Alcira. The ridiculous ideas of your father, who is meshuggene, don't have to matter to you. They don't matter to you. You have to marry a Jew, do you understand? A Jew."* Alcira, without a reply. With a certain strength she scrutinized the eyes of the old lady; with more strength she followed the movements of the old ringed finger to be certain that it was not going to perforate her empty, defenseless stomach again, and she ran to the table, which was already laid.

And the following day she committed the error. The error of the word. She committed the error of those who have words at their disposal and use them: she approached her mother and asked her the meaning of the episode and the reason for her grandmother's so-lively interest. Alcira's mother, Raquel, very Raquel, all of her, and filled with fears, settled a dry and worried gaze on Alcira, like the gazes of people who have words but do not always use them, and slowly approached the father. And after a moment of doubt she decided to be honest with him, decided not to hide from him her daughter's ingenuousness or her mother's desires (although she left buried, compressed between the walls of some of her most personal orifices, her sentiments, secret but never forgotten), and she told him the story completely and in detail. She declared: "My mother told Alcira that when she grows up she has to marry a Jew. How is it possible

that she does not appreciate the concession you make, permitting her to visit us, to remain in this house for days? It seems that behind our backs she is trying to convince the child. What do you think about that?"

And Alcira's father certainly had a very clear opinion of the facts. He said to Raquel, the very much Raquel: "How do you think I am going to feel about that? This is all your fault. Your mother is trying to convince Alcira of this foolishness because you allow it. Because you are as Jewish as she is. Shrews, the two of you. Dirty Jews. That's what you are. Now get out of here before I grab the three of you and kick you out of this house."

Like tempera, the sun, thick, melting simultaneously over the entire city, all-powerful, infiltrating itself between the grooves, plugging the openings. Injecting itself into the breath of those who run desperately, of those who walk slowly, of those who wait patiently, and of those who sleep for just a few hours. Into the breath of the plants. Of the insects. Of the corpses, stretching out in a skinlike and powerful mantle of undetainable flows and energies swelling the distinct natures of the earthly cortex with vitality.

It's killing me, Alcira feels. What's killing me is the stuffing. That makes me think that the bulky gray object that lies motionless in the middle of the street, where cars pass every once in a while, is a dead cat or a very furry little dog, struck by a truck or a motorcycle. That's why I hate the trucks that carry stuffing for the mattress manufacturers and lose it along the way. Because my mind skips from thoughts of my grandmother and the Jewish husband to the fear of what the stupid stuffing might be instead of stuffing, and it's hard for me to return. But what I want is to think about what my grandmother said, with her finger covered with thick rings entering me through my belly button, inserting itself where all the food is gathered and going down through what my mother calls the intestines, which is where all the caca is waiting to come out. My grandmother's finger, growing longer and coming out with the caca when I go to the bathroom, although I don't know what would happen, because either she jerks her hand back and takes it out and afterward washes it, I mean, before she begins to cook my mahmules *and my* mehche uaraa enab, *or else my grandmother's arm and head and body enter also, and then, just like that, all at once, she falls into the toilet.*

What can she have meant with that business of the Jewish husband? Better that she doesn't fall into the toilet, because she is good, my grandmother, and sometimes it seems to me that I love her.

The air, which still observes her and examines her closely, the winds of Rosario and its outskirts exerting pressures on the every day more ample

surfaces of Alcira's torso. Of her arms. Of her feet, which hold more weight and too much mental turmoil, when, more or less in the winter of 1965, Alcira was battling with her more or less twelve years, and the different words of her father distributing themselves, penetrating into the smallest crevice, like the sun, solid and persistent, chrome yellow, exhausting. Her father hurling his words at her: "This girl is changing schools right now. You're taking her out of public school and enrolling her with the nuns. Today. And as a boarder. Board-er. I won't hear of her leaving every day. From Monday to Friday, boarding. This very day."

And another voice, the voice of the every day more Raquel, ascertaining quietly, "And now what's the matter? Why is she going to go to Catholic school, and on top of everything, as a boarder?"

And the exasperation of that father, that father and not another, *why not another, why isn't it possible to exchange a father for one more suitable to the needs of each child*, sinking into her pores and hardening itself like cement, paralyzing any intention of flight, dismissing: "Because I say so. Because every visit of this old woman is the same story. She comes here to meddle in our private life, to try to change the decisions we made years ago. She doesn't understand that you were married in the Catholic Church to a Christian. They disowned you, they forbade you to enter your house forever, they wished that all your children would die or be born sick; they shouted this in your face. That family is no longer your family. You are a Christian, not a Jew. There are no Jews in this house. Alcira is baptized. She is a Catholic. But of course, the old lady insists. I heard her talking with Alcira in the kitchen, repeating that shit about having to marry a Jew. Why, tell me that? So they will insult her in the street? So they will shout 'dirty Jew,' which is, after all, what you and your mother are? This is not a country for Jews. Let the Jews look for another place. My daughter is not a Jew. And tomorrow she is changing schools, so there will be no doubt. And you'll speak to the nuns so they will make her take communion and give her a bed. And don't come to me saying that you take communion at eight. You can take it at any age. Leave now and register her. Now."

And a thread waving in the air, in front of Raquel's face, which is the succession of her words: "And you, since when are you a believer? From the day I met you I've heard you say you don't believe in God. What has turned you into such a practicing Catholic all of a sudden? I think the only thing you want is to humiliate us all. You ought to be a little more strict, so much strictness are you demanding of others, and follow what the

Greek Orthodox Church, your family's church, commands you. And leave others in peace."

And waving in front of Alcira's father's face, not a thread, but a rope, which is the succession of his words: "I want them to let us live. That's what I want. I don't want anyone to point at us. I don't want anyone to consider us different. We are already the anti-Peronists of the neighborhood. We don't need anything more to be the target of all these ignorant fools. And on top of everything else, you, playing at being a Jew. Get out of my sight, will you?"

They have continued conforming, reorganizing the powers, the counterposed forces, in the air that Alcira still breathes. Each time with bronchial tubes more blocked, with asthmatic sparkles in her big eyes, which begin to clamor for fresh air. Air less populated with caustic, divisive sounds. Air without any irritating particles, air that does not produce excessive phlegm in the respiratory passages, in the souls. Air only for Alcira. That only Alcira can breathe. On a yellow afternoon of that winter. Chrome sun.

That's how it seems to me. It seems to me that a person is not what others decide. You are what you are. If I was born with chestnut-colored hair, filled with curls, why do there exist people who would do anything so that I would become a straight-haired blond? What happens if the grandson of the lady on the corner, who everyone says is Muslim, one day invites me to go out? What is my grandmother going to say? And my father, what is he going to do? Are they going to wish me dead? Are they going to kill me? Because it seems to be that a person who is neither this nor that is nothing. Or maybe, is no one. And whoever is no one is dead. Or something like that. At least that is what my mother's father told her when he found out that the reason she had escaped from the house was that she was planning to get married the following day to a goy: from that moment on, she was no one. She was nothing. And that's why, as far as he and his whole family were concerned, she was dead.

When you are twenty years old in a year like 1973 in Argentina, when what you have is a country inundated with social injustice, a city with ocher skies, a Semitic-Judeo-anti-Semitic family, a sad experience of long adolescent years among nuns who wash their hands of reality and live in repression, in hypocrisy, and in resentment, some very well-known artistic inclinations and a sense of justice that grows stronger every day; you are the only thing you ought to be: a young person sensitive to everything and totally prepared to surrender even your life in pursuit of a country, a world, that is equitable and just. Or more or less that.

The House of Memory

The sun, ocher, the skies of the first half of the seventies in the cities, in the suffocating crowds, in the exterior and interior deserts, in the mountains. Inflammable and ocher, lucid and open to the great struggle. And to the illusion of possible survival. The sun.

You will always have to defend something. That is why we are here. We exist. Because there is always someone who needs to take something from another to protect what he has or to add something to his wealth.

Defending. That idea invades my mind; defending, it invades me, spreads out in me. I feel it take charge of me and it does me good. Defending what keeps me in a certain space in this world. Defending the right to follow my impulses toward Edgardo Fridman, who is two years older than I and has such green eyes that I cannot stop from staring. Defending my right to him without my father repeating the same old story he has told so many times before, always so redundant, and without him slapping me in the face, shouting, "You are not a Jew, and you're not going to get involved with that dirty Jew." The sun ocher, low, each time lower, and about to turn itself upside down on the world and suffocate it gladly with breaths of mustard. Of *sambatyon.*[1] Of mud. Taking refuge and solidifying itself in all the orifices forever.

If Edgardo were the great-grandson of Siddhartha Gautama I would feel the same. When I met him and liked him, I didn't know anything about him. What's the difference? We talked about it, and I told him the truth: I am an atheist. I don't see any god anywhere, nor am I looking for one. Neither is he. What am I? A human being. And I have the impression that that is enough. Our responsibilities are myriad, and it doesn't seem to me that all the energies we have at our disposal ought to be invested in beating children to avoid their marrying someone of one or another religion. It doesn't seem to me. That fanaticism. As if they had a magnet in some zone of the body and they moved to the rhythm of the movement of another. They don't use the power of reason to take a step aside, to separate themselves, to observe their surroundings. To ask themselves if the reasons why they moved to that rhythm were their own or whether they reached them from another direction. To question themselves about that enigmatic authority that decides for them to whom they belong. They don't question themselves. I don't know if they give themselves a reply.

I feel like crying.

What is the difference between aiding a Jew in an accident and aiding a Buddhist? I need an explanation. But it is not within my family that I am going to find that response. In myself. Only in myself am I going to find it. And I have it: there is no difference. And returning over and over to the subject is squandering the few minutes we have at our disposal in this life. That never return.

I certainly feel that there might be other differences. It would be much more difficult for me to aid an Argentine or Chilean or Uruguayan soldier, whether or not he has tortured or assassinated any of my friends with his own hands. There is where I live the contrasts. There is where, for me, things begin. Where the distinct roads begin, that each one opts to take or not. The road toward destroying one's peers or toward contributing to their basic joy of being alive. Toward being in favor of or toward being against humanity. Why am I going to want to favor those who deprive others of food, of freedom, or of life?

There is a lot of sense in the newspapers' report that more than 40 percent of the Left in this country is of Jewish origin. Why not, I ask myself? Opposing these military men means fighting against a repetition of the Holocaust. Of course they, the oh, so prolific statistics, are the least subtle manner the authorities have of establishing the two targets, two in one, of the repression that is approaching.

It overwhelms me to feel positive toward my people, to have that clarity embracing me. And it liberates me not to have any uncertainty about what the religious origin of my militant companions might be. Nor that of any of the millions of inhabitants of this country for whom I seek equality so much. For whom so many of us seek it.

I need to breathe deeply. Deeply. So that the air puts pressure on my esophagus. And my stomach. My organs, the pieces of my body. My very own.

Ocher the yellow that invades and defines everything. Not cadmium, not chrome. The years accelerate the speeds, and existence is saturated with history.

"In this house we eat pork. Po-ork. And we mix it with milk. Mi-ilk. And whoever doesn't want to work on Saturdays is a bum. Bu-um. And if you don't like it, go back to your family. No one is forcing you to remain here. And don't think that I am so stupid as to not realize that what you are hoping for most fervently in what remains of your life is for me to die, so that you can go running off to the synagogue with your sisters. Jew. That's what you are: a Jew."

The eternally Raquel absorbs the sounds, the timbres going up and down, hoarsened by the emphysema from which the words spurt forth. She no longer questions: "Since when are you a practicing Catholic?" She no longer asks questions like that. Or like others. But she absorbs, she internalizes the sounds, in which the old stubbornness makes itself tangible. And she knows that the words that pile up and stifle themselves at the end of the sentence and at the sides of her half-opened mouth must make some sense.

Terra sienna, the sky that Alcira does not have the possibility of questioning. The basement of the prison fades everything to sepia, to browns that

long for those old yellows, those jaundiced tones of the afternoon. Of the afternoons of unchanging Rosario, city with sulphurous clouds, industrial, never completely free. The Rosario saturated with family, filled with the grandmother with golden rings. The Rosario replete with insults and demands.

Toasted *terra sienna*, the air that presses against the physical surfaces of Alcira, that examines her closely, observes her, describes her and tries to understand her, that analyzes her parts, that returns her, intact, to her origins. The air that gives her form and places her in front of herself. And puts her in front of the past, which is neither more nor less than the present. The prison of her twenty-two years, the prison of her five, and the prison of her ten. And always, then and now, the same necessity of leaping toward the unforeseen and freeing herself. The sepia air of closed dampnesses and circular motions gives her form in the space of the cell and tries to impose on her the memories, images, sometimes mutilated, of her history. Of a long and meticulous film that has lasted twenty-two years now, without cuts and without ambiguities. Of an unmistakable faithfulness toward its initial model, toward the first figure of the series on a long paper, folded and overlapping, cut out with exactitude and painstaking care, so that all the figures of the frieze are maintained identical and united.

It is so repetitive, the experience is different and the same every day; there is something like a commandment in so many minds, you ought to belong to someone, to something, it is necessary to be part of a group. The idea makes me afraid. And it seduces me. But I want to be able to bring about my independence. And have the inner strength to take a leap and break away, without having disappeared from history, for that reason. And from outside, to observe my movements, my growing insanity, my mastery. I want to be myself and I want to be she, I want to be the one to whom I speak every day, and who is my you, my she, and my self.

And who else am I? More or less, besides being Alcira, I am the obsessive writer, the curious one, the one determined to try for justice, the delirious, the crazy, the impossible, the obstinate, and the curly-haired one. I am whoever I want to be. And I am Alcira.

The darkened air of the cell observes her, divides her in sections, examines her closely, and does not forget the order in which she was connected in the beginning. It studies every element that comprises her, introduces itself into her smallest corners. It analyzes her, reads her, interprets her. It reorganizes her in a different order, observes her from a distance. It attempts very diverse ways, and none seems to give satisfaction. It seems

to think profoundly. Goes on rejecting, one by one, all the options. Searches. It's trying to find her eyes. And it places them: brown and lively. And it begins the reassembly of her parts. The reconstruction in all its details. Which continues returning Alcira, in tones of yellow, to her genuine and complete forms.

Translated from the Spanish by Roberta Gordenstein

1. *Sambatyon* is, in Jewish folklore, a river that seethes with hot stones every day but the Sabbath.

Exotic Birds

Reina Roffé

During the bitterest days of my European exile, I turn to the photo album where I keep, along with more recent memories, a few images from my childhood—images that enlarged and corrected, come back to me in dreams and in disturbing moments of insomnia. That is when I see the child I was and the people I loved, and when my first and perhaps only home comes clearly into view. In that house, as if on stage or in a boxing ring, everyone defended his or her own territory with blood, sweat, and tears. Aunt Reche, however, seemed to stay behind the scenes: she didn't want to fight over the space; she wanted to leave it. I secretly shared her desire. We both believed that beyond the walls of that house a kind of salvation awaited us.

Aunt Reche waited for several years, passing up many incidents that would have given her more than enough reason to leave, until she finally found the right opportunity. One never knows when a dead branch will sprout flowers. In fact, I never did find out how that particular argument started in the kitchen, the epicenter of all the daily quarrels. I am convinced that it was nothing serious because only a few words and shouts were exchanged, but it was the drop that made the glass overflow.

I remember watching a bird trying to fly across the patio in the oblique drizzle that had been falling since morning, when I heard a clear, forceful voice:

"I'm leaving for good."

After making the announcement, Aunt Reche ran through the hallway heading toward the stairs.

She was finally running from the house and from herself. What was she like? What had she been like just moments before some alien power took

over and put her in motion? That motion was now suspended in its own impulse, in the fury of escaping, in her legs, her feet, her step, in the slight sway of her entire body.

She was a tired woman. Her tiredness was not new, it was as much a part of her as was her pale skin, her slight smile, and the eyes that revealed her disgust, her tedium, the smothered cry, and the conviction that nothing was worthwhile.

When she was little she used to walk along the dirt streets of a pretentiously named town in the province of Santa Fe, until she reached the train station where she would hide and dream of getting on the train that would take her to Buenos Aires. However, when the family finally did move to the capital, she was interested only in the port where the Sephardic Jews from Morocco used to disembark, among them her own young parents, who arrived at the beginning of the century.

As I remember her, I find it difficult to attribute her permanent air of melancholy to her nomadic appearance (she always seemed to be somewhere else). None of the stories about her provides a reason to justify her absence, the withdrawal into herself that made her invisible to everyone else.

No one ever saw her. Her apprenticeship for becoming invisible must have started very early, when she was still a child and spent long hours following the paths of the ants along the cracks in the flagstones. There must have been something in her infancy, in the solitude of her childhood days. But in her case, it was a different kind of solitude, one without which nothing was possible for her.

In the Jobson-Vera mansion, where she was born around 1925, her parents and siblings ignored her, not because they didn't love her, but because of her determination to be ignored, to become a colorless spot, an imperceptible filigree on the floor or on the walls. The teachers used to give her very high grades in school, but they complained that she was like an extension of the bench she occupied in the classroom: dull, quiet, doing what was required.

She was compliant. I know she was especially dedicated to the Friday afternoon chore she assumed when she still lived in the small town. Lacking a synagogue, the Sephardic community of Jobson, consisting of three or four families at that time, had improvised a prayer room in the back room of the store that belonged to her father, the grandfather that I never met. Seldom did the ten men needed for the rabbi to begin the cer-

emony appear. Aunt Reche had the job of going in search of those who were missing. She didn't understand this law but, although I can imagine her indignation at the fact that women's presence didn't count, I am convinced that she took her weekly duty very seriously. According to her older sister, who never kept secrets for her, once when Aunt Reche couldn't find the tenth man, she decided to take his place. She put on the cast-off clothes of the men of the house, covered her blossoming curves with a large coat, greased down her hair, put on a yarmulke, and took her place next to the other men.

She went unnoticed on that occasion and also again at the age of twenty, when she repeated the feat, needlessly, in the temple on Piedras Street in Buenos Aires, no less, which was always full. These are the only mischievous things or transgressions she is known to have committed. Later on she lost interest in everything and decided to act like a robot whose actions were preprogramed.

And in spite of that, her heart beat quickly. Even today I believe I can hear her rapid, furious puffing on the day she ran toward the stairs with the intention of reaching the last door of the house. I have her image frozen in my memory: Aunt Reche moving against a cobalt blue background; Aunt Reche who felt emotions, who felt love and anger although she was submerged in death. Certainly she expected more than anyone else did. How much more? A little more affection, a little more tolerance, the little extra promised by the lottery, the illusory bonuses of the business of life? I suspect that the magnitude of what she hoped for had become a burden, all out of proportion to what she could bear.

From there, perhaps, came her sleepless nights and the premature knowledge of failure and sorrow—a primordial, pre-existing, unyielding sorrow that nevertheless made her rebel against her own knowledge that life was only life passing by. Could her relentless, barren insomnia have been the cause of these impressions? How could she fill the void, flirt with the darkness without going crazy with the thought—first innocent and then obsessive—that all effort was in vain, that love was a meaningless fiction, nothing more than an et cetera that justified all the theories that popular philosophy at once proposed and rejected in sayings, proverbs, songs, and movies. The only real connection for her was the tick-tock of the clocks, the predictable church bells, the emergency sirens, the cat fight on the roof, the pulse of the night pounding in her head.

Her silence also added to her invisibility. Words left her mouth with great difficulty. She pronounced them one by one in a low voice, with

resistance and with a savage blush on her pale cheeks that made people very uncomfortable. For Aunt Reche words must have sounded worn out before being spoken, trivial and unnecessary. She didn't say words, she threatened to say them; in truth, they became entangled on the tip of her tongue and turned against her in an interior mumble.

The few people who could see and hear her felt little more than a platonic veneration toward her. There were never any rumors about her being in love or having a lover; she maintained her virginity intact.

In my memory and in the photos Aunt Reche seems as attractive as most of the girls of her time and social class. What's more, between the age of twenty and thirty she radiated a surprising charm that made her stand out from the prettiest girls. Perhaps in the subtlety of her ways and in her depths there was a dissuasive touch that intimidated the men, that impeded their approach, and dissolved their initiative. Those who might have wanted her quickly exchanged desire for respect.

It was a respect she probably longed for in a different order of things: in her everyday negotiations, in the most immediate reality which, to her dismay, was hostile and dull. Everything affected her, leaving its mark on her like a whiplash: the ferocity of her mother, who called her a piece of meat, the domineering men of the house, her sisters' selfishness, the neighbors' stupidity, the intolerance of certain members of the community. She didn't cry because she knew it was useless, but she acknowledged receipt with a tangible desperation. If someone had extended a hand toward her, they would have felt the tense net in which she was wrapped.

I can imagine, based on my own experience, that it was in the darkest hours, the hours of insomnia and lucidity, that all the pieces joined together to form the jungle where the trees were in flames and the beasts were screeching as if it were the end of the world. And so the day's smallest discomfort became a sharp pain. By the time night had ended, all of this anguish had left her empty, unable to share her feelings with anyone. She was uninhabited, but not dead, and that was her worst defeat.

There was a time when she did want to live like everyone else. They say that she looked for a job, begging her parents to let her work outside of the home. They permitted it; she was already twenty-five and they knew that she would be an old maid. I can imagine her on the bus, watching tired people blissfully dozing in their seats. How she would have loved to change places with the fat woman whose nostrils quivered from her heavy breathing as her energy yielded to the deep, refreshing sleep that would allow her to wake up smiling like a baby.

A pat on the shoulder, followed by a kind of envy of the lightness with which others went through life, would awaken in her the need for intense physical activity. They say that she would often walk thirty blocks to work. In the office she did her own work and that of two or three colleagues. She ate in the noisiest bars so that the chatter, the exuberant gestures and voices, the simple, spontaneous happiness flowing from the other customers would stick to her bones and break her silence. The noise enlivened her, made her eardrums tingle, her bones vibrate, her tongue click, her teeth chatter until she exploded within, mute, more alone, more abandoned than before. Some days she would end up exhausted. But she slept little; three hours was a major accomplishment. And the following morning she would be doubly tired—from her natural fatigue and from the extra physical exhaustion—thus becoming even more a phantom figure.

There was no solution. An unfailing inversion of values was at work in her. Every project she took on in an attempt to be like other people went in the opposite direction, it went astray. I am sure that with time she learned to laugh at herself, which perhaps afforded her the only intimate satisfaction that she was capable of fully enjoying. Although she was able to enjoy her own personality, which her family had declared incurable, her comings and goings began to assume the self-assurance of a saint. Rather than a transformation, it was the full deployment of the dominant traits of her temperament. Her calm manners, so habitual in her, became static. Her naturally white complexion took on a porcelain look. She seemed sculpted in marble or plaster or, more precisely, glass. Because of this transparency, she truly looked like an image carved in crystal, through which other bodies were visible in the light, as if she were an open window. When someone looked and spoke to her, they didn't address her, but rather the person behind her.

On one occasion—Aunt Reche told me this herself—she saw her younger sister in the street and, believing she was waving at her, responded by waving back, but her sister walked by without recognizing her, to meet someone else. The episode made her laugh to herself, a laugh she swallowed like a bittersweet morsel. The fact that she was still invisible at the age of forty, even when she did not want to be, tasted like a liberating elixir on the one hand (she could pass by imperceptibly like a fly's eyelash and laugh at everyone), but, on the other hand, it was like the aftertaste of the poison that had made her insignificant, like a flash that disappears at the speed of death.

Exotic Birds

Death? She showed some sparks of life at times, although they only lasted as long as a falling star. Because that day, when her mother again told her that she was nothing but a piece of meat, and Aunt Reche answered that she was leaving for good, her entire body shook with a flourishing vehemence. She ran through the hallway toward the stairs, a crucial area of the house where all the profound arguments and the most violent rejoicing took place. At that instant the steps that led to the street, as I remember them, stood out from the rest of the house like a redeeming space of arrival and departure.

It was raining, and near the back of the house a bird was flying over the patio. Aunt Reche had reached the foyer and then the first step without losing her courage. I was trying to push her along for her sake and for my own. But she needed to catch her breath on the landing. This brief pause before opening the screen door and going down to the main door stopped her, stopped her definitively.

Perhaps during that decisive moment of hesitation it occurred to her that it was better to stay with her own than to risk living among strangers. The familiar solitude had a tone less desolate than the solitude of exile. Or maybe she thought that it really didn't matter where and with whom she lived: a woman who resides only in her private world is a stranger for everyone, everywhere.

As she retraced her steps, Aunt Reche was still trembling, but she possessed the serenity of a surrender to her own battle, as if she had accepted a verdict, as if she had had a revelation. Her look was that of a game warden surveying exotic birds.

<div style="text-align:right">Translated from the Spanish by Margaret Stanton</div>

Kaddish

Graciela Safranchik

It's Reina who's coming over here. She does it so slowly that she seems to be stopping with each step. She brushes her cheek against mine, and we're so close now, one woman to another, that I can see the tiny wrinkles around her eyes. I also smell the thin, delicate perfume that hovers, ever so slightly, over her own scent, the scent of a mature woman. She murmurs something that I don't manage to understand, something about fate, and she takes me by the hand.

She too will return, with the others, to the center of the room. From there she'll look at me, she'll say, My mother is old, now what are we going to do with this old woman? And as soon as she can she'll forget me again.

Reina. My younger daughter. When did I stop wondering, What kind of woman is this, this daughter of mine?

Reina drops my hand. She lets it fall into my lap. Maybe she's surprised by this small, dead weight that she's just cast aside, which offers no resistance, because she shudders and looks away. It's cold, Mama, you should rest awhile, she tells me. She offers me a coat, a shawl: she wants to cover me up. She tries to pull her arm over my shoulders, but something stops her. The horror, I think. Let's hug Mama, cover her up, quick, she's cold. What will we ever do with her?

It's all right, dear, I tell her. It's been years and years now that my hands have been getting cold. It's age, I tell her.

Then I look directly into her eyes. I surprise her.

I'll be back, dear, Reina says, and finally she leaves me and joins the others, completing that close-knit, homogenous group of grown-ups who watch me from the middle of the room. All my children.

Kaddish

You have to keep watch over the corpse all night, the coffin closed, draped in the ritual black cloth.

Then the funeral procession. The widow and children first, then the rest of the family, friends, and neighbors.

You have to go to the cemetery and let others wash the body, everyone quiet by the gates of the garden where the tombstones bloom like flowers, they bloom beautifully, I think. And the men lift the coffin, various men, among whom are my sons.

Maybe they will be the ones to bring it to its assigned place. I can't remember this particular detail. Then they sing. A voice intones the familiar melody that will start the funeral cortege and stop by the open grave. The sons will say their prayer and tear their clothes just as the ground has been torn to receive him, their father. We will hear their chanting, in an avalanche. One chant or song will build on another and another in a measured counterpoint, like the complaint of a child who's been left irremediably alone.

We'll hug each other. Someone will come for me. Together we'll all get into the black automobiles. Other cars will come behind ours, in a procession. We'll return to the house.

There all the mirrors will still be covered.

She's put on all her jewelry—her rings, her earrings, the pearl necklace.

She's decked out in all her most costly things, her best dress, fur coat, patent leather shoes.

Anyone would say that she's about to flee, or that she's ready for a party.

She has also tinted her hair with a blue rinse that fills her face with shadows when she lowers her head. She still has a beautiful head, it's perfect, short hair scrupulously trimmed from her collar.

She's as old as anyone can get, but she nevertheless seems solid, like a building that could have been there forever. We're used to seeing her like this, it's been ages that she's looked just like herself. But Mama is old, so old that we don't know what to do with her. How to take care of her now, I mean. How to help her die without life touching her ever again, so that no other pain ever reaches her.

So many years alongside Papa and now, so calm, so fresh. Maybe she doesn't understand what's happening, not yet. It's even possible that she's happy to have us all together. Her children. Poor thing, how very sad.

The House of Memory

I take her hands. It's cold, Mama, I tell her. Your hands are icy. Can I get you a coat, a shawl? I hug her and she suddenly looks at me, right in the eyes, like a bird.

Why am I feeling this terrible shame?

It's enough to go through the door, to get the picture.

A lot of grown-ups, horrified by a dead man's coffin. And that old woman, illuminated in a corner, holding the hands of the prettiest daughter, like someone carrying a flower that could break at any time.

I hear a radio, or the flooded engine of a car. What else sounds like that?

My eyes seek out my brother who roams the room like a master of ceremonies. Seeing me, he smiles, makes faces, and shrugs his shoulders.

If he'd let me take his hand again, returning to the place where the living speak and touch, I'd go to him, my brother. But I'm planted like a tree at the door, and I can't go back or move anywhere, for that matter.

When we were little, he'd plop down on all fours, saying, Up, Sahib! Climb onto the elephant! I'd clamber on and raise my arm. Opening and closing my fist, I'd make the trunk, while he produced strange noises with his mouth.

Sometimes we'd run through the whole house like that, him shouting, me holding onto his hair. Every so often, Mama would watch us, alert, raising her eyes from her book, with such disapproval that her eyebrows, knitted together, would form a long, hard wand.

Now he looks at her tenderly. He doesn't seem ashamed to see her there, cornered, like an insect.

No matter how long someone's been alive, memory is always an amazing thing. Ultimately, everything settles down in a single place, as if we were looking at a photo album.

It's impossible to know where we were, when we stopped to catch a moment. Why that moment and not another? It's like reading stories, I think. In the beginning we fly behind the action. Then it doesn't matter, the eyes alight at random; everything's become confused, upside down, inside out, no difference.

Now I remember my father, playing on the bluff above a river. I don't know if it really happened. I mean, I don't know if I really did see my father there, if I shouted, Be careful, you could fall.

Kaddish

Maybe I'm confused, and it was a movie, or a photograph someone else took.

I imagine a noise, a loud buzz, the water maybe; it's as if I were really remembering it. There's my father, smiling at me. I look at him and yell, Be careful, you could fall into the river.

At this very moment I want to cry for him. For my father, who died more than fifty years ago. Not for my dead father, but for the young man in the photograph, who smiles and stretches out his hand as if he were trying to keep his balance, as if he had suddenly discovered that he was about to fall.

I don't know if I shout to him that it's dangerous, or maybe he's the one who's shouting, telling me not to come any closer.

Like this other image that returns again and again today. So close, of course, but so slow that it takes the course of a lifetime to reach me.

He's still in bed. I hear his labored breathing. He breathes with great difficulty and his wheezing grows louder. It's so loud that it shakes the room. It's the death rattle, I tell myself, I've just understood it.

Standing, facing the bars of the hospital bed, I look at him. The white bedspread ripples, barely tracing the outlines of a body consumed by illness. He is all shriveled, but his feet are growing. I can see them clearly, positioned here in front of me.

I throw myself on his feet, trying to stop them: they are growing so much I think they make him look really ridiculous. Then my older son pulls me away. He walks around the bed and approaches his father, holding the old razor in his hand.

He's going to kill him, I shout.

Time has passed, it's some other moment. My son is sharpening the razor against a strop of worn-out leather, he's humming something. He's crazy, I think. My son has gone mad.

I see how he slowly, scrupulously covers his father's face with a white mask. He covers his face with foam. Only the tiny hollow of a mouth remains, from which the maddening noise of death escapes. He'll be suffocated, suffocated, suffocated.

I don't fall because I am still standing by the bars of the bed, next to those feet. From there I suddenly see two strange men busy with their own ritual.

An old man is dying, resounding like thunder, and the other one, in shirtsleeves, is shaving his father for the last time as if there were nothing else to do in this life.

What's this agitated breaking that I feel so close by, so near? God! I'm the one, the woman who's suffocating! I breathe, I breathe. I have to control my body. I withdraw into myself. I sweat, tremble, throb, what a racket, what a lot of noise, of smells, all packed into me, under pressure. I'm going to explode. Up, Sahib! Can they hear me? How crazy. I have to control myself. It always happens this way, and when it doesn't, when we want to intervene, to say, now I'm going to breathe, Now I'm going to move this way, everything turns out badly, and I have to forget, forget, no one is listening.

It happened before, on the train. I thought I was supposed to wait for Reina at the station. I didn't want to take the car. There were so many people squeezed together into the aisles that you couldn't breathe. I wanted a cigarette so badly, it was torturing me, my hands trembling. I was suffocating. I'm going to die, I thought, this very day.

I tried to make myself comfortable, but the mass of bodies was packed in tighter and tighter. Then I remembered the mail car, that it should be close by. I began pushing with all my strength, moving in that direction, but with so much difficulty that I squeezed between legs and scrunched-up arms, until I finally came to the open car.

There were so few of us, you could see the dust floating in the sunlight. I lit a cigarette, inhaled, and the smoke burned my throat. I could feel the rumbling of the train. It sounded different from there, like the noise of water scouring rocks, tree trunks, things that don't float and that pound surfaces with a dry muffled thud. Like drums.

The guard was next to me, an enormous bulk in his dirty uniform.

Rigid against the closed door, he seemed self-absorbed, off somewhere else. He's as a bored as I am, I said to myself.

I took a better look at him. The clear outline of his toes pushed against the dead leather of his shoes. He had his hand in the pocket where he kept a ticket-puncher. I heard him click it, again and again, a dry, insistent click that he accompanied with convulsive shoulder movements. He'd planted himself there, as if he were expecting to trap a criminal and had forgotten about it for the moment.

Standing nearby, a boy stared at him. His face was twisted, ready to scream, his mouth half open and his crazy man's eyes glued to the guard's pocket. I couldn't resist the compulsion to reproduce his expression with my own mouth, until my jaws ached.

The boy suddenly turned toward the guard and showed him a ticket

no one had asked to see. He looked at him, his forehead so furrowed that an infinite number of wrinkles were outlined, like on a fetus. I heard a dog bark, the wheels clacking against the tracks, the water flow, the drum. The jolting movements shook me. The boy had disappeared and the guard, who hadn't moved one centimeter from his spot, dangled the ticket-puncher from a finger, like a trophy.

The shadows of the railyard buildings began filtering, in streaks, into the car. We were arriving. Once again light, noise. I walked like a robot to the central hall. There was Reina. A world of people milled about, close by, without crossing the imaginary circle that contained her, like the spotlight that follows the acrobat across the circus ring. She hadn't changed in all these years. She was wearing a long skirt that billowed with the wind and then glued itself back against her body, dissolving. It was like a blue sail held up by her hand on her waist, her gesture so slight that the patterned cloth seemed a watery reflection.

My heart jumped. I could hear the commotion on the railway platforms, the screech of the locomotive, the constant hammering of the wheels and pistons. Here I was, confused by the magic of the dress that clothed and unclothed my sister's innocent body. She was looking off into the distance, toward some other spot. I wanted to call out to her, but then I discovered the sketch unfolding on the skirt. Against the blue fabric, stretched out, I saw bodies and more bodies, with soot-blackened faces and rounded, uplifted eyes, watching.

They were prisoners, remains snatched from an old silent movie or from a scene by George Grosz. Someone shouted my name, Judith, and the skirt came toward me, unstoppable; it took me by the neck and hung onto my life, once again, like a prison term.

These rooms where we keep watch over our dead have the atmosphere of a hotel or a station.

People stir up words; they move predictable images. If you let them do that, there's nothing else, they'll all be the same. That's why I only look at what's inevitable, it's the only thing that sometimes reveals who we are. That's how I learned to recognize my children, too. Smoke signals, fragments. In the world I come from, many came to this conclusion: humanity has died.

One can learn to read fragments. This is possible. Everything else, at my age, is pointless.

The House of Memory

Humanity, humanity: what an illusion. We used to believe that we could believe in ourselves. Then it came to an end: the gods, the teachers, the victims. It's pure chance. Humanity came to an end, that's all. I mean, death is something that employees administer. A human being lives, keeps apart, shares, tries to get attention, and today, here he is, jammed into a coffin and surrounded by a bunch of people saying a lucky thing it's his turn. It'll be the poorer ones next time, the oldest ones, thank God there are others, others even older than I am. That woman who's collapsed in her chair, for example. She'll go, take our place. It'll be her turn first.

Everything's decided beforehand. A place assigned from far away, in no-man's land, one name after another, all in rows, we'll count on our fingers.

But it's not so easy to predict, today this one, tomorrow that one, and they know it. The inevitable also plots torturous pathways. This is just what I like to see. The pieces that never fit so well that we can think finally we've got everything in order.

Here comes my son Jonas. Now the place is packed. They must all be doctors, I'd recognize them with my eyes closed. They accumulate their self-assurance like prophets, like crazy men. Even Jonas, who wanted to be different, a homeopath. He's still poking around in his wizard's book, to come up with the perfect, the right combination.

Jonas brings the bitter metallic smell of the street. He says it's raining; the rain is hellish. Not much is happening inside. We don't know if it's raining, for example. Here, death has brought us all together, in one place. To get it over with, that's what we came for. To get it over with and then show, right away, how life goes on even with the grief, even with the tears. May the ritual of grief show us the way, with each of its prescribed steps. Still, it really doesn't matter how, someone always knows what to do from one moment to the next.

With the rain, Jonas says, everything will be ruined. He's satisfied that, in his own way, he's found something to communicate, something to keep himself busy.

He arranges the procession's order, determines the order of kinship, takes care of the bill, because he's discovered that his father hasn't left him anything else to deal with. No tomb, no wound. His father took care of everything before he collapsed. His place in the cemetery, even mine, too.

And although he might dispute it, Jonas, my firstborn, carries the only name and the only position possible, the one his father loved.

Kaddish

Now he worries about the umbrellas, about all the mud. There's nothing else for him to worry about. He runs to the window, pushes the others aside, looks out. There he can come into contact with certainty, with what happens in a determined manner, with what can be sorted out or controlled. Natural phenomena.

Since time began, that's something we can still busy ourselves with: the end of night, rain bursting from the sky, what we like to call time.

On his way, he encounters Judith. She can't move. She's anchored there, waiting to be chosen once again. And it's Jonas who takes her by the arm, my poor child, he says something to her, he makes her laugh against her will, like an idiot. She has her mouth open, gasping. She hopes her brother will soon disappear, that all of us will disappear.

May they die, may they all die. That's what Judith says, suspended there like a scarecrow, like a figure from the Annunciation. Nevertheless, she doesn't stop laughing.

It hasn't gone well for her, it's no easier for her. My place is the one she still fights for. Only Rudy, sweet Rudy, the one with the small hands, can save her from dying, drowned in hatred.

He'll go put himself in front of her, burnished like a mirror; he will intervene between Judith and her old mother, between Judith and her beautiful sister, and he'll love all of us women just the same.

Reina is the only one who doesn't know anything about anything. She keeps sliding along, as if she were a ballerina on a polished floor. Anyone would adore her perfect, well-ordered body, offered. Nevertheless, Reina is precisely the one who most resists.

How could she escape from herself when everyone is ready to save her, to let her die.

Sometimes I think I've always known. Before they were born, from the very moment I loved him and knew I was loved. I had to give him these children, which he loved, in order, one after the other. I had to resign myself to looking at the inevitable.

I think, It's no small matter after all. What more could a woman from the world I come from take for herself? Hardly anything, hardly anything at all. A place on the sidelines. I work as tightrope walker or as worm: there's no big gap, no great difference. Depending on how one looks at it, the glint of the embroidery needle can be like that of that of the scalpel.

Suddenly it comes to me. I'm talking like him.

It's just that we've lived so many years together. Now there's not much

left of me, just the little bit of myself that I could steal from him.

I demand attention, too. I knead a bit of life, like a bread crumb, grimy, but eager.

In a show of works by prisoners, I've seen incredible things done with pieces of bread. This is our art, perhaps, that survives.

I knew it earlier, when I tried to write in secret, when I was raising children, when I was keeping house. For centuries and centuries the steadfast resentment continues, as if we hadn't taken a single step forward since then. I mean everyone, all of humanity. What a brief existence!

People have started to come back to life. Their voices are rising. It's beginning to feel less cold.

I think about all this while I clasp hands, while I brush my cheek against more-or-less warm faces, while I smell the remnants of strange perfumes coming from all over the world.

Dear, dear Yeny, say the mouths that are moving like puppets, naming me.

Put in its proper place, a quiet world is something that attracts me.

This is new, I think. The din of the crowd used to please me. The plazas, the market, the bars, all that movement, that confusion of words that at times stood out in high relief. A single phrase like a shout, or the permanent sawing of a complaint, of an explanation, of a story told for whatever ear.

Not now. Suddenly I can't stand the noise. Perhaps because my own voice consoles me, or because I no longer want to let myself be knocked about. I'm becoming weak. I lose my equilibrium.

I easily lose patience.

The storm came, here, and brought my grandchildren and great-grandchildren. So many people, milling about with the doctors.

They don't know if I'm sleeping, if they can draw near.

I raise my head a little more and look out so they can see me. They kiss me, they rearrange me as if I were a big pillow. They bring big children, small children, and repeat the names I may have forgotten. But names are something I easily remember, although I might not know exactly to whom they belong.

I still remember anecdotes, far better than names.

Until he became sick, they came to tell me things. No one much likes to visit a sick old man. Visits from the doctor, then from doctors. This is

what we receive in the last years. But there are always books to read, memories to invent. In this sense I don't err.

I can clearly remember many faces from my childhood, some stories, which they've told me and which I myself have told again and again. Later, the desires of youth, marriage, the birth of children, the form that each of them was taking in the group.

The rest has been a long wait. I don't know for what. I never wanted to know.

We argued. I felt I couldn't make myself understood. That everything I said was held against me. I wanted to pound on something, but I didn't have the strength, not even for that.

I wanted to escape, to flee far away. But I didn't know how and there was no longer a place to go back to. Nor could I flee to any place, to some unknown site.

That's when the telegram arrived. Papa was dying. I had to do something about that. I cried all night long, huddled up against the pillow.

The possibility of Papa's death wasn't making me desperate. Rather, it was the mental paralysis that didn't allow me to understand anything at all.

Papa was eighty-seven years old. He had to die sometime. Mama was also very old but we never thought of her as having any age. I never worried about how I would take care of them. On the other hand, I wanted someone to come take care of me.

I was self-centered. I cried that night and all the next day and didn't move from the hotel once.

I also drank. I drank too much.

I didn't want to go home like this. I didn't feel that I was in any kind of shape to be meeting the others. The same old stories, and Papa dying, an old man with all his children around him. The idea made me want to puke.

Jonas called someone who called someone else who called someone else. They finally reached me. I couldn't not talk to him.

I was still crying when we had that awful phone conversation. You couldn't make out the voices very well. Jonas was shouting and his voice came and went like a ghost.

He said it was necessary for me to come, it didn't matter what I might be doing or what might be going on in my head.

Nothing's going on, I told him, absolutely nothing is going on in my

head. And I cried, and cried some more. I thought my heart would break in two.

Reina, he said, in a few hours you'll receive an airplane ticket and I hope you'll be in Buenos Aires this week. Buenos Aires. A gray, dirty, noisy place. Corrientes. La Paz. San Isidro. The river. I would see the river, I thought. The house. It's a beautiful house. Now who's going to live in that big house? Does Mama still climb all those stairs? Who takes care of the garden? Who removes the dead leaves from the swimming pool? What am I doing with my life? I don't want to go back.

And I repeated that thirty, forty times: I don't want to go back. I'm afraid. I'm afraid.

It was a little after Jonas's call that Amanda knocked at the door.

I didn't want to let her in. I couldn't stand the idea of hearing her say those awful things again

You don't know how to love, you're as empty as a shell. I hope you die. I hate you. And I am silent, as always, so she can continue. Who do you think you are, she'd say, How do you think you could do this to me? This. I was sleepy.

Amanda pounded on the door and pounded and I threw myself on my bed. Finally I opened the door. A lot of time had gone by. An eternity. She entered silently. She sat on the bench next to the bed. I want to hear you out, she said. I couldn't put one sentence together.

I'm not going to sit here all the livelong day, she insisted. It's time that you talk.

What could I tell her? My head was empty.

My head is empty, I said.

Well, then, speak with your mouth, she countered.

I said I was leaving, that my ticket would arrive soon. What for, she asked. To bury Papa, I said. I started to cry.

It was a low blow. I didn't want to do that. I know it was a low blow. However, I wasn't lying. I was only giving myself a little time.

Very well, she finally told me. They say Buenos Aires is a beautiful city.

My granddaughter lifts the baby from behind and hands him to me, his arms flailing. He is purple and crying as if he had just been born.

I don't want to take him, I tell her, but she insists, as if I were speaking to someone else.

I remember a photo, and who knows who showed it to me. A fat

woman with strong, enormous hands, like a washerwoman, holding a baby by the arms.

She was looking at the child with a peculiar expression and her head-dress, carefully placed so that it would gracefully fall, was gathered there on her hair as if it were a bride's veil.

The baby threw its head backward, stubbornly, as if it were trying to escape from the picture.

Below, the caption read, "England's Queen Victoria with her grand-daughter." But I only saw a fat milkmaid, horrified by the convulsions of the starched tadpole they had left in her arms.

Her rings appeared as spots on her fingers. The diamond brooches fastened at her collar resembled spaces of light beneath her hungry, froglike gullet. Perhaps for that reason the child contorted itself, restrained as it was by those squalid arms, sticking out from under the pleats and the foam of lace.

The child in my arms cries. I wrap him up in his blanket. Softly, I cradle him until he calms down.

Maybe we'll fall asleep together. Anyway, we both have to wait.

You anxiously awaited the spell the river would cast every afternoon, when the dense vapor arose, devouring our feet and even crawling in under our skirts, as if someone had opened a boiling pot at that very moment, when the sun set behind the porticos of Prague.

It's a circus magician's trick, you'd say, the old dry ice trick.

But the spell was repeated unceasingly, although we'd run away, as far as we could, and pretend not to be surprised. Then you'd say, It's the river ghost. It would arrive wrapped in its transparent sheets to wail through the streets, wanting to cover them so as to confuse our path.

If you can now see, here the fog doesn't nip at your ankles like a dog. It has found a way to squeeze in under pressure, to make us panic.

Where we are going, where we come from: we don't know. We barely move, amid the bandages. Half ghosts.

We lose weight and float like angels wrapped in webs of spittle, in filters of light.

I no longer have you, and words come back at me, as if I weren't the one speaking.

Judith is crying beside me, and Jonas stares at the auto's mirror. He looks at the silence bringing us together. He sees we have nothing to say to each other.

To advance under these conditions will probably be impossible. The fog has swallowed the city. We can barely see the hood of the car. We are going so slowly that it seems as if the cars are refusing to take us there, to his grave. And it rained buckets, all night long.

They'll have to bail water from the grave before they lower the coffin.

I don't know if there's some system to let it drain. A ditch or something, I guess. But they'll have to get the water out. We're not going to drop him into a puddle, into the mud.

We shouldn't have to waste any more time. We're going so slowly, it's dangerous to be on the road like this.

Cemeteries are farther and farther away from the cities these days, from the life of the city. But how to imagine this delay? Back there, inside, we couldn't know the fog was so dense.

I hope they have it all ready, that they give us time, that they take the situation into account. This sick climate, just like London's.

We always think about London when there's fog, we fall into the old cliché. But the two times I went there the sun was shining. An exception, to be sure. It must've seemed ridiculous to everyone else when I praised London's weather.

This is pitiful. Why would it happen to us, today of all days? Here we are, stopped in the middle of the road, can't see a thing. On a day like today you can't see past the end of your nose.

If we stop and get out someone could hit us from behind. You have to go along slowly, very slowly, one right after the other.

The dead man up ahead leads us toward the nothing that envelopes him. What irony! Papa would enjoy it if he could see it. Perhaps he does see, why not grant him the possibility?

He might have created this bottleneck for us. You want to come with me to the cemetery? Okay, just don't take the wrong road. And above all, make sure it's me you're following.

I'm cold, he said. The blanket your mother threw on top of me is very light.

His voice came from some joint behind the wall. It sounded hollow, as if he were shouting from some other room.

I ran into my room to look for covers but found only the baby blue crib quilt. How am I going to warm him up with this tiny thing, I shouted. I could hear how he'd laugh. When I returned to the room I called him,

Kaddish

Papa, Papa, but heard only my own voice fade into the distance. Papa, I insisted, and he moaned, I clearly heard his moan. I looked from one side to the next and soon I saw the bed hanging from the ceiling with its huge brass frame and round black casters.

Papa, you're going to fall, I said, my voice thin. I'd barely said this when the ceiling began to move and I awoke in such a panic that it took me some time to calm down.

Why did I ever dream anything like that?

It's frightening to lose someone, it's frightening not to find someone you know has to be there, to see he's no longer there, and suddenly someone looks at you, the one who's there is someone else, or else you don't know or can't know if it's really the same person.

I run to buy Papa roses, but they tell me not to. That he only wanted stones on his grave.

The roses are so dark red, so intense. I can't stand the idea of not buying them.

Mama gets angry when I select a bouquet. But finally she smiles and holds them in her arms. We'll keep them on the table for several days, she says. They're very fresh roses.

Next to the tables with flowers, flocks of children mill about, waiting for handouts from those who arrive.

They remind me of the ducks on the Moldau, the ones that chased us along the bank with no reprieve, quacking crazily whenever someone drew too close. We used to throw stones to make them go away, and they threw themselves onto the rippling water to eat them, the stones.

There are no ducks like that here, I think. Although it wouldn't surprise me to see them anywhere.

This isn't the gravedigger, it's the man who washes the bodies.

People don't approach or touch him. He's unclean. Dragging a fireman's hose and wearing a pair of rubber boots that rise above his knees, he comes out to strut before those who are waiting. It's his moment of glory, he's going to carry out his part of the ritual before these people, now halted, can complete their own.

He leaves once, twice, to look about. He carries his hose here and there before carrying out his task. Without his secret magic that no one should witness, the funeral party cannot proceed.

It will barely be an instant.

He'll open the coffin where my father is, and he'll look him in the face. As if he were a god.

The drizzle is so fine, so soft, that it feels like a silken thread against your face.

They are waiting inside, all of them, for someone to do what must be done before carrying him off to be buried. I stand at the gate. I look at the trees, like hills that undulate and spatter their green here and there against the whiteness that devours everything.

It must be the glint of the bones, I think, and I know it's nonsense. But I can't keep from seeing them gleam as they deteriorate.

Here she comes, carrying those flowers, so red that you can see them miles away.

Pale but unabashed, she resembles a Japanese doll with its mask of rice powder.

She has her head wrapped in a shawl because of the rain and the cold and she keeps her hands in opposite sleeves of her coat while holding the bouquet against her body with her arms. They are blooming on her, the buds burst open. Reina doesn't seem to belong to us. She has gone off to one side, almost mixed in with all the other people who are waiting. She looks at a child, who returns her gaze. In her hands the child holds red roses that she extends to Reina.

The woman in the shawl and the girl in the blue hood are both so beautiful, so beautiful, that the mirror containing their image fills with fear.

Even here, where tears are necessarily cried for other reasons, beauty can soften us.

I feel wounded, doubled over like a giant who has nothing over which to reign.

The men are praying and they begin to lower him. I can hear how the hinges creak, how the pulleys squeak and the ropes grow taut. The wood hits the earth. He has arrived.

They say I can cast my handful, my first, to begin covering him.

It is a moist, strongly scented earth that sticks to my palm.

My dearest one, clinging to me, the earth I cast upon you contains blades of grass and shining grains of sand. What I extend to you is a

world, albeit a small one, but large enough to fill a woman's hand.

I know it will reach you even in death.

Grief is so intense and at the same time the happiness accompanying it is so new. I ought to stay here forever, close my eyes, and listen to the rustle of the trees against the wind or run to greet those who are arriving.

In the end, it's like inhabiting the cities that I wandered like a ghost. The same incessant way of piling stone against stone, in an explicit, recognizable order. The men facing the women, the suicides in front of the wall, one beside the other, so many names I had forgotten: Yentl, Jane, Schloime, Libe, Abraham, Rifke, Itzjak.

I don't want to go back.

I put my small stone on top of the mountain covering him. A smooth red stone used in construction. They will remove it when they place the gravestone or it will stick to the mud and be forever mixed in the earth containing him. His scab of eternity.

Inside, his bones will rot, and on rainy days glimmers of light will burst forth.

I don't want to go back. Now that he is dead, let him be the one who flees from me.

What's the mouth? The seat of the soul? Or is the soul found in the eyes?

I hold my breath while the clumps of earth mixed together by the rain bounce around. I can hear the hollow sound of the wood as if he weren't there, as if he had already been consumed while waiting to be brought to his definitive place.

It's so cold that we are trembling like animals. We're stiff, glued to the task of the man with the shovel.

We see how his knotted hands slide along the handle while he wipes the drops of sweat foaming around his eyes. Like tears.

Doing this and hanging onto the fur of my mother's coat, I look like a monkey. I don't know how much time has gone by. I don't feel my feet, I can't see, my mouth hurts.

She says, Let's go, dear. Judith, it's so cold in this place that if we don't move they are going to have to cover us, too. Then I walk.

My mother drags me along, as if she could. She, so tiny, pulling along my very being. She talks and talks to me. She tells me that at home, she has to treat the tree trunks so the ants won't devour them.

*

The House of Memory

There were a lot of us. Perhaps someone has counted the number of people, so many young folks, so many old ones, until coming up with an exact number.

I see them, my relatives, what else? I have followed their trail for too long a time to give up now.

Judith is sticking to me. She doesn't want to fall. I say, Let's all go home. I'd like to go lie down. I need my bed. Yes, Mama, she answers. It's been at least forty years since I've thought of her as docile, so like the child she was.

Mama wants to rest, I tell Reina. Let her be the one who busies herself, the one who moves them along. But she says there are too many of us.

Who's going to feed all these people, she asks, horrified. She doesn't understand a thing.

Jonas won't lift a finger, I tell her. He's just buried his father and now he'll have to fuss at his mother until he's convinced.

No way can we get away from him.

What would he have to convince him about, Reina asks. She knows perfectly well what he wants.

For that very reason, I say, he'll never stop. He has to control, to prevent, I think. Falls, broken hips, memory lapses, mistakes, accidents, gas leaks, fires. He won't stop. He won't stop, I say. Not until she dies, I think. I can't say it, though.

Reina shrugs. How pale she looks.

You look pale, I say. You look like a corpse.

It's the place, she laughs. When you're here, history comes down on you, the history of all humanity. Here, there, everywhere. The world is plagued by hollow castles, tombs crammed with corpses. I'm sick of it, she cries, sick and tired of it all!

You're crazy! Don't shout! I shout in turn.

I can't believe what I hear. She, who rode about for years in carriages paid for with the money Papa sent, and now the world's too small for her.

You talk like you're full of it, I tell her. You always lived like a duchess.

Like a queen, *una reina*, she corrects me, and her crazy laugh breaks through the cemetery's forced silence.

Sometimes I would like to be like her. Turn my back on everything and then nothing could ever hurt me again.

I had forgotten these streets, or maybe they've changed some, in recent years. How much wealth is here, how much security. So many dogs, policemen, posters.

Kaddish

I'm falling, stumbling, asleep on my feet. Mama nods too, hunched next to me.

Poor thing. She must be exhausted, sleeping so poorly all these nights, at her age, and everything else, of course, there's also everything else.

I hold onto her arm. She has clamped onto her purse with both hands. I can see them, her hands with the enormous age spots. Now that the light bathes them, so near me, I can see how much they've changed. Her knotted fingers are thick at the knuckles. They are no longer the hands that played the piano, that combed hair.

These hands now clutch the purse as if there were nothing else around to hold. As if she were running the risk of someone snatching it away from her.

I tell her: a lot of trees have fallen. I never understood how these trees, seemingly so solid and strong, can be uprooted by the wind.

The storm did a lot of damage, I tell her, this mother of mine.

They're old trees, they had to die sometime, she answers. But we're almost there, Reina, we're near. Near what, I wonder.

She grows agitated, opens her purse, sorts out an enormous bunch of keys. The gate key, the one to the front door, and others that no longer serve a purpose. She wants to know if I kept my duplicates.

Of course not, Mama, I say. I don't have much chance to use them.

That's true, she answers. We can always ring the bell. We have an intercom now. You'll see. Your father saw to it before he fell ill. He had to take care of things, that's the way he was.

How was he? What kind of man was my father? Sometime I'd like someone to tell me.

The car stops, we've arrived. At last. There's an enormous wrought-iron fence around the house. I have to work some to get my bearings. I might have gone by without having recognized it.

We all get out of the cars and approach each other on the sidewalk. Mama tries to go ahead with her keys in her hand, but Jonas rushes the gate and takes out his own key case with an excessive, deafening noise.

She shudders. He takes his time about it.

That's enough, Jonas! Judith shouts, but he turns his back on us and opens. We all enter, women last.

Judith has taken Mama by the arm. The two of them hang back. They walk up the gravel path, looking at the mushrooms, the trees, as if seeing them for the first time.

I don't understand what unites them now. I can't understand.

Jonas is still opening doors when Mama reaches us. Go on in, Son, she says. You're home now.

My children are still here, seated around the table. This resembles a very formal gathering, this gathering in my dining room.

Suddenly, I don't think I understand what they're doing here. It's barely a moment, but I'd like them go out into the world. I'm thirsty, I say. Can someone serve me some tea. In the small china cups, I say.

These cups are normal-sized. They're ordinary. They aren't appropriate for passing time. The woman who sold them to me spoke of others, smaller ones. For tea, when you're old, she said.

Two old women sit down, she explained, nodding. They have a large teapot with hot water and a smaller one with tea leaves, and they fill the small cups. This is an old woman's tea.

My tea is bitter, biting. It's an excellent tea. Not yellow, but green. Completely green.

It's true that you need at least two old women for the ceremony to make sense.

She still hasn't cried. I know she cried before, when she held his hand and said tender things to him. She cried in private.

But now she can't, she can't. She doesn't know how to cry for him dead.

I'm afraid for her, and I don't want her to notice my fear, my weakness. She expects us to think of her as determined as always, ready for everything, and that we'll leave her alone. For the first time, I think we shouldn't do it. But no one can tell her anything.

Mama, dearest Mama, it's too late to begin. It's even too late to keep on being the way we were.

You're going to realize what happened, and I won't be here then, to look you in the eye.

We say good-bye, now we kiss. Don't behave, Rudy, she whispers. You've behaved your whole life.

Do you think you could stay with her a few days, I say. Until she's more comfortable, until she can look around, all this emptiness.

Reina says, Only a few days. She says that all her things are in Prague, that she doesn't have money or clothes, that she's come with a suitcase

filled with useless things. I offer some coats, whatever she wants. She hopes that you'll stay, I say. She can't get along with me. We can't talk. I fight her, you know. I don't think.

I'll hand her over to you, I think, she still cares about you, still says what one needs to hear, and she'll say it many times, Reina. She'll not ask anything inappropriate. Not from you, her beloved daughter. Nothing that can bother you. Later, you can go away forever. No one will ask you to stay, no one will hold you back.

A few days, at least, I tell her, that'll be enough. Then Rudy can take her, perhaps. We'll see.

Let her have you near for a few days, so she won't be alone.

Reina is looking at me wide-eyed. She's not worried. It's more like a look of astonishment.

What surprises you so, I ask. I didn't know you loved her so much, she says.

A woman phones. A woman for Reina.

She's speaking French. At first it throws me. Someone speaking to me in French isn't the norm. I feel important and answer courteously, Just a moment please, if you'd be so kind. That's the important part when it comes to languages.

Reina comes downstairs like a whirlwind, like when she was girl and skipped down the stairs, two at a time. She snatches the receiver from my hand. She's flushed.

Maybe because of the physical exertion. She doesn't move around much and suddenly to come down the stairs like that. No, I don't think so. It's the emotion of it all.

Go, Mama, please. I want to talk, she says. And she starts up in that language. She says sweet things, such sweet things. She speaks like a pampered child, she almost purrs, look at Reina.

Anyway, I go. It's none of my business. Ten, fifteen minutes go by. A half hour. Reina is still talking. Chuchuchú, chuchú. French sounds like that. Those lessons at the Alliance Française have served her some good, at least. To think she always went against her will. And French suits her.

One could imagine speaking each of the world's languages. But few words. Nevertheless, here she is long-distance.

I can't help being curious. I love you, she says.

A person loves everything in French. One loves ice cream, whipped cream. You know I love you, she says.

I shouldn't be here, listening. I never did it before. I don't understand.
I don't understand the words. She says, I'm jealous, or maybe I'm pretty.

Jealous. No one says I'm pretty, just like that. Not even Reina.

We women have always been jealous. Ever since they locked us up at
home and told us all those lies. Jealous of looking at the world through peep-
holes, through *jalousies*. That must be where the world comes from . . .

Don't make me suffer she says. I hear her clearly. Suffer, she says!

That's it! Her fleeing, her confusion, her upset state when we ask her
things. She's upset most of the time. . . . It was that! That kind of suffering!

She says, don't go. Wait for me a few days. I have all my things in that
damn place.

I listen from behind the door, like a thief. I'm afraid, like a thief of lives.

To be a mother is to play ignorant. I told myself that many times. Why
is it so difficult now?

It was that! Something as simple as that!

Please, I beg you, she says. She grows humble. This daughter of mine has
reason to be humble. Her pride. Please, I beg you, I implore you, she says.

I don't want to hear any more! I don't want to see anything!

But I look at her, so beautiful, pale now, speaking that language of love,
to whom does it matter with whom? I look at her from the keyhole in the
door, as a servant would look at her, on the sly, like a mother, well, that's
what I am, and she's been gone for such a long time. . . .

Reina says that the woman who called is a photographer. She's my friend.
We were in Prague because a publishing house contracted us for a book,
she says. Photographs are important, I say. You wouldn't know who you
were if you couldn't see yourself in pictures.

Do you still have that old box filled with photos, the one we'd pull out
every summer to play with, she wants to know. Then she laments: We
always had so few, because of Papa's wild idea. . . . That's something I
could never understand. Why did he resist being in pictures? Why did he
hate them so? Perhaps because he'd lost his family's, I say, but I don't know,
I never wanted to ask. It was his secret. For the first time, I tell her that
when we got married he didn't want them to photograph us together. But
he took me aside and asked me to write on a piece of paper, I'm happy, I
feel beautiful. While I was writing, he looked at me so intently that I really
was, I really felt like the most beautiful woman in the world. He always
did things his way, I smile.

Kaddish

Reina wants to see the old photographs. My dear daughter, I say to her, why dig up so many dead people? But if they're still here, she becomes enthusiastic, Let's, Mama. Show me at least one of them, the first one you take from the box . . . ! Let's play again . . . !

She climbs up onto a chair to hand down the hatbox. That hat, I tell her, the one that came in this box, is in a photo. Three young women in ridiculous hats with enormous brims. Identical hats and identical dresses. It was Pearl's idea. She thought if we looked alike they wouldn't take us for foreigners. We had fun doing it. That youthful madness was a sheer joy.

Here it is! Reina shouts as if she had found a treasure. We'll both look. Yes, it's Italy, I think. Whatever has become of them? This is the very place where we separated, when I met him. Who are the others, my daughter asks. I point out Pearl, a cousin, and Amalia, my friend from childhood. In the photo the three of us are smoking. It wasn't something just anyone would do, I mean, that women would do. The three of us with the same hat, like uniformed store employees.

Tell me about them, about the others, Reina says. Amalia went to the United States to marry some rich guy. We wrote to each other two or three times and then I lost track . . . I think I forgot about her, that's all. Pearl must have died ten years ago: I don't remember having met any Aunt Pearl, Reina says.

Never a letter, nothing, I think. Whatever became of her? We were very close; nevertheless, something happened, something that seemed so terrible that we never spoke again. Someone told me that she was dead. I was sorry. At my age you are always sorry when you learn of a friend's death.

You have so many friends, she continues. Do you still get together every Tuesday to play cards? No, dear, not anymore, I say. There isn't anybody to play with anymore.

Reina puts the photo in the box and stops the game. Why do you keep the box from that hat, my daughter suddenly wants to know. Because I was wearing it when I met your father. The three of us, dressed like that, saw him and set our eye on him. I wasn't the prettiest, I think, but he liked me.

At best, he went after the others and struck out, or so I now believe. Oh, I don't know. The three of us never again talked about him. Whenever he appeared, we'd grow silent. I'm still here, silent, and he's dead.

*

Everything here is so quiet. Tonight the dogs aren't even barking. The garden seems empty, with no soul. I can't open the window to listen to the trees whisper because it's too cold. Or because I can't stand the silence.

Nights like this one, beyond the reach of clocks, shouldn't exist. I'm afraid, as if I were a child. I'm so afraid that I would like to die and I don't know what that means: to want to die.

It's not the first time I've felt this way. I have experienced the sensation before, many times in my youth, but now it's not something I can think about easily, that I get excited thinking about. At my age, the encounter with death is all too close at hand, too threatening to seek its company voluntarily. Yet here I am wanting to die, for no reason. No reason.

Before he . . . before losing him, I also thought about this, that I want to die. I saw him suffer, writhing in bed. I didn't know what to do. I was desperate. I think I hated him for suffering so. I hated his suffering that way. It would be better for him to die, I thought. Let it be over once and for all. Let me die too. That's what I thought.

I went to sit in the waiting room. The nuns walked past like terrible angels, scraping the rubber soles of their slippers against the waxed tiles. I hated the nuns, too. Again, I thought: I want to die. I felt so alone. I spent a great deal of effort trying to remember things that could make sense of that grief that took hold of me like a prisoner. Not only the grief of losing him, but grieving for myself, for my emptiness, for my own distress.

I chose the right word: remember. It was something from the past, something that was already there, that I needed to find to defend his life. I mulled the idea over and over. What did dying mean to me? I didn't want to lose him. I couldn't stand the idea that he might stop breathing. I was controlling his breathing like one who permanently looks at a clock. I only wanted his suffering to end. I didn't know what it meant to live without him. Nor what it meant for him to stop living.

Over the years I made myself think that it would all end sometime. What good did it do me? Didn't my own death always appear as a scene? I could see my dead body perfectly, my children's grief, even my own, caused by this death of mine, parading before my very eyes.

According to my state of mind while I was having this fantasy, I either felt sorry for myself or I thought, Well, that's it, let them do something about it, their mother is definitely dead.

It was a kind of vengeance. A small one because I didn't dare risk too much in my fantasies. How do I get up my courage to represent such a

spectacle of their indifference? But when it was a question of him being left behind dead, it was different. Suddenly I knew. Death wasn't what I wanted, rather, it was the end of life, of some form of life. I couldn't bear the tension my heart had to withstand when it was so overburdened, so slow to comprehend, so laden with unspoken words. I wanted the resentment to cease, the hatred of grief to cease. I wanted to be someone else.

It was difficult, but I returned to that room where he was given over to suffering. I drew as near as I possibly could. I looked at him. I tried to recognize him under the mask that this type of life, this agony, had placed on his face. He was saying something. I thought he was delirious. Everything is going to be all right. I lied to him and held his hand. He turned his head, disproportionate for what remained of his body. He looked at me with the eyes of a crazy man, as if my presence by his side might break the mystery that made him a person, the mystery that was taking him away toward death. He clung to me with all the strength he had left, and crying, he shouted: Mama! Mommy! Yes, my dearest, I cried along with him. And I thought, here comes death to cover his mouth, nothing will be left, nothing of him, just like nothing of me is left for him.

Now I think I might have been afraid that the silence would take me away, too. But I'm being cruel to myself. It wasn't only that. I was afraid of the presence of the body that was starting to harden in the hollow of my hand, afraid of that thing that was there . . . a violent desire that they not snatch him from me.

The garden is immobile, mute. I would like to unglue myself from the window and crawl under the covers, but I can't. Here I stand, shivering, terrified. I don't want to go to bed. I can't stand the idea of being still.

When I enter Mama's room, I find her seated in front of her dresser, as rigid as a mummy. Mama, are you okay? I ask. She is annoyed, as if I had come upon her doing something terrible. She turns around and looks at me with eyes grown small from anger. Why didn't you knock? she barely whispers, because her anger won't let her talk.

I'm sorry, I say, and I flee from there. My face burns with shame. I've come across her at an intimate moment. I didn't think that Mama would have anything to hide because she's an old woman.

I'm in my room when she calls me, shouting. I run to her door, but I can't gather the courage to enter. Shall I come in, I ask from outside. Of course, she says, aren't I calling you?

She's still there, motionless before her dresser, but now she looks at me as if she were looking at herself. She wants me to come closer. I take a few steps, until I'm behind her chair. Not there, she says, and taking me by the wrist, she draws me to her side. She pulls on my arm without letting go until we're next to each other, glued.

Bend down a bit, she whispers. But Mama, I start to complain. What's the matter? You frighten me . . . Don't be silly, she smiles. I only want to look at you in the mirror.

There we both are. She has stuck her face next to mine. A cold face that has wrinkles on her chin, around her eyes, in the smile lines by her mouth. She smells of cosmetics, rouge, expensive perfume. She smells as my mother has always smelled.

We are together, looking at our faces in that strange way, but we do not see ourselves. Relax your mouth, she says, softer. Mama, I start to protest, but she looks at me again with that new fury, almost shouting, For once do what I tell you, I'm not asking much!

Then I became silent, and we look at ourselves, just like that, our heads together. I try to soften my mouth, to let it open a little in the mirror image, but my lips tremble. She asks me to pull my hair back. Now she speaks softly, sweetly. I hold up my hair with one hand, without moving from her side. My legs ache from the unnatural position I must adopt, but I don't dare change it.

That's it, she says, that's it! Although the look is sadder. Sadder? I ask. That's right, she says. I never had that sad look.

Thanks, dear, she finally says. She closes her eyes, as if tiredness were suddenly devouring her. Do you want something from me, she whispers, asleep in her chair.

No, Mama, I answer, as I walk to the door, I don't want anything that I can't wait for.

Everything around here is one big confusion, a tremendous confusion. I want him to look at me, to see me as I am. That's what I want. The world doesn't scare me. It has simply ceased being of interest. I'm out of place. Could he have known this? Could he have lingered so long because he knew that by leaving, he was abandoning me to this absence of myself? I'm tired. No one is looking now. No one can see into the past.

My mother told me that once upon a time there was a beautiful woman. She was so beautiful that all the young men of the village were in

love with her. She received their letters, their requests, their sighs. She would always think about those young men whose love she would never be able to reciprocate, and her heart was breaking. So great was her pain that she killed herself.

For the first time I think I understand the story. Today, faced with life, while my heart is breaking.

After Papa's expected death, Mama's unexpected death has unsettled all of us. I'd wandered around the house all day, not daring to speak to her. I called Judith because I was afraid. Mama seems strange, I told her, and Judith came flying. But she was afraid, too. She was always afraid when it came to Mama. The two of us stayed in the kitchen drinking tea, like when we were girls and had something to hide.

Mama didn't leave her room. I went up first, but she didn't want to open the door. After a while, Judith went up, and she told her to wait a little, it wasn't time yet. Time for what, Mama, she wanted to know. It's not time for anything, she said, her voice so clear it hung there in our ears.

At last she called us. She was lying in bed, wearing the same dress she wore for Papa's funeral. Once again she'd put on all her jewelry, and had tried to put on makeup, but her tears made the mascara run, staining her cheeks.

Sometimes it's best not to understand so much, my dears.

We were paralyzed, the two of us. Seeing her there, wearing that dress, really impressed us. She said that she loved us, that she loved Rudy and Jonas, but she didn't have the will to wait any longer. Everything was in its place. That anything we might do was okay, if it was what we wanted. I think she said this for me, although she was looking at Judith at that moment. She said she'd never believed in advice because she, for the most part, had never taken it. Life was marvelous, she said, and she regretted not having given it more of herself, of her heart.

We tried several times to interrupt her, but she stopped us by taking our hands, squeezing them tightly. I could feel how her enormous diamond ring was digging into my palm. I thought she'd deliberately turned it around so that I would feel it jab. I don't know how I could have that idea. Then she asked for tea. In the china cups, she said. I went downstairs to prepare it myself. Judith stayed with her. From the kitchen I heard her singing. I hadn't heard Judith sing in years. Mama asked, she said. Let's have our tea. It won't be an old lady's tea, but, she slyly added, neither of

you is young either. That put her in a good mood. We all laughed. She told us where we would find the other cups, like the ones we'd used. She thought it a good idea that we both have some. That any tradition at all would do, when a person felt alone. Papa and I weren't too generous with traditions, she said. We kept them for ourselves. Anyway, we might not have done them the right way, she said. One always does things poorly when doing them for others.

I think this was the last thing she said. Do you want to sleep, Mama? Judith asked her. She seemed so tired. She only closed her eyes, and with a smile and a wave of her hand indicated we should go.

We never saw her alive again.

Once again those chants are rending our souls, perhaps that's why she made me sing when we were alone, to imagine how they'd sound when we brought her here. The two stone markers will be facing each other. Papa reserved the plots. He wanted her with him, soon, as soon as possible. But I don't believe she was quite ready to follow him. Is he what she's following? Is that why she chose to die so abruptly? Is it something you can decide? To die like that? Of what? Of fear? Of boredom? What made her so suddenly tired? Did we, her children, wear her out? Anything a person does is all right, if it's what you want, she said. Even dying? Did you mean it's more worthwhile to die, when you don't want anything else? That's what you told me, yes, me, although at that moment you were looking at Reina. I know you were saying that to me. Did you know I wanted to die, too? What else did you know? One always does something poorly when it's done for someone else, she said. Was she afraid we'd do something with her, something she might not want? I wasn't going to let Jonas drag her through life. Was that why she said it? I don't understand. But it's not good to understand so much, she said. Was she speaking about Reina? Did trying to understand Reina wear her out? Did she know something? Something about Reina? About Papa? About me, perhaps?

I would've liked to have had the time to learn how to love her differently.

Mama dies and the birds sing. I never heard so many birds singing all at once. It's a marvelous day; the sun has come out, all of a sudden. Now they are both together, one facing the other, like Papa wanted. We wanted that, too. What a way they had of bringing us together—Judith, Rudy, Reina, and me. Together like before and so heartbroken.

<div align="right">Translated from the Spanish by Elizabeth Rosa Horan
and Martha Manier</div>

Part Three

On the Border: Forging Identities

Shoes: Andante, with Variations

Margo Glantz

For Beatriz Aguad

1. With the passage of time, the word *shoe* loses its original associations and etymology. Who remembers that the Spanish word *zapato* comes from the Turkish? It dates, then, from the Renaissance, and it didn't exist before then, in Spanish: other words, such as *calzas* and *calzado*, were used. In the *First Dictionary of the Spanish Language*, compiled by Covarrubias, *calzado* means someone who wears *zapatos*, as opposed to monks and nuns, whose profession involved not wearing them, in the examples of Saint Teresa of Ávila or Saint John of the Cross, commonly known as the Discalced (that is, barefoot) Carmelites.

2. The great Egyptian colossi are barefoot. The Homeric heroes, too, however we might doubt it. Moses, on the other hand, in Deuteronomy, can take pride in saying to the Hebrews: "I have made you walk though the desert for forty years, and your sandals have not worn out under your feet." This is the first written mention of footwear. Although if we reflect on this, God, when creating us, had already thought about needing to equip us with a good foundation on earth: our first shoe is what anatomy provides; the soles of our feet guarantee us a firm step. The softness and elasticity of this first footwear owes particularly to a marvelous combination of little bones, the sesamoids, located under the first metatarsus.

3. And this preamble is necessary for anyone who wants to write the story of a woman whose greatest ambition was to walk life's road wearing a pair of designer shoes.

4. She wasn't born on silk sheets or with the proverbial silver spoon in her mouth supplying her first taste of food. She worked in a provincial shoe store that sold city styles, that is, imitations or copies, at reasonable prices. This store specialized in the Elizade low-heeled pump (shiny black; austere, perfect cut) for the comfort of matrons. It also had thin-soled shoes in styles combining red and beige, or gray and black, or white with brown and navy blue. These were especially designed for ambitious young women in a working-class barrio.

5. It's time to confess that this story is autobiographical and, therefore, profoundly sincere.

6. The designer preferred by the protagonist is Ferragamo. He was born on 6 June 1898, in Bonito, Irpinia, the eleventh son in a family of fourteen children. His parents owned some farmlands. From the time he was quite small, he was obsessed with footwear, but his father (like my mother's father) regarded it as an undignified profession. One night he worked to make a pair of white shoes for his favorite sister's first communion. It was fate. Just as Leonardo da Vinci was born to paint the Mona Lisa and design revolutionary inventions, so was Salvatore Ferragamo born to design shoes.

7. When I began to write about my life, I become unsure, even though I, too, had an unassuming childhood. After I read Nabokov's memoirs, my doubts have grown stronger.[1] Truth be told, when I read things as profound as what he writes, I feel diminished, useless, and what's worse, my obsessions become somewhat inferior, like the natural history of the Americas was for Buffon.[2] How can someone whose only tragedy in life has been childhood exile from one working-class neighborhood to another compare with an exile from the aristocracy, from a country that produced Gogol, Dostoevsky, Chekhov, and of course Nabokov . . . *afterward?* My story deals with a woman who loves hopelessly, and the consequence of this fatal love is not suicide, in the style of Anna Karenina throwing herself onto the train tracks, or Madame Bovary taking arsenic because she can't cover her debts, or even the Princess of Cleves, who entered a convent to avoid carnal love. No, my heroine's tragedy consists of a slowly evolving deformation of the left foot, which produces a persistent but middling pain, lessened by analgesics. It's like the pain of a cal-

lous or an infected molar, pains wholly incomparable to the lacerating pain inflicted on Christendom's holy martyrs: the amputation of a breast, the mutilation of a limb, flaying, crucifixion. In Nabokov, tragedy often degenerates into subtle parody. In my case, parody lapses into farce, a fate similar to that of the wretched natives who were reduced to underlings when Columbus discovered they didn't have a cent. And my parents were already underlings in their own right (Russian Jews)—didn't Hitler determine that and exterminate them? My parents didn't even go to America, the real one, but to Mexico, south of the Rio Grande, where we're all deemed worthless. Had I been born in New York, I would have studied at Cambridge or Harvard and my English would be impeccable, like that of Carlos Fuentes. I insist: I was born here, south of the Rio Grande, and I insist on recounting the tragedy of a woman who loves too much. What could be more foolish?

8. Nabokov believed in God, a god formed by a kind of choir of spirits flitting about like butterflies. What kind of God could I believe in, since I don't even come from Russia, and my inheritance is only a second-rate exile? When all is said and done, my parents were the exiled ones, and their exile was less productive than Nabokov's or even that of some of the conquistadors. The other day my mother handed me the key to why she didn't return to Russia: she had nothing to boast about. If she wasn't rich or famous, why emigrate? Stalinism hadn't yet reached its height, although it was taking shape, but the act of going into exile was something grandiose, and my mother only went into exile to follow an adventurer who didn't even have a beard in those days. Things would have been better if we'd had an unusual destiny, but my father had a series of small shops, a series of moves, a series of books, a series of daughters, a series of trips, and a series of paintings and sculptures that were awaiting recognition as works of Art, like the work of the pre-Raphaelites, which were fashionable again in England. The war didn't touch us closely at all. We heard about it on the radio or we saw it on the newsreels shown at the movies, while my uncles and cousins in the Soviet Union were dying in combat, or from hunger and exposure. Perhaps this obsession with shoes that I am trying to make heroic to compensate for my lack of family heroism originates in my Uncle Ivan's line of work. He was my mother's older brother, and a shoemaker—a nefarious trade, shameful for the family, especially considering that this uncle didn't even produce a complete pair,

but just barely the upper parts of shoes, no soles, and what's more, it's not even known if he made men's or women's shoes. My uncle Allosha, who arrived in Mexico sent by my grandparents to protect my mother from exile and from my father, was also employed in selling shoe parts: he sold only the sole, made from the inside part of the hide, not even a good sole. So with the two uncles (who sold shoes, of course, in a shoe store in a mediocre neighborhood, shoes with downtown styling but at popular prices), could in no way compare ourselves to the famed Ferragamo, who turned the creation of shoes into an art as famous as that of Yves Saint Laurent with his dresses, or Bach with his fugues.

9. It should be evident, then, that there wasn't anything high-class about us. To elevate the level of my story about unfortunate love, to make it tragic, I have to construct a Herculean universe. I will try to do so. I already said that my uncle Allosha came to Mexico sent by my grandfather to take care of my mother, and when he arrived here he fell into this odious profession—or better put, he sniffed it out, since he had a leather store (cheap leather) on Jesus Carranza, a street obviously not at the height of elegance, and what's worse, he sold what shoemakers for the masses disparagingly call butchered goods. To complete the picture I must draw before proceeding to narrate my story of the woman who loved too much: my very own parents often had shoe stores in the town of Tacuba, where they sold city styles at Tacuba prices, and what's more, where they copied to perfection and without ceremony the shoes of my idol *avant la lettre*, Salvatore Ferragamo (who *par dessus le marché* was a Fascist). Amid my readings of Faulkner and Dos Passos I sat, forlorn, in the shoe store, praying to God no more customers would come so I could finish *Sanctuary* or *Manhattan Transfer;* how could I have known that later on, Ferragamo would be my idol? How could I have known that I would subsequently sink so low as to buy shoes only by that designer? Back then, or maybe when I was too young to be able to read in the shoe store, I could perceive the sadness my mother sometimes felt when she had to sell shoes and my father did nothing more worthwhile than write poetry. However, in spite of being so young, I already knew how to appreciate the elegance of those shoes (unwitting Ferragamo knockoffs) that we sold at 23.50 pesos a pair, lovingly constructed of strips of leather in green and gray, white and black, brown and beige, red and navy blue, with a marvelous, lovely, winged heel. Shoes, as I well know now, inadequate for traveling those

streets, which during the rainy season filled with mud as deep as the old lake at Xochimilco, through which you passed in canoes, or on the back of a native porter (a *tameme*) for the modest sum of fifty cents, or one *tostón*, a colonial coin.

10. As I was saying, the shoes that my mother sold were conscientiously made by hand and unwittingly imitated the Ferragamo designs then sold in Dallas's Neiman Marcus for about $40, an exorbitant amount if one thinks that we sold them for 23.50 pesos a pair when the dollar was worth 2.45 pesos. But doubts again nag at me. How can I write a book about such trivia?

11. The *Times* of July 1989 reports that the reviled and guillotined Marie Antoinette has become the darling of the French, who have absolved her of her sins some two centuries after the fact. And at an exhibition that the Caen Museum has organized to celebrate the bicentennial of the French Revolution, the most-visited object is a shoe that the unfortunate Queen lost as she climbed to the scaffold. Three architects have been commissioned to create six abstract spaces to house, in turn, that most precious piece of footwear. Curators dressed as the Queen's *Guard des Corps* carry it, protected by their white gloves, from one space to the next. The public must kneel on a white sheet, to venerate it.

12. Today I have decided to call this book: *The Story of a Woman Who Wanted to Walk Life's Road Wearing Designer Shoes* . . .

13. I must begin telling the story at the precise moment when the woman (me, that is) is walking down a street of shoemakers, perhaps that street in Lisbon, there behind a plaza, where they sell cheap shoes, similar to those sold in the shoe stores abounding in Tacuba. I would like to write a text as refined as the refined shoes designed by Ferragamo, and I can't, because the woman (that is, I) only knew neighborhood shoe stores specializing in copies for the lower middle class and for the beggars who came by every Saturday with an empty tin can to collect the prescribed small change and who on weekdays came wearing worn-out shoes, no socks or stockings, asking for work shoes at 7.50 pesos or for old women's low-heeled pumps in a shiny black with a tiny strap at 5 pesos. Only my piano teacher, chubby, wearing cotton knickers the color of lemony *mamey* cactus,

bought shoes in a grayish green that scrupulously matched her pearly-colored purse. Shoes were the only item we sold: once, *in illo tempore*, in the heart of downtown, we had a boutique called Lisette, where my mother sold hats, purses, and gloves: obsolete objects.

14. A reliable antiques magazine lists an exceptional find: a pair of seventeenth-century shoes, from a house belonging to the Lords of Northampton, sold at public auction for 20,000 pounds sterling. And here I should add, the extraordinary thing isn't in the mere fact that they might have discovered shoes from the seventeenth century. The extraordinary thing is that the pair in question is in a perfect state of repair. Remember: Marie Antoinette, like Cinderella, lost only one shoe when she climbed to the guillotine.

15. A woman walks by a store window several times. Rather, she walks down a street where shoes are sold. Her obsession is twofold, fixed on shoes and on a novel relating to the road to be walked, an obsession shared by Saint Teresa, Saint Ignatius, Saint John, and, in Mexico, by the seraphic Franciscans. The idea is to trace a comparable and allegorical parallel between the woman who must walk an amorous road, or the road in *mezzo del camin di nostra vita*, let's say, along with the seraphic friars, Saint Teresa, and Saint John, who walked unshod or with very poor sandals. I keep writing the text in which a woman wearing designer shoes walks life's road, her zeal contrasting with a martyr's calling, thus her nostalgia for Saint Teresa of Ávila and the seraphic Mexican friars; she finishes it off with Saint John of the Cross, the most important of the mystics. It should be underlined that this obsession will, perhaps, totally change the plan of her novel.

16. First she walks along streets where there are shoe stores, and when she looks at them her thoughts are indissolubly linked to the beginning of the novel, seen as a long road to walk, a road that becomes impossible to travel if her feet are not shod in special shoes, the most marvelous and soft pair, the most aesthetic ones in the universe. In her travels she comes across a shoe store in which there is a pair of shoes that fascinate her: they are on sale; nevertheless, they seem far too expensive, for she is accustomed to installment purchases, to buy in bits and pieces. Her parents were also fond of installments, as they say, because when they arrived in

Shoes: Andante, with Variations

Mexico their first encounter on the train headed off into the unknown was with a Jewish man wearing thousands of ties around his neck and thousands of hats on his head and I-don't-know-what on his hands, but he spoke to my parents in Russian and told them not to speak Russian but German, and that marked their lives. It started my father down the credit road carrying a basket full of bread on his head. Then he bought himself a horse—and where did he get it, if he had no money? I never found out, but you have to agree that in Mexico he started out down life's road on the right foot and on a horse, and this horse was to carry the bread, but while my father was riding horseback like a conquistador, an Indian, who to be precise was called Serafín, carried the basket on his head, and Serafín was like Cortés's slaves, because my father preferred to read poetry while Serafín loaded, sold, and collected the monthly payments because, although it may seem improbable, the bread was sold on the installment plan. And if I go down life's road on foot and wearing designer shoes— Ferragamo or Maud Frizon (not Christian Dior, nor Yves Saint Laurent)— then things will surely go well for me, especially if I keep my former ancestral habits, those of a person who relies on credit, and if I can get, on sale, the last pair of fatigue green Ferragamo shoes, make that demiboots, with a medium-sized heel and a cunning little buckle, a divine pair of shoes that fulfills a double function: to allow me to keep going through life in designer shoes that are elegant, perfect, and—a fundamental point—not too expensive.

17. It didn't occur to me before, but wouldn't her feet be pinched and sore because she never wore designer shoes until now? Nonetheless, I go on, and she goes on, down Bond Street, passing Armani, where she especially gasps before his suits, when she touches the fabric's texture; Ungaro, exquisite dresses, but too young (she no longer has such a narrow waist); Yves Saint Laurent, marvelous, but where could she wear such shoes? She could buy herself an Armani suit, she has the money now that they're on sale, but she's used to spending money on trifles. Her clothes take up so much space in her closet that after having totaled the cost of all of them, she could have bought herself something marvelous, but she doesn't, and she does the math again because she has the mentality of someone who buys in installments. Her blind steps lead her again to Ferragamo, where she has seen the shoes; she knows that she won't be able to write if she doesn't have good shoes to wear, she has already proven that: at this very

moment she is wearing shoes from Oxford Street, from Ravel, a cheap store for out-of-towners like herself, people who don't have much money or who, like me, have the mentality of someone who buys on installments, besides feeling an immense, tango-like nostalgia for those shoes made of colored strips, green and gray, red and gray, navy blue and white; high, narrow heels—from the shoe store of my childhood, the one Mama had— next to the shiny Elizondo pumps for old ladies that we went to Tacuba to find with Papa, when the vampish ones cost 23.50 pesos, and those for little old women cost 12.50. Perhaps I should buy myself some shoes like that: I remember a taupe pair from Christian Dior, very high-heeled, t-strap pumps like those from the 1920s, shoes I had to give away the other day, although they were still in very good condition, but I could no longer wear them, for I have bunions, and having bunions fits perfectly with the mentality of a person who buys on the installment plan, and not with stylish shoes.

18. A foot as deformed as a worn-out shoe, down-at-the-heel, no longer covering the misshapen foot, the dents or wrinkles showing a part the foot can never fill. Nothing receives the impact of reality so much as feet, in shoes or on the ground. That's why, as a girl, I wore black patent leather t-straps, flat, with a rubber heel, or white ones, and during the first days I didn't want to walk in them so as not to dirty the soles, and to avoid such a thing I walked on newspapers. That maneuver stops the effect of reality: it keeps beauty intact, as happens in still life paintings in which a few table scraps establish balance, never deteriorating because they are painted.

19. Her blind steps lead her again to Ferragamo, where she has seen the shoes; she knows she won't be able to write if she isn't wearing good shoes. She enters, inquires about the shoes; they show them to her: they are a greenish gray, with a silvery reflection produced by the treatment they have given the leather; the heel isn't too thin; it's medium-sized, with a slight curve toward the instep, like those in the Ferragamo shoe catalogue now on exhibition at the Victoria and Albert Museum. She went to the museum; she has passed through innumerable rooms piled high with erratic collections of medieval statues, blue ceramics, Persian rugs. She thinks she should stop, because Persian rugs are definitively associated with shoes, or rather with the lack of shoes, because one should never walk on them; you have to take your shoes off before entering a mosque

or a home; nevertheless, she continues on her way without stopping, the thought is useless as she treads this road trampled on by shoes: the rugs are on the wall, not even sandals could reach them. Finally she finds—oh how wonderful!—the room where the brilliant Ferragamo shoes are on exhibit. Back in the store, she tries on the shoes they've brought her after she pointed them out, there, on the round table where the sale objects are displayed. They tell her it is the only pair. She tries a shoe on the left foot, the one with the bunion; she verifies that the fit is perfect, simultaneously solving the problems of beauty and of comfort. However (and she can't avoid it) they seem too expensive, even though they're on sale. She returns to the other stores and no other shoe pleases her as much, but they still seem too expensive to her. She is used to spending her money on less expensive things, cheap things; it seems to her that those are the only things she deserves, but, and this is for sure, she also knows that the novel she wants to write can't be written if she doesn't decide to buy the Ferragamo shoes; they are her open sesame, the glass slipper from her fairy godmother.

20. At that moment what bothers her the most is the fact that she's eating too much *turrón de yema* candy, drinking too much sherry, and getting fat, and besides, she can't wear Ferragamo shoes, not even to the beach, to take them off to feel the sand, because she has bunions and, unless the sand covers her feet, her deformity is visible. She thinks about other shoes Ferragamo has made, and about those lasts made to the size of each diplomatic, imperial, artistic, or jet set foot. Then she wants to have feet like Mangano, who belonged as a child to the lower class, just as she did, and who probably wears fashionable brands, just as she does, and who has, just as she does, a bunion. Why not think about that? Ferragamo could have fashioned her a shoe last, sized to her bunion.

21. This afternoon, I thought Ferragamo's life interesting. What an odd idea for someone who has deformed feet and is at the beach, barefoot. I don't know how I could be interested in the life of a fat man who was always bent over, measuring feet and building wooden shoe lasts. Although, of course, those lasts were unique, one for each foot, because just like fingerprints, our footprints are unique, as in life or anatomy, a singular design of nature. Besides, on each one of the lasts that he made, Ferragamo inscribed the name of the owner of the shoes that allowed that

person to walk solidly on the ground. The lasts were perfect, made of an exceptional quality of wood. Now those lasts are sold at the price of gold, but you have to buy them if you want to keep your shoes impeccable. I never get tired of thinking about it; the prints of each foot are exceptional, as unique as fingerprints; but in this democratic era no one wants to admit it, and buys ready-made instead of tailored clothing: *pret à porter*, and it's redundant to repeat it, the same thing happens with shoes.

22. While she thinks about her shoes, she knows she will write a text that has to resemble an opera, one that stops both history and the sentiments, immobilizing them. In the theater those sentiments are aroused; in the opera, what seems tragic becomes grotesque, on account of the voice, the gestures, and the costumes; also because, she thinks again, she has deformed feet and they become more and more deformed each time she sings her triumphal aria, an aria in which her male companion, who loves her, always falls asleep because he can't stand opera and the scene is repeated, degraded in the shoe store, in her mind, while the music swells on the impeccable compact disc where Aída, like Nefertiti, begins her descent to Hell with her intense pure soprano voice.

23. I stop, this is very important: her main obsession comes from the idea of fame, the honor of a name. Convinced, she returns to Ferragamo, she tries on the shoes again, the clerk comments, "You were here earlier." She nods, it's decided, she buys them, but before doing so, she utters a vow, a promise made to Saint Teresa: to wear them only when she sits down at her typewriter, like she is doing now, with her shoes on, with hose of the same shade (later in Fogal she will buy several pairs, designer hose for Ferragamo shoes) and finally, solemnly, the time has come; seated like a seraphic Franciscan before the typewriter or at the computer, smoking a cigarette, listening to Bach, eating *turrón de yema* candy and drinking a glass of port, she begins the most heroic act of her existence: to write *The Story of the Woman Who Walked Through Life Wearing Designer Shoes*.

Translated from the Spanish by Elizabeth Rosa Horan

1. *Speak, Memory*, the 1951 memoir by Vladimir Nabokov, recounts his childhood and youth in Russia and his eventual exile from his homeland.

2. The Count of Buffon (Georges Louis LeClerc, 1707–1788) made the scientific knowledge of the French enlightenment accessible to readers, and formulated theories on the foundation and evolution of the universe.

The Melancholy of Black Panthers

Luisa Futoransky

Let's imagine a hailstone thawing. It slides along because of gravity—a force to which all of us animate and inanimate beings pay tribute to this day—the winds and accidents of the terrain; with its heart, its cordial hard center of ancient minerals, and a periphery that grows with weeds, obstacles, small objects that join with it, like aids to memory, or anecdotes about the terrain, until it flows together with others into a violent river, which like all rivers goes to the sea, but as the Bible proclaims, the sea does not overflow. So do I present, gather, and observe the voice of the minorities of the diaspora within the great channel of Latin American literature.

Within that palpitating and singular conglomerate that comprises the words written to tell, recount, and dream in this century of our vast literary cartography, I pause, intrigued, with the greatest respect regarding a particular period—the one between two wars—and a distinct segment of the population, which I choose to call "the mute women." I am referring to our grandmothers and great-grandmothers. The ones who were forced from their torched little villages to the *goldene medine*, innocent translation of Eldorado into Yiddish. I do not wish to signal a real absence of the word, because at times they shouted like wild animals, but the written testimony, especially that produced by the women themselves, is practically nonexistent. Of those women there remain few birth certificates, those that were not sold off or traded. Only those of death are extant and intact, which obviously they did not write.

Their first and last names, Castilianized by their children or grandchildren, appear in pitiless struggles for shares of inheritances in the registry of deeds.

The Melancholy of the Black Panthers

I want to talk about the women because the great crime of our age, because it is not codified by theological or secular laws, is omission. Lying is a sin, sometimes a crime, but guiltily omitting, silencing, laying aside, is not.

I belong to the generation of the children of Jews who came to Argentina because, between one war and another, pogrom and pogrom, they fell off the map into ships, just as the Albanians, Malaysians, Cubans, or Haitians are doing now in their own way and before them the Vietnamese; in short, the shipwrecked of all times. Those who lived from hand to mouth, and be thankful you have hands.

For those who may be familiar with the painting of the Old World that depicted the tatters with which the new one constructed its modernity in order to return them to the old in ellipses and in spirals of courage and blood, I remind them of the pictorial work of Lazar Segall, a Central European from Brazil. His scenes take place mainly in cesspools crammed with people, almost as brown as the waters of the deltas and the swollen timber of those ships. The climate breathed in his canvases is the fragile and the precarious. Even so, the picaresque of nostalgia continued building bonfires, making smoke signals in order to be understood, or simply to make the outpourings of the soul a little bit warmer.

Anxiously, the immigrants wished to become part of the country, and rapidly: that country of which they were totally ignorant and of which they demanded so much, to which the combative fury of foreign hussars and their own mad hunger had led them. It is easy to understand them, because how human is the desire to be understood quickly, or to stroll down a street whose pitfalls and ruts are known. One needs a country in order to read between the lines, to be familiar with the degrees of jealousy, the wrinkles of good and evil in the faces of the others, I mean, our own.

My relatives were not city-dwelling Jews from the capital. Neither had they been city dwellers in the places where they were born, and neither had the parents of their parents been in the impoverished sites from which they in their turn had also escaped. After arduous periodic interrogations and investigations of my relatives, almost always with negative results, I found a vague point on the map which, then as now, changed its name and flag with a certain frequency, but which always remains near a river, perhaps the only reliable and domesticated fixture of the geographical landscape. From the shores of the Dniester, it seems that some of us reached the Spanish language, the way my cousins say they reached the Portuguese of Brazil or the English of Brooklyn. None of these people—

my people—imagined seeing the ocean, just as none imagined being lost, forever.

In Argentina, at that time called "the Queen of the Plata" they came, as always, to the periphery. The ones on the periphery, aren't they, perhaps, the only ones who make the center evident? And searching for who-knows-what secret dream of redemption and Promised Land, they settled down in a place called Santos Lugares and wound up selling shoelaces and strings of garlic and onions in the town marketplace, and sewing linings for ties and corded seams for pajamas. To recreate, in short, the shtetl, the center of the imaginary, the main street of the rich and the poor, the well-read and the foolish, lunatics and saints. From the dreams of Eldorado they sensibly lowered their sights to those of silver, copper, and minerals of lesser nobility and alloy. Ending by reducing them to two: a little home of one's own, "of substance" and the son, "a doctor." And they left behind them the words of a dying language, Yiddish, on the greedy coasts of the Atlantic in order to consolidate their passage, sometimes paying in raw flesh, from utopia to the predominant culture. Like the generation that came with Moses to the Promised Land and nevertheless had to wander forty years in the desert in order to enter. That's why the second generation of immigrants, that is to say, that of our parents and our own, is just beginning to produce the saga of their future after their families had experienced, voicelessly and breathlessly, decades of poverty and trials, which they survived out of pure stubbornness. Perhaps also because the Europe they had abandoned was a conflagration where only hunger and all the familiar plagues prospered, plus other new ones of still-unknown cruelty.

Among the many things that I still have not written but would very much like to write is to give at least a pale glimpse of the life of those young women who came from villages harsh in patriarchal customs, who were reduced to the level of chattel in dialectical languages, to the pampa, the unheard-of distances, madness. They changed, altering their shtetls as best as they could, at the risk of populating the asylums with melancholy or violence, and the cemeteries with suicides. Those, the ones who were ostracized, watch from the sidelines, with their crooked gravestones, the "natural" deaths of the others.

When I say melancholy, I think of those exaggerated and obligatory mourning periods of my childhood. For years, the women of my family and the neighbor women dyed the season's clothing with black aniline in great tubs of zinc, in order to respect their rigorous mourning customs.

The Melancholy of the Black Panthers

Chronicles of entire districts were inscribed in the memory of the people because of their respect for or violation of mourning rituals. Three long years of monochromatic circumspection, which then gave way to the gamut of grays of partial mourning. At times the deficient quality of the operation recalled, because of large grease spots, the earlier print of the dress. It would tenaciously reappear in strange, superimposed designs, bringing to mind comparisons with old, exciting times that flourished despite the circumstances. A situation analagous to when I once surprised myself in the zoo, noting the backs of the black panthers. From up close their leopard spots shone through, the family memory of their origins. From that experience comes this title, because perhaps my women, in their apparent strength, distilled a dense, nostalgic "Melancholy of Black Panthers." Incapable of accepting losses. Too many, perhaps, for a single life.

Nowadays, the axe blows and stabs of the rag-picker (which furnish at any moment the fragments and splinters of our own existences) make me widen the optics of my *compatire*, of my own sharing, to experience, like my poor old mother, aunts, grandmothers, and neighbor women similar dwellings in the catalog of passion: ostracism and exile.

The women I talk about did not fit in—but they must have fit in as best they could, or supposed that they did—the suppositions of an urban imagination. Like the survivors that they were, they must have sharpened their ingenuity in the perception of the immediate. Without keys for translating the New World, they must have forced their way in with pick-locks. Repopulating life with new gestures and words. But what words. How to defend the body and oral traditions they were carrying, holding fast to them from the Middle Ages into the New World, how and when to compromise with the new realities, which required unheard-of relation-ships between man and work.

The fissures began to make themselves felt when all the fears within and without could not pass through the same coordinates of thought and word. These excisions tend to be fecund for opening precious treasures in the realm of the fantastic in literature and in art in general, but not in the struggle for life. Men's daydreams can give rise to a blazing inferno or to the sublime flying buttresses of Notre Dame. *Helás!* There's only one Notre Dame, while Hell, public and private, is innumerable. So did the closets begin to be populated with the dead and with the living men and women who could not cope with the new reality. Most of them were profound melancholics, although there also were some violent ones, those who

ended up in the madhouses with the most terrible of punishments, the strait jacket: once put on, there was no going back. Less dramatically, more amusingly and modestly, most of our women dreamt of a golem, a zombie domestic who would relieve them of the oppressive tasks of the home and defend them effectively in the hazardous world of transactions with the goyim. To calm the children of turbulent schooling, from their innermost being they invented the fear of the dark, of the unmentionable, by means of the bogeyman. This was achieved, sometimes with the opportune presence of the gypsies pronounced with *tz*, the abstract *tziganer* who would steal us away, condemning us to wander with them. Since the threat of living in absolute freedom did not instill sufficient fear in the intractable, they added the notion that they would sell us to be . . . the word "slaves" was not pronounced. The concept of white slavery, together with a panoply of sexual terrors and taboos, they inculcated into us girls much later.

Every family knew, in private, new alliances and unspoken wars in the marketplace, where husbands and boyfriends were always scarce. Unequal combat when faced with the fascination exercised by the goy, the gentile, the other. Those wars, subtle or ferocious, took place in the intimate, secret language, Yiddish.

Bashevis Singer reminds us that this language is the only one in the world that was never spoken by the powerful. A harsh destiny met this language, which arrived over waves of desperation and fury at the coasts of the Atlantic, which metamorphosized itself as best it could and knew how, passing from New York through Rio to Buenos Aires, only to expire, in an almost irremediable fashion, in the open air of its beaches.

If we observe at close range the baggage of these people, we see that in the beginning they brought rancor and alienation because of the expulsion to which they had been submitted. Under such conditions they looked at the others, who in turn looked at them, as hostile. Hostile because of their respective appearances, for not having the custom of living together, for their different devotions and sacrifices to the Divinity: exile, from the time of Babel (to not depart from the first reference in Genesis), has doubtless been and continues to be a punishment, like translation.

Because what is translating and being exiled but taking an arbitrary block of words, a planetary system of ideas, phonemes and fantasies, and transplanting it to a different, unknown planetary system. Frequently the orbits do not fit. Many words and laws, generally the greatest, the most

profound and secret, remain bouncing around like worn-out springs, out of their orbits; for that reason, translation and exile are always synonyms of loss.

Arriving in one language, living in another, and writing in a third is the literary experience of the contemporary novel; Singer, Kundera, Conrad, Nabokov, Beckett, Kosinski, Gombrovickz, or Kafka themselves confirm it. Their written language is not the one that others speak. For the great transfer of communication they realize limited pacts with language, almost impossible to translate, because sarcasm is the only inalienable weapon in the hands of the exile. Irony is capable of absorbing hatred and piety without poisoning us too much. As a result of producing such disfranchisement, the world has become a shambles inhabited by all the barbarians.

An image persists in my scenario as I ramble through these pages; it is of a painting by Francis Bacon. From a chaotic circle of greens surges a massive tree, unarmed, torn out by its roots. Without anesthesia. Like a wisdom tooth. Its roots in the air. I have a premonition that from them some grafts will bear fruit, other shoots will inevitably perish. About that line blazes, like a road, a yellow point, in full view. It might seem to be the head of a man. A little horse perhaps. The title of Bacon's work is irresistible: *Portrait of Van Gogh*.

No one better than ourselves to stand in front of the mirror of cities without hope, the jungle of all exiles. One must observe always, in order not to presume anything, that path from which we originate; it may be enough to consider, although only superficially, the treatment that the metropolises offer to each new wave of immigrants: at one or another moment of their lives, along with all the humiliations, everyone passes through this, waiting on tables and cleaning the sidewalks of the others in order, much later, to empty their pails of trash, their rubbish. It falls to the recently arrived to maintain tidied up, in short, the unconscious of the city. *On est toujours le juif de quelqu'un*.

If I am quite in agreement that's for a writer, "homeland" is where one writes, not about what or whom one writes, it is essential to poke around in the exile of those who belong to us in order to understand also our own expatriations. The fears and tremblings of those panthers of our blood, their whispers and laments through which they sift their glories and sorrows that infiltrate the imagination of the great channel of this, our Latin American writing, to which we, in their honor, also belong.

Translated from the Spanish by Roberta Gordenstein

In the Absence of Love

Ruth Behar

"When I say that I no longer loved him, I mean to say that you have no idea to what lengths one can go in the absence of love."

"Give me some idea."

"I can't."

—Marguerite Duras, *The Ravishing of Lol Stein*

In the absence of love, I am going to Cuba again. It's my seventh trip. I no longer have a reason to return. There is nothing left to find, nothing left to bring back. I have taken pictures of the forlorn houses in Old Havana where my mother grew up, where my father grew up. I have walked through the rooms of our apartment and sat on the edge of the bed where my parents once made love. I have sat on that bed with the striped bumpy spread that's under a window looking toward the sea. I have stood again under the brass lions of the Patronato Synagogue. I have stood on that same spot where a picture was taken of me when I was four, a Cuban flag half slipping out of my hand. I have gone as far as the town whose sugar slopes cannot stop weeping for the Indians and the slaves. I have gone as far as that town where my great-grandfather brought the family from Poland, only to spend nights of oblivion hunched before his account books, writing stories in Yiddish of his childhood.

I don't understand anything.

My marriage has ended, but we're staying together because neither of us has the time or energy to do anything else. We have a son who's more

attached to his father than to me. Whenever he needs anything, he calls out "Daddy!"—a wail as desperate as a shofar[1] sounding in the desert. It's the price I've paid for being a professional woman. All of my son's friends are being raised by single mothers, divorced or never married, and they watch us like hawks. They flirt with my husband and wait for me to join them.

I'm going to Cuba for two weeks. I've lost weight, so I won't feel bad this time about looking fat while everyone else goes on a national Weight Watcher's program because of all the shortages. From the sale rack of the store that has all the rayon Javanese clothes, which I usually can't wear because it's too cold here, I've picked out a short dress with a drop waist. It has thin spaghetti straps that I'll need to tie into bows to keep them from falling off my shoulders. The dress is pale gray embedded with pale pink flowers. I don't know yet what shoes I'll wear with it. Everything I have is black and too heavy for that paper-thin dress with its little girl flounce. I need sandals. And I'll have to paint my toenails a shade of dusty rose.

I don't expect anything to happen in Cuba. I mean, a love affair or something like that. I'm too cautious. I won't let myself be used by some guy who needs a plane ticket to Miami. Politically, who knows what could happen? I've always suspected I'll end up there in the midst of the final chaos, during the last chapter of the Revolution. As the book is being closed. That's the price I imagine fate expects me to pay for returning after there's nothing left to find, nothing left to bring home.

He always said it didn't matter if I didn't love him. He had enough love for the two of us. More than enough for the two of us. I wanted him to prove it to me. I don't like false promises. That's why I held back. Gave little. I think he was lying. His love wasn't boundless. It ran out. Or maybe he just got tired. Men get tired, my mother always said. I guess I pushed too hard. But I won't blame myself. It's the cultural differences—what in the world could have brought together a Jewish Cuban woman carrying too much history on her back and a bashful guy from Texas who thrives on peanut butter and sliced banana glued together with mayonnaise? Pure madness, nothing but madness.

And yet I know our good-bye at the airport will be so tender that I'll believe I almost love him. I'll beg him to wish good things for me. As I step onto the plane, my heart will shatter like glass under my feet.

Just like last year, I'm going to Cuba on a Jewish humanitarian mission. It's one of the few ways to get into the country. All expenses paid in

advance, staying at the best hotels. Bringing dried milk, powdered eggs, and potato flakes, stuff you eat in times of famine or war. For the last thousand Jews still living on the island. We're enchanted by the idea of helping the Jews who stayed behind, guarding over the palm trees. It makes us feel better about having left.

The first day in Cuba, it will be the same as always: we'll visit dead Jews first. In an air-conditioned bus they'll take us to the Jewish cemetery in Guanabacoa. I've gone many times, taken many pictures of the moldy graves and their salty Stars of David. But I will put on my new gray and pink dress and go again.

I'll leave a stone at the grave of my cousin, who died of leukemia.

I'll leave a stone at the grave of my great-uncle, who died of cancer.

I'll leave a stone at the site where they buried that sliver of soap made of sorrow and bitterness.

And before I wash my hands, I'll leave a stone by the gate.

For the losses I can't name. In case I don't return.

1. A shofar is a ram's horn, used in ancient times as a signaling trumpet, and still blown in synagogues on High Holy Days.

On the Border: Essential Stories

Miriam Bornstein

"Dondequiera que vayas verás
cosas diferentes, pero el
pueblo será el mismo"

"Wherever you go, you will see
different things, but the
people will be the same"

—Abraham Bornstein, *El llanto del Vistula*
(Cry of the River Vistula)[1]

I. The Desert: Tierra Santa/Holy Land

I come from a land of ancient mesquites; *péchitas* hanging from my mind like poems, simple in their sweet taste on children's tongues playing *a la casita*.[2] A land where *laureles* bleed as bold as Southwestern history. I have forgotten when it was that I left; but I keep returning *como una culebra mordiéndose la cola; devorándome las entrañas para encontrarme otra vez en mi desierto. Regreso al polvo antiguo después de acumular otro polvo. Huellas de otras voces; uñas incrustadas en el alma como la espina del sahuaro orgullosa de habitar su presente milenario.*/I have forgotten when it was that I left; but I keep returning like a snake biting its tail; devouring my entrails to find myself again in my desert. I return to ancient dust after gathering other dust. Imprints of other voices; fingernails inlaid in the soul like the thorns of the sahuaro,[3] proud to inhabit its millinery present. I return to my Mexican and Spanish desert,

to the land of my Indian ancestors; cultures intertwined in me like my great-grandmother's long mestiza braid and wisdom.

I now ask for her blessing and kiss her hand one more time as I remember words with memory clinging to them. Words with the essence of bones, beings dancing in the soul, working their way out through the eyes creating other eyes and more. They come like furrows to flesh and ocotillos.[4] Emptying ghosts ready for harvest under a full moon. Remembering scattered pieces of the self over sacred pyramids, fished from the sky by *sacerdotisas*; words with full headdress and filled eyes.[5]

II: Mother Is a Way of Remembering

Some of my memories of my mother include an image of her hanging clothes out to dry in the sweltering heat embracing the land; an August net cast in the still Mexican Arizona Desert. Who was to say that the glory of her red hair and the loyalty of her fair hands would be pinned to my memory, distorted by time and heat arising from the very same desert in our backyard. Her delicate fingers hanging clothes are in her children's memories like pieces of love facing the sun and truth. There, quietly, with eyes turned inward searching for life. Awareness standing on a line, like so many of the lines my family has had to cross before arriving here, on this page with this voice.

Words that have flourished against the wind behind barbed-wire fences and cement walls thick with prejudice. Memories coming to the edge of being, standing at the edge of the well. Surfaces broken over and over again by the crossings. It seems as if I have always been crossing borders, lines, fences, barricades, hedges, railings, oceans, rivers, *fronteras, sueños, miedos, tapias con vidrios puntiagudos que amenazan los ojos, castigan antes de llegar a la orilla de la esperanza./*It seems like I have always been crossing borders, lines, fences, barricades, hedges, railings, oceans, rivers, borders, dreams, fears, walls with sharp-pointed pieces of glass that threaten the eyes; punishing before arriving at the edge of hope. Undocumented memories and histories find their birthplace and slip through all the ancient holes in the night and the soul and the fence, splitting hearts in the passing between one and the other.

III: En Polonia, Abraham/In Poland, Abraham

Eres de un país donde las esperanzas se quedaron congeladas en el hielo, en las pupilas de un pueblo. El lago donde la abuela Mamishi lavaba la traviesa experiencia de tu infancia guarda las huellas de tu correteo de niño. Tus risas aun hacen eco en los recodos del bosque y en los puños de tu gente que como tú atravezaron la historia para seguir luchando.

Eres de ese país que no conozco donde igual que tú el sol jugaba asustado a las escondidas para sobrevivir la pesadilla de ser judío en esas tierras. Polonia antigua y fría desborda su corazón y te recuerda en el tañer de las campanas de Zelechów, tu pueblito al sureste de Varsovia. Atrás se quedaron las palizas de los "goím" cuando ibas por la calle jalando tu carrito vendiendo carbón y combatiendo las garras del poderoso invierno y del prejuicio. Al final del día ibas también cargando con el peso de la pobreza hasta tu cama en la vieja casa de la calle Nalewsky frente al Rynek. Regresabas a bordar recuerdos con palabras de humo en la transparencia de aquella tierra blanca y silenciosa; despertando al amanecer como el corazón de los antiguos castaños que revientan cerca de los pastizales./

You come from a land where hope remained frozen in the ice, in the pupils of a town. The lake where grandmother Mámishi washed the mischievous experience of your childhood holds on to the imprints of your running around. Your laughter still echoes in the twist and turn of the forest and in the fists of your people, who, like you, crossed over history to continue their struggle.

You come from an unfamiliar country where, like you, the frightened sun played hide-and-seek in order to survive the nightmare of being Jewish on this land. Poland, ancient and cold, overflows its heart and remembers you in the sound of bells in Zelechow, your small town southeast of Warsaw. The beatings of the goyim remained behind as you walked on the street pulling a cart selling coal and fighting off powerful winter's paws and prejudice. Also carrying at the end of the day the weight of poverty to your bed in the old house on Nalewsky Street, across from the River Rynek. You would return to dream and embroider memories with words of smoke in the transparency of that white and silent land, waking up at dawn like the heart of the ancient chestnut trees bursting near the pastures.

My father Abraham Isaac Bornstein Engel, an eleven-year-old boy in 1927, facing poverty and the rise of fascism, packed only the most essential memories and the necessary words in his eyes. Mámishi would take her children, Michalina, Lea, David, and my father, like a bouquet of flowers to "Meksiko," where for six years the old lion with the sweet and tender gaze, *mi abuelo* Mordecay Joseph Bornstein Goldboaum, *hijo de*

Nehemiah Bornstein Bielawski and Yenta Goldboaum, had earned their passage southwest across the River Vistula by selling ties on the street to gentlemen with dark eyes who stroked their land in their pockets as they too crossed a river and sent for their own families. Men who carried their need to the other side and offered the toil of their hands, enduring humiliation with *familia* strength. Men like *mis tíos*, braceros returning to Aztlán, the heartland of the ancients in *el norte*,[6] a line that I too was to cross in 1964 at age fifteen, holding on to my mother's dreams, the childhood of my little brother Abraham, and the work of my oldest sibilings, Frida, David, and Rebeca.

IV. From the Land of Abuelos: Weavers/From the Land of Grandparents: Weavers

Una cigueña stands on one leg on the roof of the synagogue surrounded by the white countryside of winter and hope.[7] It witnesses the turning of the land red with anger and hate. Balancing on the border of identities and religions, this time between Nazi and Jew, my family migrates again. Mámishi and Tatishi wove their hope out of the forest and across an ocean. Their yarn spun an unknown future and a boat carried their dreams like a prayer shawl over their heads. In their hearts they carried a blessing and the most sacred thought from Jaime Mayer Horovich Engel, my great-grandfather, and his wife, Lea Felner. In his novel, my father remembered:

> *"Nunca olvides que eres judío."*
> *El Rojo no aguantó.*
> *"¡Qué broma! Vives en un estado feudal, en pleno siglo veinte y en el corazón de Europa; ghetto escolar, pogroms, vejaciones, Hitler de vecino . . . ¡y olvidarse de que es uno judío . . . !"*

> "Never forget that you are a Jew."
> El Rojo couldn't stand it.
> "What a joke! You live in a feudal state, at the height of the twentieth century in the heart of Europe; student ghetto, pogroms, mistreatment, Hitler for a neighbor . . . and not to forget that one is a Jew . . . !"[8]

I am sure that my father carried this sentence in his proud and kind heart for the rest of his life. I see it in my children's eyes when they are called "Meskins" and told to go back from where they came even though their birth is rooted on this land.

It is said that the quota of Polish citizens immigrating to the United States was filled and in spite of having explicitly invited the tired, the poor, and the huddled masses yearning to be free, Lady Liberty pointed south. "No more Jews allowed in here," she signaled in the night, and today she is still pointing south across the river, bridge, fence to political and economic refugees speaking Spanish.

My father was to take the Zelechow of his childhood to the warmth of ancient rites and poetry, *la tierra mexicana*/the Mexican land, where he was to write in Spanish and knit sweaters for his firstborn, his daughter Frida.

V. Abraham y Cristina: My Parents

No sé dónde empezaron tus ojos, ni ese amor capaz de cruzar un océano para acurrucarse como paloma en el pecho de una mexicana, mi madre/I do not know where your eyes began, nor that love capable of crossing an ocean to cuddle up like a dove on the breast of a Mexican woman, my mother, María Cristina Gómez Sánchez, daughter of Margarita Sánchez Ortiz, my mestiza grandmother and her Spanish husband, Andrés Gómez Peral.

Mámishi almost died of a heart attack when she learned that my father was to marry outside of the faith—to a woman named Cristina *para colmo de sus males*, "oy gevalt!"[9] She wanted her to change her name to Ruth and create a melodramatic Jewish soap opera. Cristina held her ground and Abraham married her anyway in a little church, holding on to his Jewish heart, where he promised his God to stand by her, to support her in the bearing of her five children. She in turn, promised la Virgen de Guadalupe that she would support the bearing of his literary work and journeys.

It was on one of those journeys, at age thirty-six, that the car veered to the right on a stretch of highway near Lagos de Moreno, Mexico, turning and tossing my baby brother, Abraham, out the window and killing my father, killing my mother's passion. To this day I remember how deep her sorrow was, how profound her pain, always, in spite of time and grandchildren in our ancestor's land. This event has always been part of me even though I was only three years old.

The House of Memory

EN ESTOS TIEMPOS
Quizá este poema sea una elegía
o simplemente
> *se me antoje recordar*
>> *entallarme las palabras.*

Así
lanzo el anzuelo por la memoria;
tal vez recobre la imagen velada,
> *oscura tierra entre mis labios.*

Hoy
solamente me quedan:
> *algunas hojas polvorientas*
>> *(posiblemente huelen a ti)*
> *unos jirones de piel esparcida*
>> *inclinados al pasado*
> *una voz tardía*
>> *alargada por el tiempo*
una mano implícita que acaricia mis poemas.
No, la verdad es que no te recuerdo
así, con el inventario intacto de tus huesos
> *pero quisiera acordarme*
> *de tus pasos cotidianos*
> *de tus amigos, tus quesos, tus cigarros*
> *y tu amor definitivo a México.*

Sólo me queda tu perfil en un sueño
y en el hueco de la mano
> *estas inútiles palabras.*

IN THESE TIMES
Perhaps this poem is an elegy / or I simply feel like remembering / trying on words. / So / I cast the fishhook through memory; / maybe I can retrieve the hidden image, / dark land between my lips. / For now / I only have left: / some dusty sheets of paper / (perhaps they smell like you) / a few shreds of scattered skin / leaning toward the past / a belated voice / extended over time / an implicit hand caressing my poems. / No, the truth is that I don't really remember you / with the entire inventory of your bones / however, I wish I could remember / your daily steps / your friends,

your cheeses, your cigarettes / and your definite love for Mexico. / I only have your profile in a dream left / and in the palm of my hand / these useless words.[10]

VI: Mother Border Struggle

At thirty-two years of age, my widowed mother headed north to a small border town, where my little brother and I watched American tourists with curiosity and pretended to speak English by twisting our mouths, making strange faces and sounds, and then rolling on the floor laughing, holding our aching bellies.

For practical purposes, *mami* got used to widowhood, just like her mother with her six children and her grandmother with her own six children. For three generations, the curse of the widow's peak.[11] Curious strands of inherited hair became an art as she fed all of us by combing ladies' hair in the living room of our humble house in Nogales, Sonora. Pushing aside her constant tiredness and the rude remarks because her clients' straight, dark Mexican hair did not conform to the curled, blond beehive of the woman who appeared on the worn-out pages of a magazine written in English, she worked spinning smiles in her eyes as she watched her children eat with gratitude in their hearts. *Arroz y frijoles* were her offering to our future.

VII: Crossing Rivers: Vistula and Rio Grande

In spite of the kindness of our people and the fire of her fierce spirit, the harshness of life for a widow with five children and a grandchild proved too much for my mother. Again, my family headed north, this time across that boundary that only welcomes working hands, agricultural hands, hands to smooth wrinkles on clothes, hands that wash the shame of hoarding so much, invisible hands that service, feed, and clothe a nation that takes so much from so many and offers prayers on television and says grace in "English Only."

I remember my mother's hands, long and delicate beings of love and devotion. Hands that brought sustenance to the soul with every meal no matter the struggle of the day. Hands that appeared over and over again,

offering the bounty of unconditional love until crossing the border to *al otro lado*,[12] where my mother folded the Mister's underwear, cleaned dirt, and kept her designated place in a *House and Garden* home. Her hands allowed *a los del otro lado* to live without the weight of daily life, to fill their lungs with the luxury of pride, and to not ever learn the kind of dignity that simple work can bring to the spirit. Sometimes, if mother performed her duties well and there were no social engagements for which to prepare, *la Misis*[13] would grant my mother permission on a Sunday to run to the edge of Mexico and reach across the border to her children, who were not yet allowed in this country.

I remember my mother's hands, becoming small, soft, and new like baby's kisses, sneaking past uniformed, vigilant "legal" eyes through the chain-link fence, reaching for my budding adolescence and my little brother's perpetual innocence. She kissed our fingers and our hands linked, hungering for each other across our pain, our need staring at us like *púas desgarrando el corazón*/thorns tearing into the heart. A line imposed long before us by history, war, and greed now splitting the most sacred union between mother and child, our being.

All this sacrifice to become "legal aliens," but "aliens" nonetheless in our ancestor's land.

I still remember my mother's hands, now filled with the Arizona Desert, eternal time and silence.

VII: Talking of Struggles

I have always known that I had relatives of fire like an omen hanging from my neck. Ashes stuck to the epidermis fallen to this land like living molecules of long ago. Who would have said that, unfamiliar as I am to their sky, I would trace the footsteps of their words back into their Jewish eyes and learn to step around unearthed bodies scattered like forgotten residue of madness, a hate unadorned and open. I can't help but think that considering the history of my people and those who have survived across borders, rivers, boundaries of bigotry . . . my very own life could be considered a miracle. In the same context, *me impresiona imaginarme que en otro espacio, en otro tiempo mi sangre judía me delataría; mis hijos marcados por sus abuelos que no conocen serían convertidos en cenizas desperdigadas en un bosque sobre las alas de pájaros que ahora llegan a mí, a esta página, como el humo de aquellos seres arremolina-*

*dos en el rincón del miedo/*I am deeply moved upon imagining that in another space, in another time, my Jewish blood would give me away; my children designated by their great-grandparents, whom they do not know, would be converted to ashes scattered in a forest on the wings of birds that now come to me, to this page, like the smoke of those beings crowding around each other in the corner of fear.

From my father I inherited the word like the strands of *cuentos de espantos* given to my childhood by *la viejita del barrio*, the ancient storyteller who dished out images and *cocoricos* as big as *la luna llena*.[14] Holding the hand of *mi hermanito*, the way home was long, under the eye of that moon, with her ghost stories still rattling in our bones and imagination.

Finally, I would return to my mother's arms to dream of words left dancing in my eyes. Words like rivers entwined with memories as ancient as *paredes de Israel y pirámides/*walls of Israel and pyramids, where rituals assured the survival of the sun, and it is still that way.

This is my ritual, my way of keeping alive the bloods in me, given to these hands to weave a precious prayer shawl, this time a woman's cloth, a rebozo, with the colors of our own history and culture, to cross over the pain and reach the song within each of us.[15] Inherited fierce mother courage given to me to survive what is left behind and struggle for what must continue.

1. Abraham Bornstein, *El llanto del Vístula* (Mexico, D.F.: Ediciones de América, 1944), p. 158. In his short life (1916–1952) my father became a writer in Mexico and, although there are several unpublished manuscripts, this novel as well as a children's play were published in Mexico City. This novel is written in Spanish and it deals with life and the characters that lived in his small rural hometown, Zelechow, right up to the Holocaust. It ends with a description of resistance efforts in the defense of Warsaw against the Nazis, an expression of gratitude and love for his adopted country, and a lyrical cry for freedom on behalf of the oppressed and the poor.

2. Mesquite (from the nahuatl *mizquitl*) is a tree native to the southwestern United States and Mexico, which bears *péchitas*, a beanlike pods that are sweet and edible. *La casita* is when children play house.

3. The saguaro or sahuaro is a giant cactus native to the southwestern United States and northern Mexico.

4. Ocotillos are spiny, woody, furrowed shrubs found in the southwestern United States and arid regions of Mexico. They produce a long, bright red flower in the spring.

5. *Sacerdotisas:* priestesses.

6. *Mis tíos:* my uncles. The term braceros derives from the word *brazo* or arm. To meet the labor shortage of the 1940s, the United States and Mexico set up a program in which Mexican citizens worked as hired hands or laborers. By the time this form of cheap labor ended in 1964, close to five million braceros had worked in the United States. Aztlán is the original Aztec homeland in what is now the Southwestern United States. *El norte:* the north, in reference to the United States and to Aztlán, the Aztec's ancestral homeland.

7. *Una cigüeña:* a stork.

8. Bornstein, p. 156.

9. *para colmo de sus males:* to make things worse.

10. Miriam Bornstein, in *Donde Empieza la Historia* (Sacramento: Spanish Press, 1993), p. 27.

11. It is believed, particularly in Mexican culture, that when a person's hairline forms a peak on the forehead, he/she will eventually become a widower/widow.

12. *Al otro lado:* the other side of the border; in my case, Nogales, Arizona.

13. *La Misis:* the Mrs., the woman of the house who employed the domestic workers.

14. *cuentos de espantos:* ghost stories; *la viejita del barrio:* the elderly neighborhood lady; *cocoricos:* a type of cookie made with corn flour in northern Mexico; *la luna llena:* the full moon.

15. Rebozo: a Mexican shawl traditionally worn by women.

From Always from Somewhere Else

Marjorie Agosín

The Deep Breath of Exile

All exiles are like deep breaths, imperceptible in uninhabited landscapes. We abandoned our country at night. No one saw us take off. Like fugitives we gazed one more time at the Andean cordillera as the wind created ridges and scars in the dampness of our tear-drenched faces.

The Melody of Exile

My father always told me that he was always from somewhere else and that he looked at maps to invent cities. He also said that his parents had told him that he was always from somewhere else and that he was a child of the diaspora. But when he spoke to me, in 1968, about leaving Chile, this idea of belonging to a community of foreign exiles stirred within me a fear that came from vacant tables and broken mirrors.

I felt that my body was covered with a green layer of scales and bad omens. I felt cold when I heard the paper maps rustling in the hands of my parents. I didn't want to see anything new. I loved my country, its shores and its melodic language like the sweet rippling rivers. Yet I heard a voice that said: We will go to look for other islands, to surround ourselves with other seas.

My mother balanced herself within a dark and magical circle, telling us that Jews lack a national identity, that we are the most orphaned and exiled people of the earth. But I didn't want to be an orphan. I wanted to have friends and to accompany them while they left flowers for the Virgins. I wanted to sit in the folded skirts of the old shepherd who sweated in his heavy woolen garments in the summer months.

The House of Memory

Sometimes I used to hide in my pockets *milagros*, the little mass cards bearing colored pictures of the saints. But I knew that Jewish girls didn't have saints to protect them.

This time my best friends told me that I would return to the land of the Hebrews. The word *Jews* seemed too harsh, and not the least bit subtle. In fact, we were not going to Israel, the homeland of the Jews, but to the United States, the last stop on so many immigrant trails of tears.

Once again, we prepared to depart. My mother carried a handful of dirt from the southern regions of her childhood, and my father his skeletons, which accompanied him on his nights of shadows. I, on the other hand, did not know what to take with me. My cache of possessions seemed like a depository of lost objects. Memory seemed to stick to me like a covered tattoo. But I left with them and accepted the condition of being from somewhere else and from nowhere in particular.

In the evenings sometimes, I still wake up sweating, as my father does, and I don't find the maps or the suitcases, only the nightmares of being a traveler without a place to go. The experience of exile is like a sinister rainfall. No one recognizes my name or the fragrance of my skin, and no one caresses me because I am alone in a place where no one even recognizes my voice. This is how the lost and ephemeral memories of exiles are.

Suddenly, the voice of a messenger or an angel tells me that memory is right here, that it is like a music box that needs only to be opened in order to begin the process of recall.

Nostalgia

From the nostalgia-laden past, we invent countries like dreams; we sketch false rivers, imagine certain aromas, and speak the language of the homeland as if it were a ring sealing love's alliances.

＊　＊　＊　＊　＊

Letters

Seated by my side with an old and distant gaze, my father asks me if the letters have arrived—those letters from Chile that foreshadow the happiness of newlyweds and the peace of the dead, those letters that we have waited for, daily, for nearly thirty years. They are letters from distant friends, who talk to him about his dilapidated laboratory and about our

house, now inhabited by the noises made by the footsteps of others.

People in exile adjust to foreign landscapes. They hold onto letters with much eagerness and passion—a passion for memory, for past experiences, and for usurped time. I contemplate my father waiting for the letters. He has the gaze of an absent man who interrogates beings from other spheres, from countries close to an also distant sky. Exile is a state of crude recalling, of being and not being anywhere, of waiting for the arrival of the familiar in foreign places, of feeling oneself always remote.

Living in Translation

Our life in the United States has always balanced itself between the frontiers of return and the misty memory of flight. When we arrived in Athens, Georgia, we bought few pieces of furniture because we were always hoping to return to Chile. We talked about our country, wrote letters, and dreamed about the cordillera, knowing that we lived too far away from it. We ate our tasty foods seasoned with garlic and herbs, our fresh vegetables, and never tried to become part of a culture that was so foreign and distant from our own, where people greeted each other with caution, where time was a slender border of fear, and where no one dared to ask about the health of the sick. We lived in a borrowed zone, knowing that at any moment we might have to leave, as if we were waiting for the end of the war, the surrender of our furniture, and the glorious return to life.

Chile's military dictatorship lasted almost twenty years. We lost friends who disappeared clandestinely and who now have disappeared from the memory of those who knew them. We missed births and funerals. Our identity lay confused, suspended between imaginary and real borders. We lived in translation.

Now all of us reside in a type of atemporal land, in a region lost between the memory of what was and what we have fabricated across distances. We are Jews without a country. Every day we learn other languages and live in borrowed houses. I believe that if they were to blindfold us, we would find the road home.

Translated from the Spanish by Celeste Kostopulos-Cooperman

From Belarus to Bolondron:
A Daughter's Dangerous Passage

Ester Rebeca Shapiro Rok

In telling the story of my Cuban Eastern European Jewish American self, I listen closely to a competing cacophony of ancestral voices carrying 150 years of oral history and living memory, because among them I discern the currents of my own life. I must reconstruct the dislocated narrative of a family life unfolding in a turn-of-the-century Russian-Polish border shtetl village and then transplanted across three continents, two world wars, two revolutions, and five languages. Contrary as always, I insist on scrambling the official story and casting my central protagonists in contradiction to the cherished myths our family still lives by. From my earliest memories in Havana, Cuba, I grew up in the hothouse atmosphere of my father's profound attachment to his parents, Abuela Berta and Abuelo Lazaro, and his brother, Tío Noel. My father's family formed intense ties of mutual protection and loyalty in the long passage from the shtetl in Rubyshevish, Belarus, to the rural Cuban village of Bolondron. You would never have known from the way we lived our daily lives, as patrilineal as any Bedouin tribe, that my father had a sister, Tia Consuelo, whose story I carefully studied as a daughter's cautionary tale.

In Abuela Berta's family mythology, stories of shtetl hardship paved the way for the family's creation myth, her decision to undertake the arduous journey out of Eastern Europe in 1936 and book passage to Cuba. The family's voyage, like any heroic quest, required that we outwit a cruel, arbitrary fate whose small coincidences and near-misses obscured the enormous consequences. If we could catch the appointed train, we could begin a passage ending in a land of palm trees and plenty. If we missed the

230

From Belarus to Bolondron: A Daughter's Dangerous Passage

many necessary connections, we would leave the shtetl on a different train, and remain forever in Poland, strewn as smoke and ashes in Hitler's crematoria.

To hear Abuela Berta tell our family stories, her daughter, my exuberant Tia Consuelo, was a source of eternal danger requiring constant maternal vigilance until she was finally married off and became her husband's concern. Why, I wondered, was Consuelo so cruelly left out in the cold of her own family's inner circle? She herself never stopped protesting the enormity of her own family's rejection, even as she married the men they chose for her, twice by the age of seventeen. Consuelo lived a difficult life by the side of the my explosively sentimental Tio Isaac, whose profound loyalty to his own sister was forged by the crematoria fires that left them sole survivors of their Polish family. Her marriage created the haunting irony of Consuelo's life: for her husband, his sister always came first, reminding her cruelly of her invisibility to her own brothers in her own family. She lavished her generous soul's love on her son, Leon, and daughter, Leye, her six grandchildren, and her four great-grandchildren. All her thriving family are loyally devoted to the cause of making Consuelo, at long last, feel loved. At her husband Tio Isaac's funeral, Consuelo, then age seventy, told me that not a single day goes by when she doesn't remember the violence and pain of her childhood, hard as she tries to forget those bitter memories and enjoy the outpourings of love from her children, grandchildren, and great-grandchildren.

But I don't want to make it seem that Consuelo was a shrinking and pitiful presence. On the contrary, it was precisely her passionate intensity, her vivid curiosity, which overflowed the borders of our otherwise constricted shtetl family. Abuela Berta could tolerate expansive strivings on behalf of her sons, but could not make room for Consuelo's downright dangerous sensuality. Abuela Berta might have known how to manage her daughter Nachame—the name meaning "consolation" in Hebrew—under the strict rules of their shtetl life. Now, their lives were utterly unbounded by old traditions, transported into a new world that could hardly be imagined but was unquestionably filled with the dangers that had always followed Jews on their many diasporic voyages. Consuelo, as eleven-year-old Nachame, began the voyage to Cuba in 1936 and later she recast the story as a picaresque tale. At the age of adolescence, she experienced the family's terrifying train trip across an increasingly dangerous Europe as the finest adventure of her cloistered, claustrophobic shtetl life. As they waited for

the ship that would cross the Atlantic to Cuba, Nachame evaded her parent's watchfulness and took her little brothers wandering in London. Family legend tells the tale that they only made it back to the hotel by capricious chance because she located a passerby who spoke Yiddish and was able to direct them. My father's version of this story betrays his eternal conflict between a younger brother's admiration for his adventurous sister and his anxiety turned to terror that they could, at any point along the journey, be lost and surely perish as children alone in a dangerous world. When Abuela Berta related this portion of the journey she added the moral of the story to her cautionary tale, reminding us that in our family quest for survival, we could only count on fellow Jews.

Once the family arrived safely on the boat, new dangers awaited. The long trip in the ship's crowded third-class hold terrified our landlocked shtetl family. My father Jaime, still six-year-old Nachemie on that trip, and his nine-year-old brother Neiach, soon to become Noel, were free to roam the ship in Consuelo's wake, ostensibly to watch over her dangerous sense of adventure, but actually to reap the benefits of her intense sociability. Consuelo so charmed the crew and first-class passengers that she obtained far better accommodations for them, including regular access to first-class meals, the fear of hunger always a looming detail in my father's stories. After their long voyage across a darkening Europe and a turbulent Atlantic Ocean, Nachame arrived in Cuba as Consuelo, now a fully developed young woman. Her name still meant consolation, but that apparent continuity masked a world of difference and marked the ironic tensions between old world and new that characterized her growing up as well as my own.

Consuelo ripened into a voluptuous young woman, a full-faced, full-bosomed Russian beauty, with a pale yet rosy complexion, softly wavy blond hair, and lively green eyes that showed her alert curiosity and intense emotionality. Consuelo was short yet round and big-breasted as a young girl—what we would call *zaftig* in Yiddish, conveying a generous motherliness, or what we could call *sabrosa* in Spanish, conveying a generous and enticing sensuality. Consuelo's presence was further enlarged by her voice. Her speaking voice seemed to be broadcast out of larger than usual lungs, or maybe was amplified and resonant in her massive frame. She became bluntly outspoken, in an inimitable blend of Polish shtetl coarseness and Cuban *chusmeria* (slang specializing in salacious double-meanings), shattering the silence of a family where most feelings were

expressed indirectly, if at all. Consuelo always seemed to be in some excited uproar. She had replaced her shtetl Yiddish with a countryside Spanish, and her voice inevitably took on a powerful, expansive quality that filled the room, punctuated by picturesque obscenities. During my own growing up between cultures, this time in Miami after we left Cuba, Consuelo became a cherished source for scarce family images of a woman with passions and appetites. While my ascetic mother treated sexuality as a secret that reduced her to stuttering silence, Consuelo was an exuberant cook, her food fragrant with excessive garlic and cumin, her language peppered with obscenities: she sought any opportunity to call a *pinga* by its proper name. Consuelo's zest in evoking sex with its concrete, vivid intimacy remained a referent in my clandestine sexual awakening, wedged between Havana and Hollywood, in the end closely mirroring her own.

My favorite story about Consuelo's growing up as the bridge between two worlds was the family legend about her brief first marriage at the age of sixteen. To me, the circumstances of that marriage, one of those family secrets that everyone knew, captured Consuelo's history and place in the family, which I feared could so easily become my own. Mostly, the story of the brief prelude to her first marriage, which was itself of even briefer duration, captured my imagination and explained something essential to me about the family forces that denied her control of her own life. Consuelo presented my practical and implacable Abuela Berta with the terrible dilemma of bringing her daughter up as a proper young lady in an unfamiliar foreign land. She found the period after Consuelo's puberty especially demanding and treacherous, coming so soon after their immigration. Abuela Berta told me once, part proudly and part fearfully aware of the great dangers involved, that all the young and eligible young men, as well as others not so young and eligible, had fallen in love with Consuelo, including the town's chief of police. Consuelo was being asked out by a number of passionate suitors and frequently serenaded at night, in the fashion of Cuban romance. Curious as always, Consuelo found these suitor's attentions compelling proof of her attractiveness and value. Yet her interest in the local young men was completely forbidden; since there were no other Jewish families in their village, Consuelo was expected to wait patiently for an arranged marriage.

More quickly than the family could handle, Consuelo's intense curiosity and sexuality presented the problem of finding a suitable young man among the Ashkenazim of Cuba, the Eastern European, Yiddish-speaking

Jews, all of whom were referred to as *polacos*, whatever their national origin. Cuba was profoundly foreign to my family that even its Jews were unacceptable. The Spanish Jews, the Sefardim, were called *turcos* and were considered foreigners, of a different race, and hardly Jews. They might pray in Hebrew, but in the intimacy of their homes they spoke Ladino instead of Yiddish, the intimate language of our homes. One of the family's concessions to American assimilation has been accepting Sefardic Jews as permissible, although still slightly suspect, marital material. In Consuelo's time, with Ashkenazic immigrants so recently uprooted, the Sefardic Jews of Cuba were too alien to provide a needed sense of shared kinship and culture. I consider it one of the great ironies of our tribe's diasporic dispersal that my ancestors, in their inevitable transculturation with their Polish neighbors, absorbed both a far paler skin and a greater portion of Polish racism than I would have desired on behalf of my own Cuban Jewish identity.

In spite of the limited acceptable pool of potential suitors, a match was made for Consuelo through the island network of Eastern European Jewish families; this was done without the intimate knowledge of family background that characterized generations of shtetl life. The young man, whose family lived in Havana, was introduced to Consuelo, and they became betrothed. My grandparents had traveled the seven hours by bus and train from Bolondron to Havana to meet with him and his family and evaluate their suitability. They found them to be apparently well-to-do hotel keepers, which probably provided additional appeal to Abuela Berta, since her mother's father had been an innkeeper in Rubyshevish. She was relieved that this mutually acceptable family match also pleased her headstrong daughter.

Now, I have heard many conflicting versions of the story of this ill-fated marriage's abrupt dissolution, embellished by each speaker according to his or her own point of view. Abuela Lazaro told me his remembered story thirty-five years later in Hollywood, Florida, his smoke-roughened voice and thickly Russian-accented Spanish adding to the intensity of his already agitated retelling. My grandparents wanted desperately for me to appreciate their side of this sad story and had long ago accepted that I had lost my Yiddish in our United States transplantation. Spanish was now the shared language of family intimacy. Abuela Berta let him take the lead, but inserted necessary details to fill out the narrative and persuade me that they had done all they possibly could for their wayward daughter. As my

grandparents told the story, Consuelo arrived in Havana after a proper Jewish wedding in Jovellanos and at some early point discovered that her new husband and his family were the owners not only of hotels, but also of brothels, which were legal though not respectable in Cuba. Abuela Lazaro angrily remembered that Consuelo had called them in tears, telling them what she had learned about her new husband and in-laws and asking that they take her home. Abuelo Lazaro even suggested that this man expected Consuelo to help out in the family business (as a receptionist or record-keeper?)

Abuelo Lazaro and Abuela Berta's brother-in-law, Tio Loba, married to her sister, Tia Anita, went into Havana together. They severely beat Consuelo's husband and his father, and they brought Consuelo home. According to Abuelo Lazaro, they were taken to court for assault but fully vindicated by the judge, who confirmed that they had acted appropriately in defending the family's honor. Abuelo Lazaro was furious and indignant at this terrible deception and blow to the family's reputation. As a secondary concern in his approach to the court, our family demanded the dowry paid for Consuelo returned, and was vindicated by the court in forcing the money's return. Through the haze of remembered outrage, Abuelo Lazaro proudly recalled the opportunity to rescue his daughter, avenge the family's dishonor, and receive return of the money by his own decisive action. The courts of this exotic new land did deliver a familiar justice.

I later asked my father what he knew about the story of Consuelo's first marriage, and told him what Abuela Berta and Abuelo Lazaro had told me. Father laughed and said my grandparents were either misremembering the story or deliberately re-embroidering it. He had been told by Consuelo herself, when she came home weeping, that her new husband had told her he loved another woman but his real love had been unacceptable to his family. He had agreed to the arranged marriage with Consuelo to satisfy his parents, but he did not love Consuelo and would continue seeing the woman he truly loved. Since, my father continued, Consuelo had been in love with this man, she was heartbroken and refused to continue in the marriage. To me, my then eleven-year-old father's version sounded suspiciously like what Abuela Berta would come up with as an acceptable way of explaining the situation to her impressionable youngest son. The key dramatic elements of my father's version—the young man torn between filial loyalty and romantic love and, of course, choosing filial loyalty—

provided precisely the explanation of events that Abuela Berta was most drawn to, as I learned over the years.

More recently, when my cousin Edith, my Uncle Noel's older daughter, was visiting Boston, she inquired about my writing and I mentioned that I was still working on our family stories. I told her that the best story so far described the family's arrival in Cuba and Consuelo's brief first marriage. Edith, eager to set the facts straight, responded quickly, "Oh, my mother told me that story." Consuelo went to her marriage bed, her husband discovered that she was no longer a virgin, *era una puta*—she was a whore—and he sent her back to her parents. She added that her husband, Joel, was friends with the first husband's son from his second marriage, and could confirm these facts. The story of Consuelo's marriage as seen through my aunt's eyes did not surprise me, because I recognized in it the kind of moralistic cautionary tale used to terrify Edith into protecting her own virginity in the turbulent permissiveness of our shared North American adolescence. I was instead astonished by the extraordinary news that Joel knew a version of the story from the divorced first husband's son. I was frankly shocked by the evidence that our intergenerational lives had continuity, did not drop off the edge of time like amber photographs of a vanished shtetl, of a vanished Cuba. We immediately asked Joel, "So what do you know about this story?" Joel dismissed as fiction the story of Consuelo's lost virginity. Consuelo had been too hurt that her husband had agreed to an arranged marriage while loving another woman, and she had insisted on her right to a love of her own. The story of her lost virginity had been generated by the young man's family, who had been trying to keep Consuelo's dowry payment after the marriage was dissolved, claiming that Consuelo and her family had committed a breach of the arranged marriage contract, which was all about social obligations and mentioned nothing at all about love.

While disagreeing on the motive, everyone agreed that following these events a divorce was quickly arranged. Consuelo immediately met and married Isaac, in 1943 a recent arrival from Poland whose heart and eyes burned with the fires and ashes of the crematoria. Hitler had destroyed all but his sister Rivkeh, the sole witness to a vanished world. As I remember Isaac from when I was growing up, he was a black-haired, mustachioed, portly man, effusive and affectionate in a maudlin way that was embarrassing to us as children. Father and Noel always regarded Isaac as a sentimental clown in the classic Russian style, not to be taken too seriously.

From Belarus to Bolondron: A Daughter's Dangerous Passage

Over the years they were often on and off of speaking terms with him because of Isaac's frequent objections to their failure to give their sister her fair measure of love, respect, and financial support.

After her marriage, Consuelo moved in with her husband and his sister Rivkeh's family, and from that time on was more involved with her husband's family than her own. Yet Consuelo never stopped trying, in the face of repeated failure, to feel more included in the tight family circle that Berta, Lazaro, and their two sons became over the years. Consuelo's relationship with her family finally changed during the months of Abuelo Lazaro's illness and in the period after his death in 1984. At age fifty-seven, Consuelo finally began to feel included as a potentially valued member of her own family, an inclusion still interfered with by Isaac's combative temperaments and by Consuelo's own anguish at a lifetime of rejection. At age seventy-one, so recently a widow, with Abuela Berta's recent death marking the end of a generation, Consuelo may finally be offered a more substantial place in her family as this installment of our shared story continues to unfold.

While I was growing up, the story of Consuelo's marriage and the turn her life had taken terrified me, even when I was too young to understand my fears. I was horrified, as I reached adolescence, of an early marriage within the approved Cuban Jewish family circle and of the claustrophobic life that would follow. As an oldest daughter who had been disappointing to the family for failing to be a firstborn son, I identified with Consuelo. I was destined to share her character, disrespectfully outspoken and with a dangerous tendency to disobedience. By early adolescence I also shared her unhealthy interest in boys, goyim and North American Jews alike. I had been taught, as a Cuban Jewish girl, that whatever my intelligence (regarded suspiciously as related to my disobedience and family disloyalty), my contribution to my own and my family's future well-being would come with my success at attracting a suitable mate. Fully part of my own North America world, I could not at that age visualize myself married, although my competitive self felt that vying for the sexual attentions of men was a fine idea. I ended up applying this family principle rather farther than was acceptable, resulting in violent struggles over my sexual behavior during my adolescence.

In what was my most intense encounter with Consuelo at the intersection of our lives and fates, she talked to me at some length about her attempt to be a loyal daughter and obey her mother's wish that she marry

Isaac. The conversation took place in Consuelo's apartment in Queens, where she lived down the hall from her two married children and her sister-in-law's family. My sister, cousins, and I had all gone to visit Consuelo and her family during Christmas vacation of my senior year in high school.

During that entire visit, Consuelo plotted to engineer my betrothal to her daughter Leye's brother-in-law Enrique, linking me more closely to her family through a marriage within her own extended family. Enrique was a very bright, affectionate, serious older man, an alluring twenty-five to my rebellious seventeen. I enjoyed the romance and the satisfying sense of conquest in our relationship for as long as my adolescent attention span held out. For everyone else in that branch of the family, the whole affair had the serious weight of courtship. During that endless two-week visit, Consuelo would take me aside to explain marriage as it really was, so as to better prepare me for this next, imminent stage in my life. At one point, she was telling me that marriage was a matter of yielding to practical realities. She herself had not known what marriage really demanded when she married Isaac, but she learned to make the best of things.

Warming to her words, as always, she began to speak increasingly loudly and to race around the small apartment, throwing her weighty body from room to room as she seized props to better illustrate her points. As she tried to tell me that marriage involved intimate relations with a relative stranger who often had disgusting habits, and conditions and compromises of that sort, she ran into the bathroom and came out with a towel, screaming, "I even wipe my face with his towel, which is soiled with the pus from the sores on his skin!" She rubbed the towel on her face, exemplifying wifely devotion and sacrifice, which presumably would soon fall to me as well.

It seems extraordinarily ironic, looking back on it, that Consuelo of all people should have tried hardest of all to marry me off at the significant age of seventeen. I'm not sure if she was aware of my parent's despairing, futile attempts to control my sexual relationships with boys to the limits of proper feminine virtue. Perhaps she felt an early marriage would in my case, as in hers, succeed in channeling my sexual energy and curiosity to the proper object, before my virtue was lost. (Little did she know how lost it was already.) Maybe she felt my parents and grandparents would be grateful to her for providing me with such a good match and at the same time saving me from the dangers of my impetuous character. After all, my

cousins were already talking about my disobedience and sexual effrontery, saying *"que se portaba como une puta"*— how I behaved like a whore. Consuelo became absorbed in taking control of my life at the same age and in the same way that others had taken control of hers, by arranging an early marriage.

At the time of my visit to her home I felt a peculiar sensation of being party to a Russian courtship. The unfamiliar winter setting in a snowy New York added to my eerie feeling of participating in the romantic rituals of another world, as if the lost world of the Polish shtetl had been parachuted into Queens. In Consuelo's living room, thick, red velvet curtains were always drawn, and the ornate lamps cast a darker glow against the heavy furniture. My American ideas about my place as a liberated woman reminded me that this scene could not possibly be for real. Yet the strain of ancient expectations collided with my own view of my life and began to seem too close to a possible reality, no longer a hilarious cross-cultural romp I could later share with my hippie friends. For the first (and last) time, I called my father and begged to return home early.

Consuelo and I have remained close, and she understands how deeply I appreciate her indomitable personality and the dilemmas it created for her in our constricted Shapiro clan. Consuelo has developed an intimate relationship with her own daughter, and has never repeated her own sad history by devaluing her older daughter in favor of her younger son. Consuelo's children's and grandchildren's filial loyalty and capacity for expansive expressions of love for one another has always seemed to me to be Consuelo's enduring legacy.

When I saw Consuelo at the wedding of her then twenty-two-year-old granddaughter, Lisette, I went to sit with her for a brief while, she huge and resplendent in a white lace hand-beaded dress, her blond hair carefully lacquered, her diamond and gold jewelry bountiful evidence that she had made material success of her married life. I remembered that we had recently seen each other at a family event, and she had contemptuously looked at my ethnic beads and asked me in her characteristically brusque way, *"Oyeme, chica, cuando tu marido te va a comprar joyas de verdad?"*— when is your husband going to buy you some real jewelry? Two years later, I was divorced and at the wedding alone. We had one of our customary, searingly intense talks about our intertwined lives. She asked me if I was planning to have a child on my own, as it was too important a piece of living to sacrifice, with or without a man, and to hell with what

people thought. I told her I was planning to do exactly that if I remained single much longer, and she offered her approval and support. I mentioned that I had continued to write about her and the family, and wondered if I had her permission to publish this work sometime. She said that she had always been proud of her ability to live her own life rather than be dominated by her parents, with their fears and prejudices. *"Yo siempre hice lo que me dio la gana"*—I always did what I felt like doing—she said proudly. "I don't care who knows it." I thanked her for this gift of her life, made with her customary generosity and seasoned with her *picardia*, her sense of mischief, sharing her desire that in our self-important, self-protective family, all hell should break loose.

Biographical Notes

Writers

Marjorie Agosín (Chile, 1955) moved permanantly to the United States in 1968 with her parents, who were themselves the children of exiles from Eastern Europe. She is a poet, essayist, critic, and international activist. Her many books include *Always from Somewhere Else: A Memoir of My Chilean Jewish Father* (1998), *A Cross and a Star: Memoirs of a Jewish Girl in Chile,* (1997), *Dear Anne Frank* (1994), and *Scraps of Life: Chilean Women and the Pinochet Dictatorship* (1987), among many others. Winner of the Letras de Oro Prize and the Latino Literature Prize, Agosín is chair of the Spanish department at Wellesley College.

Ruth Behar (Cuba, 1956) came to the United States in 1962, immigrating with her Cuban parents. Her love for the island of her childhood has been a central theme of her writings. She is professor of anthropology at the University of Michigan and has won many awards including a MacArthur grant. Her works include *The Vulnerable Observer: Anthropology That Breaks Your Heart* (1996), and *Translated Woman: Crossing the Border with Esperanza's Story* (1993), an account of her friendship with a Mexican street peddler. Behar is the editor of *Bridges to Cuba* (1995) and coeditor of *Women Writing Culture* (1995), an anthology about the creative writing of women anthropologists. Behar is currently writing a memoir.

Miriam Bornstein (Mexico, 1950), a poet and literary critic, was born in Mexico to a Mexican mother and a Polish father, whose family fled Poland just before the Nazi takeover. Bornstein's family immigrated to the United States when she was fourteen, settling in Arizona, where Bornstein earned her Ph.D. This bicultural border experience continues to influence Bornstein's poetic voice. She is the author of *Bajo Cubierta* (1976) and *Donde Empieza la Historia* (1993). Her poetry has appeared in national and international anthologies, including *Daughters of the Fifth Sun* (1995) and *Floricanto Sí: A Collection of Latina Poetry* (1998). Bornstein is associate professor at the University of Denver, where she teaches Chicano/a and Latin American literature and culture.

Alicia Freilich de Segal (Venezuela, 1939), daughter of Yiddish-speaking journalist Máximo Freilich, grew up in a home filled with Venezuelan Jewish writers. After receiving her Ph.D. in literature from Venezuela's Universidad Central, she began publishing critical essays and cultural journalism in leading newspapers and magazines. The author of two prize-winning works of fiction, *Claper* (1987; tr. *Claper*, 1998) and *Colombina descubierta* (1991), Freilich de Segal also represents prominent Jewish organizations in Venezuela.

241

Luisa Futoransky (Argentina, 1939), a born traveler who often calls herself a perpetual gypsy, is a poet, novelist, and short story writer. Futoransky, who typically considers Jewish themes in her work, has received several international prizes as well as a Guggenheim fellowship and the Chevalier des Arts et des Lettres granted by the French government. In Spain she received the Carmen Conde Prize for her book of poetry, *El divan de la puerta dorada* (1984). She is also the author of one novel, *Son cuentos chinos* (1983), the story of her life in Peking as a radio announcer. She currently resides in Paris and is a translator for UNESCO.

Margo Glantz (Mexico, 1930) is a writer, essayist, and professor of literature at the UNAM, the National Autonomous University of Mexico, in Mexico City. Glantz is the author of many books of essays and short stories. *Las genealogías* (1981; tr. *The Family Tree*, 1991), an autobiographical memoir about her father, Jacobo Glantz, is her most well known work. Others include *Erosiones* (1984) and *Síndrome de naufragios* (1984). In addition to her prolific writing career, Glantz is also cultural attaché to London.

Angélica Gorodischer (Argentina, 1930) moved to the city of Rosario after studying at the University of Buenos Aires. She is a prominent cultural figure and activist in her adopted city. Also a short story writer, novelist, and essayist, Gorodischer is the author of ten novels. She is best known for her science fiction writing, in particular for her character Trafalgar, an extraterrestrial being who converses with Rosario's writers in cafes. She has received much acclaim for *Trafalgar* (1990), as well as for her novels *Mala noche y parir hembra* (1983) and *Bajo la jubeas en flor* (1973).

Sonia Guralnik (Chile, 1924) has lived in Chile for almost sixty years. Although her native language is Russian, she began writing in Spanish when she was almost forty years old. Guralnik has published numerous short stories in Chilean newspapers, a book of stories called *El Samovar* (1984), and an autobiographical novel, *Recuento de la mujer gusano* (1991). Most of her work deals with issues of Jewish identity in Latin America. Guralnik, who is also an acclaimed chef, lives in Santiago.

Rosita Kalina (Costa Rica, 1939) trained in comparative literature and received her master's degree in English literature. She then became professor at the University of Costa Rica. Kalina's poetry, essays, and fiction have appeared in several of her country's newspapers. Her book *Los signos y el tiempo* (1988) won the National Prize for Poetry. Other books include *Esa dimensión lejana* (1997) and *Cruce de niebla* (1980). Currently, she is director for cultural affairs at the Department of Education.

Alicia Kozameh (Argentina, 1953), born to a Jewish mother and a father whose family belonged to the Greek Orthodox Church, was baptized a Catholic and sent to a Catholic boarding school. Her political activities led to a three-year prison sentence in Rosario and Buenos Aires, a period of her life detailed in her novel *Pasos bajo el agua* (1987; tr. *Steps Under Water*, 1996). In addition to novels, Kozameh writes short stories, memoirs, and screenplays. She now lives in Los Angeles, California.

Biographical Notes

Clarice Lispector (Brazil, 1925–1977), who was born in the Ukraine, arrived in Brazil when she was two months old. A well-known author, Lispector was also a journalist, contributing numerous essays to Brazilian newspapers. Among her many books are *Laços de Família* (1960; tr. *Family Ties*, 1972), *Maçã no escuro* (1967; tr. *The Apple in the Dark*, 1986), and *Agua viva* (1973; tr. *The Stream of Life*, 1989), which was recognized by the French philosopher Hélène Cixous. She died in Rio de Janeiro and was buried in the city's Jewish district.

Barbara Mujica (Chile, 1949) is a novelist, short story writer, and critic who has lived much of her life in the United States. Her book-length fiction includes *The Death of Don Bernardo* (1990), *Affirmative Actions!* (1999), and *Far from My Mother's Home* (1999), a collection of stories. A two-time nominee for the Pushcart Prize, Mujica won the E. L. Doctorow International Fiction Competition in 1992 and has received a number of grants for her work. Mujica writes extensively on Spanish Golden Age literature and is professor of Spanish at Georgetown University. She also directs El Retablo, a Spanish-language theater group.

Angelina Muñiz-Huberman (Mexico, 1936) was born in southern France as her parents were escaping the Spanish Civil War. The author of almost thirty books including novels, essay collections, and poetry collections, Muñiz-Huberman has won many prizes in Mexico including the Xavier Villarutia for her work *Huerto cerrado, huerto sellado* (1972; tr. *Enclosed Garden*, 1988), and the Sor Juana Ines de la Cruz Prize. Among her works are *De magias y pródigos* (1987) and *De cuerpo entero* (1991). Muñiz-Huberman teaches at the UNAM in Mexico City.

Rosa Nissan (Mexico, 1939) grew up in a Sephardic household in the Jewish community of Mexico City. The mother of four children, Nissan went against family tradition by enrolling in journalism courses. She went on to participate in workshops directed by famed Mexican writer Elena Poniatowska. Beginning in 1983, Nissan published sixteen short stories, followed by two novels, *Novia que te vea* (1993) and *Hischo que te nazca* (1996). She continues to live and write in Mexico City.

Teresa Porzecanski (Uruguay, 1948) is a writer, anthropologist, and professor of cultural anthropology at the Universidad de la República in Montevideo. She is also a poet and an essayist. Her recent fiction includes *Invención de los soles* (1981), an erotic novel, *Ciudad impune* (1986), and *Historias de vida de inmigrantes judios al Uruguay* (1986).

Reina Roffé (Argentina, 1951) studied journalism and literature at the University of Buenos Aires. In 1979 she won the Borges Prize for her first work, the short story "Profanation." She traveled and studied in Europe and the United States and began to write nontraditional novels that question stereotypes of sexuality and gender. Among such works are *La rompiente* (1987) and *El cielo dividido* (1996). Roffé, like so many of her generation, left Argentina in 1976 and moved to Madrid, where she still resides and works as a journalist and writer.

Ester Rebeca Shapiro Rok (Cuba, 1952) was born in Havana to an Eastern European family that had arrived in Cuba shortly before the Holocaust, and left it for Miami shortly after the revolution. She is associate professor of psychology at the University of Massachusetts, Boston, and director of health resources at the Mauricio Gaston Institute for Latino Research, Pubic Policy and Community Development, and has published several books in the field of psychology.

Graciela Safranchik (Argentina, 1953) lives rather reclusively in Rosario. Her published works include *Cruce de niebla* (1995) and *Kadish* (1993).

Ana María Shua (Argentina, 1951) writes novels, short stories, children's books, and essays. Among her many books are *Soy paciente* (1980; tr. *Patient*, 1997) and *El libro de los recuerdos* (1994; tr. *The Book of Memories*, 1998). The grandchild of Jewish immigrants from Poland and Lebanon, Shua often writes about relations between first- and third-generation Argentine Jews. The recipient of a Guggenheim fellowship in 1993, Shua has also worked in journalism, advertising, and film.

Alicia Steimberg (Argentina, 1933) has received numerous literary awards throughout her career. In 1983 she was awarded a Fulbright to join the International Writing Program at the University of Iowa. Her many works include *Músicos y relojeros* (1971; tr. *Musicians and Watchmakers*, 1998) and *Cuando digo Magdelena* (1992). Steimberg, who lives in Buenos Aires, continues to conduct frequent lectures and workshops at universities in the United States and Latin America.

Ana Vásquez (Chile, 1947) was born into a German-speaking family. She studied psychology at the University of Chile and practiced until 1973 when she left the country during the Pinochet dictatorship. After settling in Paris, where she specialized in rehabilitating victims of torture, Vásquez began to write in both Spanish and French. Among her works are *Abel Rodríguez y sus hermanos* (1981), a novel about political betrayal and exile written during the Pinochet period, and *Mi amiga Chantal* (1991). Vásquez still resides in Paris and writes for feminist journals and human rights periodicals.

Credits

Marjorie Agosín, excerpt from *Always from Somewhere Else*, copyright © 1998 by Marjorie Agosín. Translation copyright © 1998 by Celeste Kostopulos-Cooperman. Reprinted by permission of The Feminist Press at the City University of New York.

Ruth Behar, "In the Absence of Love," copyright © 1999 by Ruth Behar, published by permission of the author.

Miriam Bornstein, "On the Border: Essential Stories," copyright © 1999 by Miriam Bornstein, published by permission of the author.

Alicia Freilich de Segal, excerpt from *Cláper*, copyright © 1987 by Alicia Freilich de Segal, reprinted by permission of the author. Translation copyright © 1998 by Joan E. Friedman, reprinted by permission of University of New Mexico Press.

Luisa Futoransky, "The Melancholy of Black Panthers," copyright © 1999 by Luisa Futoransky, published by permission of the author. Translation copyright © 1999 by Roberta Gordenstein, published by permission of the translator.

Margo Glantz, excerpt from *The Family Tree (Las genealogías)* copyright © 1981, 1986 by Margo Glantz, reprinted by permission of the author and Serpent's Tail Ltd. Translation by Susan Bassnett copyright © 1991 by Serpent's Tail, reprinted by permission of Serpent's Tail Ltd.

Margo Glantz, "Shoes," from *Desde la literatura*, copyright © 1994 by Margo Glantz, reprinted by permission of the author. Translation copyright © 1999 by Elizabeth Rosa Horan, published by permission of the translator.

Angélica Gorodischer, "Camera Obscura," copyright © 1999 by Angélica Gorodischer, published by permission of the author. Translation copyright © 1999 by Roberta Gordenstein, published by permission of the translator.

Sonia Guralnik, "Sailing Down the Rhine," from *Relatos en sepia*, copyright © 1987 by Sonia Guralnik, reprinted by permission of the author. Translation copyright © 1999 by Martha Manier, published by permission of the translator.

Rosita Kalina, "Golem," from *Esa dimensión lejana*, copyright © 1997 by Rosita Kalina, reprinted by permission of the author. Translation copyright © 1999 by Roberta Gordenstein, published by permission of the translator.

Alicia Kozameh, "Alcira in Yellows," copyright © 1999 by Alicia Kozameh, published by permission of the author. Translation copyright © 1999 by Roberta Gordenstein, published by permission of the translator.